C000150176

NO SHAME

NO SHAME SERIES BOOK 4

NORA PHOENIX

No Shame (No Shame Series Book 4) by Nora Phoenix

Copyright ©2018 Nora Phoenix

Cover design: Vicki Brostenianc

Editing/proofreading: Angela Campbell

All rights reserved. No part of this story may be used, reproduced, or transmitted in any form by any means without the written permission of the copyright holder, except in case of brief quotations and embodied within critical reviews and articles.

This is a work of fiction. Names, characters, places, and incidents either are the products of the author's imagination or are used fictitiously. Any resemblance to actual persons, living or dead, businesses, companies, events, or locales is entirely coincidental. The use of any real company and/or product names is for literary effect only. All other trademarks and copyrights are the property of their respective owners.

This book contains sexually explicit material which is suitable only for mature readers.

www.noraphoenix.com

PUBLISHER'S NOTE

This novel depicts mature situations and themes that are not suitable for underage readers. Reader discretion is advised. Please note there's a trigger warning for mentions of domestic abuse, sexual abuse, and sexual violence in this series, including rape.

1

M iles Hampton awoke to the sensation of his cock being sucked. Quite expertly, as a matter of fact. A hot, wet mouth with a devious tongue that licked him top to bottom and back, then teased his slit. A throat that seemed to lack a gag reflex, as it sucked him in all the way, with pressure that drew his balls up tight after mere seconds. He clenched his fists as his orgasm barreled through him.

"Thank you," he managed.

Warm hands cleaned his cock with what smelled like a baby wipe, then put it back in his pajama bottoms. "You're welcome. Sleep well."

He was halfway back asleep when it hit him. Who the fuck had just sucked him off? Had he seen him before? Yes. Yesterday, he'd quietly slipped into the room as well. Dark hair, tanned skin, gorgeous brown eyes. A quiet little mouse, who could suck cock like it was all he did.

Miles dreamed of him, that slick mouth, that perfect tongue. What was his name?

It was hard to stay awake with so many drugs in his

system. Painkillers, sedatives, whatever else he needed to not die. He kept waiting for his balls to start hurting, but they never did. Had they started giving him hormones after all?

He came in his sleep. Or had he been awake?

He woke up, knowing he'd orgasmed again, but his pajama bottoms were dry. What the hell?

The next time he roused when warm hands dragged down his pajamas. He reached out, slower than he'd liked, but still fast enough to catch the guy's hand. Slim. Soft.

"Who are you?" he croaked.

"I'm Brad. Can I suck you off?"

"Hell, yes. Please."

He put his hand on dark messy curls, so soft to his touch. He held it there until he came hard, groaning as he spurted cum into that perfect mouth. Who the hell was this?

Brad.

Brad with the perfect mouth.

"Thank you."

"You're welcome. Sleep well."

Hadn't he said that before? Deja vu.

Pain radiated from his heavy balls into his cock, his legs. It had been too long. He moved his hand down, vicious pain stabbing him in the ribs, reached inside his pants. Rock hard, of course. That never changed. Fuck, he hated this.

He jerked himself once, biting his lip from crying out as the uncoordinated move sent a wave of pain through him. The door opened, and he was too slow to pull out.

Shit. What would they think? Pervert. He was a fucking pervert.

"I'm sorry. I'm here now."

Before he could say another word, his hand was pulled off his cock, and that mouth descended. Wet heat, tongue, hard sucking. He exploded, tears forming in his eyes as his balls furiously emptied. Fuuuuuuuuck.

He looked up, met apologetic brown eyes. "I couldn't make it here earlier. I'm so sorry. Do you need another one?"

"Brad?" he asked.

"Yeah, it's me."

"You suck cock like a champ," he heard himself say, his eyes drifting shut again.

A low chuckle. "I'll take that as a yes. Close your eyes, I've got you."

It took slightly longer, but when his second release hit him, he fell asleep instantly.

CHARLIE STUDIED himself in the mirror above the bathroom sink. A month after the assault, his face finally looked normal again instead of the black-and-blue freak show that had slowly transformed in multiple shades of purple and blue. Zack had hit him straight in the face, multiple times, and it had shown. Fuck, his face had looked like a freaking rainbow flag, only less pretty.

Goddamn Zack. Fucking asshole.

Nope, he still wasn't over his anger. Noah had talked to him about stages of grief, had offered to listen whenever Charlie wanted to talk. And Charlie had poured his heart out, but not to Noah. He'd shared what had happened with Brad, who was a way better listener than many people gave him credit for. Still, he couldn't tell him everything, not when it was so stupid, so unbelievably stupid. He'd been such a fucking idiot.

Noah had said the process of grieving over what had happened with Zack started with denial, which in Charlie's

case had lasted for months. Why the hell had he stayed that
long? It had been months since the first time Zack had hit
him—and he'd still stayed with him. He'd known the guy
was a massive dick, and not in the good way, but he hadn't
wanted to admit it to himself, let alone to others.

To Brad. That's what it came down to, didn't it? He
hadn't wanted to admit to Brad that Brad had been right all
along. He'd warned Charlie against Zack from the day he
met him, back when Charlie had been too starry-eyed and
impressed that the sexy cop was even giving him the time of
day to listen. God, Charlie had been such a fucking naive
kid. Brad had been a loyal friend, but he'd warned Charlie
repeatedly. And fuck him to hell, he'd been completely
right. Of course.

At least Zack hadn't given him any VDs, what with all
his cheating Charlie had already suspected and that Brad
had confirmed. He didn't blame Brad for not saying
anything—he'd been in an impossible position, since
Charlie hadn't been open to hearing anything negative
about Zack. The one outing he'd done since the assault had
been to a clinic to get tested, and thank fuck everything had
come back negative. But what a fucking asshole Zack had
been, to even approach Brad for a fuck.

Charlie hadn't made it past the second stage yet: anger.
Deep, raging anger. He felt it bubbling inside him at times,
making him all restless and edgy. The fact that he'd been
fired from his job—working as a virtual personal assistant to
a fashion designer had been kinda hard after the assault,
and the man had fired him days later, the jerk—and couldn't
do his drag act either, which he loved so much, didn't help.
He was going stir crazy.

Maybe it was time to go job hunting, even if the thought
of going outside scared the fuck out of him. Outside was

where Zack was, and so far, he'd shown no sign of giving up on finding Charlie. He'd called relentlessly, until Charlie had changed his number, and Brad had resorted to that same tactic since he'd been inundated with calls as well. Even Blake had been approached. It was only a matter of time before Zack would find him...and going outside would only increase his chances of being found. No, he'd stay inside for now, in this safe place where people were nice and friendly.

He checked himself again. He'd always been on the pale side, but right now his skin was downright ghostly, contrasting starkly against his dark hair. His eyes looked even bigger than they usually did, probably because he'd lost some weight he couldn't afford to. He was already so fucking frail. The cute, pint-sized twink—what a horrible cliché. And he fucking oozed rainbows out of his pores without wanting to, alerting everyone in his vicinity that yes, he was gay, thank you very much. *Fuck my life.*

He made his way downstairs. Brad was already at work, but Noah was on the couch doing something on his iPad with Indy curled up against him, reading a book. Ever since Indy had come home, those two had been inseparable. Charlie had sighed with the warm and fuzzies more than once, watching them kiss, or cuddle, and touch.

And yet, despite the joy that was apparent over their reunification, there was a lingering sadness in both their eyes, especially Indy's. Was it a residue of the trauma he'd been through? Charlie wasn't sure.

"Good morning," Indy greeted him, friendly as ever.

"Hey, Charlie," Noah said, looking up from his iPad.

Max, Brad's dog, was on the floor in the living room and lifted his head for a sec to check who it was, then went right back to sleep.

"Hi. Did you guys have breakfast already? If not, I could make some?"

"You're the guest here," Indy protested. "Shouldn't we be making you something?"

Charlie grinned. "Sugar, I've been here for a month. Pretty sure we're past the guest stage. Also, in case you hadn't noticed yet, your boyfriend can't cook. He managed to burn an omelet the first week I was here. That in itself is quite the feat, actually."

Indy laughed. "I know, but he has other redeeming qualities to make up for it." He shoved Noah playfully, who shot him a quasi-indignant look in retribution.

"Yeah, somehow, I didn't think you picked him for his culinary talents," Charlie said.

Something flashed over Indy's face that was gone too fast to interpret, though it had looked a hell of a lot like sadness.

"It's not like Brad is much better," Noah fired back.

"Oh, I know, but he's not my boyfriend."

Noah and Indy shared a look that Charlie refused to interpret. He was pretty sure they had their thoughts about him and Brad. After all, he and Brad were two gay, single men who were really close and who had been staying in the same room now for a month. It made sense that they'd be together, right? Fuck, they had no idea.

"Speaking of that," Noah said. "We need to ask you something."

Charlie lowered himself on a chair across from them. Was this when they were telling him it was time to move out? He couldn't blame them, not after staying way past his expiration date already. Anyone else would have kicked him out weeks ago.

"We're not kicking you out, Charlie," Noah said, his

voice warm and kind. The guy was damn good at reading minds, Charlie had noticed on more than one occasion.

"You know about Miles, right?" Indy asked.

Miles. Sure. The gay, hunky FBI agent who was daily reaping the benefits of Brad's extraordinary cock sucking skills. Not that Charlie would know from experience, of course. Brad didn't see him that way, would never even approach him for something like that. No, he only knew from Brad's stories, because while the guy was a total introvert with Indy and Noah, he gave Charlie a daily recap of his sexual encounters in private. It was the sweetest torture.

He merely nodded at Indy.

"He'll be released from the hospital in a few days. He has no close family, and no friends nearby that he can stay with. We'd love to invite him to stay with us as well, but we wanted to make sure you'd be okay with it."

Charlie shrugged. "Sure. It's your house anyway."

"We want to make sure you'd feel safe," Noah stressed.

Charlie frowned. Why wouldn't he? The guy was an FBI agent, for fuck's sake. Then it hit him. "Just because one cop turned out to be a massive asshole who beat up his boyfriend doesn't mean I won't ever trust cops or authority figures again. I think you have a pretty accurate bullshit meter, Indy, so if you say he's a good guy, that works for me."

"And if Brad and Miles continue their...sexual activities while he's here, that wouldn't bother you either?" Noah asked.

The question was so unexpected that Charlie couldn't keep his face straight as his insides clenched painfully. Fuck, even the thought of having to watch Brad with another guy... It had always bothered him on some level, but he hadn't truly admitted it to himself until he'd moved in here with Brad, until they had spent so much time together. Until he'd fallen so hard and so deep he knew there would never be anyone else for him.

"Oh, Charlie," Indy said, his voice soft and sad. "I'm so sorry. If I had known, I would've never asked Brad."

Charlie raised his chin. He refused to feel shame about his feelings. Love was not something to be ashamed of, ever. "Brad doesn't know, so I'd appreciate it if you didn't say anything to him."

"Don't you want to tell him?" Indy asked.

Charlie sighed. "Noah, you're pretty good at reading people. Does Brad strike you as the type to be open to a declaration of love?"

Noah hesitated. "He's hard to read," he admitted. "I like him, and it's clear he's super smart, but he's closed off. He's hiding big parts of himself."

God, you have no idea what Brad is hiding. "Exactly."

"But he's different to you, Charlie. He talks more with you than with anyone else, and he's tender and sweet toward you," Noah added.

"He feels responsible for me, always has."

Indy quirked an eyebrow. "How long have you two known each other?"

"Five years. We met when I was in my senior year in high school. Brad was my math teacher," he explained. "It was pretty clear that I was gay, and I was getting bullied for it. Brad stepped in when a couple of jocks were giving me a hard time, physically, I mean, then started sort-of mentoring me. He signed me up for jiujitsu lessons with his brother Blake, insisted that I'd learn to defend myself. He's had my back ever since, and we became close friends once I graduated. But he sees me as someone he has to protect, that's it."

"I don't think it's quite that simple," Noah said. "There's

a lot more to Brad than he shows, but you two need to figure that out yourselves."

"Charlie, if you don't want Miles here, we'll find a different solution," Indy said. "The last thing I want is for you to feel awkward, or hurt."

"Or the fifth wheel in a house with two couples," Charlie commented dryly.

Indy grinned. "Or that. I love your humor, by the way."

"You should come see me when I perform as Lady Lucy," Charlie said. "She's way funnier than I am."

"I'd love to. When are you going back to performing?"

Charlie's face fell. "I don't know. I'm... I don't know." How could he explain that he was scared to even leave the house, afraid Zack would be there?

Indy gave him an encouraging smile. "It's okay. We'd love to come watch you when you're ready to perform again."

Charlie nodded, grateful that they weren't giving him a hard time about it. "And I'm okay with Miles coming here, honestly. Right now, he makes Brad happy, and that's all that matters to me."

It was true, in a way. Brad loved pleasuring the FBI agent, so that part was true. It did make him happy, in as far as Brad could ever be truly happy. Charlie would just have to get over the fact that it was Miles who was on the receiving end of Brad's attention, and not him. Even after spending a month in a room together, Brad was still not touching him beyond those sweet, way too short kisses and a whole lot of cuddling.

Fuck my life.

2

S oft voices beside his bed. Miles opened his eyes. Indy. And some handsome guy with a massive upper body. It took him less than a second to recognize him from the pictures in Indy's file: Noah.

"Indy," he said, his voice was barely audible. He coughed, sending a wave of pain through his chest.

"Don't clear your throat," Noah said. He grabbed a cup from the night stand. "It's still tender from the intubation. Here, take a sip of water."

Strong hands held him as he drank. "Thank you."

"No problem. I'm Noah, by the way. It's good to see you awake."

"Yeah, you too. I mean...It's good to meet you."

Damn, his brain still acted like molasses.

Indy stepped closer to the bed. He looked good. Rested. The constant stress on his face was gone.

"How are you feeling?" Indy asked.

"Much better now that I've seen you," Miles said, smiled.

"You flirting with my boyfriend?" Noah asked.

Indy smacked his arm. "Cut it out, Noah. He's been out

of it for a week, so he has no idea what happened. He's merely happy to see me."

At that rather unfortunate expression, Miles' cock perked up. With thin pajama bottoms and only a sheet covering him, there was no way he'd be hiding his erection.

Two pairs of eyes traveled south, where the sheets slowly moved upward. Miles froze inwardly, thanking his lucky stars once again that he never blushed. Didn't mean he wasn't embarrassed as hell.

God, he wished for one day where his body wouldn't let him down. One single day where he could be normal. Maybe he should close his eyes, pretend to fall asleep again. They'd leave then, right?

Indy turned toward Noah, jammed a finger in his face. "Not. A. Word."

Noah kissed his finger with the cutest gesture ever, then turned his eyes on Miles. "I'm sorry for you. Indy told me. Can't even imagine how inconvenient and frustrating that must be."

Miles let out his breath. He rarely talked about his issue, and when he did, he not often encountered understanding. Most people thought it was either hot—I wish I would be horny all day! No, you don't. Really, it's not nearly as awesome as it sounds—or didn't believe him.

"Thank you. It is. And no, I was not flirting with Indy. Last time I saw him we were in some storm shelter in Kansas, and everything was going to hell in a hand basket, so I was indeed happy to see him alive and well. And with you."

He added the last words for good measure, wanting Noah to know he had no designs on Indy. He honestly didn't. Sure, the kid was cute, but he didn't chase guys who were already in a relationship.

Wait, why was Indy here with Noah and not in FBI custody?

"Why are you here? What happened?"

"Someone took out the top three of the Fitzpatricks, including Duncan. There's no more contract on my head, and the threat is gone. I'm still testifying against the remaining lieutenants, but they're all in jail. Those that managed to avoid being arrested don't have the funds anymore to take me out. The FBI confirmed that the contract that was out on me has been canceled. So, I'm home. With Noah."

Miles' head swirled with the news. "That's fantastic. God, I'm happy for you, Indy. You deserve it."

A look passed between Indy and Noah that made Miles' heart ache. Noah kissed Indy softly. "He does," he said.

"Stupid question, but how am I doing?" Miles asked. "I mean, they've talked to me, but it's hard to remember when your brain is mush. How long will I have to stay?" He vaguely remembered his boss, Wells, coming in and talking to him at some point, but the details were rather fuzzy.

"You're doing well," Noah assured him. "Aside from bruises all over your body, you had a severe concussion, three broken ribs, a broken nose, a hairline fracture in your clavicle, and most importantly, you had internal bleeding from your spleen, which they had to remove. The surgery went well, and you're expected to make a full recovery, in time."

Miles tried to process it, but it was a lot to take in. These assholes had worked him over good, apparently. He couldn't remember anything after feeling his body give up on him in that storm shelter in Kansas.

"What happened?" he asked Indy, his head hurting with the effort of thinking.

Indy sent him a soft smile. "I used your phone to call an ambulance for you and took off as soon as they arrived. They operated on you immediately."

"You saved my life."

Indy shrugged, looking embarrassed.

"You did, Indy. Thank you." He didn't add the perfunctory "I owe you one", because it wouldn't work that way with Indy. Not with himself either. You didn't owe people for saving your life. You simply had to be grateful and be worthy of their sacrifice. Still, Indy had done an extraordinary thing, dragging him out of that barn. The kid could've easily left him there and hightailed it outta there.

Wait, was he still in Kansas? If so, how the hell did Indy and Noah show up here? It was a long way from New York.

"What hospital am I in?"

"You're in Albany General, the hospital I used to work in," Noah said. "We talked to your boss and had you transferred from Kansas as soon as you were stable."

"Why?"

Indy reached out to him, put his small, strong hand on Miles' arm. "I hope you're not mad with us, but we overheard your boss saying you had no next of kin and no valid emergency contact. They didn't want you to stay in Kansas without a support system, but in DC you wouldn't have had anyone either. I convinced them we'd become friends."

Miles closed his eyes. Of course. He'd never changed the information in his FBI file, so Casey had still been in there. "My boyfriend broke up with me a few months ago, so yeah. Should have changed that, I guess."

"No parents or family?" Noah asked.

"My parents and my sister were killed in a boating accident a few years back when a drunk guy in a speedboat rammed their sailing boat."

"Oh, Miles," Indy breathed, the compassion in his voice clear.

Miles opened his eyes again. "Thank you. For bringing me here and visiting me. Friendships are not easy in this line of work."

Indy squeezed his arm one last time, and of course Miles' traitorous cock reacted immediately.

"Do you want me to stop touching you?" Indy asked, his eyes trailing to the tented sheet.

"No. Please don't. I mean..." He swallowed, lost for words. How did he explain how lonely he was, how starving for touch? He was so scared to connect with others, knowing he'd get hard. It was pathetic, but the simple sensation of Indy's hand on his arm made him desperate for more. Not sex, but simple human touch. Connection. Friendship. God, he was a pathetic fucker.

"Look, Miles, there's something you need to know about us," Noah said. His voice was warm and kind, and his eyes held nothing of the contempt and anger Miles had grown accustomed to and had come to expect. "As far as sex goes, we're not exactly normal." Miles remembered Indy's file, the suggestion he was living with three other guys. "Me and Indy, we shared a house with Josh and Connor, and we were very open with each other about our sexual activities."

Indy grinned. "That's the polite way of saying we're a bunch of kinky fuckers."

Noah shot Indy a grin. "All this to say that we're not easily offended, or weirded out. What you have, how your body responds, it's okay with us. We won't take it the wrong way."

Stupid tears were clouding his eyes. It was a sad testament to how rarely he encountered compassion and understanding for his struggles. "Thank you."

"You're being released from the hospital in a week or so, they told us. Is there anywhere you want to go?" Indy asked.

His heart sank. He really was pretty close to being pathetic, wasn't he? "No. I'll have to return to my apartment in DC, hire a nurse, I guess."

"You can come home with us, if you want."

Indy said it so matter-of-factly, it took Miles a few seconds to process it. "What? Why?"

Another deep look of love between Indy and Noah. "Indy thinks you're lonely, and he can't stand to see people in pain. He wants to take you home, make sure you're okay."

Miles swallowed. In the short time they'd spent together, it seemed the kid had him pegged. He wasn't sure if he should be grateful or feel mortified he'd come across as a charity case.

A gulf of pain rolled over his body. He slowly reached for the morphine drip button and pushed it. He had a few minutes before the stuff would knock him out, and there was something else he needed to ask.

"Do you guys know a man named Brad? Dark curls, brown eyes?" He wanted to add "sucks cock like it's nobody's business" but thought better of it. Being kinky fuckers was one thing, but fuck knew how they would respond to a crude remark like that.

Indy smiled, a slow, sexy smile that made his face light up. "You like him?"

Miles' eyes narrowed. "Did you send him?"

"Yeah. When you were transferred here, I realized you had a problem, considering your...condition. So, I arranged a solution for you. Brad. How's he been working out?"

Were they really talking about this? It sure seemed so. Indy's eyes were dancing, his face pulled up in a mischievous grin. He was obviously very pleased with himself.

"His visits have been...highly satisfactory," Miles said, trying to maintain at least a hint of modesty, then giving up on that notion. In for a penny, in for the whole thing. "Oh, what the hell. He sucks cock like you wouldn't believe. I'm not kidding."

Indy elbowed Noah. "Told you."

"Indy," Miles said. "I really appreciate you doing this for me. It's incredibly considerate of you. But who is he, and why is he okay with doing this? I'm a complete stranger to him."

"I can't tell you why he does it, that's up to Brad to share. Or not. But rest assured, he's doing it voluntarily. We're not forcing him. Or paying him."

A sense of relief flooded Miles. He hadn't dared to ask, but the thought had occurred to him that Brad might be a prostitute. That wouldn't make him less grateful, but it would have been different. As a federal agent, he couldn't exactly engage in illegal activities, no matter how good they felt.

And holy fuck, Brad did feel good. His hot, slick mouth on Miles' cock. That tongue of his that lapped him up like he was a delicious treat. He wanted to fuck his throat, stuff his mouth completely full and come down his throat again. And then do it all over again.

"He's drifting off," Noah said. "The morphine is kicking in."

Miles blinked, fought to stay awake. Exhaustion was battling with arousal, since he was still hard from Indy's touch and their conversation. Fuck, he hoped Brad would stop by. Soon.

"You wanna come home with us?" Indy asked.

"God, yes," Miles heard himself say. "I'd love to."

His eyes drifted shut again.

"We'll see you tomorrow, okay?"

He was already half asleep, when voices at the door woke him up again. Who were Noah and Indy talking to? The door closed, then was locked.

He fought to open his eyes. Brad. Thank fuck.

"I'm so damn hard," Miles said.

That sexy, low chuckle. "That's what I'm here for."

"Wanna fuck you."

The sheet was whipped off his body, his pajama bottoms shoved down. "You'd have to be awake for that, champ. How about you fuck my mouth instead?"

"Okay," he mumbled.

Slick heat engulfed his cock, and he let out a deep moan. His hands sought, found, caressed those soft curls. The slurping sounds aroused him even more than he already was.

"Mmmm. You're so good at this."

Brad pulled his mouth off Miles' cock with a delicious plop. "Would you like me to play with your balls? Your hole?"

"Fuck, yes. Everything. Everywhere."

His right testicle was sucked into Brad's mouth, setting his entire body on fire. Miles' hips bucked.

"Oh, damn."

The left testicle was next. Then Brad wet his finger and put pressure on his hole. Miles moaned. It had been so long since someone had done that. He bore down, and Brad's finger slipped in. Electricity danced down his spine.

"Coming," he warned.

Brad's mouth took him in, all the way in. He increased the grip on his head, lifted his hips of the mattress. Brad's finger followed the movement, sunk in deep, creating that perfect friction in Miles' ass. His cock thrust deep into the guy's mouth, then again, and again, and he came so hard. So good. Hot damn.

"Sorry. Did I hurt you?"

"Not at all. I love to be skull fucked."

Skull fucked. Miles had never heard that expression before. It was dirty, and perfect. He sighed, relaxing as all tension left his body. It wouldn't last, but he'd enjoy it for now.

"Thank you," he said. He couldn't open his eyes anymore. Too tired. "You're perfect."

3

He was crazy. This was crazy. Bradford Kent argued with himself the entire elevator ride up to the ninth floor of Albany General, as he had done every single time he'd gone up to Miles' room. Yet the end result had always been the same: him slipping into Miles' room, locking it behind him, and bringing the gorgeous FBI agent to a shattering climax. Man, the guy could come. And come. And come again.

Even stuck in a hospital bed with bandages everywhere and almost as pale as the sheets covering him, the man was rip-roaring hot. Tall, blond, fit, and with a cock that tasted like heaven.

Okay, that was even more crazy, Brad admitted. Most men, even gay men, wouldn't say that. He did, however. He'd thoroughly enjoyed sucking Miles off. He could only hope it would last a bit longer, because surely as soon as the guy was recovered enough to go home, it would end. He had to have a long list of willing bed partners to gratify him.

Brad hesitated shortly before he opened the door. Would Miles be awake again this time? He was getting more and more lucid, whereas before, he'd been half out of it. If Brad hadn't felt his erection every time, he would have worried about sucking him off without the guy being able to give consent. But what Indy said had been true. Miles was hard all the time, and if he wasn't, it took one touch to get him fully erect.

He'd been too cute last time, telling Brad he wanted to fuck him. The man was nowhere near ready for that, yet, but if he was, Brad would bend over in a heartbeat. If blowing him already felt so good, Brad could only imagine how deeply satisfying it would be to be fucked raw by the guy. Yeah, as he said, he was out of his fucking mind, and a pervert to boot. What else was new?

Miles was watching TV when he stepped into the room, a first. Brad jammed his hands into his pockets, suddenly nervous and shy. "Hi," he said.

Miles sent him a blinding smile, turned off the TV instantly. "Hi. I was hoping you'd come by."

"Yeah. Of course. I mean, I've been here twice a day, most days."

"I didn't realize. I've been pretty out of it." He gestured toward the morphine pump. "That stuff is powerful."

"How are you feeling?" Was that a stupid question to ask? Brad sucked at small talk, never knew what to say, or when it got awkward.

"Wanna sit down?" Miles asked, pointing toward the chair beside his bed.

"Don't you want me to..."

Miles swallowed. "Yeah. If you want. But maybe talk first?"

"Oh." That was unexpected. And major uncomfortable. What the hell would he want to talk about? It wasn't like they had much in common. Still, Brad lowered himself on the chair, folded his hands in his lap.

Miles smiled. "Your name is Brad, right?"

He nodded.

"I'm Miles."

"Yeah, I know. I mean, nice to meet you. Officially?" Way to go, bubbling idiot, he cursed himself, but Miles didn't seem to mind.

"I guess we hadn't been officially introduced, even though you seem to know me quite well in other ways."

"Indy said it was okay," Brad said quickly. Was Miles upset with him? Had he done something to displease him?

"It is. It was. Hell, yes. Thank you."

He relaxed again. "You're welcome."

"Indy explained to you what I have?"

He nodded. "Yeah. He said it would hurt like hell if nobody took care of you."

Miles let out a soft sigh. "It gets quite painful. Why do you do this? I mean, you don't even know me."

Brad's face tightened. There was no way he was sharing this with Miles. He'd be repulsed for sure. Even Charlie didn't know the whole story, and Brad trusted him with his life.

"It's okay," Miles said. Did he sense his discomfort? "You don't need to tell me. I was curious, but above all, I'm grateful."

"You don't need to be. I love doing this."

"You love sucking cock."

He raised his chin. This much he would admit. "Yes."

"You're really, really good at it." Miles' voice was so sincere, Brad didn't doubt the truth of his statement even for a second.

Brad's face lit up. "Thank you. Please tell me if there's anything else you like. I can bring a dildo to fuck you while I suck you off, or give you a hand job if you'd prefer. I don't know if you like it a little rougher, add a touch of pain, or what."

He clamped his mouth shut. Total verbal diarrhea and so fucking eager. Would he ever learn?

"I'm going home in a couple of days, if all goes well," Miles said, studying him with an indecipherable look.

Damn. That was it, then. He had a few more days with this perfect man, and then he'd be back to scrounging favors off total strangers in gay clubs. He'd known it was temporary anyway. Miles wouldn't want him once he had options, and Brad needed something the agent would never be able to give him. He doubted anybody could or would, especially once they realized how truly fucked-up he was, but that didn't keep his stubborn heart from hoping.

"Okay."

"I'm going home with Indy and Noah."

He was? How crazy was that? He and Charlie were still staying with them, too. Charlie's ex was still too much of a threat to even consider moving back into Brad's place, since that would be the first place Zach would come looking for Charlie. Brad had been surprised Zack hadn't made a move yet, but Charlie said he'd been out of state for three weeks on some kind of training that had been scheduled months in advance.

Brad had asked Indy repeatedly if he was okay with them staying there, especially since he'd just been reunited with Noah, but Indy had assured him it was fine. Josh was still at the mental facility, so maybe when he came home it would be time to leave? It would certainly make things interesting with Miles moving in as well.

Brad's eyes lifted from the floor to meet Miles'. He saw

uncertainty there, an implicit question. Was Miles asking him what Brad thought he was?

"I could...continue helping you there, if you want me to," he offered, almost holding his breath.

"Would you? I don't even know where you live, or what you do for a living," Miles said.

Brad exhaled. He'd have him for a little while longer, thank fuck. Still, he was so not answering that last question. The guy would be bored to death in seconds. Besides, he wanted to pleasure Miles, not become BFFs. This could never be about more than sex, about Miles' need to come and Brad's own sick need to please.

"I live pretty close to their house, ten minutes maybe? But I'm staying in one of their guest rooms right now with Charlie, my best friend. He was assaulted, and needed a place to recover. So it wouldn't really be a bother."

Miles looked him straight in his eyes, those misty blue eyes demanding truth. "And you are absolutely certain you don't mind doing this? I respect your privacy, but consent is a big deal for me."

Brad nodded vehemently. "I love it, I swear."

"And your friend Charlie, he won't mind either? I don't know if you two are..."

"We're just friends," Brad assured him, though he had to force himself to keep his eyes level when he said it. Of course, he and Charlie weren't mere friends. Charlie had wanted more from the beginning, but Brad had always kept him at a distance—at least in that sense. Charlie deserved more and better. But all that was kinda unnecessary to explain to the Fed, wasn't it? Need to know, and all that. "And he knows, and he's fine with it." That part, at least, was true.

Miles's face softened. "In that case, yes, please. Your

mouth or your hands, it doesn't matter, as long as I come. If you can play with my ass at the same time, even better. A dildo is perfect, or your fingers, whichever you prefer. The more often you make me come and the more intense my orgasm, the longer I'll last, but I will never put pressure on you to do more than you want to, or feel comfortable with."

The sheet around his groin was tenting, evidence of his massive hard on. Brad felt himself stir, a rare occasion, though it died down quickly. "I'll bring lube next time," he said. "Didn't want to do that without your consent."

Miles hand reached out to touch Brad's hand, sending a spark through his body. "Brad, you can do anything to make me come. Anything. Unless I explicitly say no, anything is fine. My need to come trumps any shame or embarrassment I have."

Brad's mouth dropped slightly agape. Was the guy serious? Hmm, they would have to see if he meant it. Maybe "anything" meant something else entirely to the agent than it did to Brad.

His skin burned where Miles was touching him. "I'd love to suck you right now, if that's okay."

Miles' eyes burned into his. "Lock the damn door."

Brad jumped up, locked the door. When he turned around, Miles had kicked down the sheets and was shimmying out of his pajama bottoms, his forehead frowning with effort and probably a bit of pain.

"How many do you need right now?" Brad asked.

"As many as you can spare. I'm on the edge, so the first one should be easy."

Brad licked his lips. "Okay."

He reached out for that perfect cock, all ready and glistening against Miles' stomach. It was weeping already, so eager for his touch. He circled it with his hands, admired the fierce head, almost purple in its desire to come. A thick drop of precum pearled on the top, and he swiped it with his thumb, used it to wet the crown.

How much pressure did Miles like? He'd have to find out. He circled the base with one hand. Grabbed the top of his cock with his other hand and started rubbing. Up, down, increasing in pressure.

"Ohhh," Miles let out. "Fuck. Little harder. Yeah, like that. Oh, dammit."

He groaned low and deep, and his cock exploded in Brad's hand. The guy hadn't been kidding that he was on the edge. Thick ropes of cum flew onto Miles' belly. Brad didn't miss a beat, swiped some of it with his fingers while he kept jacking Miles off with his other hand.

"Raise your legs," he said, smiled when Miles obeyed without delay, though with careful moves. His index finger found Miles' hole, eased inside, aided by the man's own cum. His left hand jacked off, his right hand finger fucked his ass. Being ambidextrous really had advantages.

He swiped more cum off the man's belly to wet his cock, which made jerking off so much more pleasant. You could use lube, sure, but there was something inherently dirty about using cum. Miles didn't seem to mind. He had his eyes closed and let out a stream of soft moans and groans. Brad's insides sighed with content. He was doing this. He was bringing this gorgeous man pleasure.

Miles' tight channel eased around his finger, signaling he was ready for more. Brad added his middle finger, turned his hand to find that spot. He fucked, felt, fingering him until he found that slightly spongy spot that was just a little different to the touch than the surrounding area. He hit it straight on, jacked him off hard with his other hand.

Miles let out a loud curse. "Fuckohfuckohfuckohfuck."

Yup, he'd found it, alright. He repeated his move, and the man's cock went off like a rocket, squirting fluids all over Brad's face. Brad licked a drop of cum off his lips, smacked.

"Oh, shit, sorry," Miles panted, his face falling. Did he think Brad would be upset over cum in his face? He got off on shit like that. The dirtier it got, the better.

Brad responded by burying his face in Miles' crotch, nuzzling his balls. Miles' hands came up to touch his hair, as he'd done before. Brad loved it when those big hands caressed his curls. The slight pressure of Miles' hands added to the sensation of being used.

He proceeded to lick Miles clean, his fingers still knuckle deep into the man's ass. Miles was definitely not a top only, because he'd taken Brad's fingers with ease and had obviously loved having something in his hole. Brad filed that information away. He held his fingers still for now, wanted Miles to concentrate on something else.

Those big balls were a perfect fit for his mouth. He took the right nut in, sucked gently. Miles gasped, increased the pressure on Brad's head. Hmm, he liked that, huh? Brad smiled with his mouth full of testicle, let it slip out. He licked around it a few times for good measure, because, damn, the man tasted so good. Sweaty, musky, all male. He doted on the other nut with the same attention, licked it even more, because he couldn't get enough of it.

Miles was thrashing on the bed by now, his head rolling left and right, his hips bucking every now and then. Those strong hands were digging into Brad's skull, begging him to finish it.

He took mercy on him, took him into his mouth, sucking him all the way in until his balls hit his chin. He never gagged, courtesy of a lot of practice. Then again, he'd never had much of a gag reflex to begin with. Miles' hips came off the mattress as he thrust into Brad's mouth, probably without realizing it. Brad echoed the move, thrusting into Miles' ass with his fingers.

Miles moaned obscenely loud, fucked his mouth again. Brad did the same in his ass. Fingers dug hard into his skull, as Miles fired off hard thrusts, Brad doing his best to keep up. It wouldn't take long anyway, not when...Miles's body tensed up completely, his legs and arms stiff as a board.

"Fuuuuuuuuuck..." he moaned, as his cock spurted out his third load. Brad swallowed happily. Hmm, next time he wanted to swallow the first load. This was way more translucent, less tasty.

Miles fell back on the mattress, his hands sliding off Brad's head. The man was done. Good.

Brad cleaned him up as best as he could with his mouth, slowly pulled his fingers from that tight heat. He'd brought baby wipes, as he had before, because they were the easiest way to clean Miles, since he couldn't very well shower yet. Brad didn't want to leave any traces for the nurses washing him. He took them from his jacket, cleaned Miles nice and fresh, including swiping his hole to remove the last traces of cum.

The dirty baby wipes still clutched in one hand, Brad pulled Miles' bottoms over his bare ass and flaccid cock. He'd rarely seen it so peaceful. Three orgasms must have done the trick. When he looked up, Miles was staring at him. Brad jolted, as if stung. Somehow, he'd expected Miles to be asleep again.

"Thank you," Miles said.

Brad licked his lips, couldn't help it. "You're very welcome."

He threw the wipes in the waste basket, washed his hands in Miles' bathroom. He threw some water on his face, washing off the remnants of cum, patted it dry with a paper towel. There, all presentable again. No one who'd see him would have any idea of what he'd done.

Miles was as good as asleep when he stepped out. "I'll see you tomorrow."

TWO MORE DAYS before Josh got home. Indy couldn't fucking wait. The reunion with Noah had been truly special, and they still had a hard time not touching each other when they were together, but there was a Josh-shaped hole in Indy's heart and his life.

He'd come back, expecting to find Josh home with Noah, but instead Noah had told him about Josh's stay in the clinic. Apparently, he'd had a brutal breakdown there during his stay, causing him to extend his treatment. He'd been gone for over five weeks now, and Indy couldn't even imagine what Josh had been through. Indy himself hadn't seen Josh in almost three months, and it was killing him.

Indy had thought Connor's disappearance had been a ruse when Miles told him about it back in Kansas, but Noah had assured him it was real. The cop had actually broken up with Josh on the day Indy had gone into protective custody. It went against everything Indy had believed about Connor, and even now, he had a hard time understanding what had moved Connor to do it. Had he felt threatened by Noah's friendship with Josh after all? He had to have known Josh would've never done anything without Connor's approval.

No wonder Josh had experienced a rapid deterioration in his mental health. Losing Connor must have been a devastating blow for him. Josh had loved the cop with all his heart, of that Indy had no doubt.

For a second, when he heard the news about the sniper shooting, Indy had thought Josh was behind it. It was too much of a coincidence, what with Josh being a sharpshooter who could pull it off and all. But when Noah had told him about Josh's stay in the clinic and about his psychotic break-down, Indy had chalked it up to coincidence after all. He would have been too hopped up on meds to make sense, let alone to plan an attack like that. It had to have been someone with a gripe against the Fitzpatricks. Fuck knew the list of people who hated them was miles long.

What would Josh be like when he got back? Vulnerable, probably. Indy vowed to take care of him the best he could. Maybe they could...

The doorbell interrupted his thoughts, and his heart rate jumped. Noah had gone to physical therapy a few minutes before, Brad was at work, and Charlie was in his room doing fuck knew what. It was okay. He could open the door. The danger was gone, but it took some getting used to. It was fine, he told himself.

He walked over to the front door and opened it. His heart dropped, then jumped right back up when he saw him. He didn't even think, launched himself right at him.

"Josh!"

Josh opened his arms wide, caught Indy with ease. Indy wrapped his legs around his waist, held on to him for dear life, as Josh's hands circled him to hold him close. He breathed in his smell, put his cheek against Josh's. It was like a missing piece of his heart slipped back into place.

"God, I missed you so much," he whispered in Josh's ear.

Josh hugged him as if he never planned to let him go. "I missed you like crazy."

They held each other for maybe a minute before Indy leaned back to look at him. "How are you?"

He narrowed his eyes when he took in Josh's clear eyes, the slight flush on his cheeks, his swollen lips.

Josh lowered him carefully to the ground, shot him a look of love. "I'm good," he said. "I'm doing really good."

"You just got fucked," Indy said slowly. "And it wasn't Noah, because he's off to therapy. Plus, he wouldn't have done it without telling me. But there's no way you would sleep with anyone else, which means...Connor is back?"

Josh smiled. "I told you he would figure it out!" he called over his shoulder.

Connor stepped into view from beside the house, his hands stuffed in his pockets. "Hi Indy," he said. "It's good to see you back home."

Indy's head dazzled. Josh looked way too healthy for someone who just had a major breakdown, even if he had stayed in the clinic for a few weeks afterward. And Connor didn't look guilty at all, which he should have if he really had broken up with Josh. Which meant that he hadn't, that he'd only pretended, because...why? What reason could Connor have to pretend to break up with Josh and go back to Boston?

Indy looked from Josh to Connor, and it clicked.

"Oh, damn... It *was* you."

Tears filled his eyes, and he lifted his hands to cup Josh's cheeks. "You did this for me, for us."

Connor stepped in, and Indy dragged his eyes away from Josh to look at Connor. "And you helped him. I don't know how you did this, how you set it up, but it was you. Both of you."

Josh placed his own hands on top of Indy's, looked him straight into his eyes. "We'll never talk about this ever again, you hear me? Ever."

Indy blinked. "But Noah, he'll..."

"Noah won't know. He won't figure it out like you did, because he doesn't see me like you do. In his eyes, I'll always be the weaker one, the one who needs protection. It's you and Connor who see me differently."

Indy realized at once how accurate Josh's statement was. Noah loved Josh with all he had, but Josh was right. Noah would never be able to fully let go of his protectiveness toward him, developed over years of having his back. He would've never thought Josh was strong enough for this—but he was. He had been. Josh had done the only thing that set Indy free.

"God, Josh, you saved me. What you did—"

"Was nothing more than what you did for me by going after my attackers. And we both did it for ourselves as much as we did it for the other. You belong here with us, Indy. We belong together, as a family, and I would have done anything to make that happen."

Indy nodded, tears still streaming down his face. Josh kissed his forehead, then let go of his hands. Indy dropped his hands from Josh's cheeks, turned to Connor. He hesitated for a second, then opened his arms and hugged the big man. Connor's arms came around him, and soft lips pressed a kiss on his head. "It's wicked good to see you back home, kid," Connor said, his voice a little hoarse.

Indy released him, stepped back. "What explanation are you gonna give Noah for your return?"

Connor and Josh shared a quick look. "Undercover work for the Boston PD, which is sort of true. Don't ask me for details, Indy, because I'll never tell, but I was in Boston the whole time, working on the Fitzpatricks' case. If Noah asks, we can tell him I helped collect the evidence against them used in the raids."

Indy nodded. "That'll work. I don't think Noah will get

suspicious." He looked from Connor to Josh. "Does Connor know..." His voice trailed off. Maybe he should've asked Josh this in private. Damn. That fucking filter of his was still not functioning.

"Yeah. I knew Connor wasn't really breaking up with me, and he gave me permission to let Noah fuck me, when necessary. It was, both for Noah and for me. God, Indy, I've never seen him in such a dark place. It scared me. Losing you, he took it hard."

"I know. I wish it had been differently, but I don't know what else I could have done. And thank you, for taking care of him." Indy suddenly remembered, slapped his forehead. "Oh, shit. Miles is coming to stay. And we have Brad and Charlie here as well, with Brad's dog, Max."

Josh's eyes widened. "They're still here? And who the fuck is Miles?"

Indy quickly caught them up on what had gone down in Kansas and what the deal was with Miles, including his condition. He figured it would be wise, especially with Connor around. Josh wouldn't care, but Connor's reactions weren't always predictable yet to Indy.

"Miles is a great guy, honestly. Be careful, though. He's smart. Really smart. The guy's got a degree in psychology, and he's fucking sharp. Don't even drop a hint, because he'll catch on."

Josh sighed. "Well, great."

Indy's shoulders hunched. "If I'd known Connor would be coming back, I would've never invited him."

Josh bent over, kissed his head. "It's fine. We'll make it work."

"It's a lot of people, though," Connor said.

Josh smiled. "Then that twelve-seat massive dining table I ordered for the kitchen will come in handy, won't it?"

"I had a different purpose in mind for that table," Connor growled.

Indy laughed. "We christened it for you. Noah and I are happy to report it's sturdy and at the perfect height."

Josh spontaneously hugged him again. "God, it's so good to see you, hear your voice."

"Why are we still standing outside? Let's go in," Connor said.

4

This could either be the biggest mistake of his life, or the best decision he'd ever made. Only time would tell which one it was, but Miles had to admit he was a little apprehensive as he sat in the back of Noah's car.

"Let's go home," Indy had said. Miles envied him that, a sense of truly being home somewhere. He'd lost that feeling when he'd lost his parents and sister, had never regained it. His apartment in DC was not even close to being a home. It could have been a hotel—it sure felt like it to him at times.

Noah and Indy's house would be different, he was sure. Indy had made another reference to them being very open about sex. Miles wasn't entirely sure what to expect, but at least he didn't have to fear a negative reaction about Brad helping him.

Which he would around five, according to plan. Apparently, he had to work late—he'd said something about a meeting—but after that, he'd promised to help Miles. *Help.* Now, there was a nice euphemism.

He'd made him come three times last night, so Miles

should be okay till later. Though maybe he shouldn't think about Brad too much, lest his cock decided it wanted to get a head start on things.

"This is it," Indy said as they turned into the driveway of a dark red farmhouse. Not at all what Miles had expected. "We've given you the former in-law wing for now. It has its own entrance and bathroom, so you'll have more privacy than when you'd be staying in one of the guest rooms."

"Wow, thanks. Who did I kick out of their own bedroom?"

Indy laughed. "That would be me and Noah, but we're fine. We confiscated the last empty guest room, and we can share a bathroom with Josh and Connor."

Something told Miles Indy preferred sharing a bathroom with them, but he kept his mouth shut. He'd discover soon enough what the deal was with these four. Or not. He'd not yet met Josh and Connor, but according to Noah and Indy, they were fully on board with Miles moving in temporarily, even though Brad and his friend, Charlie, were also still staying there.

Noah parked the car in the driveway, as close to the front door as possible. "I'll get Connor to help," he said. "I don't fully trust my leg yet, so I can't support you."

Miles nodded. Noah had lost a leg in Afghanistan, he'd read in Indy's file, and had recently needed surgery to amputate even higher up, due to complications. "Okay."

The man who stepped outside with Noah a few minutes later was massive. Broad arms and chest in a tight Red Sox shirt, strong legs. Miles recognized him from the pictures in the file. Ignatius O'Connor, called Connor by everyone. The last Miles had heard, the guy had been balls deep in the Boston crime scene, so he had no idea what had happened there.

Connor's cheeks were flushed, as if he'd been doing something physical, and he and Noah were arguing about something.

"I don't believe this," Indy muttered, threw open his door and left it open as he stepped out. "Seriously? You guys were fucking again? At the rate you're going, poor Josh won't be able to sit for a week."

Connor shrugged. "At least he'll know who he belongs to."

Noah shook his head. "You're a regular fucking caveman, O'Connor. You would have done great with the dinosaurs."

"Now why would I want to fuck a dinosaur? You're not making any sense," Connor said, his Boston accent thick.

Indy opened the door on Miles' side. "Let's get this guy inside so he can rest."

Another man stepped outside. Tall, lanky, with cute, boyish looks. That had to be Joshua Gordon. He walked carefully, as if something hurt. Miles' eyes narrowed. Had Connor hurt him? Josh took another careful step, and the source became clear. His ass. Had Indy been right? Holy crap, what kind of people were they?

Connor turned to watch Josh, and a look of pure love painted his face. Damn, but this was way more than mere fucking. Like with Noah and Indy, the love was palpable.

"You okay, babe?" Connor asked.

Josh leaned in, kissed him. "Yes, Connor." Connor's face lit up with happiness and a deep satisfaction.

"Shit, guys, sometime today, please?" Indy said, tapping his foot.

Connor came over. "Sorry. Connor," he said, holding out his hand.

Miles grabbed it. There was time for questions later. "Miles. Thanks for having me."

"Not a problem, glad to have ya. Need a hand getting out?"

"Yes, please," Miles said. No need to be proud when it hurt like crazy.

Connor reached under his arms, lifted him up like he weighed nothing, then gently put him on his feet. Wow, badass much? He leaned heavily on the guy as they walked inside, but at least he walked. No fucking wheelchair here.

Connor led him straight to a sunny bedroom, where a king size bed was waiting for him. He sat down on the bed, panting with the effort. A gorgeous black Labrador trotted in, apparently curious what all the commotion was about.

"That's Max, Brad's dog," Indy said, kneeling to take off Miles' shoes, while Josh slung back the comforter and fluffed the pillows. It wasn't hard to see who the homebody was here. "He loves to cuddle, but we can keep him in the living room if you want."

"That's fine. I like dogs," Miles said.

"Want me to take off your pants?" Indy asked.

"Nah, that's okay." He was hard again. No fucking way was he showing that to these four men.

"Miles, they don't care," Indy said. "If you want to stay here, you gotta trust us that we're okay with you. We want you to be able to be yourself. Nobody gives a fuck. I told you, we're all sexual deviants here."

Noah grinned, while Josh chuckled. "It's true," Josh said. "Connor's cum is literally dripping out my ass as we speak, since he came right when you guys pulled up."

"Joshua!" Connor's voice sounded stern, but the twinkle in his eye belied his anger. "Do you need another spanking?"

Miles' eyes widened. What the fuck?

"Yes, Connor. I mean, no, Connor."

Yeah, that slip up had been completely intentional, Miles had no doubt.

"I don't care what you do, as long as you're not hogging the shower again. I have plans with Indy for that shower," Noah said.

"Okay, okay." Miles raised his hands. "Take the damn pants off. Holy fuck, I feel like I walked onto the set of a porn movie."

Indy giggled. "Actually, it often looks like that here. That's why we installed you here, so you can choose to limit your exposure to our...activities."

With quick hands, he undid the waist strings of Miles' jogging pants. "Lift your hips," he said. Miles raised his ass off the bed, and Indy dragged the pants down, revealing Miles' tight white boxers that were barely containing his raging hard on. Nobody so much as batted an eye, however, as if a hard on was the most normal thing in the world here.

"When's Brad coming home?" Indy asked conversationally as he folded Miles' pants and put them on a chair.

"Around five, he said."

"Good. If you need anything, press the buzzer. It rings a bell in our kitchen. If you want something to eat, you'll need to tell Josh. He's our best cook. I can make a decent meal, but Noah and Connor will feed you crap, so choose wisely."

Miles nodded.

"You said you wanted to take a shower? Do you think Brad would help you? The shower here has extra handrails and shit, including a shower bench, so that makes it easier. If you need more help, Connor would be happy to help you."

Miles doubted the big guy was okay with Indy so casually offering his help, but when he looked over to Connor, he was nodding in agreement. Huh. Interesting dynamic here. Indy seemed to be at the center of it all, which Miles had not expected.

"I dunno. I'll ask Brad, but if not, I'll ring for help."

Indy nodded. "We'll let you rest. Miles..." He waited till Miles looked at him. "This is your home now. You would honor our hospitality by truly making yourself at home. Do whatever you want, okay? There's no need to pretend here. And FYI: we have enough sheets to change the bed daily."

His heart welled up with warmth. What had he done to deserve this friendship? It was an unexpected gift he intended to treasure. "Thank you. All of you. You have no idea how much this means to me."

They walked out, smiling and joking with each other, Max following them out. Connor slapped Josh's ass playfully, and the taller guy kissed his cheek in response. They were absolutely fucking nuts, but he'd never felt more welcome anywhere.

He took his shirt off as well, then decided to go completely nude. Fuck, he loved the sensation of his bare ass against the sheets. The downside was that it didn't help with his boner, but he felt so free. He laid down on the bed, inhaled deeply. The sheets smelled fresh, like lavender, and the crisp cotton was cool against his heated skin. So this was what a home smelled like. He fell asleep in under a minute.

Hmm, something delicious was teasing his toes. Wet, hot, sucking. He arched his back, moaned.

His eyes flew open. What?

He lifted his head, watched in amazement as an almost naked Brad sucked on the toes of his right foot. He was sporting a black pair of loose fitting boxers on a tight, lean body. Not an ounce of fat. Miles' big toe disappeared into Brad's mouth and that delicious, sinful tongue lapped, sucked.

Damn, his cock was throbbing. Who knew that having your toes sucked was so damn erotic?

"Brad," he breathed.

Brad looked up, shot him a shy smile, as he let the toe pop out. "Hi."

"Don't stop," Miles said. "Please, don't stop."

With that, Brad sucked his big toe right back into his mouth, went down on it like it was Miles' cock. His head nodded and his cheeks hollow, he sucked on it with a force that had Miles gasping for breath.

Brad gestured to pull up his legs, and Miles quickly obliged. His toe was sucked right back into that hot mouth, then Brad reached for his cock, fisted it tightly. One, two, three hard jerks and Miles was coming.

His cum landed everywhere, but he didn't care. Fuck, that had been good. "Damn, that's a turn on," he said to Brad when he'd caught his breath.

Brad let go of his foot, shot him a sexy smile. "We're only getting started."

"Why are you still wearing underwear?" Miles asked. The smile on Brad's face disappeared. Miles frowned. What had he said wrong? "It's okay," he said quickly. "You can... It's okay. Whatever you prefer."

"I don't like being naked," Brad said. "I prefer to leave my boxers on."

"Okay, that's fine."

Miles let his head rest back on the pillow. Leaning on his arms was starting to bother his ribs.

"I brought some toys," Brad said. "And lube."

"Have at it. Whatever you like."

He should care, but he honestly didn't. The orgasm had barely taken the edge off, and his balls throbbed painfully. When it got to that point, it was hard to think. All he wanted was to come, preferably hard and long so his balls would empty.

"O-o-okay."

He'd stuttered. Was there something wrong? "I meant it when I said everything is fine with me, Brad. Whatever you feel like, or feel comfortable with."

He closed his eyes, suddenly tired again. The bed moved, and warm hands touched his face. A cloth was pulled over his eyes, then Brad tied it. "Don't look," he told Miles.

Okay, that was unexpected.

"Are you clean?"

Miles frowned. Wasn't that a bit late to ask? The guy had given him dozens of blow jobs by now. "Yeah. Got tested three months ago and haven't had sex since."

"Three months? Holy fuck."

"You?" Yeah, he should've have asked that sooner, too.

"Yeah. I always use condoms, and I'm on PReP, but I get tested every month."

Every month, while taking PReP? Wow, the guy must have a serious sex life. Should he trust him? It was a little late to talk safe sex now.

"I can show you my last results if you want," Brad said more softly.

"No. It's fine. I trust you. I've never gone bareback, that's all."

It was weird to talk when you couldn't see the person you were talking with. Made him feel more vulnerable, yet at the same time it was easier to say shit.

"Not even with your boyfriend? Indy said you got out of a relationship a while ago."

Miles sighed. "No. He didn't want to, and in hindsight that made sense because it turned out he was screwing around for months. Guess I should be grateful he at least protected me from STDs."

Brad was quiet for a few beats. "Are you sure it's okay? We can use condoms, it's no biggie. It's just that it's a hassle to have to switch condoms every time you come, 'cause I intend to make you come a few times in a row."

Fuck, yes, please. Paradise was around the corner, Miles could taste it. "No. It's fine. I trust you." It didn't make sense at all, but he really did.

The bed moved again, and Miles felt Brad touch his legs. A cap was flicked open, lube squeezed out. "Pull your feet up. Now raise your hips."

Pillows were stacked under his ass, lifting it off the mattress. Miles was completely focused on hearing, feeling, now that he'd lost his ability to see.

A slick finger pushed against his back entrance. "Let me in," Brad said.

Miles pushed back, sighing when the finger popped past his ring. He'd never been a strict top, but it had been a while since he'd been fucked. Casey had been the last one and even that had been months before he'd broken up with him.

In hindsight, there had been a great deal of issues with their relationship, and Casey being a bottom only who hated to top had been one of them. Miles loved to fuck, but he loved bottoming as well. He'd rarely gotten the opportunity with Casey, one of the many signals their relationship was never as solid as he had thought it to be.

Brad rubbed his pucker with his finger, circled it a few times, before adding another one. Wordlessly he pushed, circled, scissored, and stretched. Miles bit back a moan. Everything this man did felt so delicious, setting fire to his skin and insides.

Brad pulled his fingers out and Miles let out a whimper

of disappointment. Brad chuckled. "You like that, huh? No worries, I got something better."

A slick pressure demanded to be let in, and Miles bore down. A dildo. Brad pushed slowly until it was completely in. It created a hot burning that spread from his ass to his balls, and all the way to the tip of his cock. It made him want to fuck, badly.

Again, something he hadn't done in a while. He'd had a few one night stands since Casey, but they had been highly unsatisfactory. Most men could not appreciate a premature ejaculation—and the mere act of fucking turned him on too much to keep himself from orgasming.

"You like having something in your hole?"

He nodded. "Yeah. It makes my orgasm more intense. Especially when it...ohhh!"

Brad had pulled the dildo back, then slid it back in, aiming directly for Miles' prostate. "Fuck, yeah, like that..."

Brad repeated the move, causing goosebumps all over Miles' skin. "Do you prefer stopping when you come, or continuing, so your orgasms come right on top of each other?" Brad asked.

"If I can keep going, fuck straight through an orgasm, 'cause the next one is way more intense."

Nobody had ever asked him this kind of shit. Not even Casey. He'd merely wanted to know how Miles got off quickest, not what felt best for him.

"Can I try something?"

"Brad, my love, you can try whatever the fuck you want, as long as you..."

The dildo was yanked out of his ass, then shoved back in. Miles let out a yelp that transformed in a deep moan when Brad repeated the move. His balls buzzed with excitement, hiding flush against his body. Come on, come on, so close...

"Ooooohhhh..." The moan was so loud everyone in the house would be able to hear it, but he didn't care. His balls contracted, then emptied as his cock spurted. The dildo was rammed right back in, causing him to emit another load onto the sheets.

He was still panting, when he felt a weight on his legs, then a hand on his dick, which was still trembling with aftershocks. The damn thing was still hard, of course. What was Brad doing? His answer came when his cock was pressing against something warm, tight, then popped in.

"Shitshitshit...whatareyoudoing? Ohmyfuckyoufeelgood," Miles babbled. His cock speared straight into a tight, slick heat, aided by his own cum and what felt like some extra lube inside of Brad. Brad was fucking him. Holy shit, he was riding him.

His hands sought, found Brad's hips. He was still too weak to help him lift up and sink back down, but at least he could touch him. Brad had the perfect rhythm going, fast enough to rebuild his orgasm from the ground up, but not so slow it would take forever.

"Fuck, I want to turn you over and fuck the shit out of you," Miles groaned.

"When you're healed, you can have my ass as long as you want to. This one is on me."

He moved his hand toward where Brad's cock had to be, but his hand was slapped away. "Don't touch my dick."

"I want you to come, too," Miles protested.

"This isn't about me. Do not touch me, or I walk away."

For a second he wondered what the issue was with him touching Brad, but then his arousal got the better of him. He raised his hips as Brad moved downward, moaned with satisfaction at the increased force.

"You're so fucking responsive. It's like taking candy from a baby. I love it," Brad panted.

Was it Miles' imagination, or was Brad more free with him now that Miles couldn't see him? Interesting.

Brad shifted slightly and the next move downward was so deep, it made Miles' teeth rattle. "I'm close," he warned.

Two thrusts later, he lost the battle. He shouted it out, as he came inside Brad, who sat down on him and stopped moving. A second later, he reached backward and shoved the dildo back into Miles' ass, straight at his prostate. He was still orgasming when his balls erupted all over again, sending wave after wave of white, blinding pleasure through his body. He shuddered, winced as pain traveled through his battered body, then ground his teeth at the force of his release.

His lungs drew in a desperate breath, as his legs jerked once more. Holy fuck, he'd never, ever come that hard. He'd had what felt like two orgasms at once. "What the fuck was that?" he managed.

"You like?"

"You damn near killed me."

Miles' soft cock slipped out of Brad's ass, a testament to how intense his orgasm had been. He was truly sated, and that didn't happen very often.

"Don't take your blindfold off yet," Brad said. The weight from Miles' hips disappeared, leaving him strangely lonely. He'd felt connected to Brad, even with the blindfold on. But if Brad needed him to not see him naked, for whatever reason, he'd respect that.

Seconds later, the blindfold was untied and he blinked against the sudden light. Brad leaned over him, kneeling on the bed, his boxers back on. His cock was soft, so he must have come, though Miles had no idea how or when.

"Hi," Brad said, with that cute, shy smile.

"Hi back atcha. That was pretty intense, man. The good intense. I've never come so hard."

The proud smile on Brad's face did funny things to Miles' insides. Why did the guy take such pride in pleasing Miles, a complete stranger? He was an enigma, this one.

"They say an anal orgasm is different from a penile one, so I wondered how it would feel for you to have them both on top of each other."

"Really, really, really good. That's how that felt, in case you were wondering."

Brad grinned. "I got that impression, yeah."

"Any chance you'd be willing to help me shower?"

5

Brad's post-fuck exuberance vanished instantly. It had felt so good, Miles' thick cock inside him. And that double-orgasm had wrecked Miles in the best way. The bliss on his face had been all Brad had hoped for.

Now, the man wanted to shower. Showering meant being naked. There was no way in hell Brad was stripping completely in front of Miles. He was already insecure as it was, afraid Miles would spot it even with his boxers on. Charlie had said it wasn't visible unless you knew or really paid attention, but Brad wasn't taking any chances. The man was an FBI agent, after all.

"It's okay if you want to leave your boxers on," Miles said. "You can borrow a pair of mine afterward."

Did he know? Brad hadn't seen him study his groin, but still. Or maybe he'd picked up on his reluctance to be naked and wanted to respect that? That seemed more likely.

"Okay," he said. He could hardly say no. Miles needed to shower, first of all, and who else could help him? Even more, Brad wanted to take care of him, serve him. If it hadn't been for the entirely naked requirement, he'd jump at the opportunity right away. It was still a risk, but he didn't see any other way.

"Thank you."

Miles was so polite, always thanking him. He had no idea what pleasuring him meant to Brad. He didn't need the thanks.

"I need to take off these bandages first. Noah will put new ones one later," Miles said.

"I'll do it."

Brad kneeled next to Miles, helped him sit up on the bed. He swiftly unwound the bandage around his chest. There were still some blood crusts underneath, but it didn't bother him. The incision on his belly was healing well, as far as Brad could tell. He'd only ever had the one surgery, but he'd seen his brother Blake after his and that had looked pretty similar—though Blake's wound had been way bigger. No wonder, they'd had to cut him open entirely.

He rolled off the bed, held out both his hands so Miles could pull himself sideways. He did, but it cost him effort. Brad leaned in to help him stand up, then slung the man's arm around his shoulders so he could take part of his weight. Step by step, they made it into the bathroom.

He helped Miles sit down on the bench in the shower. Mighty convenient that this shower was handicapped accessible. At least Miles could sit down the entire time. Brad turned on the shower, waited till the water had the right temperature, then handed Miles the shower head. "Here, hold it on yourself. I'll wash your hair."

They barely spoke as Brad shampooed his hair, then helped him rinse it. He'd found washcloths in a bathroom cabinet, had taken one. The shower gel smelled fresh, ocean-scented. He squeezed out a healthy amount and started washing Miles from his neck down.

Miles groaned, not unlike he did when Brad was pleasuring him. "Feels good?" Brad asked.

"You have no idea."

By the time he'd rinsed Miles, the guy was looking mighty pale again. Time to rest, Brad reckoned. He toweled him off, noting with deep satisfaction that Miles' cock stayed soft. He'd worn him out for now, which according to his information was no small feat.

He helped him back to the bedroom, still half wet himself and wearing soggy boxers. They were not coming off, though. Not in front of Miles, anyway. He quickly helped him into a pair of soft pajama bottoms.

"There's boxers of mine in the drawer," Miles said. "Feel free to grab a pair."

Brad did, closing the bathroom door behind him as he dried himself off completely and put the boxers on. They were a little wide on him, but he preferred that. He always bought his underwear at least a size bigger so it would conceal more.

Miles' eyes were closed when he stepped back in. Must have fallen asleep again. Brad got dressed quickly, making as little noise as he could.

"You can sleep here tonight, if you want," Miles suddenly said.

Brad turned around, startled. "Oh. Erm, thank you, but no. I wanna hang out with Charlie, and I have to work tomorrow."

Miles opened one eye. "Yeah, so? You can come back after spending time with Charlie and get up early. I don't mind."

Brad put his jacket on, grabbed his backpack. "I do mind." He sighed. Better make this crystal clear. "This is sex, Miles, nothing more."

Miles opened his other eye as well, leaned halfway on his side to make eye contact. "It could be more, maybe. I like you."

Brad scoffed. "You like that I can satisfy you sexually, that's all. You don't know me at all."

"Maybe I want to get to know you."

Brad walked out. With the door knob in his hand, he looked over his shoulder. "I don't want you to get to know me. I want to make you come, but that's all you're gonna get from me. Get some rest."

MILES WOKE UP GROGGY, unsure of where he was for a second. He blinked, turned his head to investigate the noise that had woke him up. Brad was sitting on a chair across from him, tying his shoes. Max was right next to him, observing him, it seemed.

Right, he was in Indy's guest room.

"Hi," he whispered.

Brad looked up. "Hi. Sorry if I woke you up. I left my shoes here yesterday."

"S okay. Where are you going?"

Brad looked at him as if he was stupid. "Work. It's Friday morning."

Miles pushed himself into a half-sitting position. "Right. Sorry. Not entirely awake yet." He dragged a hand through his hair, discovered that it was standing up straight, way past what he could pull off as a bedroom look.

Would things be weird, after Brad's parting words yesterday? It had been potentially humiliating, to admit you liked someone, only to be shot down like that. Yet it hadn't felt that way to Miles. There was a hell of a lot more going on with Brad than a mere rejection because he didn't like Miles. No, this guy was hiding stuff, which made Miles all the more determined to keep digging.

Brad himself looked a tad pale. It was hard to spot considering his slightly darker complexion, but Miles was a trained observer. Brad was tired. "Did you get any sleep?" Miles asked.

Brad rose, looked down on Miles with surprise. "Shouldn't I be asking you that? You're the guy with all the injuries and shit."

He'd expertly dodged the question, Miles noted. What was it with Brad that he kept everyone at a distance? Why was even a simple inquiry like this too close for comfort for him?

Miles offered him a slow grin, despite his thoughts. "It is a very comfortable bed."

"You and I will have to make sure to thoroughly test it," Brad said.

Miles was hard instantly. Brad was so uninhibited about sex. Aside from the fact that he wouldn't let Miles see him naked, that was.

Brad noticed his arousal, shot him a semi-exasperated look. "Not now, I have to leave for work. I can't be late."

"Then don't say shit like that. Massive turn on, man," Miles complained. He reached for his cock, rearranged it so it wasn't as uncomfortable.

"Oh, what the fuck. I'll suck you off. But you better fucking come fast, you hear me?"

Completely dressed, he kneeled beside the bed and gently pulled Miles toward him. He whipped Miles' cock out of his pajama bottoms before Miles could say another word. Fuck, he loved it when Brad got so wanton. He was such an enigma, shy and struggling for words one second, and then all sexy and almost desperate the next.

Miles' hands went to Brad's head, dug into his curls. He loved holding him like that when Brad sucked him off. Holy fuck, the boy could suck cock. Miles already felt his orgasm building.

A door squeaked, and Miles stiffened, but Brad was unrelenting. He sucked him in deep, let Miles fuck his throat. Someone was coming into the room, dammit. Should he let go of Brad's head? Brad's grip on his base intensified. Footsteps came into the room. Miles' hips bucked, his body prioritizing orgasming before anything else.

"Brad?"

Oh, fuck, that had to be Charlie. Miles hadn't seen him yet, but he recognized his voice from hearing him talk to the others in the living room yesterday. He stepped into sight now, the cutest face Miles had ever seen. Charlie spotted them on the bed, and his eyes widened.

Brad would have to stop now, right? Miles was so close, dammit. Brad held up a finger to Charlie, as if to indicate he needed one more minute. Miles wouldn't, not if he kept sucking like that.

"Oooohhh!" Miles groaned, jerked into Brad's mouth as he came.

Brad licked him clean efficiently, then tucked his cock back in. "There, that should tide you over till I get back. Should be around four fifteen."

He rose, licked his lips in a gesture that did strange things to Miles' insides. "Hey babe," he said to Charlie. "Sorry, needed to get my morning protein shake in."

He kissed Charlie on the lips, and the kid crumpled his nose. "I can still taste him on you," Charlie said.

Brad chuckled. "Little protein for you, too, then. He tastes good, you know. Anyway, I gotta go. See you this afternoon, okay?"

He kissed him again, and Charlie didn't seem to mind. Definitely too affectionate for casual friends. What was the story with these two? Seconds later, Brad was out the door, and Miles was left with Charlie and Max.

"Hi," he said gamely. He managed to push himself up into a sitting position, made sure to cover himself completely. What the fuck did you say when a complete stranger saw you getting a blow job? "I'm Miles, as you've probably figured out."

"The constantly horny FBI agent," Charlie said.

Miles winced. "Yeah, that would be me." He cleared his throat, acutely embarrassed. "Sorry you had to see that."

"No worries. Brad gives me a play by play anyway, so it's not like you had any secrets to begin with."

Miles swallowed. "He what?" That had to be a joke, right? Brad, who you had to force to reveal anything, had told Charlie about the sex with Miles? What the fuck?

"He didn't tell you?"

"Brad doesn't tell me much of anything."

Charlie let out a sound that appeared to be a laugh. "Too busy making you come, huh?"

Miles didn't know what to say to that one. "But apparently, he tells you a lot, huh?"

"More than others anyway."

Imagine that, Brad did actually confide in someone. What did Charlie have to do to make Brad trust him?

"How did you two become friends?" Miles asked.

"He was my teacher," Charlie said.

"Come again?"

"Brad. He was my math teacher in high school. I was a

junior, and he was a substitute for my real math teacher who had a heart attack. He was fresh out of college and substituting when he saw me getting stuffed into a garbage can by some jocks who objected to my sexual orientation. He intervened, and became a sort of mentor to me afterward."

Miles' mouth was slightly open. "Brad's a math teacher?"

"Yeah. He teaches middle school now. You didn't know?"

"No. I asked him what he did for a living, but he wouldn't tell me." And now Miles wondered why. It wasn't like math teacher was a profession to be embarrassed about. Why had Brad not even want to share that with Miles?

Charlie looked at him, his gaze surprisingly sharp considering how damn early it still was. "Do you like him?" he asked.

Miles could pretend he didn't know who Charlie was talking about, but there was little sense. "Yeah, I do. He's a puzzle to me, one I can't seem to figure out."

Charlie sighed. "He's not easy, but he's worth getting to know. If you want to, that is."

"I'd love to get to know him better, if he would let me."

Another puff from Charlie. "Brad's defensive mechanism is highly developed," he said.

"I'll say. I've encountered porcupines that were less prickly than him. But I also saw how sweet he can be, with you just now, for instance." Miles let the implicit question linger.

"He's different with me," Charlie affirmed. "He always has been, but I think it was because I was so young when we met. I didn't start out as his equal, so to speak."

Miles frowned, trying to make sense of what Charlie was saying. What was going on with Brad? Did it have something to do with whatever secret Brad had that he was trying to guard, something both Charlie and his cop-boyfriend had known?

Noises were drifting into the room that Miles didn't recognize.

Charlie cocked his head, seemed to listen as well. "It's, erm, Connor and Josh," he said, looking sheepishly. "They're quite expressive."

Seconds later, more sounds joined in, and Charlie sighed. "And that would be Noah and Indy. Sorry, it can get crazy like that here."

They both listened for a bit, as the sounds intensified. Charlie sighed, then walked over to the door and closed it.

"Let's watch some TV until they're done," he said.

"You wanna hang out here with me?" Miles asked, surprised at the level of trust Charlie displayed here.

"Sure," Charlie said easily. "Brad likes you, and that's enough for me. He's never wrong about people. Plus, the fact that you're staying here says enough. From what I understand, these are not trusting folks by nature, yet they took you in and set you up with Brad. That must mean you're a good man."

"Wow. Thank you. That's unexpected, but thank you."

They installed themselves, each on a side of the king size bed. Miles sat up against the headboard, pillows propped in his back for comfort, while Charlie lay on his stomach on the bed. He found a morning show for them to watch, and Miles relaxed. Max walked around in a few circles, before deciding to plop his butt down on the carpet, and seconds later, the dog was napping.

It sure was a nice set up Indy and Noah had in their bedroom, and Miles did feel a tad guilty for making them sleep in the guest room. Well, he didn't make them. Hell, he hadn't even asked them. They'd willingly offered. And judging by the sounds, it wasn't like it was hindering their sex life. Holy hell, Indy had not been kidding when he said they were open about sex. It took some getting used to, that was for sure.

"You're hard," Charlie said suddenly, pointing at Miles' tenting pajama bottoms under the sheets.

He hadn't even noticed, caught up in his thoughts and used as he'd become to his body's reactions.

"Yes."

Should he explain? But if Brad told Charlie everything, he'd already know, correct?

"Do you need some privacy?"

Miles blinked. Fuck, the kid was considerate. "Erm, no, but thank you. This will go down by itself, since Brad...Yeah, anyway."

"Okay." Charlie turned his attention back to the TV, and when he didn't say anything else Miles slowly relaxed again. Miles covered his groin with a pillow to at least spare Charlie the sight of his hard on. For almost an hour, they watched the morning shows companionably, commenting on some crazy segments, and laughing at the antics.

Someone knocked on the door. "Guys?" Indy.

"Come on in," Miles called out. He muted the TV.

"Good morning. We were wondering where you'd gone, Charlie."

The unspoken question was clear. Indy wanted to know what the fuck Miles was doing here with Charlie. It warmed him, this care.

"The morning sex was getting a little loud for our comfort, so we retreated in here," Charlie said before Miles could say anything. Miles swallowed. Apparently, Charlie didn't have much of a filter when it came to sex, either. He'd never considered himself to be a prude, but compared to these people, he damn well was.

"Oh. Right. We're done fucking, for now, so do you guys wanna come into the kitchen for breakfast? Josh is making pancakes from scratch."

THE SCENE WAS ALMOST surreal to Charlie. Here he was, sitting in this picture-perfect kitchen on a Friday morning, surrounded by gay men, eating the best damn pancakes he'd ever had. All that was missing was Brad, who was at work. It was like a scene from a cheesy commercial or something, except for Miles who was obviously in pain.

Miles hadn't asked Charlie anything personal when they'd hung out. Charlie had figured the man had to be wondering why Charlie was staying there, but maybe Brad had at least shared bare facts of the assault with him? Charlie had felt self-conscious, but only for a little, and then Miles had gotten a boner, and he'd stopped feeling sorry for himself. Now there was a guy with a problem. Holy hell, he would not want to trade with him.

Next to him, Miles struggled to cut a piece of his pancake, his movements stiff. It must still hurt for him to put pressure on his hand.

"Here," Charlie said softly, "I'll do it." He cut off a piece for Miles, held it out on the fork.

"Thank you," Miles said before taking the bite.

Charlie took another piece himself. Man, these pancakes were so good. Josh should be a fucking chef. He caught Max's pleading look and sneakily snuck him a piece of pancake, too.

He reached for Miles' plate, cut the pancake into little pieces. "Can you get them, or do you want me to help you?"

"This will work. Thank you."

Miles was nice. Truly, honestly nice. Charlie could easily spot the reasons for Brad's attraction to Miles, even if his friend swore up and down it was just sex. He always said that, but it was never just sex with Brad, only he fucking refused to acknowledge that. His self-preservation instinct was so damn strong he'd do anything to prevent getting hurt. Charlie had given up on trying to confront him. It would work itself out. Or not.

Either way, Miles was hot, a classic California surfer boy. More importantly, he was kind. Smart, too. He was seeing way more of Brad than his best friend realized, and seemed pretty determined to figure him out. Should Charlie be concerned or jealous? He mulled it over. Interestingly enough, he was neither. He was curious, and maybe actually rooting for Miles to get through to Brad? Somebody had to, because he seemed hell-bent on getting hurt.

"What's the plan for today, guys?" Noah asked.

"I have jiujitsu in an hour," Indy said, "and Blake asked me to stick around for the women's class he teaches. He's looking for another teacher and thought I might be interested."

Noah's look of surprise told Charlie that was news for him.

"You think you'd like that?" Noah asked.

Indy nodded, beamed. "Yeah. Now that I don't need to hide anymore, I'd love to see if that's something I could do."

"You're certainly good enough," Miles said, carefully bringing another bite of pancake to his mouth. "He kicked my ass back in Kansas."

Indy grinned. "You were a little overconfident, dude."

Miles looked sheepish. "Word. To be fair, Indy totally downplayed his jiujitsu skills. I thought he was a novice. He humiliated me, then proceeded to beat another agent as well." He stilled, and the smile on Indy's face disappeared. "Fisher was a total homophobe and a major asshole, but he was a good agent."

From his words, Charlie deduced this Fisher guy had died. Brad had said something about Indy being attacked while in FBI custody.

"That's how you met, right?" he asked Miles.

"Yeah. I was one of the agents on Indy's protective detail. We erm, kinda bonded, I guess."

Indy snorted. "We didn't bond. You wouldn't leave me the fuck alone, and then when you attended to my injuries after my bout with Fisher, you got a massive boner."

Charlie's eyes grew big. How would Miles take this? He still wasn't entirely sure what the deal was with him and his...condition. It seemed so far-fetched when Brad had explained it to him.

"It wasn't a massive boner. I got a little excited, that's all."

"Dude, I walked in on you jacking yourself off. There was nothing little about it."

There were snorts and laughs all around the table.

"And thanks, Indy, for making me relive that moment. It's a few more hours till Brad gets home, okay, so have mercy on me?"

Charlie look sideways to Miles and let his eyes travel down, to where the man's erection was clearly visible. Miles met his eyes when he finally could tear his eyes away, and his gaze was so vulnerable it hit Charlie deep.

"You really are hard all the time," Charlie said in wonder. Brad had told him, but it had been an abstract concept to him. To be fair, he'd suspected Miles had blown

up the whole thing. Sure, some men had more sex drive
than others, but who the fuck needed at least four orgasms a
day? He was starting to see the deep truth behind it, though.
Despite all the joking and teasing, this was a real problem
for Miles.

The group grew quiet. "Yes," Miles said. "I swear to God,
it's not personal, Charlie. But if it bothers you even the
slightest, I'll stay out of your way, okay? I usually wear two
tight boxers so it doesn't show as much, but I didn't think of
it since everyone here's been so relaxed about it. I can do
that, if you want, or I'll find another place to stay."

He was nervous, Charlie realized. The super cool FBI
agent was babbling. "It's okay," Charlie said slowly. "I'm
more...curious."

Miles swallowed. "Ask."

"Ask?"

"Anything. I've never talked about this before, but
everyone here knows, and they haven't run me off with pitch
forks so far."

"We're waiting till you get better," Noah joked. "It's no
fun bringing in pitchforks when you're injured."

Charlie let his gaze wonder down again, where Miles'
pajama was still tenting. "How do you cope with the embarrassment?" he asked.

Miles' eyes grew soft, almost moist, it seemed. "It's not
easy," he admitted. "People take it personally, you know?
They think I'm some kind of perv, because I get hard in
inappropriate circumstances, or they fear that I'm after their
boyfriend. They don't understand it's a purely physical
response to stimuli, and that there's nothing I can do
about it."

"You must have a ton of strategies to protect yourself,"
Noah remarked.

Miles nodded. "Yeah. As I said, double underwear, extra tight. Luckily, we usually wear suits, so they're a little roomier than jeans, but on the farm in Kansas that wasn't an option. I barely watch TV or movies, because they tend to get me excited easily. I keep my distance, avoid touching people. That's what got me into trouble with Indy, the fact that I needed to touch him to check his injuries. Even the slightest touch can...you get the idea."

"I can't even imagine what that must be like," Josh said. "We're all so touchy-feely here, and to miss out on that..."

"By nature, I am, too, but I've discovered people don't take it well when a casual touch makes me aroused. Imagine I'd hug you, Josh, and you'd feel me grow hard. You'd be uncomfortable at best, offended at worst, and that's not to say what would happen if Connor saw. No offense, man."

Connor looked pensive, scratched his chin. "None taken. Solid point, though."

Miles looked down at himself with a dramatic gesture. "Solid, for certain," he joked.

He must want to lighten the mood after sharing something so personal. Charlie's heart went out to him. How did the man survive like this? He had to be incredibly lonely. "How long has it been like this?" he asked.

"This condition? Started when I was a teen, but all guys are horny at that age. Went to the doctor when I was in college, 'cause I got worried. They ran a whole battery of tests and came back with this. I'm thirty-two, so it's been a while."

"And nobody touches you?" Charlie asked.

"Right now, Brad. Before that, no one. I had a boyfriend, but..." Miles' sigh was deep and sad, and Charlie's heart contracted in response. "Casey couldn't deal with it. Well, that was one of the reasons he dumped me, but yeah. I tried one-night stands, but that was too embarrassing to deal with."

The kitchen was quiet as Miles' pain hummed around for everyone to feel. Brad should have been there, Charlie thought, should have heard and seen this. If Brad had seen Miles' vulnerability and how loving these men had reacted, maybe it could have helped him to realize no one was gonna reject him for his issues.

Then again, being Brad, he'd need more than that. What, Charlie didn't know. Fuck knew he'd tried over the years to give Brad what he needed, to be who he needed, but it had not been enough. Or it hadn't been the right thing. Brad needed something, beyond mere understanding for his issues, but damned if Charlie knew what it was. He could only hope he'd either discover what it was and help Brad, or that Brad would find what he was looking for before his reckless sexual behavior would hurt him. Charlie loved him, more than Brad would ever know, but one of these days he'd encounter the wrong guy and get hurt. Much like himself, come to think of it.

Miles let out a huge yawn. "Sorry, guys. I'm off to bed again. Thanks for the delicious breakfast, Josh."

"Make sure to take your pain killers, Miles," Noah said. "There's no need to be in pain. Your body needs to rest and heal."

Miles nodded as he carefully got up from the table.

"I'll help you to bed," Charlie offered without thinking.

Miles turned his head to look at him, surprise painting his face. "You sure? You don't have to, I can—"

Charlie put his hands on his hips, shot him a deadly glare. "If I didn't want to, I wouldn't have offered. Don't treat me like china, just because I was stupid enough to let my boyfriend beat the crap out of me. I'm a lot stronger than I look."

Hello, anger. It was still there, clearly.

Miles' face went from relaxed surfer boy to authoritative in one sec, and Charlie watched, fascinated. "Don't ever call yourself stupid. You're not to blame. He is. This not on you, no matter what you said or did. He's the motherfucking asshole, not you."

Charlie nodded, impressed with Miles' tone as much as his words. Wow, that had been seriously cool. Hot, even.

Mile's eyes softened. "And I'm sorry for making you feel like you were delicate. It wasn't my intention."

Charlie swallowed. "I know. I'm...it's touchy for me. Because of my size and shit, people always assume I'm some fragile flower that needs protecting. I can take care of myself."

"I won't make that mistake again," Miles said, a hint of a smile on his lips. "I'd appreciate your help."

Charlie grinned, desperate to break the sudden tension. "I'll even tell you a fucking bedtime story."

Miles slowly walked toward his bedroom. "What kind of story?"

Charlie walked next to him, ready to extend a hand if the man needed one. "Well, Brad always entertains me with his fuck stories, but I guess with your condition that would be kinda rude, no?"

Miles held out his hand, a gesture that packed a deep meaning. Charlie grabbed it, smiling, as they walked together. Max followed them, maybe hoping for more treats from Charlie.

"I could always retreat into the bathroom, rub one out," Miles said.

Charlie grinned. "True. In that case, I'll tell you about

the time Brad thought he met the perfect man, this big, furry bear—only to discover the guy had...Well, that's what you're about to find out."

In the kitchen, the others exploded in laughter, apparently still listening in to him and Miles. It felt good, joking around, even if his insides were still burning with anger, Charlie thought.

6

"Keep your arm strong, don't let me push it down," Blake told Aaron. "Let's try it again."

Aaron did better this time, holding his arm tight while Blake tried to break through his defense. He still could if he wanted to, obviously, but that was not the point. Aaron was getting better at jiujitsu. He wasn't a natural talent like Indy, and he missed that fighter's mentality, but he made up for it with a deep willingness and desire to please Blake. The kid would walk through fire if that was what Blake told him to do. It was an honor and a responsibility Blake took seriously.

"That's it for today," Blake announced. "Let's do some cooling down."

Aaron immediately took off his white belt, decorated with three small black strips to indicate he was well on his way to earning a grey belt, then got rid of his gi jacket. Blake laughed when he took off his gi pants as well, leaving him in nothing else but a pair of cute, pink boxers. It was a good thing they were alone in the studio, with the front door still locked. God, he loved Sundays. He got to spend the whole day with his puppy.

"I didn't mean a literal cooling down," Blake said.

Aaron giggled. "I know, but I'm sweating my ass off."

Blake slapped his ass playfully. "Such a cute ass it is."

He'd gained some weight, Aaron had. His muscles were more defined after training with Blake, and it looked good on him. Blake loved the feel of that lean, tight body against his. He had ample opportunity to enjoy that particular sensation, because Aaron loved nothing more than touching Blake.

He didn't even realize it half the time, but he intuitively always sought Blake's body. Sometimes he'd simply put his hand on Blake's leg, or foot, or arm, but more often he wanted to feel Blake against him. His favorite spot was still at Blake's feet, no matter if it was on the floor, on the couch, or in bed. He could sit there for hours and be absolutely, perfectly happy.

Blake took off his own gi, stripping down to his underwear. He wasn't particularly sweaty, but maybe he could entice Aaron in a little play before they showered? Or maybe during the shower?

"Blake, will you do something for me?" Aaron asked.

"Anything, puppy. What is it?"

Aaron crumpled his nose in that cute gesture that made Blake's stomach swirl. The kid had no idea how ridiculously cute he was.

"Why is that always your first reaction, to give me what I want?"

Blake stepped close, Aaron looking at him with serious eyes. "Because I love you, and I want to make you happy. There's little I wouldn't do for you, you know that."

Aaron closed the distance between them, circled his

arms around Blake's neck and put his head on Blake's shoulder. Blake breathed his scent in, pulled him close against his body, his hands possessively on Aaron's ass. His cock was already hard, but that was often the case when Aaron touched him. He was addictive as shit, and Blake never seemed to be able to get enough of him.

"I'm so happy when I'm with you," Aaron sighed.

Blake smiled. "You make me happy too, my little puppy."

Aaron's tongue licked Blake's chest. He decreased his hold on Aaron, giving him room to do as he pleased. He rubbed his cheek against Blake, before trailing a wet path to Blake's left nipple.

Blake had gotten better and better at reading Aaron's signals. There were times when all Aaron wanted to do was explore Blake's body, and bring Blake pleasure. The kid could give amazing blow jobs, would suck his balls, and rim Blake until he saw fucking stars.

Other times Aaron had this desperate need to be filled, taken. He would care about nothing else but to have his own needs met. Blake could fuck the living daylights out of him then, and he'd come and come and come until he was too spent to even lift a finger. Blake had the feeling this happened when Aaron was upset, or emotionally out of whack about something, but he hadn't discussed it with Aaron yet.

Aaron was licking his way down. After lavishing both Blake's nipples with wet, hot attention, he was moving south.

"You taste so good when you're sweaty," Aaron said happily. "Well, you taste good, period, but I cannot get enough of you like this."

He dragged Blake's underwear down without asking, buried his nose in Blake's pubes, then nuzzled his balls.

His puppy had come a long way from his first tentative touches.

Blake let out an appreciative sigh, while Aaron lapped the precum from his cock.

"Come on," Aaron said, standing up straight.

"Wait, what?"

Aaron grinned. "I want you inside me. In the shower. Easier to clean up after."

He didn't wait for Blake, sauntered into the locker room, confident Blake would follow. Of course, Blake would follow —he'd trail Aaron everywhere if he had to. Blake left his gi on the floor, stepped out of the underwear still pooling at his feet and made his way into the locker room as well.

Aaron stood buck naked against the shower wall, hands leaning against the wall, ass pushed all the way back.

"Hurry up, would you?" he asked.

Blake fumbled with the wallet in his jeans, managed to get the packet of lube he wanted. Seconds later, his cock was coated.

He took position behind Aaron, put his hands on the boy's hips. "You want my cock, puppy?"

He teased him with the tip, pressing against his hole without entering.

"I swear, Blake, if you're not inside me in ten seconds..."

He sure loved it when Aaron was like this. Sexy, wanton, impatient to be fucked. And shit, that ass was made to take cock. Aaron loved it when Blake breached him without prep.

He bent over Aaron, brought his mouth to Aaron's ear. He licked the sensitive spot behind his ear, then gently bit his lobe. "Or you'll do what?"

"Shit, Blake, fuck me already, would you?"

When Aaron started swearing, he'd reached his fucking

limit. Blake took mercy on him, pulled his hips back and surged inside him in one powerful thrust.

"Ooohhh, fuuuuuck," Aaron moaned.

Blake straightened himself, dug his fingers into Aaron's hips, slid in again. He loved it when he had control like this, could angle his thrusts exactly so he'd hit Aaron's sweet spot.

Slick, sopping noises filled the shower as Blake built a steady rhythm. Aaron didn't come as quickly as he had in the beginning, when all he needed was Blake's cock inside of him, but he still didn't last very long. Blake could tell he was already close, by the tension in his body and his clenched fists against the wall.

"Come for me, puppy," he grunted, slammed in hard. Aaron could take everything you threw at him, and Blake fucking loved it. No need to be careful here, no holding back. Blake fucked hard, and Aaron took it all with pleasure.

"Blaaaaaake!" Aaron whined. His body jerked and his cock exploded against the shower tiles.

"Good boy," Blake praised him. He didn't stop, didn't need to. Aaron loved it when he fucked him through his orgasm. Sometimes he'd come again in under a minute. The kid sure had a faster recovery time than anyone Blake had ever fucked.

"Bend over, Aaron. You know you want my fat cock in your hole. Push that sexy ass back. Yeah, like that..." Blake groaned.

He'd discovered that proper, prim Aaron loved it when he talked dirty. The kid still didn't curse outside of the bedroom, had trouble even saying "fuck" or anything similar, but he totally got off on Blake getting all dirty with him.

He fucked him hard, deep, loving every second of it. "You're so hot and tight around my cock, Aaron. Is my cock

filling you completely? You like that burning in your ass
when I breach you? No prep for you, 'cause your hole is so
fucking eager for me...You were born to be fucked, puppy,
born to be mine. I will never, ever get enough of your sweet
ass."

Aaron whimpered, moved back against Blake's thrusts.
His eager Aaron, so desperate for more. Blake's skin prickled, his balls pulling tight against his body. He buried
himself balls deep in Aaron one last time, then surrendered
to the orgasm blasting through him. His cock jerked inside
Aaron as he came, depositing his seed right where it
belonged. Aaron followed him swiftly, convulsing in his
arms.

Panting slightly, Blake loosened his grip on Aaron's hips.
It was always a sad moment when he had to pull out, but at
least he got to see his cum smeared all over Aaron's ass.
Within minutes, it would start dripping down—his favorite
thing to watch. He pulled Aaron up, his body still limp,
kissed his shoulder blade before he spun him around. "Love
you."

Aaron sighed against him, melted in Blake's embrace. "I
love it when you come inside me," he whispered.

"You love it when I talk dirty, too," Blake said, smiling.

Another sigh. "I do."

Blake held him, dropping light kisses on Aaron's neck,
his cheeks, his mouth until both their heartbeats had
calmed down. Their spent cocks cuddled as well, happy to
find each other well-sated.

"You ready to shower, puppy?"

"Yeah, I guess. I love being held like this."

Aaron had missed out on so much physical affection in
his childhood, Blake had reasoned, that he still had a lot of
catching up to do. He was no psychologist, but this seemed

pretty straight forward to him. Apparently, today was a needy day, as Blake called them in his head, a day where Aaron needed his proximity.

"I don't have a lesson till this afternoon. I had planned to do some admin, but I could do that at home on the couch, so you could sit with me if you want?"

Aaron nodded. "I'd love that." A wave of sadness flashed over his face.

"What's wrong?" Blake asked gently. He didn't talk easily, Aaron. Even after months of being together, Blake still had to coax him to share every single time. "Does this have something to do with what you wanted to ask me earlier?"

Aaron's shoulders hunched. "Will you ask if we can visit with Josh? Maybe for lunch?"

How telling it was that Aaron didn't dare to call his own brother to ask if he could come over. Things between him and Josh had improved, somewhat, but Aaron still felt like an outsider, a nuisance—and not entirely without reason. Josh seemed to have little need for Aaron in his life, happy as he was with Connor, Indy, and Noah.

Even his stint in the clinic hadn't made a difference in that. Selfishly, Blake had hoped Josh would come to some sort of insight there, some revelation that he needed Aaron in his life, too, but he hadn't even contacted Aaron immediately when he'd gotten back. They still hadn't seen each other since Josh had gotten back five days ago. Blake wanted nothing more than to fix this, but he couldn't. The only thing he could do was be there for Aaron, and help him as best as he could.

"Sure, sweetheart. No problem."

"You might run into Brad. Are you sure you'd be okay with that?"

"He's a grown man, Aaron, making his own choices. As

long as it's what he wants, I won't interfere. Besides, from what I heard, this FBI guy is a decent fellow."

He kissed Aaron's forehead. "Ready for that shower now?"

"Five more minutes. Please?"

Blake pulled him close again. "Anything for you."

AARON'S STOMACH rolled a little as Blake made the turn into the driveway. Why was he still anxious about seeing Josh? It was his brother, for heaven's sake.

He'd been so nervous he'd initially even put on one of the few boring polo shirts he had left from old Aaron, as Blake liked to call it. Blake had sent him straight back to get changed, though, telling him he wanted sexy Aaron to show up.

So he'd chosen a dark blue tank top with a sheer tunic over it that had a gorgeous abstract pattern in all shades of pink, ranging from the subtlest pastel to bright fuchsia. After debating for at least five minutes, he'd even put on a touch of mascara and a bit of lip gloss.

Maybe he was nervous, because he knew it would be a big group today. More people meant more chance of messing it up, of saying or doing the wrong thing.

Then again, Charlie, he loved. Aaron was only too happy to see him again. Brad wouldn't be an issue, either. He'd been acting differently since Aaron had come back, had tried to make an effort to be nice to him. He could still be aloof and abrasive at times, but Aaron felt that was probably more his character and not personal. He did that to Blake too, at times. That left only Miles, the FBI agent, which was ridiculous, because Aaron had nothing to fear from him.

No, his trepidation was because of Josh. His own brother made him sick to his stomach. How sad was that? He let out a small sigh.

"You okay?" Blake asked as he parked the car.

"Yeah." He felt like a total idiot that he'd had to ask Blake to call Josh. It was just that the thought of calling him with the possibility of being rejected was too much for him.

Blake shut off the engine, turned Aaron's head toward him with a soft grip on his chin. "It'll be fine, puppy. I won't let anything happen to you, you know that."

He nodded, a warm feeling replacing his fear. Blake had him. He had nothing to worry about. "Let's go inside."

Indy let them in, and the solid hug he gave Aaron made his stomach settle a little. "It's lovely to see you, Aaron."

Apparently, Indy had forgotten about the awkward first encounter they'd had, where Aaron had asked him out. Even thinking about it made Aaron cringe inside. He'd been such an idiot back then.

Then Charlie came right up to him, and hugged him tight. "Aaron, honey, it's so good to see you!"

Aaron held him close, reveling in the feeling that someone was actually happy to see him.

Charlie gave him a thorough once-over when he'd let him go. "That top looks gorgeous on you!"

"Thank you," he said, touching it self-consciously.

Charlie reached up to cup his chin, critically studied Aaron's very basic makeup. "You could do with a bit more color, honey, especially on your eyes. I can show you if you want. I've got my whole kit here."

Aaron blushed, acutely aware of everyone watching their exchange. Charlie meant well, but this was the last thing Aaron wanted, to have everyone focus on how feminine he looked. "That's okay, really."

He felt a hand on his shoulder and looked around to find his brother behind him. "I think that would look great on you," Josh said, squeezing his shoulder.

Aaron tried to blink away the sudden tears in his eyes. This was so not what he had been expecting. "Thank you," he managed, his voice barely audible.

Josh gave his shoulder another squeeze before he let go. "You've got time before we eat."

Emboldened, Aaron nodded to Charlie. Charlie held out his hand, and they walked over to his bedroom. "Sit," Charlie pointed and Aaron obediently sat down on the bed.

Charlie rummaged around in a closet and came back with a huge makeup kit. "How have you been?" Aaron asked, unsure of how to word it.

Charlie sighed. "I'm okay, I guess. Physically, I've healed."

He started wiping Aaron's mascara off with a makeup remover wipe. "And emotionally?" Aaron dared to ask.

"I talked to Brad a lot," Charlie said after a while. "It helped. A little. But I still feel stupid as fuck for staying so long. I mean, you saw me when I did your makeup that night Blake took you to Flirt. You knew he'd hit me. Why did I go back?"

Aaron kept his eyes closed since Charlie was still busy removing the little makeup he'd put on, so he could only guess Charlie's state of mind by the tone of his voice. What could he say to make him feel better? Was there any such thing? Words seemed woefully inadequate. Still, he would try.

"All I can remember feeling since I hit puberty was shame. Shame over my body's response to stimuli. Shame over being attracted to boys." He swallowed. Charlie deserved honesty here. Pretending wouldn't help him. "And then shame over pretending to be someone and something I wasn't. Shame over how I treated Josh. Shame over this desire to be pretty. Shame over wanting Blake to take care of me."

Charlie had stopped cleaning his eye, so he opened them. "I grew up in a culture that seemed aimed at making you ashamed of who you were. And it's wrong. Shame is a debilitating emotion that sucks you dry and leaves you with nothing but hatred and bitterness toward yourself. That's not you, Charlie. You're light. You're happy. You have this joy inside you. Don't let shame steal that. Don't let Zack take that from you. He's not worth it. You have nothing to be ashamed of."

He wasn't sure if it made sense, what he had said. It sure had sounded more eloquent in his head.

"He's right, sweetie," Brad said. Aaron turned his head to find him leaning against the doorpost. "You have nothing to be ashamed of, and especially not where it concerns Zach."

Brad's tone was different than Aaron had ever heard him before. Softer, gentle. He'd known Brad and Charlie were best friends, but it was good to see Brad so caring toward him.

Charlie sighed. "My head knows you're right, but my heart doesn't want to accept it yet."

Brad walked over, kissed Charlie on his head. "You'll get there."

Aaron was watching Charlie when Brad kissed him, and for a second Charlie's face displayed such love, that Aaron knew instantly he was in love. With Brad. Wow, how would that end?

Brad wanted to let go, but Charlie grabbed his wrist. "The same is true for you, Brad."

Aaron frowned. What was Charlie talking about?

Brad shot Aaron a dark look, as if threatening him not to say anything. Yeah, like he was that stupid. He wasn't getting anywhere near this, whatever it was.

"Drop it, sweetie," Brad told Charlie.

Aaron noticed that even though Brad's eyes were shooting daggers, his tone toward Charlie was still soft. This was mighty interesting—not that he was gonna get himself involved in any way. He wasn't touching this with a ten-foot pole, not now that Brad finally seemed to warm up to him a little.

Charlie sighed. "Okay, but we'll talk about this later."

He turned back toward Aaron. "Okay, I'm thinking shades of pink since it will match your gorgeous tunic. Sound good?"

Aaron nodded.

Charlie opened his massive makeup kit and started rummaging through it, taking out items and lining them up. Aaron had to smile a little. Charlie took his makeup very seriously, and it was heartwarming to see.

"Can I watch?" Brad asked.

"I don't care, do you, Aaron?" Charlie asked. Aaron loved that he checked.

"It's fine," Aaron said. He kept his face as neutral as possible, but inwardly he was grinning like crazy. How did these two not see they were in love with each other?

"Close your eyes, honey," Charlie said. "I'm gonna start with a little primer, just like last time."

He expertly put on various layers of eyeshadow while Brad asked him questions every now and then. Aaron was content to listen in, enjoying the unspoken attraction between these two.

"Okay, open your eyes," Charlie told Aaron. He held out a mirror for Aaron to study himself. "See what I did? It's three shades of pink. It's subtle enough for now, but you can make it much bolder for a night out. Or throw in a little glitter eye shadow. Now, let's do the mascara."

Putting on mascara was hard, Aaron had discovered. He still poked himself in the eye every now and then, which made your eye tear up, which in turn made your mascara run. And he still hit his eyelids regularly, or the skin between his lower lashes. That was infuriating, because getting that off meant also removing the makeup underneath. It took a steady hand and a lot of patience, he'd discovered.

"You're really good at that," Miles' voice suddenly sounded.

Charlie let out a little squeal and jerked his hand, which caused Aaron to clinch his eyes shut in reflex.

"Shit! Dammit, Miles, you scared the crap out of me!" Charlie snapped. "Didn't they teach you to never scare a man putting on mascara?"

Aaron opened his eyes again. Miles stood next to the bed with a sheepish expression. "Sorry," he said. "They didn't cover that at the FBI academy."

Charlie sighed. "Well, now you know. Okay, honey," he said to Aaron. "Let's see what the damage is. I could have taken out his eyeball, you know?"

Aaron assumed the latter part was aimed at Miles. "I'm quite attached to my eyeballs," he quipped.

Charlie smiled, the anger dissipating from his face. "You should be. They're beautiful. And I would kill and die for your skin. It is so smooth and perfect, it's practically glowing."

"You're not so bad yourself," Miles said. "I mean, I'm no expert but your face looks plenty healthy to me. Like, radiant, I guess."

Charlie's face broke open in a big grin. "You are the sweetest thing, sexy. And such a smooth talker."

Miles jammed his hands into his pockets. "It sounded better in my head."

Charlie blew him a hand kiss. "I'm sure it did, sexy, but I recognize a compliment when I hear one. So thank you. You have redeemed yourself, and I will no longer be upset with you for making me stab Aaron in the eye."

"I'm sure he was shaking in his metaphorical boots about you coming after him with that mascara wand," Brad said.

Was that a joke Brad had just made? Aaron grinned. The times most certainly were a-changing.

"He should be, because hell hath no fury like a makeup artist scorned," Charlie fired back.

"Duly noted," Miles said, smiling again. "Though no offense, Charlie, but I think I could take you on."

"Says the guy who was flat on his back in under ten seconds the last time he said that to someone. Didn't Indy cure you of the notion that size matters?" Charlie rebuffed him, meanwhile removing the smeared mascara with a cotton swab and some remover.

"Ow, burn, baby! That one hurt," Brad laughed.

It was rare to see him laugh, Aaron realized. His Blake was a serious man by nature, but Brad even more so. This carefree laughter was extraordinary.

Miles raised his hands in mock surrender, his face split in a broad grin. "I give up. I can't win if you two are ganging up on me."

"Victory is mine!" Brad declared, making a V with his fingers on both hands.

"More like mine, since I made the winning punchline, but I'll be magnanimous and share it with you, because I'm a benevolent ruler," Charlie said. He put down the cotton swab, looked at Aaron from all sides. "There. Perfect, honey."

Aaron studied himself in the mirror. Charlie was right. It was perfect, his blue eyes popping with the shades of pink around them. "Thank you," he said softly.

Charlie smiled at him. "Anytime. You're gorgeous like this." He started to put the makeup back in the kit. "Go show Blake," he said.

Aaron nodded. Blake was in the living room with the others, lounging on the couch. Aaron shyly walked up to him, as always insecure of how to approach him when others were present. Blake made it easy for him, because he immediately pulled Aaron close. "Let me look at you, puppy." Aaron sank to his knees, and Blake lifted his chin to study him. "God, that's beautiful on you. Absolutely stunning."

Aaron blushed. He wanted to crawl on Blake's lap and hide his face, because everyone was looking at them, and it was too awkward. Blake petted his head, held him in place. "Maybe we should get some more makeup for you to experiment with, hmm? I really like these colors on you. How about I ask Charlie to recommend some for you, since he'll know what works?"

Aaron nodded. He still found it hard to believe that Blake accepted him the way he was, with all his strange quirks, including makeup and all, but he did. The others, he wasn't too sure about, but Blake loved him exactly the way he was.

Blake pulled him up, placed him on the couch beside him so Aaron could snuggle close. That sense of safety he experienced whenever he could physically feel Blake, it had never gone away. The man could calm him with a simple touch. He rubbed his head against Blake's shoulder, letting out a soft sigh when he was rewarded with a little neck scratch.

He looked up to find Josh studying him, but not with hate or irritation. It was more like wonder, as if he was seeing something new. Aaron gave him a tentative smile and was rewarded with a nod and a smile from his brother. He was happy to listen to the others talk after that.

"I need to get back to the kitchen to prepare the last things for lunch," Josh said a few minutes later. "Aaron, you wanna help me?"

Aaron sat up and bit his lip. "I'm not really handy in the kitchen."

Josh grinned. "I'm used to Noah, and I'm pretty sure you're not as bad as him. Come on, I'll go easy on you."

It was an olive branch, a big one, and Aaron grabbed it with both hands. "In that case, I'll be happy to help. Just keep it simple."

He followed Josh into the huge kitchen. A few minutes later, he was cutting bell peppers into small slices. Julienne, Josh had said, before laughing and explaining what that meant when he caught Aaron's baffled expression.

"How are you?" Aaron asked carefully. Josh looked well, but Aaron had no idea how he really was doing. Then again, maybe he didn't even want to talk about it.

"I'm better than I was," Josh said, meanwhile mixing oil, vinegar and some other ingredients into what looked to be a vinaigrette. "It was hard, being away for this long, but I'm glad I did it. It was the right thing to do for me, but also for the others."

Aaron understood about not wanting to be a burden. It was the story of his life, especially since he'd come out. He'd felt nothing but a burden with Blake at first, but since he'd come back from his trip, as he called it, it was much better. He was slowly accepting who he was—and that Blake loved him exactly the way he was.

"How are things going with Blake?" Josh asked.

Aaron's face lit up and he looked up from his cutting board. "Very good. He bought a play pen for me, and we..." He stopped, caught himself.

Josh sent him a reassuring smile. "You guys played in it? What did you do?"

"We played with a ball...and then we...Not sure you want to know more, actually." He felt a blush creeping up again.

"Is it kinky? Then I definitely want to know," Josh teased him.

Aaron studied him. Where had sulky, stand-offish Josh gone? It's like Josh had come back a different person after his stay in that clinic. All Aaron could do was be grateful and go with it, even if he was beet red. "We both got naked, and we wrestled... I love touching him like that, licking him everywhere."

"Mmmm. He's an edible man, your Blake, so I can imagine."

Aaron had to put down the knife, because the tears in his eyes were making it impossible to see what he was doing. A sob escaped him, and then he felt Josh's arms around him, hugging him from behind. His big brother put his head on Aaron's shoulder. "I'm sorry, Aaron. I...I wasn't ready."

Aaron turned around in his arms and clung to him tightly. "I missed you, Josh. I missed you so much. I thought you would never stop hating me for what I did."

"Oh, Aaron, I'm so sorry. I blamed you for the things that were never your fault. It took me too long to see that."

There was a peace in Aaron's heart that he'd never experienced before, even as he was still sobbing in Josh's arms. How he had missed that, his brother holding him.

Josh kissed his head, gently rubbed his back. "I love you, baby bro."

7

The lunch was surprisingly relaxed. Brad had worried about tension what with him and Blake still not back to where they were before—which was completely his own fault, as he'd fucked up royally. Added to that was the tension between him and Miles at times, because the Fed kept pushing his buttons—though they'd shared a few laughs with Charlie when he was doing Aaron's makeup. And of course, there was the lingering animosity between Josh and Aaron, though that seemed resolved. Brad was happy about the latter, because he liked them both and hated to see them at odds.

Next to him, Charlie yawned. He still didn't sleep well, weeks after Zack has assaulted him. Nightmares kept waking him up, and since they were sharing a bed, Brad as well. Truth be told, he was dead tired as well. Being around so many people wore him out as an introvert, but it was more than that.

As much as he loved taking care of Charlie, the constant focus on making sure Charlie was okay was draining Brad's energy. He could never think of Charlie as a burden, fuck no. Being with him was...perfect and yet so fucking hard. It was being close to everything you wanted, yet knowing you would never have it.

The fact that he was still servicing Miles, as the others had started to call it, added to that pressure. As much as he loved sucking off Miles or riding him while he was blind-folded, there was no denying it was tiresome as well.

But he'd agreed to help him out, so he could hardly say no now. Plus, the man needed it. He really was hard all the fucking time. He'd discreetly sucked him off right before lunch—one of the reasons why Brad wasn't all that hungry right now. He really should stop swallowing all the time. It was messing with his digestive system.

Still, it was Charlie who bothered him most. Not bother as in being a pain, but he worried about him. It was weeks since Zack had beaten him up, but Charlie still hadn't set a foot outside. He kept making up excuses, but Brad knew the truth. He was scared of Zack, deadly afraid of running into him, or worse, of Zack figuring out where he was stay-ing. Brad understood, but it wasn't healthy. It also wasn't fair.

When Charlie yawned again, he leaned over and whis-pered in his ear, "You wanna take a nap?"

Charlie's forehead crinkled the way it did when he was worried about something. "I can't sleep if I'm alone."

"I'll come with you."

"You will?" The surprise in Charlie's voice hit Brad deep. Did Charlie really not grasp Brad would do pretty much anything for him?

"Sure thing, sweetie. Let's lie down for a little bit."

The others had no problem with them taking a nap, so he led Charlie into their bedroom, Max following them, then softly closed the door behind them. They both stripped to their boxers, and Charlie crawled into bed, yawning again.

Brad would never admit it, but he loved sleeping next to Charlie. There was something so sweet and comforting about feeling that much smaller body snuggled against him. Max found a spot right next to the bed on Brad's side, and Brad smiled. He loved how Max was never far from his side.

Charlie immediately nestled close against Brad and put his head on Brad's shoulder, flinging an arm across his abdomen. It was Charlie's favorite position, Brad had deduced, because he always curled up like that against Brad. It was the sweetest torture, to hold that gorgeous man, that perfect body, to want him so much...and know he'd never be good enough to deserve him.

"Does Miles know?" Charlie asked out of the blue.

Brad had to think for a second what Charlie could be referring to. *Ah. That.* "About me? No. It's just sex, Charlie, that's it."

"How long do you think you can keep having sex with him with your underwear on, or with him blindfolded?"

"As long as I have to."

"You don't think he's getting suspicious? Or maybe I should say curious."

Brad sighed. "Maybe. Probably. I don't care. I'm not telling him shit, babe. It's none of his fucking business."

Charlie was quiet for a bit. "I think he wants more than just sex," he then said.

"I don't." Brad's voice was definitive. He was not discussing this with Charlie. Charlie was such a romantic at heart. He never fully understood why Brad did what he did in the club, and he certainly would never understand the complicated thing he had with Miles. "Get some rest, babe."

Charlie gave up, apparently, and fell asleep in minutes.

Brad waited fifteen minutes to make sure his friend was truly asleep, then wiggled from under his body. He was too wound up to sleep, the thoughts in his head not slowing down.

He dressed quietly, checking one last time on Charlie before he left. Even in sleep, Charlie's face showed signs of stress. He was never fully relaxed anymore. God, that fucker had to pay for what he had done.

He waited till Max had trotted out, then closed the door behind him softly. Everyone was still gathered in the living room, Miles spread out on the couch and the others on chairs, or on the floor—that would be Aaron, siting at Blake's feet, obviously. For lack of a chair, Brad lowered himself to a large pillow on the floor, leaning with his back against the couch where Miles' feet were parked. Max found a spot on the floor, too, his head on Brad's lap.

"How is he?" Blake asked. "He looked tired."

"He is," Brad said. "He still doesn't sleep well."

Miles was studying him, and out of a newly acquired habit, Brad checked his crotch. All was quiet there, thank fuck. Four orgasms this morning all in all should tide the man over till tomorrow, hopefully. Miles caught his look, grinned. He was so sexy when he smiled like that. Made Brad's stomach do back flips, as much as he hated to admit it.

"Does he have nightmares?" Noah asked.

Brad hesitated. He hadn't asked Charlie if he was okay with him sharing this, and he didn't want to violate his privacy.

"It's okay," Noah said. "You don't have to answer. Let him know he should ask his family doctor for sleeping aids, if he needs them."

"That would mean seeing his doctor, and he's afraid to

leave the house," Brad said quietly. "He's scared Zach will find him."

Noah nodded. "I noticed. He knows he can talk to me anytime, right?"

Brad nodded. "He does. He talks to me, a little, but...I'm not good at saying the right things."

Noah sent him a reassuring smile. "Listening is often the most important thing, and you've got that part down. He trusts you."

He did, and Brad vowed he'd be worthy of that trust. It was one of the reasons why he'd never start anything with Charlie, no matter how much he wanted him...and how sweet Charlie looked at him, with eyes that spoke volumes about what he wanted Brad to do to him. No, he wasn't going there. Right now, that trust meant finding a solution for Charlie's problem.

"How are we gonna nail this son of a bitch?" he asked.

Miles eyebrows rose high.

"What?" Brad snapped.

"Nothing. Not the kind of reaction I was expecting from you," the agent said.

"I told you: you don't know me. At all."

"Clearly," Miles said, but he didn't sound angry.

"Sorry. He's my best friend. I'm still really fucking pissed."

Miles held up his hands. "I understand. I wasn't criticizing you. I was merely surprised."

"We can't do anything, not until Charlie gives us permission." That was Blake, of course. Practical, reasonable Blake.

"He'll never stand up to Zack. Does that mean he gets away with it?"

"I understand you're mad, bro, but it has to be Charlie's decision. We can't take that power away from him."

Brad leaned back against the couch, felt Miles' foot touching his back, rubbing it. Was he doing it on purpose? It seemed so.

"At least he hasn't found him here yet," Blake added.

"Not yet," Brad said. "But with the resources he's got, it will be easy for him to find him anywhere."

"What resources?" Miles asked, sharp as ever.

Brad winced. Damn, he hadn't meant to let that slip. Noah knew, but he hadn't said anything. The guy took patient confidentiality seriously, even when he wasn't formally working anymore. That meant this was new to everyone else, including Miles by the way. How the hell was he talking his way out of this one?

"His boyfriend is a cop," Aaron said.

"Aaron!" Oy, Blake was angry with his puppy, that much was clear.

"No, Blake, you're wrong about this one. I know you don't want us to say anything, but we've got a cop here, a federal agent, and men who know what this is like. Surely, we can trust them."

It was good to see Aaron had a backbone when it was needed. Then his choice of words registered with Brad. Men who knew what this was like? What the fuck was Aaron talking about? Brad knew about Indy—in general terms, at least. The details of his rape at the hands of that guy he'd killed were pretty well known. But Aaron had said men, not man, so who else?

"Aaron is right. This is not about what Charlie wants. This is about a cop abusing his power, pretending he's above the law." Josh's voice was clear. It earned him an affectionate kiss on his head from Connor. Was he the one? He had to be. There was something inherently strong about him that screamed survivor.

"Does anyone have a last name for me, so I can look up this guy?" Connor asked. His face was neutral, but his eyes displayed anger.

"Zachary Waitley," Brad supplied. "Albany PD."

"You're shitting me," Connor said.

"You know him, babe?" Josh asked.

"Hell, yeah. Worked with him. Didn't even know he was gay."

"He's bi, technically," Brad corrected him. "Had a girlfriend before Charlie. Has a daughter with her, but he never sees her."

"She local?" Connor asked.

"Dunno. Charlie said it was because his ex was a bitch and refused to let Zack see his kid, but I know for a fact he's a lying, cheating asshole, so who the fuck knows what's true."

Connor looked pensive. "He cheated on Charlie?"

"Hell, yeah. Men, women, everyone he could get, if you ask me. Came after me as well. He was dead drunk, cornered me a while back when Charlie was performing at Flirt. Told me to suck him off, or he'd tell everyone I..."

Fuck, he'd dug a hole for himself there, hadn't he? They'd done an IQ test on him in elementary school, had told his mom he'd scored off the charts, but surely if he were that smart he wouldn't do dumb shit like this.

Blake cleared his throat. "Brad has something he would prefer others did not know, let's leave it at that." Thank you, big brother. The guy was a fucking saint, saving his ass all over again, even when he didn't deserve it.

"What did you do?" Miles wanted to know.

Brad shrugged. "Told him to go fuck himself. He knew I had way too much dirt on him for him to ever sell me out. I would've fucking buried him."

Was that admiration he saw in Miles' eyes? Sure looked like it.

"He's a nasty piece of work," Blake said. "But for some reason, Charlie loves him."

"He's known Zack since he was fourteen," Brad said. "He fucking idolized him. The guy did some volunteer work in the community center Charlie was a part of. Charlie's parents didn't want much to do with him, so he was looking for a father figure, I guess. They kept in touch, became friends, then more the minute Charlie turned eighteen."

Brad caught a meaningful look between Connor and Miles.

"I'm on it," Connor said, then Miles nodded.

"Thanks for letting us stay here," Brad said.

Indy sent him a warm smile. "Sure thing. We love having you guys here."

"We're running out of rooms, though, so let's not take in any more strays, okay baby?" Noah said, kissing Indy's head.

"I can sleep on this couch if need be," Miles joked. "It's pretty nice."

Indy grinned, then laughed out loud as Noah shot him a look. "What? He's right, it is a damn comfortable couch."

"Yeah, and thank fuck it has washable covers," Josh muttered.

Brad looked at the couch, then at Miles. "Holy shit, and here I thought I was a horny fucker," Miles quipped.

For one second, everyone seemed to hesitate, not sure if he was serious or not, but then they burst out laughing.

"I'm telling you, if that couch could talk..." Indy said, laughing.

"If it had a camera built in," Josh added. "That would make for some serious heavy porn."

Those two were now rolling against each other, laughing, while Noah and Connor shook their heads.

"Come on, Josh, we're embarrassing Blake and Aaron. They're not as kinky as the rest of us," Indy finally managed.

Brad's mouth ran off again. "You're talking about the puppy, right?"

The second he said it, he froze. He hadn't meant it in a derogatory way, but it sure could be perceived as such. *Fuck, no, please let Aaron and Blake be okay with it.* He'd already made them feel like shit about their relationship once, and Blake had rightfully called him out on it. Nothing hurt him more than Blake being angry with him.

He looked at Aaron, all but pleaded with his eyes that it had been a joke. Blake's eyes were on Aaron to see how he would respond. Aaron seemed to search for words for a second, then threw his head in his neck and barked. He fucking barked! Max lifted his head up, looking around in confusion, as if wondering where that other dog had come from all of a sudden.

More laughter ensued, and Brad exhaled in relief. He found Aaron's eyes, and the man nodded at him as if to say he'd gotten it. Aaron smiled, seemed genuinely grateful to be included in the group. Maybe he had been, Brad realized. Aaron always seemed to be at the fringes, much like himself. Maybe he had actually appreciated Brad's attempt at leveling the playing field. They were all kinky in some way, right?

Blake petted Aaron's head, and Aaron turned his head. He first kissed Blake's hand, then licked it. It was incredibly cute, in a weird way, and the first time Brad had seen him be so open about his puppy-play. He'd been weirded out at first, but there was no denying how happy Aaron made his brother. Blake's eyes shone with love for the man, and that was all Brad needed to see to accept him wholeheartedly.

He smiled, turned to check in with Miles, found the agent's eyes fixated on him. His eyes dropped, lower, to where Miles was sporting an erection. Brad widened his eyes on purpose in pretend shock. Miles shrugged. Brad held up four fingers, shook his head. He was rewarded with that same sexy grin he loved so much.

"What are you guys signaling about?" Indy asked.

Brad loved that about Indy: much like himself, the guy seemed to lack a filter. He was unabashedly curious and said whatever the fuck he wanted. Still, he wouldn't embarrass Miles, so he bit his tongue.

"Oh, Brad was a little surprised that after all his hard work this morning, I've still managed to get a boner."

Brad almost gasped. Wow, Miles was really putting himself out there. He had to feel mighty safe in this group to say something like that. Then again, there was no one here who didn't know already what he was dealing with.

"Did the four fingers mean that you..."

Brad nodded, smiling at Josh's question.

"Wow. Sweet. You and I need to swap strategies, friend," Josh said.

"Joshua!" Connor said sternly, but the snickers around the room signaled they all knew how fake this threat was.

"Yes, Connor?" Josh asked innocently.

"Do I need to take you to the bedroom to show you what happens when you embarrass me?"

"Erm, yes, please?"

Indy's hand clamped down on Josh's leg. "Hell, no. You're not going anywhere. We're all fucking hard, but you'll have to suffer through it, like the rest of us. Now, Brad, if you want to share, feel free."

"Ew, TMI," Blake said, his eyes dancing. "That's my brother, dude."

Indy snorted. "Don't go all prude on me now, man."

Brad pondered Indy's words as the others switched topics. How could Indy be so open about sex, joking about it even, after everything he'd experienced? He didn't understand. He was doing everything to keep his trauma a secret —though he was hesitant to even call it that since it was nothing compared to what Indy had been through. And Josh, too, he surmised. How could these two joke about sex, be so open about it?

Maybe talking was a strategy he could try. Aside from his brothers and Charlie, no one knew. He gently scratched Max's head as his eyes traveled to Miles, who'd fallen asleep on the couch, amidst all the talking. Would he be a safe place to start?

He'd been pleasuring Miles for almost two weeks now. He'd kept him at a distance, obviously, but Miles kept asking questions, chatting him up, indicating he wanted more than mere sex. Which was ridiculous considering sex was the whole point of their relationship, for lack of a better word. Miles needed to get off, and Brad, well he got his freak kicks satisfied.

He loved being here, though, loved spending so much time with Charlie and being in this house. These men were something else indeed. They were unapologetic about sex, and how they enjoyed it. When Connor was spanking Josh —or whatever the fuck he was doing—it was audible in the entire house, but nobody batted an eye. Brad had seen the pure bliss on Josh's face afterward and had concluded this was as consensual as it got.

Being open and joking about sex might help Indy deal with his trauma, but maybe that was because he was a people person in the first place? Brad was anything but. Teens, he had no problem with, funny enough, but adults? His tongue got all tied into knots at every attempt at small talk. He always said the wrong stuff, offended people, or plain pissed them off. And sooner or later, people always left him, rejected him.

He'd never found anyone he trusted enough to be himself with, not even Charlie. He knew more than most, but even Charlie didn't know everything. If Brad told him what he wanted, what he so desperately craved, Charlie, too, would walk away from him.

No, Brad would do it his way. He'd keep his distance from Miles. A few more days and Miles wouldn't need him anymore, wouldn't want him anymore. Then Brad would walk away with his head held high and his dignity intact.

8

Miles groaned as he pushed himself up to a sitting position in bed. Recovery was frustrating as fuck, since his mind wanted to go way faster than his body could handle. He could be up for about an hour, two if he pushed it, but that was it. He was still spending way more time napping and resting than he wanted to.

Noah had told him this was normal, especially considering his injuries. It had taken a while for Miles to realize just how lucky he had gotten that Indy had called Noah and asked for medical advice. If he'd left him as Miles had told him to do, Miles would have died from internal bleeding. It had been a sobering realization.

Wells, his boss, had contacted him several times to check up, and his latest call had been a not so subtle reminder that his mandatory counseling would start as soon as he was fit enough. They'd send a trauma shrink to him if necessary, his boss had told him in no uncertain terms, but the sooner he'd start, the better.

He knew it was the right thing to do. A trauma like he'd

survived was not to be taken lightly. They had shot both Nunez and Fisher at point blank. He still didn't know if he'd been spared simply because they'd gotten to his room last, or because Crouch had somehow chosen him to be interrogated. He liked to think the first, because the second made him sick to his stomach.

Crouch. Now there was a depressing thought. He hadn't even told Indy, but Wells had informed him they'd found Crouch's body a few miles from the farm. He'd been executed with a single shot, the bullet matching the one used to kill Nunez. They'd simply shot him when he'd outlived his usefulness.

Turned out his sixteen-year-old daughter had been kidnapped the day before the raid on the farm, thus ensuring Crouch would cooperate and not alert his boss. She'd been held in an abandoned warehouse in her hometown of Rockville, Maryland, but had managed to escape, much to everyone's relief. She had survived, but her dad hadn't. It was an unimaginable tragedy for the family.

The FBI had caught the men who attacked the farm— but only because of the shooting in Boston. They'd made the mistake of contacting lower level lieutenants already in police custody because of the raids the Boston PD had done for days after. Their informant had delivered them a ton of solid intel on the Fitzpatrick's organization on a silver platter, and they'd used it. There was nothing left of the empire.

The FBI was still trying to figure out who had tipped off the Fitzpatricks where Indy was held, though, and how they had known Crouch was the agent in charge. It smelled like an inside job, and that was deadly dangerous.

They were also still investigating the shooting in Boston, in cooperation with the Boston PD. They had zero leads. Zero. Sure, they'd had a ton of tips on the crime tip hotline, but none that had proven useful. Wells had reported the shooter was a fucking ghost, and he'd said it with equal amounts of admiration and exasperation. Technically, it was a job for the Boston Field Office, but since it was tied to the Fitzpatrick case and thus to the murder on that Boston DA Merrick, FBI headquarters had gotten involved.

Miles was intrigued and had asked Wells to keep him posted, even though he was off-duty while recovering. There were so many questions surrounding both the raid on the Kansas safe house and the shooting in Boston, that Miles had a hard time letting it go.

A timid knock sounded on his door, interrupting his thoughts.

"Yeah, come in," he called out.

Charlie walked into the room with Max on his heels. "I didn't wake you?"

Miles smiled as he pushed himself up farther, leaned back against the head board. Charlie's face broke open in a happy smile that made Miles' belly weak. God, Charlie was so fucking gorgeous, but hardly aware of it himself, it seemed. "Nope, I was awake already. What's up?"

Charlie seemed to hesitate for a second, then climbed on the bed and faced Miles, pulling his legs up. "I'm bored."

Max gave them both a long look, then decided that the floor looked appealing and plopped right down. He had to be the easiest dog Miles had ever seen, always content as long as there were people to hang out with.

"No one home?" Miles asked.

"Noah has classes, Indy is teaching a jiujitsu class, Brad won't be home for another half hour, and Josh and Connor have a session with Master Mark, a Dom."

Miles' eyes widened. "They have a what?"

Charlie's eyes gleamed. "That got your attention, huh?

Apparently, they visit a local Dom regularly and he teaches them more skills, I guess? Josh said they'd do something today called shi..shibatsu?"

"Shibari," Miles supplied. "Bondage. It's an artful way of tying someone up with ropes."

"Yup, that's it. Josh was really excited about it."

Miles cocked his head. "You okay with all of that? I mean, they're quite the over-sharers here in this house."

Charlie shrugged. "Sure. I mean, I don't know half of the stuff they're talking about, Josh and Connor I mean, but I can see how much they enjoy it, so why not?"

"It doesn't embarrass you, this open talk about sex or hearing them go at it?"

"Nah. Well, maybe the first week or so with Noah and Indy, but after that, I got used to it. They're so open about it that it's hard to feel embarrassed. It's not like some dirty little secret or something."

Miles hummed. That made sense, actually.

"But it must be harder for you, I guess?" Charlie added.

Miles grinned at the unintentional innuendo. It took a second for Charlie to register his own pun as well, and he giggled. It was a beautiful sound that filled Miles' heart with joy.

Miles swallowed back the joke that was on the tip of his tongue. He still didn't know Charlie that well, and he didn't want to hurt him, or trigger bad memories with an ill-timed quip.

Charlie's smile dimmed. "You're doing it again," he said.

"Doing what?"

"Treating me like I'm breakable. You wanted to say something. I could see you hold back."

Miles sighed. "I wanted to make a stupid joke and then thought better of it. I don't want to hurt you, Charlie. That has nothing to do with me thinking you're fragile or some shit and everything with not knowing you well enough to be aware of where you're sensitive."

Charlie's jaw set. Miles was pretty damn sure that wasn't supposed to make him look even more adorable, but it totally did. "I'm not sensitive," Charlie said between clenched teeth.

"Sure, you are. We all have our trigger issues. Doesn't mean we're weak or fragile."

Charlie scoffed. "Bullshit. If that's true, then where are you sensitive?"

Miles kept his face neutral. "Holidays, for instance, especially Christmas. I can't stand it when people complain about how busy it is, or how they don't like their family coming over, or whatever. I would do anything to celebrate Christmas with my parents and sister one last time. They were killed in an accident years ago, and I still miss them like crazy."

Charlie's face fell. "Oh, god, I'm sorry. I'm a horribly selfish person at times. Brad says so, too."

"I don't believe that," Miles said. "I don't think you're selfish. I think you've been dealing with so much that your brain was too occupied with coping with your own shit to have the mental capacity to invest yourself in other people's shit. You're not selfish. You're a survivor. Big difference."

Charlie's eye grew big. "Is that how you see me? Not as weak and fragile? Everyone always does."

"Charlie, there's nothing weak and fragile about you, other than maybe your body in comparison with, say, Connor. You're not delicate china. You're like one of those tin cups that come in all kinds of colors. Really pretty, but strong as fuck. Unbreakable."

It started with a sob that escaped Charlie's lips. "He tried to break me."

"I know. But he couldn't, could he?"

A bigger sob tore through the slender body. "He beat me. Who the fuck beats someone he claims to love?"

Miles knew what was coming, had seen it enough in witnesses and crime victims. He mentally braced himself, could only hope Charlie would trust him enough to seek comfort. "I know, love."

"He cheated on me, did Brad tell you? All the time. Who does that?"

"I know."

One more big sob, and then he broke. Miles saw him crumble, right before his eyes. He watched as the dam burst that had held back Charlie's emotions, witnessed as it shattered into pieces, was washed away by the avalanche of emotions.

Charlie let out a blood-curling scream, then another one, and another one, until his voice broke and it turned into sobs. Big, body-wrecking, angry sobs.

Miles held out his arms, and without a second doubt, Charlie crawled toward him, took shelter in Miles' arms. Miles kissed his head, held him close as he broke into pieces.

The door to his room opened, and Brad came running in, coming to a sudden halt when he saw Charlie bawling his eyes out in Miles' arms. Miles' eyes met Brad's, and they filled with tears. Underneath his prickly exterior, he was such a softie. And he really cared a lot for Charlie, if not more. Miles had seen him look at Charlie in a way that suggested way more than friendship, but as always, something was holding Brad back.

Miles gestured with his chin that Brad could hold

Charlie from the other side. As much as Miles loved being here for Charlie right now, maybe Brad was who he really needed. Brad nodded, then climbed on the bed and took position behind Charlie. Charlie grabbed his hand and pulled it around him, but he made no indication he wanted to let go of Miles, so he kept holding him. Brad hugged him tight from behind, while Miles held him from the front, and Charlie kept crying until he hiccupped one last time, and promptly fell asleep.

After a few minutes, Brad whispered, "Thank you. He really needed that release."

How could he be so sweet when it came to Charlie and be so defensive toward Miles? Miles didn't understand. "I don't mind."

"I can move him to our room?"

Miles studied Brad, his pale cheeks and the dark circles under his eyes. "He can stay here. I don't mind. I need to nap myself as well."

The relief on Brad's face was palpable. Then his eyes traveled south. "Do you need a release?"

Miles' dick was, of course, hard. How could it not be after that whole talk about sex and then holding Charlie? There had been nothing sexual about it, but it had been so long since he'd held someone like that, that his body has responded fiercely. But to ask Brad under these circumstances, when the man was obviously tired himself and while Miles was holding a sleeping Charlie? It felt so wrong. Times like this he truly hated himself, hated his stupid body that wouldn't cooperate.

"I don't mind, honestly," Brad said.

Miles sighed. "Please," he acquiesced. "I'd really appreciate it."

"I like sucking you off," Brad said softly, carefully getting off the bed to make it to Miles' side. "It's very soothing for me, especially when I'm stressed."

Huh. That was interesting.

No more words were spoken as Brad expertly took him in and brought him to climax in minutes. Miles' eyes were already sinking shut when Brad was still tucking his cock back into his bottoms. "Thank you," he managed.

"My pleasure."

Miles felt the bed dip again. Was Brad staying? He was almost asleep when Brad spoke again. "It's always my pleasure."

Brad was in his car two minutes after dismissal. Teaching had been impossible today, his head a chaotic mess. Luckily, his students were good kids, for the most part, who seemed to sense something was off with Mr. Kent today, and didn't take advantage.

He'd fallen asleep next to Charlie. In Miles' bed. He had woken up hours later, completely disoriented, and hadn't been able to sleep again. Charlie had eaten a little bit, and had gone right back to bed. Miles' bed. Where he had slept peacefully for the first time since the attack. Miles had been quietly snoring through the night as well, relaxed after Brad had given him a hand job.

Brad had been too worried to fall back asleep. What did this mean, the fact that they were in bed together? Was this becoming a thing now, the three of them together? It was all becoming too fucking complicated, though he couldn't deny the idea of being with Miles and Charlie made his blood pump faster. They both had something he craved.

The joy Charlie exuded was so calming to Brad. Just being with him, reveling in his sweet kindness made Brad happy. Plus, he was so beautiful it took Brad's breath away at times. Sharing a room with him all this time, it had been perfect and horrible at the same time. He wanted what he would never have, and there were times it physically hurt.

With Miles, it was something else entirely. Admittedly, the guy was easy on the eyes, but it was the thought of sucking him that got Brad's heart beating faster. His head was always so busy inside, but with Miles' cock in his mouth it quieted down. It was peaceful, as fucked-up as it may sound.

They hadn't fucked, or more accurately, Miles hadn't fucked him again. God, Brad had wanted him to, but he didn't know how to make sure Miles would be blindfolded again. He couldn't let him see his junk, deformed and mangled as it was. Charlie could claim all he wanted it wasn't that noticeable, but Brad knew better. Fuck no, no one could look at that and still want anything to do with him. Miles would boot him out the door instantly. The guy could do so much better, and they both knew it.

No, the thought of the three of them together was a pipe dream. Maybe Miles would develop a thing for Charlie. He seemed like his type, and Miles sure as hell was Charlie's. It was good that they hung out while Brad worked, right? It gave them a chance to grow closer, maybe develop something deeper?

A deep stab in his heart made Brad swallow. It would be perfect, Miles and Charlie together. Charlie needed someone he could trust, someone honorable. Plus, Miles wasn't a strict top, so that worked out well since Charlie definitely wasn't a bottom-only, despite looking like the perfect twink. No, the guy loved to fuck. Never got much chance to, with his asshole boyfriend, but now that he'd finally gotten rid of that loser he'd have a chance to build something real. He deserved it.

Brad sighed deeply, rubbed his temple. He should help them find each other, be happy for them. It wasn't like he had a chance with either of them anyway. Even if Miles did like him as much as he claimed to, he'd stop as soon as he knew about Brad's dick.

Besides, Miles couldn't fulfill the void Brad so desperately wanted to see filled. He was too young, for once. Too perfect, too. Too kind and smart and composed. Not the type to be the sick fuck Brad was and needed.

And as for Charlie, fuck no. The kid was too sweet, too nice and kind. He deserved so much better than Brad with all his fucked-up issues. No, they were better off as friends because anything more would only end with him hurting Charlie and Charlie walking away.

Brad drummed his fingers on the wheel as he drove, lost in thought. He jerked as suddenly police sirens went off right behind him. What the...

Oh, fuck. Zack. He should've known. Thank fuck he came prepared. He'd known this would happen at some point since Zack didn't know where Charlie was, and Brad was easy to track through his job. He was more surprised it had taken Zack this long to make a move. Charlie had said Zack had been gone for some kind of training, so that must've delayed him.

He twisted his sneaky little dash cam sideways and pulled over, stayed seated with the engine off and his hands clearly visible on the wheel. Zack had never liked him—and that was the understatement of the year. He could guess what the cop's game was here, but he wasn't giving the asshole any excuse to use force.

He checked his mirror. Zack was not alone in the car.

That might be his way out of this. He waited till Zack had walked up, signaled for him to turn his window down. He turned the engine briefly back on to power the windows, slid the driver's window down. "Officer Waitley," he said. "What can I do for you?"

"Where is he?"

Okay, then. No small talk. He could lie, of course, but why would he? They both knew the truth. "If he wanted you to know, he would've contacted you."

"You tell me, or things will get very unpleasant for you."

Brad took a deep breath, forced down his anger. "As unpleasant as they were for Charlie or did you have something else in mind?"

The smile on Zack's face was scary as fuck. "I wouldn't put my cock inside you if you paid me, you fucking man-whore. Don't think I don't know what you do at the club, sucking cocks left and right. You're filthy."

"Two minor corrections. I'm not a whore, since I don't charge for my services. And secondly, I'm a clean cock sucker. Unlike you, Mr. Gonorrhea. Unfortunate little accident there, right?"

Zack leaned over in the car, brought his face close to Brad's. Perfect, in full view of his dash cam. "You have no idea what I can do to you."

"Actually, after seeing what you did to Charlie, I have a pretty good idea. You beat him up, you fucking asshole."

Brad's voice was calm, but he was shaking with anger.

"He's mine, Brad, so I can do whatever the hell I want. Don't think for a second you can keep him from me, you deviant, sick fuck."

Fuck, he would lose it if this motherfucker kept this up. The only thing making him keep that last, thin grip on his temper was the knowledge that not only would Zack throw his ass in jail, he'd discover the dash cam and everything would be for nothing.

"On that, we disagree, asshole. He's not yours, he never was, and he never will be. Now, are you gonna charge me with anything or can I go home?"

Zack retreated from the window. "You were doing fifty in a forty zone."

"Bullshit, and we both know it. But what the fuck, write me a ticket. I'll contest it in court, see how the judge feels about abuse of police power."

"I'll let you get off with a warning this time, but be assured, Brad, I'm watching you. You'd better tell Charlie to come back, or there will be consequences."

Brad's hands shook as he closed the window. He didn't even wait for Zack to get back in his car, but took off. There will be consequences...it was like a bad movie script. Who the fuck did this guy think he was? At least he had it all on cam, so hopefully Connor would be able to do something with it. Or Miles.

He took the first street to the right, then turned left, then left again. He parked at a flower shop, wanting to make absolutely certain Zack wasn't following him. After ten minutes, he took off again, but kept looking in his mirror until he pulled in the driveway.

Josh was in the living room, reading a book, but he was the only one there.

"Hi," Brad said. "Where's everyone?"

"Hey man," Josh said. "Erm, lemme think. Connor has a job interview, Noah is at uni, Indy is shopping, and Miles and Charlie are in Miles' room."

Charlie and Miles were together. In Miles' bedroom. Maybe his fears would come true sooner than later. Brad swallowed back the sudden tightness in his throat. "I'm gonna check on them," he said.

Josh nodded and dove back into his book. Brad walked into the hallway. The bedroom was all quiet, so he opened the door softly. He found both men in bed, plus Max, who was napping on the floor. Brad kneeled next to his dog to hug him and received a couple of licks as a heartfelt greeting.

Charlie was closest to the door, sleeping on his stomach in a shirt and boxers, the sheets kicked off. He looked so young, so frail like this.

Miles stirred when Brad walked over to his side. He'd put underwear on underneath his pajamas, Brad noted, probably as a consideration to Charlie. It said a lot about the kind of man Miles was.

He sat down on the bed, put a hand on Miles' stomach, underneath his pajama top. The man's misty blue eyes opened immediately, dark with want, and his face tightened.

"It hurts," were the first words out of his mouth, barely audible. "Dammit, I'm so fucking horny."

Brad's eyes softened. Poor guy. "Bathroom," he simply said. "Come on."

Miles was in pain, Brad could tell from the way he moved. He was walking with O-shaped legs, stumbling into the bathroom. Brad shut the door behind them. "What do you need?" he asked.

"God, I'm sorry. Please, Brad, I'm sorry. Didn't wanna jack off with Charlie there. This is not...it's bad, right now. It fucking hurts."

Brad cupped his cheeks, forced Miles to make eye contact. "It's okay. I'm here, tell me what you need."

With unsteady fingers, Miles got rid of his top, then his bottoms. "Can I fuck you? I need to..." His body shivered violently.

The one advantage of this house was that there was literally lube everywhere, including in this bathroom. Brad grabbed it from the bathroom counter, squeezed some out.

Miles was standing with shaky legs, his cock purple and his eyes glazed over with need. Brad wordlessly coated the man's cock, then turned his back toward him and started stripping.

When he reached his underwear, he hesitated. No, Miles needed him. This was not the time to be difficult. Besides, the guy was too far gone to even notice, probably. Hopefully. He took it off as nonchalantly as he could, shivering with tension. Apprehension battled with the deep contentment stemming from Miles' need for him. He grabbed some more lube, spread it inelegantly in his own hole.

He walked toward the sink, gripped it with two hands and bent over.

"Come on, big guy, I'm ready for ya."

Miles walked over, unsteady. "Prep," he said. "Don't I need to prep you?"

Brad looked over his shoulder. "I'm good. Ease in slow, okay? After that, you're good to go."

Shaky fingers grabbed his hips, and he opened wide. Brad's cock was soft, as was to be expected, but a thrill of excitement ran over his spine. There was something very masculine and raw about Miles right now, and Brad craved it. Miles' tip pushed against his outer ring, then breached it. Brad bore down, let him in. He canted his ass, pushed it back further and leaned on his arms.

"Fuckfuckfuckfuck," Miles stammered as he burned his way inside, filling him inch by inch until he was fully seated. "Won't last long."

"I know. Keep going. Fuck through it," Brad encouraged him.

"You okay? Please, Brad, tell me you're okay. I'm not hurting you?"

"I'm good, I swear. Let go, babe." The word slipped out. Hopefully Miles would be too out of it to notice.

Miles groaned, pulled out and slammed back in, fucking the breath out of Brad's lungs. "Oh, fuck," Miles said, his voice tight. He slammed in again, made the bottles on the counter rattle. "Brad!"

Brad's heart clenched as Miles shouted his name when he climaxed inside of him. He was damn proud that he could offer this to the man releasing inside him. He did this. This was his doing. Miles' breaths turned to sobs as he fucked straight through his orgasm, the cum dripping down Brad's legs. He took it, bent over even deeper as Miles unleashed on him—deep, brutal thrusts that made his teeth rattle.

The bathroom door opened, but Miles didn't hear it, blind to his need. Brad looked under his arm. Charlie was standing in the doorway, his mouth dropping open as he watched them. Brad sent him a reassuring smile. He didn't care if Charlie saw him, saw them. Wouldn't be the first time his friend watched him get fucked. Charlie had watched him suck off complete strangers in the club, even witnessed him getting fucked a time or two.

Miles' body jerked, and he deposited another load inside Brad. Good. That had to offer some relief. He should have done more this morning. Clearly, that one blow job had not been enough. The four orgasms of yesterday had been awesome, but the man still couldn't last longer than twenty-four hours. At least this should tide him over till tomorrow, right?

He was so lost in thoughts that he didn't notice Miles'

hand sneaking around until it was on his cock. Brad's completely limp cock.

"Oh, no." Miles' words were soft, but Brad felt them in his very soul. "What have I done?"

Miles pulled out with incredible gentleness as Brad buried his head in his heads on the sink, too humiliated to face him. What a pathetic excuse for a man he was, that he couldn't even get it up when this hot, sexy man fucked him so perfectly.

"Brad..."

"Go away," Brad said.

"I'm so sorry..."

Yeah, that's what he needed, pity. Fuck, no. He was done with this. He'd known it wouldn't last, that Miles would be repulsed as soon as he knew. Who the fuck wanted a limp freak like him? No one.

A trembling hand softly landed on his shoulder. He shook it off. "Get the fuck out."

Cum was still dripping down his legs, a sorry testament to the only thing he was still good for. Without that, he'd have nothing left.

"Brad, I..."

He pushed himself up, spun around. "Get the fuck out!"

Miles looked dead pale and stricken, as if Brad had slapped him. He stumbled back, almost tripping over his own feet. Brad looked past him, where Charlie stood, eyes wide. One look at the pure shock on his best friend's face and Brad crumpled. His legs gave out and he sagged to the floor.

"No, Brad, no. He thinks he hurt you," Charlie said, his voice surprisingly firm. Brad looked up, as Charlie held out a hand to stop Miles from walking out. "You didn't hurt him."

"Look at him! He can't even look at me..." Miles' voice was broken, as if he'd been cut to pieces. Funny, because that's exactly how Brad felt.

"You have to tell him, babe," Charlie pleaded.

This was to Brad, obviously. No way in hell was he embarrassing himself even more than he already had. He dropped his head on the floor, content to pretend he was a rag.

"Stop walking away, dammit. You misunderstood. He's not in pain, not physically anyways."

Brad closed his eyes. It seemed he didn't need to embarrass himself. Charlie was doing a damn fine job for him.

"I don't understand." Miles sounded confused. What the fuck was there to be confused about?

Wait. Why was Charlie going on about Brad not being hurt? Did Miles think he... Oh, shit. He'd interpreted Brad's lack of arousal to pain. He thought he'd been too rough.

He opened his eyes, pushed himself into a sitting position. "You weren't hurting me," he said gruffly.

Miles turned around, his cock gone soft by now, slapping against his bare leg. "Then what the hell is going on?"

Brad met Charlie's eyes, who were pleading with him to tell the truth. Oh, he might as well now. Miles was done with him anyway after this drama. He slowly rose, forced himself to uncover his groin.

"I had testicular cancer. They removed one testicle."

Miles eyes dropped to his groin. "Yeah, so?"

Okay, not the reaction he was expecting. "I have one ball. The other one is an empty sac."

Miles crossed his arms. "I gathered as much from your previous statement, not that I can spot the difference from here. Is that why you wouldn't let me touch you?"

"Erm, partly. I, erm, also have been experiencing erectile issues. You know, trouble getting hard."

"Is that caused by the cancer? Did they damage any nerves?"

"No. Everything is normal physically. They say it's psychological."

Miles arms uncrossed and his eyes went all soft. "You could've told me."

"Yeah, 'cause it's such an easy thing to open with. Hi, I'm Brad. Oh, yeah, before I forget: I have a limp dick and only one testicle."

"Sarcasm is kind of your defense mechanism, isn't it? That, and being plain rude. Why the fuck would you think I'd care, other than that I'm sorry for you?"

Brad frowned. "Because it's hella not sexy, and a big turn off."

"Do you realize who you're talking to? Brad, my love, I would really appreciate a turn off, if that were the case, but sadly, your one-ball-body does not turn me off in the least. Neither does your limp dick, as you called it. In fact, if you would be so kind as to lower your attention to my cock, yes, there it is, I am hard once again. If there is any reason for me to rethink our arrangement, it's because you turn me on too much, not the opposite."

All Brad could do was stand and look at Miles. He had to be kidding. This had to be some kind of misguided attempt to make Brad feel better, because why would anyone be turned on by him?

"You mean you're turned on when I touch you, suck you off, or let you fuck me," he said.

"No, idiot, I'm turned on by you. Apparently, I have a thing for prickly, rude guys who are unfailingly kind to their best friend. Plus, I love your tight body and your sharp mind. Dammit, Brad, I told you I like you. Why don't you believe me?"

The words echoed in his head, demanding to be heard, felt. "Nobody has ever liked me," he said slowly.

"Maybe because you never let anyone close enough?" Charlie piped up.

Brad's eyes traveled to his friend, who stood determined behind Miles. "I let you close."

"Yes, after much nagging from me. And you know I love you, I always have."

"That's different," Brad protested. "We're friends."

Charlie smiled, a smile so sweet and sad at the same time it made Brad's skin tingle. "We were never just friends. There's always been a promise of more, but you held back."

It wasn't the first time Charlie had said something like this. "You're eight years younger, sweetie, and my student," Brad offered the excuse he always had whenever Charlie had hinted at more.

"Oh, fuck off. I haven't been your student in a long time, and who gives a fuck about the age difference? Zack is sixteen years older than me."

Brad took a step forward, eyes blazing. "Zack is a fucking pervert, an abuser, most likely a rapist, and a sadistic son of a bitch who should be in jail. Don't you dare compare me to that piece of shit."

Charlie's eye grew wide, then moistened. Fucking hell, now Brad was making the one person cry he wanted to cherish more than anything or anyone.

"I'm sorry, babe. That was mean of me. Don't cry. I know you love him."

He stepped in, past Miles who watched them with kind eyes. He opened his arms and thank fuck, Charlie accepted his embrace, snuggled close. It was a little awkward with him being naked and Charlie dressed, but what the hell. It wasn't like Charlie had never seen him naked before. He kissed his head, held him carefully so he wouldn't hold him against his will.

"I don't love him," Charlie muttered against his neck.

"What was that, babe?"

"I don't love him. I'm not sure I ever did, but if I did, I sure as hell stopped the first time he hit me."

Brad pushed him back gently, so he could see his face. "Then why did you stay with him?"

It took a long time for Charlie to answer and when he did, his lip was quivering. "Because I was ashamed and embarrassed, and I didn't know where to go."

Brad frowned. "To me. You could've come to me."

"I know."

"Then why didn't you?"

Charlie gently shook his head. "It's complicated," he said.

Brad forced himself to be accepting. It's what Blake had taught him most, that domestic abuse was incredibly complicated and that victims had conflicting feelings about their abuser. All you could do was listen, be there, and let them sort it out. "Okay, babe. If you're ever ready to talk, I'm here. And please know that you are always welcome to stay with me, as long as you want."

"Really?"

Charlie acted as if that was news to him. "Of course! I thought that didn't need saying."

"You don't think I'd hamper your style?"

Hamper his style? What was Charlie referring to? Oh, sex? "You're talking about sex? Like I give a shit whether you're there or not. You just watched me get pounded by

Miles, doesn't bother me in the least." A thought occurred. "Does it bother you? Make you uncomfortable?"

"Not with Miles," Charlie said.

That was it, then. There was no one else at the moment, since Miles kept him plenty busy. Well, provided Miles did indeed still want him. Besides, he rarely took guys home, but maybe Charlie didn't know that. He usually kept it restricted to quick bathroom blowjobs or fucks.

"You two need to take a shower. I'll wait." Charlie kissed him on his lips, a soft kiss that made Brad long for more, so much more.

He watched as Charlie walked out, his head a scrambled mess of thoughts and feelings.

10

Miles didn't know whether to kiss Brad or slap him, though he was severely tempted to go through with the first option. Maybe he could kiss some sense into him? The man was so fucking blind. How could he not see Charlie loved him? Not as in best friends love, but was completely in love with him? One look at Charlie's face had made it crystal clear to Miles.

He'd bet good money that he knew why Charlie had stayed with Zack—or at least, why he hadn't gone to Brad's. Miles' guess was that the pain of staying with a man he didn't love was more bearable than moving in with one he thought didn't love him back. Miles wasn't too sure about Brad not loving Charlie back, though. The way he held him, the way he'd flinched when he'd realized he'd hurt him— those were not the actions of a man who didn't care. Miles would bet his money on Brad loving Charlie right back. Something else was holding Brad back, other than his erectile issues, but as usual he was damn hard to read.

"Do you want to shower?" Brad asked, subdued. "Or do

you need…" He gestured at Miles' cock which was a half mast.

Miles pursed his lips. "Are you offering?"

How would Brad respond? Ever since Brad had told him about his issues, Miles had wondered why he seemed happy to pleasure Miles. What did Brad get out of it? Not a boner or sexual pleasure, that much was clear.

"Sure."

He meant it. Everything on his face, in his tone, in his body posture indicated his offer was real. What the fuck was going on with him? "Why?"

"Why what?"

"Brad, why are you doing this?"

Brad looked at him defiantly. "What the fuck do you care as long as you get off?"

It hurt. He knew Brad was lashing out in self-defense, but it hurt. It was the same as when he'd told him it was just sex, that he didn't want Miles to get to know him. For some reason, he was deadly afraid of letting people in. Anyone except Charlie, it seemed. But how should Miles respond?

"You know that's not true. I am interested in you, but you're determined to keep me at bay."

"I told you, this is just sex."

Miles crossed his arms. "Well, I'm afraid that doesn't work for me anymore."

Brad scoffed. "Like you can afford an attitude like that. You need me."

Damn, the man knew where to hit hardest. Miles bit back an angry response. "No, Brad, I really don't. I'm immensely grateful for what you've done for me, but it's still my choice. Right now, I'm deciding that I'm done with being used by you."

Brad balled his fists. "Used by me? What fucked-up version of reality is that? You need me. You're using me to get off. How the fuck could I be using you?"

"You're getting something out of this. I haven't quite figured out what and why, but otherwise you wouldn't be doing it. You're using me, and until you tell me why, you're not touching me."

Brad took a staggering step back. "You're rejecting me?"

The pain on his face was so horrific, it broke Miles' heart. "No, honey, I'm not." He made sure his voice was kind. "I want you, but I want more than your body. You're rejecting me, not the other way around. Tell me why you're doing this and you can do whatever you want with me. Until then, you're not touching me and neither is anyone else."

The hurt was replaced by anger. "We'll see how long you can keep that up."

"You have no idea how stubborn I can be. I can handle the pain, Brad. The question is: can you?"

"I'm gonna take a shower," Brad snapped. He muttered something under his breath that sounded like "fucking asshole", but Miles wasn't sure. It had to be something along those lines, though, considering the thunderous look on Brad's face.

Brad turned on the shower, his back turned toward Miles. Miles sighed, grabbed a washcloth from the cabinet and proceeded to clean his cock. He'd last for a while after two orgasms, but by his estimation he had about twenty-four hours before it would start to get mighty uncomfortable. He could only fucking hope that Brad turned out to be less stubborn than he himself was.

Charlie was asleep when he got back to the bedroom, lying on his stomach on his side of the bed. Miles smiled, as he carefully got into the bed next to Charlie. It had only been a few hours, and he already thought of that as Charlie's side of the bed. Would he be comfortable spending the night there again? Miles hoped so. It had been unreal, sharing his bed with both Brad and Charlie, and despite everything that had just happened, he hoped for a repeat.

Charlie was so strong and yet vulnerable. He was such an intriguing mix of sweet and sassy, of insecure and bossy. Miles was drawn to him, wanted to take care of him and let Charlie fuss over him at the same time. Physically, Charlie still seemed to be recovering, judging by how often Miles found him napping. Then again, Brad had mentioned nightmares, so maybe he didn't sleep well at night? Miles could only hope Charlie would recover mentally as well.

And then there was Brad. Prickly, defensive Brad who was such an enigma. Miles wanted to kiss him silly, fuck him till he'd stop being such an ass, and then hold him and tell him everything would be okay. Preferably with Charlie on Brad's other side. Miles wasn't sure what had happened with Brad, but something told him the man needed a whole lotta love. If only he would accept it.

Miles surrendered to the fatigue claiming him and fell asleep. He woke up more or less refreshed two hours later. A quick look sideways confirmed Charlie was still beside him. Brad had apparently left them by themselves.

It was six thirty, so maybe it would be good to wake him up so they could grab some dinner? They'd planned a BBQ with some friends, Josh had told him, as the man was dying to try out his brand new, shiny, big-ass Weber. Miles had never in his life said no to a juicy, well-grilled steak, and he had no intention to start now.

He carefully moved toward Charlie, put a soft, tender hand on his bare shoulder. He was so small, his skin so perfect now that all the bruises were gone. How could you hurt something so frail and beautiful? "Hey, Charlie, wanna wake up?"

Charlie groaned, shifted a little, but that was it. Miles shook him gently. "Sleeping beauty, time to wake up."

"Don't wanna fuck…" Charlie muttered.

What? Was he still stuck in a dream, or something? "Wake up, babe," Miles said again.

"Leave me alone, please."

He still sounded completely out of it. Maybe it would be better to let him sleep a little longer. He was about to pull his hand back, when a tremor tore through Charlie. The whimper he let out gave Miles' goosebumps.

"No, please, no…don't hurt me."

Was he half awake and thought Miles was his boyfriend? Or was he stuck in some nightmare? Either way, Miles needed help. He rolled over to his side, pressed the buzzer Indy had shown him on the first day. It only took a few seconds for Brad to come in, a worried look on his face.

"It's Charlie. He's out of it, and I don't know what to do," Miles whispered.

Charlie jerked, then whimpered again. "Please, Zack, please. You're hurting me."

"Oh, shit," Brad said. "Is he dreaming again?"

Brad had hinted before that Charlie wasn't sleeping well and that he had nightmares. Apparently, this was a recurring event. Was that why Brad was getting so little sleep?

Brad took off his pants, then his shirt. He climbed in bed from the foot end, slid in close to Charlie on his side, so their bodies touched. He put a hand in Charlie's neck, scratched it softly. "Hey sweetie, you wanna wake up? You're having a bad dream, but I'm here."

Charlie whimpered again.

"You're safe, babe. I'm right here with you. Wake up, Charlie."

"Brad?"

Miles exhaled in relief.

"Yeah, sweetie, it's me."

Charlie's body moved, as he turned to his side. His eyes opened. "It hurts so bad."

"I'm so sorry, babe."

"I dreamed that you had left me, that you were angry with me."

Brad moved in for a quick kiss on his lips. "I could never be angry with you. And you know I would never leave you."

"Will you hold me?"

The tender way in which Brad cradled the fragile body in his arms made Miles' insides go liquid. When Brad let his formidable defenses down, he was truly irresistible. He had such a big, kind heart, such infinite kindness for the wounded and hurt.

Charlie took shelter in Brad's arms, there was no other way to describe it, the two bodies completely plastered together. It was almost too private a moment to watch, yet Miles couldn't tear his eyes away. It was heartbreakingly beautiful, and also erotic as fuck. Holy fuck, Charlie was gorgeous. And him and Brad together, it was almost too much to take.

"You okay now?" Brad asked, his cheek pressed against Charlie's.

Charlie turned his head, brought their lips together. Miles swallowed. There was such tension when these two kissed, even if it was a short kiss. How Brad could ever miss that and mistake it for mere friendship, was beyond Miles. The sparks were pretty much visible.

He raised his eyebrows when the kiss continued, deepened. Brad seemed to stiffen for a moment, then gave in. Tongues came out, invaded, sucked, making noises that had Miles hard in an instant. Should he leave? Surely, he was the third wheel here. But fuck, it was so mesmerizing, so fucking beautiful.

Charlie tore his mouth away, and the two looked at each other, panting slightly. Brad's face was completely open, no trace of the guarded expression he usually sported around Miles.

"What are you doing?" Brad whispered.

"I want you."

"Charlie..."

That one word was so full of longing, Miles' heart ached for him. What was holding Brad back?

"Please, make me feel good, Brad." It wasn't a question, more a desperate plea.

"Charlie...are you sure about this?"

"I need your mouth on my cock."

"Babe, I don't wanna hurt you..." Brad said. Miles could hear the internal battle Brad must be waging in his voice.

"Dammit, Brad, stop talking and put your fucking mouth on my cock. Now. I need you."

Miles' eyebrows raised. Boy, Charlie was a bossy little twink, wasn't he? Who the fuck could say no to a request like that?

Brad leaned in, gave him a scorching kiss, before scrambling on his knees. There was no foreplay here, no touching or exploring. He gave Charlie a gentle push to roll him on his back and took Charlie's boxers off.

When Brad rolled flat on his stomach, Miles caught a good look at Charlie's package. Holy crap, his cock was way bigger than Miles would have expected on such a small guy. Charlie was packing a serious tool there, rivaling Miles in size. They sure were equally hard.

Brad licked the head of Charlie's cock, making him groan softly.

He should go. This was not meant for him to see. They must have forgotten he was there. He tried to move off the bed as quietly as he could, but Charlie rolled his head sideways and met his eyes.

"Stay," he said.

"This is between you two," Miles said, his voice hoarse.

"No, it's not. You're fucking him, too. Plus, he likes being watched."

His cock disappeared inside Brad's mouth. There was no way Brad hadn't heard the exchange, but he said nothing. His head bobbed as he sucked Charlie, slurping sounds filling the room.

Charlie's hand traveled to Brad's head, much like Miles himself liked to do when Brad was sucking him off. Charlie moaned, sighing at the same time. "Fuck, you're so good at this," he said.

"He is," Miles heard himself say. "He sucks cock like it's the last thing he'll ever do."

Charlie's chuckle transformed into a soft moan as Brad sucked him deep, hard by the looks of it. His hand caressed Brad's hair. "You're a good little cock sucker, aren't you?"

What. The. Hell.

Brad didn't seem to mind being called this, on the contrary. His expression was hard to make out, what with his mouth full of cock and all, but it looked like he was beaming. Why?

He'd told Miles he loved sucking cock, and he hadn't lied. Apparently, Charlie knew this, too. Now Charlie had indicated Brad liked it when someone watched. And sweet, small Charlie had just bossed him around, ordered him to suck his cock, and Brad had obeyed instantly—loving it, by all accounts. How did this all fit together?

He kept watching as Brad brought Charlie to the brink, let him hover there for a bit, before sending him over. Charlie bucked as he came, and Brad swallowed greedily, taking every drop. He let go of Charlie's cock, licking his lips. "Damn, you taste good," he said. He scrambled higher, gave Charlie a kiss.

"More," Charlie demanded. "I love tasting myself in your mouth."

Brad grinned, kissed him again, with tongue this time.

They. Were. Killing. Him.

At this rate, he wouldn't even last another hour, let alone a whole day. Fucking live porn right in front of him. He moved off the bed, his cock hard as a rock.

"You need help with that?" Brad asked behind him.

Miles turned around. Brad was on his back now, Charlie on his side beside him, a hand splayed on Brad's abdomen, right above the waistband of his boxers. Boxers that contained, if Miles was not mistaken, one hard cock. Huh. Whaddayaknow, Brad could get hard under the right circumstances, apparently.

"Not unless you're willing to tell me what I need to know," Miles said. "You need help with that?" he pointed to Brad's erection.

Charlie moved his hand lower so it rested on Brad's cock. "I told you he likes to be watched."

That's what got him hard? Being watched? Miles didn't buy it. If that were the case, he would have been hard in the bathroom, when Miles was fucking him while Charlie watched. No, it was more than that. Charlie knew it, too, because his pointed look at Miles was a little too deliberate.

Charlie's hand squeezed Brad's cock and Miles could swear he felt it in his own dick. "You're so fucking hard, Brad. Tell him why."

"Charlie..." if it was meant to sound angry, or even remotely like a threat, Brad failed spectacularly. It came out more like a breathy moan. Who the fuck would have thought the dynamics would change so completely? Charlie had Brad's number, and he played him like a fucking fiddle.

"As soon as I'm better, I'm moving in with you...and I'll demand you suck me off every morning."

Charlie's hand slipped under the waistband, and he took Brad's cock out.

"Every single morning, I want your hot mouth around my cock, because damn, you suck me so good. And I'll have you rim me."

He fisted him, his hand around the top of Brad's cock, his thumb pressing on his slit. Miles watched in fascination as Brad closed his eyes, leaned into Charlie's touch.

"I'll have you eat me out, fuck my hole with your tongue until I can't stand it no more. What do you say, Brad, you want your mouth on my hole?"

Brad moaned, the first time Miles had ever heard him make a sound like that. Charlie was jerking him off for real now, using the drops of precum Brad was producing.

"And when I'm so hard my cock could pound nails, I'll nail you instead. I'm gonna bend you over and take your tight ass. You don't need no prep, do you babe? Your hole was made to be fucked, and I'll fuck it hard and deep. You know I got staying power, babe. I'll fuck you till you can't bear it no more."

Brad bucked, his hips coming off the mattress. Charlie increased the tempo, fisting him hard and fast.

"Oh, you like that idea, huh? I knew you would. It's what you live for, isn't it? To be fucked. To have your mouth and your hole full of cum. That's what you are, babe. You're a little cum slut."

With an inhuman roar, Brad came, his hips jerking and his body shaking like a leaf. The cum was flying out of his cock, landing everywhere. Thick, creamy spurts that showed Miles how long it had been since the guy had come. A week, at least, but probably longer.

Charlie slowly let go of Brad's cock and rolled on his back, panting with effort.

"Charlie..." It was half a sob Brad let out, seeking Charlie's cum-covered hand.

"I know, babe. I know. It's okay."

"I'm sorry."

"Sorry for what? For giving me a mind-blowing orgasm? For being sweet and kind? For taking such good care of me? You know I love you the way you are. Now, go clean up. You came all over yourself."

"Yeah," Brad sat slowly. He sat up, avoiding Miles' eyes, rolled off the bed and walked into the bathroom, closing the door behind him.

"What the fuck was that?" Miles asked, still trying to process what the hell had just happened.

Charlie sighed, wiping his hands off on the sheets. "That was his first orgasm in maybe three months."

GROWING UP, Indy had always dreamt of having his own family one day. Not the fucked-up kind he grew up in, with a drug-dealing mom who sold him to pay off her debt. Hell, he didn't even know who his dad was. One of his mom's johns, probably, but he had no idea. She'd never said a word about him, and the few times he'd dared to ask, she'd exploded, so he'd learned to let it go. He'd wanted a real family, some day.

But now, as he looked around the yard, he realized he'd become part of a true family. It was a different kind, one forged not by blood but by choice, but a family it nonetheless was. It was Friday evening, and both his house and his heart were filled with friends who'd become family.

There was Noah, his strong man, willing to start from scratch to fulfill his dream to become a shrink. He was so protective of those he loved, willing to sacrifice everything. The love between them was deeper than Indy had dared hope for, and it still grew every day. He'd learned to handle his pain, though his stump had bothered him way less since the new amputation. It had healed well, and his mobility had improved. Still, the pain management course he'd taken had made a big difference in how he handled pain. Sex was no longer his go-to method.

Beside him, Connor was flipping burgers on the new grill. Built like a tank, he had the heart of a lion. Yet he had such a tender side, especially when it came to Josh. There was literally nothing this man wouldn't do for the love of his life. Josh walked straighter because of him, had become more resilient.

Over on the grass, Blake had stretched out on a fleece blanket, simply enjoying the sun. Aaron lay curled up at his feet, reading a book. Every now and then Blake would scratch Aaron's head, or rub his neck, and Aaron would send him a look so filled with gratitude it almost made Indy tear up. Theirs was anything but a conventional relationship, but damn if they didn't make it work.

Miles had parked himself on a reclining chair, studying those around him. He was good at that, Indy had come to learn, figuring out patterns and relationships. No wonder, with his psychology degree. He was healing well, though still nowhere near his old self. Indy wondered what Miles would do when he got better, if he would return to his old job. He'd been so lonely, and had found friendships and relationships here he'd never had before.

Charlie was on an identical chair right beside him. Those two had sure hit it off. There was an easy familiarity between them, as if they'd known each other for years. Yet Indy had also caught Miles looking at Charlie with less-than-brotherly desire. Sure, the FBI agent was constantly horny, but this was something else, something deeper.

Brad was sulking on the grass with his back against a tree, Max at his feet. Indy still couldn't figure out what his deal was. He was wicked smart for sure, kind to a fault when it came to Charlie, but there was always something aloof about him. You never felt like you got to see the real Brad, as if he was always holding something back. And he'd had some kind of falling out with Miles, or Charlie, or maybe even both. Considering his relationship with Miles, Indy's money was on it having something to do with sex. Sex always complicated things, now didn't it?

Suddenly long arms wrapped around him from behind, a tall body enveloping him. "Hey, baby," Josh said. "What are you thinking about?"

"Family," Indy said, sighing. He leaned back against Josh.

Josh chuckled. "It's a bunch of kinky fuckers we've collected, isn't it?"

"Much like ourselves," Indy said.

"Yeah, we're not much better, are we?"

They stood like that for a bit, watching their ragtag family. "I miss you," Josh said.

Indy turned his head to look at him. "What do you mean?"

"Since Connor is back, we haven't slept in the same bed, since he's not working night shifts anymore. I miss that. I miss waking up with you draped all over me."

Indy smiled. "I miss that, too." He turned his back again, happy when Josh pulled him close like he had before. "So, Connor is turning into a bit of an exhibitionist, isn't he?"

Josh laughed. "You mean what happened in the bathroom this morning?" Indy had walked in on Josh sucking Connor off. Considering they hadn't locked the door, he was quite sure they'd wanted someone to see them.

"That, and yesterday's hallway fuck." Connor had fucked Josh against the wall—one of the most erotic sights Indy had ever seen.

"He won't admit it, but he does get off on it. He likes to watch others as well. Fuck, he'd spank me for telling you this, but he loves watching you and Noah fuck. Yesterday, he happened to watch from the hallway as Brad went down on Miles in the living room. That's what initiated the whole hallway fuck. He was so damn hard. It's hard for him to let go of his inhibitions, I guess, but he's getting there."

"Good. He's got little use for them in this household."

"No shit. What's up with those three?" Josh gestured toward Miles and Charlie, where Brad had now hesitantly taken up a spot at Charlie's feet. The three of them were eating burgers, devouring them, to be more precise. "I'm picking up on some serious sexual tension there."

"You too? I thought it was just me. I think Miles has got the hots for them both."

"Charlie definitely has a thing for Brad," Josh added.

"He does?" Indy asked.

"Fuck, yes. Watch those two interact. The way they kiss each other, that's you and me, baby."

Indy smiled, turned around in Josh's arms. "But we're not together," he said, pouting.

Josh held out his hands. "Jump," he said.

Indy smiled, jumped up and circled his legs around Josh's waist. Josh's hands held him tight on his ass. He pressed them together, Josh's cock undeniably hard. Josh's mouth came close to Indy's ear, his breath causing goose bumps. "You know better, Indy. We are together. We always have been. And one of these days, Noah and Connor will see it, too."

Exhilaration raced down Indy's spine. Was Josh saying what Indy thought? Did he want him as much as Indy needed him?

"You and I, we'll make love again, and we'll let our men watch, because that's how we roll. You'll top me again, and we'll kiss all fucking night long."

Indy drew in a much needed breath, saw everything he needed to know painted on Josh's face. "You think Connor will be okay with that?"

"If he gets to watch, hell yeah."

Indy wasn't so certain. "I thought he was jealous of me, of Noah, that he didn't want to share you."

"He was, but he's changing. He's starting to see that my love for you doesn't take away from my love for him; it only adds to it."

Indy couldn't help it, he had to kiss him, had to taste that sweet mouth, feel that hot tongue against his. Josh let him in, kissed him back with equal parts desperation and sheer lust. They got lost in the kiss, their groins rubbing against each other until Indy's entire world was the want thundering through his veins.

"Hey, you two, you wanna maybe get a room?" Noah called out.

They pulled back at the same time, breathless. Indy turned to look at Noah and found him watching them with love, probably mixed in with lust as well, but no anger. He let his gaze wander further, to Connor. He looked surprised, but not mad either.

"Fuck, you're right," he whispered.

Josh waited till he had Indy's attention again, then slowly and deliberately kissed him one last time—a hot, wet, searing kiss. "Soon." He lowered Indy to the floor. "I think your man needs a quick fuck. I know mine does, and I'm willing to oblige since you've got me so damn hard." He slapped Indy's ass playfully. "Off you go."

Indy shook his head, smiling. What had gotten into Josh? He loved this sexy, confident side of him. Still, letting his ass get slapped like that was beneath his dignity. He spun around, hooked Josh's legs and took him down on the grass, rolling on top of him and pinning him down securely. Josh looked shocked for a second, then burst out laughing.

"Uncle," he said.

Indy rolled off him. "You're no fun," he said. "Too easy."

He jumped to his feet. Fuck, he had too much energy, needed to burn some off. He looked at Brad. "You wanna have a go?"

Brad smiled. "Do I look stupid to you? Pick someone your own skill level, like my brother."

Indy put his hands on his hips, shot Blake a smile. "You wanna play?"

Blake shook his head. "Sorry, but not right now. I'll kick your ass some other time."

He pouted, still bursting with energy. And his dick was still so fucking hard. Maybe he should take the man up on his advice. He sauntered over to Noah, who was watching him with an amused smile. Connor had walked off to discuss something with Brad, from the looks of it. The last few yards, Indy ran, then jumped, Noah catching him with ease.

"Hey babe," Noah said, holding him tight. Indy circled his arms around Noah's neck, wrapped his legs around his waist like he'd done with Josh minutes before. "Little horny from making out with Josh?

Noah knew him so well. "You could reap the benefits?" Indy said hopefully.

Noah laughed. "I'm second choice, huh?"

Indy sobered. Would Noah really think that?

"I'm teasing you, babe. It's fine. Connor's not ready yet."

What the hell? How could Noah possibly know what he and Josh had been talking about? "Can you read lips or something?" Indy asked.

"No. But I can read you and Josh pretty well. The two of you have been patient, babe. Hold off a little longer. Connor will get there if you give him time."

Indy saw nothing but love and understanding in Noah's eyes. "You're okay with this," he said slowly.

"Yes. Completely. You love us both, and I get that. Your heart is big enough for us both, and so is Josh's. You are special, the two of you, and I won't stand in the way of that."

"I love you," Indy breathed against Noah's lips.

"I know, babe. And I love you, too. Now, let's go inside so you can use me to release your sexual frustration. It's a dirty job, but I'm willing to sacrifice myself."

Noah carried him inside, Indy peppering his face with kisses. His heart was bursting at the seams, and he couldn't do enough to make Noah feel the depth of his love. They didn't make it further than the couch, where Noah unceremoniously dumped him.

Indy whipped off his shirt, dragged down his shorts and boxers in one move. He yanked the drawer under the coffee table open, where he found the bottle of lube he needed. Meanwhile, Noah had undressed as well, though he'd left his prosthesis on. Indy squirted some lube out, coated Noah's cock, smeared the rest on his own hole.

He kneeled on hands and knees, opened his ass wide. "I need you inside me, Noah. Now."

Noah's hot, strong body covered his, as his cock lined up. "I love it when you go all bossy on me. You don't need prep?"

Indy shook his head. "Nah. Go slow."

There were times when he needed Noah to take his time, but right now, he wanted to feel the burn, wanted to be reminded how lucky he was with the men he'd found. Noah's cock pushed in, breached his outer ring as Indy breathed out, welcoming him. Noah inched in, completely in tune with Indy's body, as always.

"Fuck, Indy, I'll never get enough of this. Ever," Noah whispered, covering Indy completely with his body. "You fit me like a glove."

He filled Indy completely, bottoming out. Indy breathed away the burn, until there was nothing but fullness. Noah moved slowly, every stroke deep and precise. Indy had wanted a quickie, but what he got was infinitely more. It was Noah's love song, sending Indy higher and higher until he shattered, spilling his load. Only then did Noah finish with a few deep thrusts, filling him with his seed.

He stayed inside him as they calmed down, kissing his

nape, his shoulders. "Even if I were your second choice, Indy, I'd take it any day over not having you at all. You make me complete, baby."

He moved out of Indy, giving him room to turn around. Indy ended up with his bare ass in his own cum, but he didn't care. He kissed Noah, sweet and tender. His heart was finally at peace, knowing he could have it all.

11

They had ended up in Miles' room. After everyone
had left, Charlie had wanted to watch TV, but it
seemed Indy had had a little...accident on the
couch. Yeah, right. They'd fucked on that damn couch, that
much was clear. Josh had taken the covers off to wash, so
Charlie and Miles had retreated to Miles' room to watch a
movie, and Brad had trailed along, not knowing what else
to do.

It had been fun, though, watching Miss Congeniality
together. Charlie had kept a running commentary on the
hairdo's, makeup, and dresses, while Miles had chimed in
with everything the movie got wrong about the FBI—but in
a fun way. Brad had watched and listened, feeling strangely
included even though he never spoke a word. He'd been
literally between them, as if they hadn't want to give him an
easy way to escape.

Charlie had promptly fallen asleep near the end of the
movie, and Brad hadn't had the heart to wake him so they
could relocate. Miles had fallen asleep a while ago as well,
his face turned toward Brad. Even Max had settled in in a

corner of the room, deeply asleep. So he'd sucked up his own unease, and had tried to will himself to sleep, so far unsuccessfully.

The fact that Charlie felt so comfortable with Miles said a lot. It seemed he really was developing a thing for Miles. Brad couldn't fault him. Miles was hot, first of all. Insanely hot. Tall, blond, ripped—how the fuck could you not love that? Brad's insides jumped up every time the guy smiled at him. The dude was smart, too. And fucking stubborn.

He had to be getting uncomfortable by now. That little show Indy and Josh had put up—that had been scorching hot. Even Brad's cock had stirred. Briefly, but still. If it turned him on, he could only imagine what it had done to Miles.

Hell, Indy and Noah had gone for a quickie, Brad had seen Josh and Connor return with flushed cheeks half an hour later, and even Blake and Aaron had disappeared for a few minutes. Everyone had gotten off, it seemed, except the three of them. Miles had to be bursting to unload.

So Brad would wait. He had the patience. All he had to do was wait till it became unbearable for Miles, and then he'd give in. It felt cruel, if he was honest, but what was the alternative? Giving in to Miles' ultimatum to share why he was willing to humiliate himself and pleasure him? Yeah, so not happening. It was nobody's business, but his own.

Charlie knew, but that was only because Brad had gotten drunk that one time when it had all become too much, and he'd spilled the beans. And even then, he hadn't told him all of it. Sure, Charlie said he loved Brad, and he knew that to be true, but how long would that last if Charlie knew it all? If Charlie knew what a sick fuck Brad was deep down, that love would soon disappear.

If only he'd been healthy, normal, he would have been

able to offer Charlie something. He knew the kid had liked him for years, had wanted more than mere friendship. It had been messed up, of course, what with him being with Zack back then, but that was life for ya. It was never as black and white as in the movies.

How could he start something with his best friend, the only one who knew him better than anyone—if still not completely—and yet loved him? He had nothing to offer Charlie but a limp dick and a fucked-up mind. He'd fuck up, inevitably, at some point, and lose him, too. And that was something he couldn't risk, not when his feelings for Charlie were too damn big already as it was. He wouldn't survive Charlie rejecting him, too.

Miles stirred, his hand reaching for his cock. The tension on his face was obvious, and he winced as the movement undoubtedly caused him pain. Brad almost reached out to free that beautiful shaft from its confines, suck him in deep. Damn, the man tasted so good.

Miles' eyes shot open, his face distorting for a second in pain. He seemed to realize where he was, turning his head and met Brad's gaze head on. His look was deadly, absolutely fucking intimidating. The flippant remark died on Brad's lips. This was not a man he wanted to fuck with.

"Miles, you're in pain," he whispered instead.

"You think I don't know that? Tell me what I need to hear."

Brad's mouth set in a thin line. "No."

Miles rolled on his side, wincing all over again. "Brad, this is a battle you will not win. Trust me."

Brad scoffed. "You'll be the one suffering, not me."

Miles' face became surprisingly soft. "That's where you're wrong, but you'll find out soon enough."

He clumsily moved his left hand inside his pajama

bottoms, slowly dragged out his cock. The damn thing was hard as a fucking diamond, of course. Miles fisted the top of his shaft, moaned as he squeezed it.

"I'm so fucking hard," he whispered, and Brad felt the words reach deep inside him. "I'm at that stage where pain and pleasure go hand in hand, you know? Where every time I touch my dick, I wince in pain, yet at the same time I can't stop because I need to come so bad."

With slow, deliberate moves he fisted himself. Brad couldn't peel his eyes away.

"My balls...They're so heavy right now, so full. Once I come, they'll explode. Nothing beats that feeling of release, of tension dissipating, of my cock spewing out cum."

Brad balled his fists. He wanted that cock in his mouth so badly. Wanted to bring Miles pleasure, to use him, fuck him. Dammit, what the hell was wrong with him?

"Ask me what I'm thinking of right now, when I'm jacking myself off."

Brad held back, though he wanted to respond more than anything. Sweat pearled on his forehead, his breathing rapid and shallow.

"Ask me, Brad!"

"What are you thinking of?" he gave in. This man was impossible. He fucking knew exactly what buttons to push.

"You. Charlie. The two of you kissing. Fuck, that kiss you shared was so hot. I almost came from watching it." Miles moaned, a low sound that reached deep inside in Brad's very core. "Your mouth on his cock, knowing how unbelievably good that feels. Him jerking you off, with those filthy words coming out of his mouth."

Behind Brad, the bed moved. Charlie moved close against his back, his dick undeniably hard. He brought his mouth close to Brad's ear, bit his ear lobe. Brad's skin prickled. "Suck him off, Brad."

"No." Even to his own ears, it sounded more like a plea than a statement.

Charlie chuckled, had picked up on it, no doubt. "Suck that gorgeous cock off, babe. You know you want it."

A sob-like sound tore from his mouth. "I hate this!"

"I know, babe. Stop fighting. It's okay."

"It's not okay. It's fucking humiliating."

Charlie kissed his neck. "No, it's not. It's who you are, and you're perfect."

The dam inside him broke. "I'm a slut, okay? Always have been, even before my surgery. I need to be used, bossed around, humiliated, whatever. Nothing makes me happier than pleasuring others, especially at the expense of myself. Please, Miles, please let me make you come. I'll do whatever you want."

It wasn't the whole truth, but it would have to be enough for now. If Miles had smiled, looked triumphant even for a second, Brad would have still pleasured him, but he'd hated himself for doing it. But Miles didn't do anything of the kind. Instead, he got that look in his eyes, that dominant, alpha-as-shit look that made Brad's insides liquid.

"Your mouth on my cock, now," Miles said.

Brad scrambled up. "Thank you."

If Miles thought it was completely fucked-up Brad was thanking him, he didn't show it. Instead, he shoved his dick in as soon as Brad had opened his mouth and was in position.

Brad gagged, tears forming in his eyes. Fuck, yes. He wanted this, needed it. He sucked, taking Miles in as deep as he could. Before, Miles had been somewhat passive when he'd blown him, content with letting Brad set the pace, and merely holding his head. This time was different. Miles fucked his mouth, hard, unrelenting until tears and drool were streaming down his face.

Brad felt the orgasm coming, Miles going completely tense on him before shooting his load. He swallowed as much as he could, the rest dripping down his chin as Miles kept abusing his mouth, his throat. Brad relaxed, his mind going blank. Finally, peace.

He sucked, breathed when Miles pulled out for a few seconds, sucked again when that cock was shoved down his mouth again. Somewhere he registered Charlie yanking down his boxers, then jacking off behind him, encouraging him, saying the dirty words that affirmed who he really was. A slut. A fucking dirty, filthy boy, born to take cock.

Miles pulled out of his mouth, leaving him whimpering with disappointment. He closed his eyes, was pushed to his back and simply lay there, his eyes closed, desperately sucking in breaths.

When the first stream of cum hit him he jerked, opened his eyes. Miles was on his knees to one side, jacking his cock, Charlie on his other, doing the same. It was Charlie's load hitting his chest, then his face. Miles erupted seconds later, painting his legs, his arms.

"Fuck him," Charlie said. Brad turned his head to face him. What did he mean? "He hasn't had enough yet, Miles. Fuck him."

Charlie leaned in carefully to kiss Brad deeply. "You're so fucking beautiful when you surrender. Let go, babe. We've got you."

When he ended the kiss, Miles was still looking at them as if they were speaking Chinese. "Which part of 'fuck him' was unclear to you? Lube your cock with the cum on his body and fuck him. He needs it."

Brad giggled. When Charlie got all bossy, he was so fucking adorable, so perfect. His hand shot out, dragged Charlie's head toward him, still careful not to hurt him. He wanted that mouth, wanted more of it. Charlie met his tongue, stroke for delicious stroke, hot and hungry.

"You think that's funny?"

Brad vaguely registered Miles' words, the agent's hands on his body. Hands swiping the cum on his stomach, his legs, while Charlie was devouring his mouth. Fuck, the kid could kiss. Then wet fingers found his hole, demanding entry. He let them in, two at once, spreading a furious burn through his ass.

His legs were bent double, rough hands yanking him in position. He lost Charlie's mouth, whined as a result. "Charlie..."

He didn't get the chance to say more, Charlie's tongue invading his mouth again at the same time Miles' cock spread his hole wide open. He bore down, let him in. Charlie tasted so sweet...Miles' cock burned so good.

Then Charlie's mouth disappeared, and Miles kissed him. The man kissed the same way he fucked, with absolute dominance. He simply took over Brad's mouth, made him surrender in every way possible. His tongue swept Brad's mouth, exploring, tasting, while his cock steadily filled him. Brad was bent in two, taking Miles cock and tongue at the same time, and hot damn, he loved it.

He searched with his hand. Where had Charlie gone?

"I'm right here, babe," Charlie said. His fingers touched Brad's, then took his hand, wrapped it around a cock. Charlie's cock. "Jack me off, babe," Charlie commanded, his voice hoarse.

Miles fucked him so good, ramming inside him with powerful thrusts. His ass was on fire, still accommodating

Miles' size, but it felt fucking perfect. Brad curled his hand tight around Charlie's cock, swiped the precum on top around to make it slick. Miles inside him, his hand now fisting Charlie's cock, Brad was in heaven. He let go of everything and anything else.

"You love this, dontcha?" Charlie whispered. "Your ass full of cock, your mouth still tasting Miles' cum, your body covered with our loads, and we ain't done yet." His words pierced through the fog in Brad's brain, demolishing the belief he couldn't get hard. His cock filled, swelled with sweet discomfort.

Miles tore his mouth away. "Charlie was spot on. Your ass was made for cock. And I'm still holding back because of my injuries. When I'm all better, I'm gonna fuck you till you can't walk anymore. You want that, Brad?"

"Yes." The word was barely audible, yet it felt massive to him. His hand fisted Charlie harder, faster.

"Or I'll fuck your ass while Charlie fucks your mouth... We'll fill both your holes with cum. And then we'll switch and do it all over again. Would you like that, Brad?"

"Yes." Louder, this time, the word coming out more easily.

Miles slammed into him, hit his prostate head on and Brad moaned. "Look at him," Miles muttered. "He's in fucking heaven."

"I know, right? Such a perfect little slut for us. You like having two men to please, dontcha, babe?"

A sob escaped from Brad's lips. "Yes. Fuck, yes."

"You know what we should do, Miles, when you're fully recovered? Double team him. His hole would love two dicks at the same time, right, babe?"

He'd never even dared to allow the thought in, but now that Charlie mentioned it, it was all he could think about.

The image filled him, demanded to be seen, accepted. "Please," he whispered. "Oh, fuck, please."

Miles groaned, low and sexy. Brad was on the fucking edge, almost there. Then he opened his eyes as he heard a sound, watched as Miles and Charlie kissed—sweet, and so fucking dirty. Miles sped up, firing off a series of rapid thrusts until he blew his load inside him. Brad's hand tensed around Charlie, making him come, too.

Tears pooled in his eyes, as his own release stayed just outside of reach. He wanted it so badly. Why the fuck wouldn't his body cooperate?

"Fuck, that was good," Miles said, pulling out roughly and turning on his side. "How 'bout you Charlie?"

"Damn fine hand job," Charlie commented, rolling out of reach of Brad as well.

He was left alone, his breath panting, his ass leaking cum, his skin itching where the previous loads had dried and crusted, his cock rock hard, and so fucking miserable after the peak of bliss he'd been in. Tears streamed down his face.

"Do you want to come, babe?" Charlie asked.

Brad hmm'd to affirm.

"Use words. Tell Miles."

The last bit of resistance inside him crumbled. He scrambled to his knees, every thought of dignity gone. "Please, Miles, I need to come."

A look passed over his head between Miles and Charlie. "I could use a fourth orgasm. Rim me, Brad, then fuck me with your fingers to make me come. If you do, we'll let you come, too."

Brad was on him before he'd even said the last words. He pushed back Miles' legs, opened his ass. He buried his face in his balls, breathed in deeply. Fuck, he smelled so good. He took the left nut in his mouth, less full now that Miles had come already, sucked it gently. Miles responded with soft hums of pleasure that made Brad ridiculously happy. The right testicle got the same treatment, and Brad all but licked his lips. He swirled around Miles' balls with his tongue, then nibbled his way back.

He lapped at his crack, one big, wet lick from bottom to top, shivered with delight. The other way around was equally good. He teased Miles' puckered hole with his tongue, smiling when Miles' body jerked in response. The guy was so responsive, reacting to every little thing Brad did. Every lick was delicious, the sweaty, musky taste ambrosia to him.

"Stop teasing him, babe. Fuck him with your tongue," Charlie said.

Why was it that he could not resist Charlie's commands? It was ridiculous, because the guy was eight years younger, at least three inches shorter, and built like a fucking elf—and yet he had the power to make Brad obey. It was mind-blowing, really. Good thing Charlie had never abused it, would never either.

He dug in, fucked Miles' hole with his tongue, rimming him and eating him out until he was thrashing on the bed, his body preparing for yet another orgasm. There was something to be said for his sexual stamina, because by fuck, Brad got his fill with him. He dribbled saliva down the man's hole, ruthlessly shoved a finger in and curled it, going straight for his prostate. Miles bucked, swore loudly in colorful terms.

"Oh, he likes that, babe," Charlie said, delighted. "Do that again."

He did, with pleasure. Miles made another obscene sound, indicative of how far he was gone. Brad was about to

take pity on him and jack him off, when Charlie beat him to
it. Brad watched in fascination as Charlie's small hand
curled around Miles' cock and started fisting him. It only
took three, four jacks and Miles' body froze, his cock
pumping out cum that looked like it had to come from his
very toes.

"Fucking hell," Miles sighed, panting. "The two of you
are gonna kill me."

Brad giggled, strangely proud of what he'd done. He was
a fucking mess, dried cum everywhere, and the sheets
hadn't fared much better. But holy crap, what a ride it had
been. He couldn't believe they'd had a threesome. He looked
at Charlie, who was watching him with love. "Did you
mean it?"

In credit to Charlie, he knew immediately what Brad
was referring to. "If Miles wants to, hell, yes."

Brad turned to face Miles, scared of what he'd see on his
face. Surely this had been a heat of the moment thing.
There was no way a federal agent would actually be game
for a three-way, right?

He found Miles studying him with a pensive look, before
his eyes shifted to Charlie. "We'll need to talk first, because
if we do this—and if I didn't come four times in the last
hour, I would be fucking hard merely thinking about it—
we'll need some ground rules. I don't want you to get hurt,
Brad."

Brad sat up, shrugged. "It won't hurt me. I like my ass
full. Have never tried DP before, but I'm pretty sure I'll
love it."

"Honey," Miles said, the first time he'd ever called Brad
that. "It's not physical hurt I'm worried about. Your ass was
made to be fucked. But you're more fragile than you think."

Brad raised his eyebrows. "Me? You mean Charlie, no

offense, babe." Charlie shrugged, didn't take offense apparently.

Miles shook his head. "It's not Charlie I'm worried about. He's strong as fuck, especially mentally. No, honey, it's you that has me worried."

"Why?" Nobody was ever concerned about him. Well, Blake maybe, but even he had never voiced it this explicitly.

"Because we promised you we'd make you come if you brought me a fourth orgasm. You have, yet you haven't even mentioned it. You have erectile dysfunction, and I understand that's complicated for you. You did come with Charlie, however, but only after he talked to you in a very explicit and specific way. That tells me that deep down, you don't think you deserve pleasure, and that worries me. I have no qualms about bossing you around, using you, or humiliating you sexually, if that's what gets you off. All fine by me, not to say I love that shit. But I will not, you hear me, I will not affirm your negative thoughts about yourself. If your craving to be a cum slut, or whatever the fuck you want to call it, is fueled by a sexual or psychological inferiority complex, I'm not okay with it. You deserve pleasure, as much as Charlie, or me, or anyone else."

Every word hit him like a jackhammer. How the fuck had Miles managed to see him, all of him, the real him? Nobody ever had, not even Charlie. "What are you, a fucking shrink?" he said.

"Knock off the sarcasm, Brad. Won't do you any good. If you want this to work, you have to let us see the real you."

12

Charlie held his breath, waiting for Brad to respond. Miles' words had been flaming swords of truth, cutting deep. They'd made Charlie ashamed that he'd never spoken them. He'd wondered, at times, where Brad's sexual hang ups originated in, but he'd never dug deeper than Brad had allowed. Which was quite shallow, to be honest. He'd been scared to lose his friendship, because damn it, Brad could be brutal when he was backed into a corner.

"You wanna be all kumbaya and share? How about you tell us why your boyfriend broke up with you?" Brad fired back at Miles. Yup, there was the grenade Charlie had expected Brad to launch.

Miles' flinched, then straightened his shoulders. "Fair enough, though your tone could use improvement. Casey was a lawyer, we met through my job. We started dating, fell in love—or what I assumed was love, moved in together. At first, he loved that I was always in the mood for sex. The sex was great, plentiful, and I thought we were happy. That didn't last long, and he started complaining about my sex drive. He felt I was pressuring him constantly to have sex, which made me feel very guilty, then told me my issue was either fake or psychological. I started doubting myself, debated taking the hormones after all. It took me a year to find out he was fucking dozens of other guys behind my back. When I confronted him, he told me he knew I had cheated, too. There was no way I hadn't, not when all I wanted to do was fuck...He never believed me when I assured him I had never done anything else but jack myself off as long as we were together. He left, and moved in a week later with a guy he'd apparently fucked a few times before. In hindsight, I can see that there were a great many things wrong with our relationship, and that I fucked up, too, but that's another story. That enough detail for ya?"

Like Charlie, Brad was subdued. This was not the story Charlie had expected to hear, and he figured it was the same for Brad.

"I'm sorry," Brad said. Did Miles recognize the sincerity in his tone? "That was a shitty thing to do to a man who holds integrity in such high regards."

Miles' eyebrows rose. "What?" Brad said defensively. "You think you're the only one who can read a person?"

"Oh, Brad, you sarcastic little shit. Why do you react so fiercely? It wasn't criticism. I was pleasantly surprised by your faith in my character."

Brad mumbled something.

"To my face, Brad. Say it to my face."

Fuck, Miles was unrelenting.

"It's self-defense," Brad said, louder this time.

"I know it is, honey, but I'm telling you there's no need for it. I won't hurt you."

"Sure, you will." This time, Brad's voice rung out crystal clear.

Miles' face was all compassion. "Tell me, honey, why have you never started a relationship with Charlie?"

"With Charlie? But we are friends, best friends."

"You know he wants more, and I'm pretty sure you want it, too."

Charlie froze. Was Miles right? He'd always thought his attraction was one-sided. Sure, Brad liked him, that much was clear. There was sexual tension, but Brad had always held him at a distance, at least in that regard.

Brad was quiet for a long time. "I've got nothing to offer him," he finally said. The emotion in his voice brought tears to Charlie's eyes.

"Nothing?" Miles asked.

"I got a steady job, but that's it. Emotionally, I'm fucked-up. I don't wanna expose him to that. He deserves better, and God knows what could happen."

"What do you fear would happen?"

Brad's shoulders sagged and he dragged a limp hand through his black hair. He opened his mouth, then closed it again. "I wanna take a shower," he finally offered.

"Okay," Miles said easily. "Let's shower. The damn thing is big enough for the three of us."

Charlie bit back a smile. That could not have been what Brad had in mind. Indeed, his head jerked up. "You want us to shower together?"

"After what we shared before, a shower should be easy, right?"

Brad turned to make eye contact with Charlie, who made sure he sported an innocent look. "Fine with me," he said. "I'm sticky all over."

Brad grumbled as they all climbed off the bed, but he didn't protest. Miles and Charlie started the shower, while Brad hunted up towels and wash cloths. By the time Brad joined them, the water was perfectly hot, and Charlie let out a happy sigh. "Fuck, this feels good."

He caught the wash cloth Brad threw at him. Behind him, Miles gestured and Charlie understood. "Sit down on the bench," he told Brad.

Brad looked confused. "Why?"

"Trust me, babe," Charlie said.

Brad lowered himself on the bench, looking from Charlie to Miles and back, as if he knew they were up to something. Miles smiled at him. "Trusting doesn't come easy for you, does it?"

Brad sighed. "It really doesn't."

Charlie reached for the shampoo, squeezed some out. "Close your eyes," he said.

Brad blinked once, twice, then did as Charlie asked. Charlie brought his hands to Brad's hair, started shampooing the dark locks, always a tad too long. Seconds later, Miles' hands joined him, and together they washed Brad's hair inch by inch, softly massaging his scalp. Every now and then a soft moan would float from Brad's lips.

Miles had been spot on. Brad was always focused on taking care of everyone else, including Charlie. He'd become used to it, to the point where he'd completely missed the underlying beliefs Brad harbored about himself. When had Brad started believing he wasn't good enough? When he'd said he had nothing to offer, man, that had hit Charlie hard. How could Brad possibly think that? Yet he'd been speaking what he believed was true.

Together, they rinsed out his hair, again massaging and finger combing his hair until every last fleck of foam was gone. Charlie knew what was next. He took the wash cloth, soaped it up. "Stand up," he ordered Brad.

He kept his eyes closed, but dutifully rose. Charlie sat

down, figuring Miles could do the top while he did the bottom. They washed Brad's body thoroughly, soaping every inch of skin. Brad's eyes were closed, his chest rising and falling with rapid breaths. This was hard for him, being taken care of. How the hell had Charlie missed that all these years? He'd taken and taken, never once realized how little Brad took back.

They were a study in contrasts, Charlie mused. Miles was so tall and blond, the ripped alpha of their threesome. Brad was his opposite, with his dark hair and brown eyes, his lean body. He had a long-distance runner's build, not an ounce of fat on his frame. And then there was Charlie himself, the quintessential twink with his small, slender frame. His dark hair was more similar to Brad's, but his fair skin color stood out, and his blue eyes were more like Miles'.

He washed Brad's ass, taking his time to clean his crack and hole. It was strange, yet so familiar to touch him like this. He'd saved the man's cock for last, not sure how he should proceed there. If he should. Brad had always been extremely sensitive about men seeing him, even Charlie. As if losing a testicle had made him less attractive, less of a man. You couldn't even notice it, not unless you knew and were pretty damn close to him.

When he gingerly touched his remaining nut, Brad's eyes flew open. "Charlie," he warned.

"You're beautiful," Charlie said, not letting himself be deterred this time. "Miles was right. I do want you, always have."

"You deserve more," Brad said.

Miles had been right. How had Charlie not seen this? "More than what, babe? More than you? A kind, loving man who's never treated me with anything less than respect, who's always been there for me? Brad, you've been my rock since day one, when you busted those guys for stuffing me in that trash can. You have taken care of me as much as I've allowed you. What more could I possibly deserve?"

Brad's face distorted in pain. Did this have something to do with his parents, his brothers? Charlie knew tiny slivers of Brad's past, shared when he was drunk, but he'd never gotten the whole picture.

Miles shut the shower off. "We'll talk about this tomorrow. We all need sleep right now."

Silently, the three of them toweled off. "I'll remake the bed," Brad said. Without waiting for an answer, he walked into the bedroom, still naked. Did he realize he was already growing accustomed to Miles seeing him like that? Charlie doubted it.

"We'll back off for now," Miles said softly.

Charlie nodded. "It's hard for him."

Miles' hand cupped Charlie's cheek. "I know, love. It's worth it. He's worth it." Electricity sparked between them. "You surprised me, bossy little man."

Charlie smiled. "Not your typical twink, huh?"

"I don't like the meek ones," Miles said. "The ones who passively bend over and take it."

"Not much chance of that with me."

"You told Brad you'd top him."

"You thought I was a bottom, didn't you?"

Miles hesitated. "Yeah, I did. Highly stereotypical, I know."

"I'm vers, like you, though honestly, I prefer topping."

"How did you...?"

Charlie snorted. "Dude, you liked it way too much when Brad played with your hole. You're definitely not a strict top."

"And Brad?"

"Shouldn't you be asking him?"

"I'm asking you."

Charlie relented. "He's a bottom only guy, even before his surgery. He's topped in the past, but it's not his thing. He loves to be on the receiving end."

"Charlie, my love, are you sure this is okay with you?"

"What, us you mean?"

"Yes. You're coming out of a relationship you haven't even formally ended."

"Trust me, it's over. We're over. I may have been stupid enough to take it a few times, but this? This was inexcusable."

Miles searched his face, nodded when he'd found what he'd been looking for. "When you're ready, I'll listen. No judgment."

Charlie followed his instinct. He stepped in, raised his face and offered Miles his mouth. He took it, gently and tender. It was the sweetest of kisses, making Charlie float.

"Brad gets your heat, and I get your heart. You're a man of contrasts, Miles," Charlie whispered against his mouth.

Miles' lips pulled up in a sexy grin. He kissed Charlie again, equally soft. "He's not ready for my heart, and you're not ready for my heat."

He had a point, Charlie mused as they walked into the bedroom, where Brad was finishing up remaking the bed. The dirty linens were in a pile on the floor. "We'll have to help Josh do laundry," Brad said, a look of guilt on his face.

"Something tells me he's used to washing sheets," Miles said. "The way these guys fuck, he's gotta be doing laundry daily."

They got back in bed, the tension gone for now. By unspoken agreement, they took the same spots as before, with Brad in the middle. Charlie turned on his stomach, his favorite sleeping position. He sought Brad's hand, put it around him.

Brad chuckled softly. "You're such a cuddler," he said. Still, he obliged by turning on his side and snuggling close to Charlie, his arm protectively around Charlie's waist.

The bed moved as Miles took position behind Brad, spooning him from behind. He nuzzled Brad's neck, kissed his nape. "Sleep well."

Brad's eyes widened, and Charlie held his breath to see if he would accept this affection from Miles. Brad let out a long sigh, his body releasing the tension, then closed his eyes.

The poor guy. He'd never even gotten his orgasm, not even after making them both come so many times. Miles had been right, there were deeper issues than Brad's limp dick, as he referred to it. But they'd wait till tomorrow. For now, they'd sleep. The three of them sharing a bed, and feeling wonderfully right.

Charlie fell asleep with a smile on his face.

MILES WAITED three whole days for Brad to bring their conversation up himself. When he didn't, Miles knew he was in for a fight. Brad still didn't realize Miles was willing to go to war over this. He was stubbornly clinging to the illusion that what they were doing was nothing more than sex. Fucking idiot. A child could see Charlie's heart had gotten involved a long time ago, and the same was true for Brad.

As for Miles, he kept telling himself falling in love in this short a time was impossible, especially when it concerned not one, but two guys. Yet his feelings were way too big, too demanding to be mere infatuation. So he'd fight for it, for them. But first, he had bigger fish to fry.

Charlie was napping in Miles' bedroom, so Miles waited in the living room till Brad got home from work. He walked in at four-thirty, looking tired and pale. Miles frowned. The guy was so busy taking care of everyone else, that he forgot to eat properly. And he certainly wasn't getting enough sleep. Miles made a mental note to make sure that would change.

"Hey," Brad said, dropping his backpack near the front door. "Where's Charlie?"

"Hi," Miles said. "He's napping in my room. How was your day?"

Brad's eyes widened as if he were surprised someone was even interested in him. "It was okay. State testing is in two weeks, so we're cramming the last chapters in."

Miles wanted to hear more, but Connor walked in, per his request.

"Brad," he nodded.

Brad did a half-ass awkward wave that Miles thought was endearing. He could be so clumsy and clueless at times.

"Let's talk," Connor said. He lowered his impressive body on one of the chairs.

Brad crumpled his nose. "Talk?"

"Yeah," Miles said. "I asked Connor to meet us here. We need to talk about Charlie's boyfriend."

"Ex-boyfriend," Brad corrected, plopping down on the couch. "And what does this have to do with you?"

Miles sighed. "Really, Brad? You don't think the fact that I am an FBI agent, let alone the reality that the three of us are involved gives me the right to discuss this?"

Brad had the decency to look halfway embarrassed. "I was handling it with Connor," he said.

"Fine. And now you can handle it with Connor and with me. Start talking."

Connor barely reacted, but his eyes sparkled. "I asked my former partner to do a little digging on Waitley. Turns out, he's the kinda cop that gives the rest of us a bad name. His ex-girlfriend filed charges for assault and battery twice, but retracted them both times."

Miles cursed softly. "Classic for battered wife syndrome."

"Yeah," Connor said. "His former partner says he stalked her as well. He reported it to Internal Affairs, but Waitley found out and laid low."

"What about the dash cam video?" Brad asked.

Miles frowned. "What video?"

"You didn't tell him?" Connor asked.

Brad shook his head.

"Waitley pulled him over a couple of days ago," Connor said. Miles' stomach turned sour. "Our Brad here had a dash cam installed, one that not only records video, but sound as well. Waitley wanted to know where Charlie was, threatened Brad in a non-specific manner if he didn't tell. The good news is that he all but confessed to the domestic abuse."

"And you didn't share this with me, why?" he asked Brad, his voice ice cold. Brad shifted on the couch, crossed his arms, then uncrossed them again, but didn't say anything. "This is not something you keep from me, Brad. This is the kind of thing you tell me immediately."

"Why? It's none of your business. What we have is sex, man, nothing else. That gives you the fucking right to know shit."

Brad's defense mechanism was in fine form again, Miles noted. In situations like this, he was damn grateful for the training he'd had to stay in the present, to keep his mind engaged, rather than let his emotions take over.

"I swear to God, Brad, if you ever say something like that again, I will spank your bare ass, do you hear me? Do not, I repeat, do not insult my feelings for you and for Charlie by referring to it as mere sex."

Brad's mouth dropped open slightly. "You wouldn't dare."

Miles' eyes narrowed. "Don't tempt me. If you insist on acting like a brat, I will fucking treat you as one. Feel free to deny your own feelings, but don't you dare disrespect me and Charlie like that. I know you're scared, but that doesn't give you the right to decide for us what we feel."

"I'm not scared." Brad was adorable when he tried to be all tough, but his voice came out trembling.

"Honey, you're scared as fuck. I haven't quite figured out what you're scared of and why, but I'll get there. Do we have an understanding, Brad? Do you hear what I'm telling you?"

"You'll spank me if I say it's just sex," Brad said slowly, his voice throaty.

Connor chuckled. "He likes the idea," he said. "Look at him. His pupils are dilated, he's flushed, and he's breathing fast. He's fucking aroused."

Connor would know, considering his activities with Josh, but Miles had already come to the same conclusion. "Is he right, honey?" he asked Brad. Brad's eyes shot down to the floor, as he fidgeted with his hands. "I asked you a question, Brad."

His eyes flew up again. "I don't know, okay? Yes, maybe. How the fuck would I know? I've never... How would I know?"

Miles nodded, satisfied. They'd have to revisit this topic at a later time, preferably not in front of Connor, and with

Charlie present as well. "Okay, I'll accept that. Now tell me about the video. Is it usable?"

"Yes and no," Connor said. "It's legal in New York to record police officers without their permission, so the video will be admissible in a court of law. The problem is that it would only be useful if Charlie decided to press charges for assault. Without that, there's not much you can do. Legally."

"Will he press charges?" Miles asked Brad.

He'd looked confused when Miles had shifted the conversation so quickly back to the video after their spanking discussion, but he was alert now.

"I honestly don't know," Brad said. "He's scared of him. He refused to go to a hospital because he was scared Zack would kill him. I don't know if he meant that in the literal sense or was more expressing a general sense of fear of retribution."

Connor dragged a hand through his short hair. "He's got reason to be scared, especially after what Waitley did to him. Was this the first time?"

"No. I've seen him with bruises a few times, but he denied it was Zack. Blake let him stay at his house a while back when he spotted Charlie being hurt. Charlie admitted he'd been beaten, then, but still went back."

The hurt and self-blame was easy to spot. "It's not your fault, honey," Miles said, his voice soft.

"I should have dragged him away from that fucking asshole," Brad said.

Connor sighed. "I know you feel that way, but the truth is that abuse victims cannot be helped until they're ready to accept help. Charlie made his own choices, Brad, and my guess is that he doesn't blame you at all."

He doesn't have to, Miles thought. Brad was blaming himself way more than Charlie ever would or could. "Let's assume Charlie doesn't want to press charges. Where does that leave us?" he asked.

"Legally, nowhere," Connor said.

"You keep using that word, legally," Brad remarked. "What do you mean by that? Are you implying there's another route, illegally?"

Miles smiled. "I think Connor is testing the waters, considering he's no longer on the force, but I am still a federal agent."

Brad harrumphed. "As if you wouldn't walk through fire to keep Charlie safe."

The casual way he once again expressed his belief in Miles' character hit him deep. "How can you say that, yet not believe I have feelings for you?"

"Holy fuck, can you let it go?" Brad snapped. "Let's focus on the problem at hand, okay?"

"You wanna watch your tone there, Brad. I'm getting mighty tired of you taking my head off all the time."

"Fuck you. You're not my dad!"

Max woke up from his slumber on the floor and raised his head to check what was happening. Brad jumped off the couch and stormed off into the bedroom, though still managing to open and close the door quietly because of Charlie. Max got up, seemed to shake his head at Miles, then followed Brad to the bedroom, softly howling until Brad opened the door to let him in.

Miles leaned back, rubbing his neck. One step forward, two steps back.

"He's a good kid, deep down," Connor remarked.

"The best," Miles agreed. "You should see how tender he is with Charlie. It's me he graces with his lethal defenses."

Connor leaned back in his chair. "Sometimes we hurt the ones we love the most to see if they'll stay."

Miles sighed. "Yeah. Doesn't mean it doesn't fucking hurt, though."

They shared a comfortable silence for a bit.

"I was surprised to find you here when I arrived," Miles changed the subject. He'd been dying for a one-on-one with Connor to put his feelers out, and here was finally his chance. "Last thing I heard you were in Boston, recruiting, and weeks later I find you back here with your man. Or men, I should say."

Connor smiled. "The Feds keeping tabs on me?"

"You knew we were. Anyone connected to Indy was being watched, but you were of interest especially."

"I'm flattered."

Miles smiled. The guy was a Marine and a cop—and it showed. He was every bit as cool as Miles under pressure. "You wanna fill me in on the truth?"

Connor got up, slapped him good-naturedly on his shoulder, which left him reeling. "Nah. You're a wicked smart man, Miles. You'll figure it out."

Miles mulled it over, as Connor walked off. He'd gotten to know all the people that had once been names in a file so much better. Indy, the ultimate survivor who hadn't merely build a new life here, but was thriving. He was at the very center of this house, keeping everyone together with sheer love.

Then there was Noah, whose love for Indy was palpable. He came across as aloof and stern, until Indy entered the room, and then that face lit up like a Christmas tree. Miles had heard of the expression being the light in someone's life, but he'd never seen it in reality, until he'd seen how Noah responded to Indy's presence.

Added to the mix were Josh and Connor, the sweet intro-vert and his bossy cop who knew exactly what Josh needed.

And who, apparently, seemed to accept that Josh and Indy had a special relationship as well. If Noah and Indy together were light, Josh and Connor were fire...but Josh and Indy were like the wind. You couldn't quite catch it, but boy, did it have power.

It's why the whole story didn't make sense to Miles. Connor in Boston, cozying up to criminals with a known hate for the Fitzpatricks. Him breaking up with Josh, who was clearly the love of his life, on the same day Indy was taken into FBI custody. Josh, who by all accounts suffered a brutal mental breakdown in the veteran hospital he'd been admitted to. Miles had seen the file, courtesy of his boss, and the list of meds Josh had been administered would knock an elephant out.

Then there was Noah, still physically recovering from his amputation surgery, when he was dealt a severe blow by Indy's departure. Noah and Josh back together according to the file, Indy in Kansas, Connor in Boston. What were the chances that these four who were more intimately linked than any men he'd ever met before had been truly apart? He didn't buy it.

He'd looked over the files and reports of the shooting in Boston. The cops had worked with the Feds and other experts to determine what had happened. They'd figured out where the shots had come from—an apartment building across the street—but that was it. Speculation was rife, with theories ranging from the CIA's involvement to Russian sharpshooters being hired by a rival mobster family.

One fact had puzzled everyone on this case: the accuracy of the shots. The shooter had nailed them in rapid successions with shots straight to the heart, and all that from a long distance, with a standard military issue rifle.

A standard military issue rifle. The one army snipers used, like Specialist Joshua Gordon. His army file had been thick with praises about his accuracy as a sniper. The same Joshua Gordon who'd been drugged out of his mind in a mental health care facility, all documented, yet who had shown up here doing remarkably well for someone who had a complete breakdown weeks before.

It had to have been Josh who shot them, somehow aided by Connor. The fact that Connor had been on an undercover job with the Boston PD and had been in Boston when that shit had gone down? Too much of a coincidence. The FBI had thought he'd been recruiting for the Fitzpatricks, but Miles' suspicion was that he was the guy who had managed to organize a mutiny against them—and handed them all on a silver platter to the Boston PD.

Miles had no idea how they had pulled it off—Connor and Josh, because Indy had not been involved, that much Miles was sure of, and Noah probably neither—but he would bet all his money on Josh being the shooter. And now he was living in his house, enjoying his hospitality. It was crazy as fuck, wasn't it?

Miles should care, on some level. He was a federal agent, and he had no business condoning vigilante justice, not even implicitly. And yet he had felt zero urge to report his suspicions.

Instead, he found himself admiring the sheer balls of this particular operation. And having read the bulging file on the crimes of the Fitzpatricks, especially the vicious attack on Stephan Moreau and the brutal murder on DA Merrick and his family, Miles couldn't say he was sorry these men were dead. The legal system had failed Stephan and others, but in the end, justice had been served.

It had truly been the only solution to bring Indy freedom. Even if the justice department had succeeded in getting a conviction for the top Fitzpatrick leaders—and that would have taken a year at least—Indy would've always had to look over his shoulder. He was truly free now. Plus, three of the lowest lowlifes were dead. Miles could not have a problem with that, as much as he maybe should.

Maybe it said a lot about his motivation, or lack thereof, for his job. He'd loved it at first, but the last few years had been tough. It was a somewhat sobering realization he'd made since staying in this house, how fucking lonely he'd been. He'd kept people at such arms' length that he'd been starving for contact, both emotionally and physically. Being here, in this house, with all these men, it was like water for his barren soul. And fuck, the physical contact...people touching him, hugging him without caring that he'd get hard. It brought tears to his eyes at times.

It was the first time as long as he could remember that he'd felt truly accepted. Even with Casey, he'd always had to hold back. Here, he walked around with just PJ bottoms on, no double tight boxers, and no one gave a shit of they saw his pants tent. It was a freedom he'd never had.

And interestingly enough, he could already sense a difference in himself, even physically. At first, every casual touch had gotten him hard, desperate as he'd been for human contact. Now, it had become easier. He was still hard half the time, but not as quickly.

More important were the friendships and of course, Brad and Charlie. Miles had no fucking idea where the three of them were headed, but he wasn't ready to walk away. And as soon as he was back on the job, he would have to walk away. Aside from the fact that the FBI might not tolerate a ménage relationship, Miles himself didn't want it. If nothing else, his failed relationship with Casey had taught him that his job didn't mesh with a relationship. Maybe it was time to start looking for something else.

So yeah, he did value the friendship with all of these men over doing his duty, especially when that duty would bring nothing good. The Fitzpatricks were dead, justice had been done, and those that remained in the organization would get their day in court. Case closed, as far as he was concerned. Maybe in a few years time, he could ask Josh and Connor how the fuck they had pulled it off.

But right this moment, he had two more pressing problems. Well, three actually. The most pressing one was that he needed to come, since the pressure in his balls had been building up to a damn uncomfortable level. Then there was Brad, who needed a good night's sleep, a solid meal or two, and a massive orgasm. After that, they had to come up with a plan to keep Charlie safe from his ex, because the kid hadn't left the house since he got here, and that couldn't continue.

Miles nodded. Now that his priorities were sorted, he knew what to do.

13

Fuck, he was tired. As much as he enjoyed cuddling with Charlie after he'd just woken up from a nap, Brad's head throbbed with a nasty headache brewing behind his eyes. He hadn't slept well for weeks, but the last three nights had been particularly restless, courtesy of the two men he'd been sandwiched between.

He was so on high alert to make sure Charlie was okay, that he couldn't fully surrender to sleep. And Miles' presence was...unnerving, to say the least. He saw so much. Too much. It was only a matter of time until Miles figured it out, figured him out, and then he'd dump Brad for sure. Fuck, he wanted to run, wanted to preserve what little dignity he had left, but at the same time couldn't drag himself away.

"Do you need anything?" Brad asked softly, kissing Charlie's head that was resting on his shoulder.

"No, he doesn't," Miles said, jolting Brad. He hadn't even heard him come into the room. "You, however, need a good meal, some decent sleep, and an orgasm. You look like shit."

Brad almost laughed at the brutal honesty Miles threw at him. Almost, because he wouldn't give in that easy. He turned his head to face Miles, who was watching him with more kindness than he'd expected considering his tone.

"I wasn't asking you," Brad pointed out. "I was talking to Charlie. He can damn well answer for himself."

Charlie untangled himself from Brad's arms, pushed himself up carefully. "Miles is right. You look pale and tired."

His tone was much nicer than Miles, but that didn't make the stab in Brad's heart any less. "You're choosing his side?" he asked, incredulity lacing his voice.

Hurt flashed over Charlie's face. "No, you idiot. I'm choosing your side."

Brad's eyes darkened. When had Charlie ever taken a stand against him? Had the two of them been talking about him behind his back? Maybe they'd come to the conclusion that three was a crowd, that they really didn't need nor want him. They'd be perfectly happy with the two of them, without his fucked-up problems.

"What are you, my dad? Fuck off. I can take care of myself," he fired at Miles, his heart painfully contracting. He was losing them, even Charlie. God, what would he do now? He'd known he would fuck up. He always did.

"Fucking hell, Brad, we're trying to take care of you! What the fuck is wrong with you that you won't let us?"

Charlie's eyes were full of hurt as he hurled the words at Brad, and he flinched. His shoulders sagged and he closed his eyes for a second. He was so tired. Exhausted, really. Fuck, his head hurt.

"Brad, you have five seconds to get off that bed and move your ass to the kitchen, where you will sit down and eat."

Miles' voice was deceptively calm, but Brad recognized the steel underneath. His eyes flew open. Miles meant business. What would he do if Brad refused? He wouldn't really spank him, would he? There was no way the serious FBI agent was that kinky and stern. No, he was bluffing.

"Five...four..."

Brad found himself scrambling off the bed, angry with himself for responding to Miles' tone. It reached somewhere deep inside him, made him want to obey as much as be even more of a brat, as Miles had called him.

Miles took his arm with enough force to make Brad wince. "Let's go. Now."

He let himself be dragged to the kitchen, where he discovered Blake and Aaron hanging out with Indy and Noah. Oh, hell no, he was not doing this in front of his brother.

Blake's eyes fell on Miles' hand and became ice daggers. "You wanna remove that hand from my brother's arm," he said coolly.

Pandemonium ensued as everyone started talking at once, Aaron saying something to Blake, and Indy asking Miles what he was doing, and Charlie telling Noah it was all right, and Max was barking his head off, which he never did, and Brad couldn't think, couldn't breathe, couldn't stand it anymore.

"Shut up!" he screamed, his voice breaking with the force.

All that was left was his own ragged breath, as every face in the room turned to him in shock. Max whined, and came over to rub his head against Brad's legs.

"Bradford, what the hell?" Blake snapped.

A sob worked its way up, escaping before he could force it back. "I'm leaving. I'm going home."

He yanked his arm free with more ease than he'd expected, realized Miles' hold had been more in his mind than in physical force.

"Brad..."

That was Charlie, his face pure shock. Brad swallowed. "You should be with Miles. He's good for you. He'll make you happy. I...I can't, Charlie. I can't do this."

"Brad, talk to me..." Blake got up out of his chair, but Brad stepped back.

"No. These are your friends, Blake, not mine. I don't belong here."

He walked out before the dam burst, as he knew it would, his loyal Max on his heels—the one being in his life who would never choose someone else over him.

Five seconds after he walked in the front door of his own house, his hold on his emotions broke under the pressure. He let himself drop onto his bed and gave up, cuddling Max in his arms and crying hot tears into his fur.

MILES' first impulse was to stop Brad from leaving, but he held himself in check. He'd seen the pure terror on Brad's face. The man had somehow reached a limit, and he needed to walk away. Didn't mean Miles wouldn't bring him back, kicking and screaming if he had to.

"What the fuck did you do to my brother?" Blake asked, stepping into his personal space. Behind Miles, Charlie whimpered in fear.

"Blake, sit down. You're scaring Charlie," Indy said, his voice calm and steady. He put a hand on Blake's forearm. "Walk away if you have to, but you can't do this."

Blake was so close, Miles felt his breath on his face, before the man stepped back. Blake swallowed, turned to Charlie. "I'm sorry, love. I didn't mean to scare you."

He opened his arms and offered Charlie a hug, which he accepted after a slight hesitation.

Miles breathed out in relief. Phew, that was a close call. He would've needed Indy's help to keep Blake at bay had the man decided to get physical, that much he knew. He was no match for a black belt, especially not in his current condition.

"I apologize," Blake said, his voice stiff and formal as he faced Miles again. "I usually have a better grip on my temper, but I'm protective of my brother."

Miles nodded. "Accepted. I understand, but I need you to know I wasn't hurting him. Not like that, anyway."

Charlie stepped forward until he stood beside Miles, their arms touching. "It's true, Blake. We're trying to take care of Brad, but he won't let us."

Blake sighed. "Yeah, he sucks at that. Always has, even as a kid. He's always taking care of others, but he finds it hard to accept it when others do the same for him."

"He doesn't want to be a bother," Charlie said, moving toward one of the chairs and sitting down.

Blake took his spot at the table again, but not until after kissing Aaron on his head. As soon as he sat, Aaron reached for his hand. "I've told Brad multiple times he should see a shrink, but he refuses."

Miles frowned. "Why would he need to see a shrink?"

"To talk about what happened with our parents. The abuse, my mom dying, I'm sure it's what's messing with Brad's head. I did the best I could, but I don't think it was enough."

Miles' head reeled. Abuse? What the hell was Blake talking about? His confusion must have shown, because Blake sighed. "He didn't tell you, did he?" Blake turned to Charlie. "Did you know?"

"Not the whole story. Brad only talks when he's drunk, so he's shared tidbits, but never the whole story."

Miles found a seat as well, his legs suddenly rubbery. "Look, you shouldn't say anything if that means breaking his confidence. I didn't know, but then again, there's very little I do know about Brad, because he doesn't talk to me."

Blake's eyes were sad. "It's not a betrayal of his confidence. It's what happened to us, to him. He doesn't want to talk about it, and if you ask me, that's the whole reason he's struggling."

"What can you tell us?" Charlie asked, seeking Miles' hand. Miles loved that he spoke of "us", that there still was an "us." Somewhere, somehow, they had failed to make Brad safe and secure enough in their threesome, but they'd correct that. They belonged together, and they'd figure out how to fix them.

The room got quiet as Blake spoke, his voice filled with pain. "My dad was an abusive drunk, always had been as long as I can remember. He hit my mom, and us too, if he got really angry. Mostly her, but as the oldest two, me and Burke got slapped around every now and then as well. He mostly ignored Brad and my youngest brother Benjamin, but that was also because Benjamin was mentally handicapped and Brad was really adept at being invisible. He did anything to avoid getting my dad angry, including helping my mom in the house and taking care of Benjamin."

Miles' throat closed as he thought about the little boy Brad had been, always afraid he, too, would get beaten up.

"My mom left him once, took us with her. He found her, of course, and beat the shit out of her. We tried to step in, me and Burke. Man, we fought him as best as we could, but he was big and mean. Brad, he wanted to help, too, but I locked him and Benjamin in our room, told him to stay out of it. He may have gotten a smack to his head once or twice, but it wasn't as bad as it was for me or Burke."

Aaron had listened quietly this whole time, but the sadder Blake got, the more restless he became. Finally, he got up and squeezed himself on Blake's lap. Blake's arms came around him with a sigh of contentment. He clearly appreciated the comfort Aaron brought.

"My mom died of a heart attack a few weeks after my eighteenth birthday. We had no other family, so after much deliberating with family services, the judge granted me custody of Burke and Brad, with the provision that there was a supervising guardian from child protective services as well. Benjamin was placed with a foster family because of his special needs, and they ended up adopting him."

Miles couldn't believe what these brothers had endured. "How did Brad react to your mom's death?" he asked.

Blake shook his head. "I fucked up there. Burke started acting out, so I focused on keeping him straight. Brad did what he'd done for years: make himself invisible. He took care of all of us: cooked, cleaned, did the laundry, you name it. And I was grateful, because I was working two jobs and trying to keep Burke in school. I was actually glad Brad was so helpful, did so well in school. He's fucking brilliant in math, did you know?"

"Is he?" Miles asked, surprised.

"Yeah, off the charts brilliant. He could have gone to some expensive university, even had a partial scholarship, but he refused, went to a state school instead. I mean, he still got a degree, but he could have done so much more, except..."

Blake hesitated, and Miles and Charlie looked at each other.

"Except he didn't think he was worth it," Charlie said

softly, voicing Miles' thoughts exactly. "I, for one, am grateful he became a math teacher, because otherwise I would have never met him."

"I know, love, and I'm glad he has you as a friend," Blake said. "But you have to understand: he's my regret. They say everyone has one big regret in life. Well, he's mine. I fucked up with him, allowed him to stay invisible. I never saw him until it was too late, and now he's all messed up because of it."

Miles leaned back in his chair, ordering the information in his head. The dots connected, and suddenly it clicked. It was so crystal clear that he wondered why he hadn't seen it before. The sarcasm, the self-defense, his need to please, his disrespectful behavior, the psychological erectile dysfunction, the interest in discipline—it all made sense.

There was a giant void in Brad's life, a void that had never been filled. The question was whether Miles was willing and able to fulfill the role Brad needed.

Craved.

My God, Brad craved it, desperately. Everything had been there, but Miles simply hadn't seen it because he'd never thought to ask about Brad's parents. He'd never known the shit his man had been through—shit that had robbed him of his sense of worth, his sense of security, and his sense of being lovable.

He squeezed Charlie's hand gently, looked at him. "Charlie, my love, are you up for a little road trip? We need to get Brad back, and it cannot wait till tomorrow."

Charlie hesitated. "I can't."

Miles' heart sank. "Why?" he asked, making sure his voice was kind.

Charlie's hands clenched into fists, and his shoulders

hunched. "Brad's house, it's the first place Zack will look for me."

Miles had known Charlie was afraid of his ex, but he hadn't fully realized to what degree until he saw the pure terror in his eyes just now. He cursed himself for allowing Charlie to cultivate his fear this long. They should have helped him sooner, encouraged him to get out of the house.

"You don't think I'd ever let anything happen to you, do you?" he asked softly.

Charlie still refused to look at him, instead kept focusing on his hands. "You don't know what he's capable of. He's... He's not like all of you. He has no honor, no moral compass like you all do. I'm scared for Brad, even now. If Zack is waiting for him when he gets home... He hates Brad. Truly, deeply hates him."

"Brad can take care of himself," Blake said in a placating tone.

Charlie's head snapped up, his eyes spewing fire. "No, he can't dammit. You always say that, but it's not true. He can't take care of himself. If he encounters Zack, he'll open his sarcastic little mouth, antagonize him, and get the shit kicked out of him. And if he doesn't... He's by himself right now, convinced that nobody loves him and nobody wants him. How the hell will he survive this? He can't take care of himself, Blake. He needs us, Miles and me. He needs us to take care of him."

If ever there had been any doubt as to the depth of Charlie's feelings, it was all gone now. This spunky pistol was head-over-heels for Brad, and it warmed Miles' heart. "So come with me, Charlie," he said. "Help me show him that we're here for him, that we do want him."

Charlie's eye showed his internal battle. "I wish I—"

"We all need to go," Noah interrupted him, the first time

he had spoken since they'd walked into the kitchen. "If he feels like we are not his friends, like he's not truly wanted and welcome here, we should all go. And nothing will happen when you're with us, Charlie. Your ex may be a mean asshole, but he won't be stupid enough to try anything with all of us there."

Miles' heart filled even more. He thanked whatever deity would listen for the day he met Indy, because that encounter had led him right here, to this amazing group of...family. That's what they felt like, family.

Charlie's face lost some of the tension. "Okay," he said finally, squaring his shoulders. "But somebody better bring a gun, just in case."

Miles grinned inwardly. Charlie was such a bossy little shit at times, and he loved it. Connor's eyes gleamed, but he kept his face neutral otherwise. "I always carry, kid," he said.

"So do I," Josh said calmly. "And I don't miss."

Somehow, that statement removed the last bit of tension from Charlie. "Okay." He took a deep breath. "Let's do this, then. Let's bring Brad home."

14

Charlie's heart beat fast and his hands were clammy as he sat in the back seat of Noah's car. It wasn't even Zack he was afraid of—though it was certainly on his mind. He hadn't fully realized how scared he was and how safe he'd felt holed up in Indy's house until Miles had asked him to leave that cocoon. Fuck, he was pathetic. If he continued like this, he'd end up an agoraphobic hermit. Still, that was not what had him so nervous right now. No, his mind was on Brad.

What if Brad hadn't gone home? What if he'd left in search of someone who would fuck him, make him forget? It's what he did when his demons got the better of him. Charlie knew, he'd known for years, but he'd never understood. God, he'd failed Brad in their friendship. All these years, and he'd never known how deep his sense of rejection was. What if it was too late now?

He'd never heard Brad yell, ever. He could be snarky and fire off deadly verbal attacks, but he'd never broken down like that. He'd been a time bomb waiting to go off, but Charlie had never had the guts to confront Brad. Not like

Miles, who'd simply refused to budge. The man was simply not deterred by Brad's defenses, seemed to be able to take hit after hit. In that sense, he was perfect for Brad.

Charlie's breath caught as his own thoughts registered. In a way, he was thinking the same thing Brad had voiced. He'd expressed his conviction that Charlie and Miles were good for each other, and now Charlie was doing the same for Brad and Miles.

It was hard to find his place in their threesome, to discover how they fit together. They did, that Charlie was convinced of. Brad needed him as much as he needed Miles, hell, they all needed each other, even if they all hadn't figured out what piece of the puzzle they were.

"We're here," Noah said. He parked the car behind Brad's car next to his duplex. Charlie let out a sigh of relief when he spotted the car. Thank fuck Brad had gone home. He wanted to get out, but Miles held him back. "Let Connor go first, check to make sure Zack isn't here."

Charlie nodded, relieved to see these men taking care of him. Connor got out, hand on what Charlie presumed was his gun, and looked around methodically. Josh did the same, and it was interesting to see the usually shy man be hyper alert. Charlie waited till they signaled for them to come out.

"How do we do this?" Indy asked when they'd all gotten out.

Noah and Miles looked at each other, then at Blake. "He's your brother," Noah said.

"Yeah, but I'm not sure I'm the best person to talk to him right now."

"I think you should talk, Noah," Miles said. "He's pissed at me, maybe at Blake, too, and you're a neutral party here. You could tell him he's wanted in your house."

Noah nodded. "I can do that."

Charlie took a deep breath. "No. I'll do it."

All heads turned to him. "Charlie, love, he'll rip you to shreds," Miles said, his voice sad.

"No, he won't. He never has. I've always been the only one he trusts, and he's never hurt me. He loves me, even if he's too damn scared to admit it." He straightened his shoulders.

"We'll back you up," Noah said with a smile.

It was a strange procession that made its way to Brad's house. Grim faces, a ripple of determination making its way through the group. They wouldn't leave without Brad. He belonged with them. Charlie praised himself lucky for finding these men.

Charlie didn't pause when he reached Brad's door, simply knocked. Not a sound was coming from inside, but Brad was home, Charlie was sure. Not only had he spotted his car, but moreover, he felt him. Somewhere inside was Brad, and he needed him, needed them.

"He's not opening the door," Noah said.

Charlie smiled, his first smile that night. "Good thing I have a key."

He opened the door without qualms, not giving a shit about Brad's privacy. "Brad, we're coming in so if you're naked, put some clothes on."

A sound traveled from Brad's bedroom. Charlie stepped inside, and everyone made their way inside Brad's house, which was suddenly crowded with so many people.

"We'll wait here," Noah decided, and the others nodded.

Charlie looked at Miles, who hesitated. "Do you think I should come?" he asked Charlie. It was the first time Charlie had seen him insecure, and it was disconcerting. Maybe Miles hadn't figured out how they fit together, either.

"Yes. We're in this together. I'll talk to him, but I need you there."

Miles took his hand as they walked into Brad's bedroom. Brad was on his bed, hiding his face in Max's fur, his body tense.

"Brad..." Charlie said, his voice suddenly emotional. What if he couldn't get through to him? What if he said the wrong thing, and fucked it all up?

"Why are you here?"

He was talking, that was good. And it wasn't downright hostile. He'd sounded more surprised than angry. "Because we're not complete without you. We miss you when you're not there."

Miles squeezed his hand, shot him an encouraging look.

"I don't want you to see me like this."

"Tough luck, because I'm here, and I'm not leaving without you. We need you, Brad, and you need us."

"We?"

"You didn't think I came here by myself, did you?"

Slowly, Brad's head turned toward them. His eyes were all red and blotchy, and he looked like he hadn't slept in weeks. Brad flinched when he spotted Miles.

"Why did you bring him?"

Nope, Brad wasn't truly angry. He was trying to be but couldn't pull it off. "Miles is here for the same reason I am, because he cares about you, and wants you back where you belong. With us."

Brad closed his eyes, the sadness on his face so heart-breaking it took Charlie's breath away. "I don't belong with you, babe. Or with Miles. Or with any of them. They're all good men, and I'm... You're too good for me, Charlie, too sweet and kind. You have so much joy, and I don't want to diminish your light. And Miles, he's perfect, and he'll give you the life you deserve."

God, how had he missed this all these years? How had he not seen how Brad suffered? "You're wrong on all accounts, sweetie. I love you. You know that, I always have for as much as you've let me."

Brad's eyes flew open. "How can you love me? I don't understand. How can you love someone who is so fucked-up, and broken, and so damn needy all the time?"

Charlie put his hands on his hips. Time for some tough love. "Open your fucking eyes, Brad. You're so caught up in your own shit, that you don't see everyone around you is just as broken and fucked-up, only in a different way."

"What do you mean?"

"God, look at our friends. Do they, I dunno, seem normal to you? Have you realized the company you're in?"

Brad still looked at him as if he was an alien. How could he be so fucking blind? "Guys, little help here?" Charlie called out.

One by one, they stepped into Brad's bedroom, filling the entire space. Brad's face was pure shock.

"What the fuck?" he gasped, before scrambling up into a sitting position. "What the hell are you all doing here?"

His face was crimson red with embarrassment, and Charlie almost took pity on him. Almost. "Anyone here want to show Brad he's not the only fucked-up person in the room?" Charlie asked.

Chuckling reverberated through the room.

"I'll go first," Aaron said, surprising not just Charlie. He stepped forward, raised his chin. "I grew up with parents who only loved me as long as I adhered to their standard of perfection. I've never felt loved, never felt accepted for who I was, never felt safe and secure. I may be an adult, but I often regress to childlike behavior and neediness—the puppy behavior you've witnessed. I physically and emotionally need Blake to take care of me, the way my parents never have."

Charlie had met Aaron multiple times, and always thought he was a good guy, if a bit weird, but this explained a lot. It took balls to admit this, especially to his brother in law.

"My mom sold me to a known mobster when I was fourteen to pay off a debt. I was his whore for years, before he gave me to another man to settle a debt. That guy raped me before I killed him. My ex found me, and beat me up with the help of others."

Indy's voice was quiet, with little trembles betraying the depth of his emotion. He turned his back toward Brad, lifted his shirt. Charlie couldn't hold the small gasp in when he saw Indy's scarred back. He'd never seen anything like it, his whole skin one maze of scars.

"They poured acid over my back. I ran and I hid, until I met Noah and Josh, and Connor. I never knew what love was, what it felt like, until I met them. They taught me what love is, what family is."

He turned back around, dropped his shirt. Noah pulled him close, as Josh reached out to hold his hand.

"I have PTSD, caused by a sexual assault when I was in the army." Josh's voice was barely audible, yet it floated through the room straight into everyone's heart. He was witnessing something special, Charlie realized. "Three of my fellow soldiers raped me, and shortly after I watched my best friend get blown up. I spent two weeks on a closed ward, and I've been treated for depression, anxiety attacks, nightmares, and other shit ever since." He lifted his chin. "I need regular Dom/sub sessions with Connor to keep my mind clear. He spanks the stress right out of me. Without Connor's love, Indy's heart, and Noah's friendship I wouldn't be here today."

"I'm so fucking proud of you, Josh," Indy said, stepping in and hugging Josh tight. Connor kissed his head at the same time, showing the beautiful dynamic between these men. Charlie couldn't figure out what Indy and Josh were to each other, but it was clear they were more than mere friends.

It was quiet for a few seconds. "I've never told this to anyone else, but Josh, Indy, and Noah," Connor said. He cleared his voice. "I was a Marine Sergeant, leading a mission I knew was doomed to fail, when I was captured by the Taliban, with my best friend, Lucas. We were..." He swallowed, and Josh hugged him tight. "They tortured us. Waterboarding. Lucas didn't make it. I got out, but I was a robot. It's still hard for me to talk, to feel. Josh...he cracked my defenses. His love, it's healing me. That, and my family."

Noah's head whipped around. "Your family?" His tone was sharp.

"Yeah, me and Josh and Indy and you. We're family."

Noah's face broke open in a smile that lit up the entire room. Holy fuck, the guy had a smile that could power a small city. Charlie felt the effects in his entire body and he wasn't the only one. "Damn, O'Connor, you say the sweetest things."

"Fuck you, Flint."

"Not with that monster you have, but thanks for offering," Noah quipped, breaking the tension in the room.

Indy and Josh laughed, while others grinned. Charlie had heard rumors about Connor's cock, which apparently was somewhat oversized.

"Brad, don't you see? Everyone here is fucked-up,

whether it's emotionally, physically, or sexually. There is no normal. That's something that only exists in your head. You've blown your own hang ups so out of proportion that you've lost sight of the reality."

Miles sat down on the bed as he spoke, tugging Charlie on his hand to join him.

Brad's eyes were big as he looked at them. "But what about you two? You're both perfect," he whispered, his voice filled with pain.

"Oh, sweetie, we're not. Not even close." Charlie swallowed. Should he tell him? How could he not, after what the others had shared? "I let Zack fuck me every time he wanted to, since I was fifteen... I knew he had a girlfriend, knew he was using me, and still I let him, because his attention was the only love I'd ever known. He used me, and I let him, and he abused me, and still I stayed. If that's not seriously fucked-up, I don't know what is."

"Charlie!" Brad's voice was so pain-filled it made Charlie's eyes tear up. He rose to his knees, hugged Charlie. "You're worth so much more...I'm so sorry. Why didn't you ever tell me?"

This was Brad, too. This infinite kindness and compassion, this tenderness and care.

"Because I was ashamed for being this stupid. He played me like a fiddle, Brad, knew exactly what to say to a lonely, love-starved kid like me."

"You're not stupid. This is all on him. He was the adult, sweetie. You were just a kid."

Charlie untangled himself from Brad's arms, cupped his cheek with his right hand. "So were you. Blake told us a little about what happened with your parents."

Brad stiffened, his face closing down. "What the fuck

does that have to do with anything?" Yup, the defenses were back up. Charlie sighed.

"I failed you," Blake said, stepping forward.

"No, you didn't. You took care of us all," Brad said, but his voice was emotionless.

"No, Brad, you did. You cooked and you cleaned and you did everything. And I didn't see it until it was too late. I kept Burke out of trouble, but you took care of both of us, like you cared for Benjamin before Mom died."

Brad's eyes shifted restlessly. "I had to, because he was all alone. Mom always focused on keeping you and Burke quiet, so you wouldn't anger Dad. Benjamin was all by himself."

"And who took care of you, Brad?" Miles asked, his voice so full of love Charlie got goosebumps. "Who looked after you?"

"He only hit me once or twice. It was way worse for Blake and Burke." Brad's voice had dropped to a whisper.

"That's not what I asked, baby. Who took care of little Brad?"

"They didn't want me."

Brad's shoulders sagged, and his eyes went down to his fidgety hands.

Blake inhaled as if to say something, but Miles stopped him with a finger. "Who didn't want you, baby?"

"No one. No one wanted me. Matt and Julie, the couple who adopted Benjamin...I'd thought that maybe they'd want me, too, but they didn't. They only wanted Benjamin."

This time Miles couldn't keep Blake quiet. "You never told me you wanted to go with Benjamin."

Brad looked up. "You never asked. You asked Burke if he'd be okay with you as guardian, but you never asked me. No one asked me."

Blake looked stricken. "You didn't want me as guardian?"

"I wanted a family! For once in my life, I wanted someone to see me, love me, care enough about me to spend some fucking time with me. The only one who ever loved me was Benjamin, and that's because he didn't know any better!"

Brad's chest was heaving with ragged breaths, his voice broken. Max licked his hands, and Charlie's heart melted at witnessing the dog's loyal love for Brad.

"I love you, Brad. I know I fucked up, but you have to know I love you." Desperation laced Blake's voice, and Charlie felt for him. Couldn't be easy for this guy to hear all this, knowing he'd messed up.

"Well, you have a funny way of showing it. You take care of everyone else, Blake, you always did. Burke never got away with shit, and it was you who made him into the man he is. You run this amazing program for abuse victims. You open up your own house for people who need shelter, for fuck's sake. God, you take care of Aaron like it's nothing—no offense, Aaron. But when have you ever been there for me? You knew I was self-destructing, was letting everyone and their brother fuck me, but you never gave a damn. Not enough to call me out on it."

Tears streamed down Brad's face, his eyes still red and swollen from previous cries, yet he'd never looked more beautiful to Charlie. For the first time ever, he felt like he was seeing the real Brad. It was painful to watch, and it hurt to see him suffer so deeply, but it was liberating at the same time. They'd broken through Brad's defenses, which meant there was hope.

∾

HE'D DONE some pretty humiliating things in his life. Sucking off complete strangers, letting himself be fucked by guys whose name he didn't even know. Nothing topped being stripped of all his defenses, however, in front of all these men. What the fuck was wrong with him that he'd broken down like this, had admitted way more of the truth than he should have? Any chance he'd had of a relationship with Charlie and Miles was now definitely out the window. God, he was pathetic.

It was true, what he'd said. All of it. The anger at Blake he'd kept hidden for so long had finally risen to the surface. "I failed you", Blake had told him. And what the fuck did that buy him?

"I'm so sorry," Blake said, his voice broken.

What the fuck was he supposed to say to that? Of course, Blake was sorry. He was a good man. Fuck, he'd only been a kid himself at the time, had done the best he could. Didn't make it right, though. Brad's head was fucked-up, probably forever.

"Guys, would you wait for us outside? I need to discuss something with just the three of us," Miles said.

Blake wasn't happy, but Aaron held him close and led him out of the room, following the others. Miles gave some kind of signal to Josh, who whistled for Max, and coaxed him to follow.

Brad held his head high. He knew what was coming. This was it. The end of his short-lived fantasy with these two perfect guys. Indy was the last one out, and he closed the bedroom door behind him, then the front door. All that was left were his own irregular breaths.

"I know what you're gonna say, okay? So save yourself the trouble. It's over. We're done. I get it."

Charlie gasped, but Miles didn't show the reaction Brad

had expected. Instead, he shifted on the bed until he had two feet on the floor, his back turned toward Brad. Miles took an audible breath. "Come here, boy."

His voice was deep, steady, and oh, so damn authoritative. It pushed all these needy buttons inside that no one had ever reached.

Brad's eyes widened slightly, but his mouth set. "No."

"I'm gonna count to three, and if you are not on your feet in front of me at three, there will be severe consequences, you hear me?"

The air sizzled with electricity, as Charlie's mouth dropped open and Brad froze. He couldn't be serious. What was Miles playing at now?

"One."

The muscles in Brad's jaw ticked, his body completely tense.

"Two."

Charlie gasped, pushed against Brad. "Go!"

Brad stubbornly shook his head.

"Three." Miles's hand shot out, grabbing Brad's ankle before he had a chance to pull it away. If Brad really wanted to get away, he could. Miles was still hurt, so one well-placed kick against his ribs would do the job. He let Miles yank him off the bed on his knees to the floor.

"Stand up."

Brad rose slowly. Miles' eyes were completely focused on him, shining with sheer determination. Without words, he unbuckled Brad's belt, unbuttoned his pants and shoved them down. One hard pull by his wrist and Brad was across Miles' lap, his bare ass sticking up.

The slap as he hit Brad's ass echoed through the room. It stung like a motherfucker, and Brad eyes welled up. Again. Another roaring smack hit his cheeks, then another and another. It hurt so badly, yet so good at the same time. Brad went slack on Miles' knees, not struggling even in the slightest.

Behind him, Charlie gasped.

"Tell him," Miles said, his hand coming down hard and steady. Between his legs, Miles' cock swelled until it was rock hard. "Tell him how much you want this. Tell him what you want to call me right now. Say the words. Your secret is out, boy."

How the fuck did Miles know? How had he figured it out? His ass stung like crazy, but Brad refused to surrender. Fuck, no, what would Charlie think? He'd never even look at him again.

His cock hardened faster than he'd ever felt it react since his surgery. A sob worked its way up through his lungs, and he had to let it out. God, his ass had to be crimson by now. It felt so damn good.

Miles' hand halted, and Brad whimpered in protest. "Do you want me to stop, boy?"

Nonononono, he couldn't stop. Not when it was so perfect, and he was so close. To what, he didn't know, but his whole body tingled, and there was the promise of something good, barely out of reach. If Miles would continue just a little longer. Oh, God, please.

"You're a stubborn little shit, boy, but you've met your match in me. I will not give up, and I will not walk away. I see you, Brad. All of you. Tell me what I want to hear. Tell me what you need to say to me."

"Don't stop." Brad hated the plea in his own voice, but he needed more.

"Speak up so Charlie can hear you, too."

"Don't stop. Please don't stop."

"Don't stop, what? What do you call me?"

Another sob tore through him, and he gave up. He was so damn tired, and Miles would simply keep battering at his walls until they crumbled. "Please, don't stop. Daddy."

"That's a good boy."

Miles's hand came down again, softer this time, and it felt like water on dry land. Miles settled into a steady rhythm, slapping both cheeks until they burned to his very core.

"I'm spanking you because you've been disrespectful to Charlie and to me when we were trying to take care of you. When I'm done, you will apologize to us, you hear me?"

Brad's mind shifted, somehow. The crazy cacophony of thoughts inside his head quieted down.

"I asked you a question, Brad. Answer me."

Peace. There was peace in his head.

"Yes, Daddy."

He humped Miles' leg, thrashing and twisting to get away from Miles' hand that kept descending ruthlessly on his ass, yet seeking it at the same time. Miles' hand came down one last time. Brad's ball drew up unexpectedly, and he came violently, a white hot explosion thundering through his entire body.

He'd come. How the fuck was that possible? One minute his ass had been on fire, shockwaves of pain radiating everywhere, and the next he'd come from humping Miles' leg.

"That's a good boy."

Miles' words rang in his ears as his body hung limp over the man's legs. Snot and tears were dripping down his face, probably mixed in with saliva from his mouth, because fuck, it had hurt. Still did. Yet the sweet praise reached deep inside, somehow.

How had he known? Brad had never told anyone, not even Charlie. He'd been deadly afraid to ever reveal this sick desire inside. If Charlie knew, it would be the end of their friendship.

He knew now.

Oh, fuck.

The reality of what had transpired settled in. Miles had spanked his ass bleeding red, and he'd called him daddy. The FBI agent had taken the role Brad had never even dared him ask, because first of all, it was sick as fuck. And secondly, the guy was only two years older than he was. Who would have thought he'd be suited as the authority figure Brad had dreamed of?

"What do you need from me, boy?" Miles asked, still in role.

More. He needed more. If he was going down, he would do it after experiencing everything he'd dreamed of.

He couldn't ask. He'd do, instead.

Brad slid off Miles' legs, not caring that his pants were still somewhere around his ankles. He kept his head low, avoiding Miles' eyes as he reached for his buckle. He unbuckled him with one hand, rubbed his stiff shaft with his other. Miles' hand shot out, blocked him from unbuttoning him.

"What do you need to ask, boy?"

Miles was gonna make him say it, give voice to the deep need inside him that was too embarrassing to think, let alone give words to.

"Please, let me suck you off, Daddy."

Miles' hand released his, moved to his head where it affectionately rubbed his hair. "I'd love that."

A weight he'd never consciously experienced before released from his shoulders, his heart, as his hands made fast work of his Miles' pants. They whipped out that perfect cock that was always ready for him. He bent his head, sucked it in deep. The first release needed to come fast, Miles was on the edge. It only took seconds before his mouth filled with cum. He couldn't even keep up swallowing, let some of it drip along his mouth, his chin, where it joined in with the remnants of saliva and snot. He was a fucking mess.

"Nobody sucks cock like you," Miles said. "Give me another one."

Yes.

He licked him clean, started sucking all over again. His jeans were still on, making it too tight for him to do much else. He pulled back.

"Fuck my mouth, please, Daddy?"

Miles stood up and Brad took position. That delicious cock was pushed all the way inside his mouth. He angled his head back, relaxed his throat. He wanted to make this as good as possible. Pleasing him, that was all that was important.

"You're such a good cock sucker, boy. No, no, don't fight me. Trust me. I know when it's too much. That's it," Miles praised him. "Mmmm, feel my cock fill your mouth, your throat? You're so hot and wet and tight."

His mind went blank again as Miles thoroughly fucked his mouth, holding his head with two strong hands.

"Damn, I love your mouth as much as I love your ass. Is your ass ready for me, boy? Because I'm gonna fuck you hard. No prep for you, huh? I'm gonna burn my way in, make you feel all full inside. And you know what I was thinking? I think you need your mouth full, too, so you're gonna suck our Charlie off while I pound your ass."

Brad didn't know if the words were meant for him or for Miles himself, or maybe even for Charlie, but damn, they were a turn on. Miles was getting close again, and Brad's own cock was stirring again, too. He groaned around the fat cock in his mouth.

"You like that? You're a little boy slut, aren't you?"

His jaw hurt and his eyes were red rimmed from tears, but he'd never felt happier in his life. The cock inside his mouth jerked and he barely managed to pull back a little before the next load of cum was deposited. He was gasping for breath by the time the cock was pulled out of his mouth.

"Hmm, that was nice. Now, on the bed on hands and knees, and open fucking wide."

Brad still didn't look at him, couldn't bear to see his eyes. He was playing along, but what was he thinking? It was too sick, right? Calling him daddy, then sucking him off and getting fucked. It was some twisted sexual deviancy inside him that made him crave this.

He kicked off his shoes, pulled off his pants and socks, followed by his underwear and shirt. His ass stung like a motherfucker. No wonder with that spanking. It had been so fucking perfect.

He yanked open his bedside drawer, threw lube on the bed for Miles. He climbed on the bed, couldn't avoid Charlie who seemed to be waiting for him.

"Kiss me," Charlie demanded.

Brad hesitated. He couldn't be serious, right? Getting sucked off was one thing, but kissing, that was personal. Intimate. Kissing signaled affection. Acceptance, even?

"Hurry the fuck up. I want to taste him."

Charlie meant it. Brad crawled toward him. Charlie reached for him as soon as he was close enough, fused their mouths together. Fuck, he always tasted so good, so sweet. Brad kissed him with all he had, sharing the remnants of Miles' taste with him.

Charlie moaned in his mouth. "Mmmm. Love how he tastes in your mouth. Strong."

What a massive turn on, to have Charlie taste Miles on his tongue. He moaned right back, as his cock grew hard.

"Do you want to suck me off, babe?" Charlie asked him, their faces pressed together. If he wanted to stop, Charlie had just given him the perfect out. He was basically asking Brad to confirm that yes, this was what he wanted. This was his chance to deny it, say it had all been a game, a bit of sexual play. But he couldn't lie anymore.

"Yes. I love sucking you off, and I want to do whatever Daddy asks me to."

He held his breath, waiting for Charlie to reject him. Instead, Charlie smiled affectionately, and then a soft mouth was pressed to his in a short, sweet kiss. "Off you go, then. And I'd better not feel any teeth when he's fucking you."

"Thank you," Brad said, his voice tight. "I'm...Thank you."

"I love you," Charlie said.

He'd said it before, but it felt different this time. Bigger. Deeper. Brad's heart skipped a beat. This was not a friend telling him he loved him. This was a man, a lover, declaring his deepest feelings.

"Even with this?"

"Especially now. You're letting me see the real you for the first time."

"How can you love me, knowing this? You watched me get my ass spanked red by Miles, and I fucking called him daddy."

"Yeah, so?" Charlie looked puzzled. "Did you think I'd be weirded out?"

"Well, yeah. Because it is weird. It's sick. Miles is two years older than I am, and I'm calling him daddy."

His head hurt, trying to wrap his mind around it. Behind him, Miles had moved to the bed as well, sitting down for now.

"Babe, does it feel good when you call him that?" Charlie asked, his voice kind.

Brad nodded.

"Did it feel right when he spanked you?"

"Fuck, yes. It hurt, still does, but in a good way."

"Did you want him to spank you, and call you boy, and dominate the shit out of you like he did?"

He shrunk. "Yes. Even more than he already did."

Charlie wasn't fazed, however. "What more would you like him to do?"

Behind him, Miles came close, spooned him. He'd gotten rid of his clothes, at some point. The sensation of that strong body behind him gave Brad the courage. He took a breath, took the plunge. "I want him to tell me to clean my room, do the dishes, eat my fucking veggies. I want him to discipline me, punish me when I'm being a brat, or mouthing off. I want him to fuck me as hard and as often as he can, because I love being used by him. Fuck, yes, I want you two to double stuff me, split my ass wide open. I wanna do anything for him, suck him, rim him, fucking hold his dick while he pees, anything he tells me. I just wanna be taken care of..." His voice died, his face burning as much as his ass.

This was it, then. The brutal truth.

Charlie's eyes shifted to Miles'. "You on board with this?"

"Completely. He's tired, you know? Exhausted. He's been taking care of people since he was a kid. It's time someone takes care of him. I can give him what he needs in terms of discipline, but he needs your sweet love, too. How do you feel? Think you can handle this?"

Charlie bit his lip. "What about you and me, or me and him? How will this work?"

"This is what he needs from me. With you, it's different. What you guys have is sweet and sexy. Nothing needs to change there. As for you and me..." Miles' voice was uncharacteristically hesitant. "I would love it if there was an 'us' as well."

Charlie's face broke open in another one of those sweet smiles. "Me too. I want there to be an us. You, Brad, and me."

It was strangely comforting, the way they were talking about him in his presence. Brad leaned back against Miles, a tiny act of surrender that earned him a kiss on his nape.

"We'll figure it all out, I promise. My suspicion is, things will change over time. Brad's needs are raw and desperate right now, but I suspect once they're fully met, he'll become less needy. But for now, it's fine."

Miles' hand reached between Brad's legs. "Raise your leg and open up. I wanna be inside you when we discuss the rules."

He pulled his leg up, turned his ass so Miles could access it. His hard cock pushed against him. "Hand me the lube," he told Brad. Miles could have easily grabbed it himself, but the rules had shifted already, Brad realized. He angled for the bottle, handed it to Miles.

"Your ass hurting? It's glowing something fierce," Miles said.

"Yeah. It's burning."

"Good," Miles said, satisfaction dripping from his voice. "Then you'll remember to watch your tone with us."

His slick cock demanded entrance. Brad's muscles, already worn out from the spanking, protested, clamped up. "Let me in, boy."

He wanted to obey, forced himself to relax. He was

breached, then slowly filled, taking his breath away. Miles didn't go easy on him, pushing in without stopping until he was balls deep.

"Let's talk," he said. "You can call me Miles or daddy during the day. I don't care, but when you need me to be strict, you'll call me daddy. I will push your limits, Brad, because you need it. You'll fight it, especially the humiliation, but we both know you crave it, right?"

He moved his hips, lazily fucked Brad's ass with slow, languid strokes.

"Yes."

"We do this in the open. No hiding from the others, no pretending. If I give you an order, I expect you to obey, even when I'm not there. I'll ask Charlie to tell me if you've been disobedient, you understand?"

Miles could talk and fuck at the same time, Brad discovered. Very well, actually. He was thrusting in slow, but deep, each stroke bottoming out.

"Yes."

"I promise I'll take care of you, sweetheart. You've missed out on a lot as a kid, and I'll do my best to give you the structure and attention you need."

His head spun. "I won't always accept it," he said carefully.

Miles grinned. "I know. I'll discipline the shit out of you if need be. Don't you worry, I've got you. You can be as bratty as you want, honey. I won't walk away."

His words lit a light inside Brad that had been extinguished for a long time. Hope. For the first time in forever, he had hope.

"Does he need your permission to be with me, or you know, play with me?" Charlie asked.

"No. I would never come between you two. All I ask is that you tell me, and don't keep it from me."

Brad nodded in relief. He would have hated not having free access to Charlie.

"Let's agree on a safe word, for all of us. Yellow means slow down, red means stop immediately. Brad, you can use it if you feel unsafe, or threatened, or if I do something you truly don't want. Charlie, love, you should use it, too, if we're doing something you're not comfortable with, okay?"

Charlie nodded.

"And Charlie, my love, you and I will need to talk about your sexual preferences as well, okay? Something tells me you're dying to experiment a little, too."

Brad blew out a shaky breath as Miles fucked him so intensely, yet so slow. Every stroke was measured, precise, every thrust deep and full.

Brad clenched his ass muscles, teasing Miles, and was rewarded with a low moan. "You little shit," Miles said affectionately. "Think you can speed me up, huh? Doesn't work that way. You get your mouth on Charlie's cock while I keep fucking you, because I ain't coming till he does. We're gonna pump both your holes full of cum, so get going, boy."

Charlie laughed. "I'm already loving this arrangement."

Brad lowered Charlie's pants enough to take his cock out. The guy was fucking hard, so it wouldn't take long anyway. The joy of being young and horny. He took him in his mouth, making sure he was in a comfortable position.

"Talk to him, honey," Miles said. "Let's remind him what a good little cock sucker he is."

Charlie's hips bucked off the mattress, shoving his dick deep into Brad's throat, and he gagged before relaxing again. Miles' thrusts were unrelenting, his ass burning and throbbing.

"I know. He sucks cock better than anyone else. How's his ass?"

Miles grinned. "Fucking heaven. He doesn't need prep, you just take him and his hole will open up. This ass was made to be fucked, seriously. He's gonna fucking die when we double stuff him."

Brad sucked hard, saliva drooling down his chin, reveling in how different Charlie tasted than Miles. Miles was saltier, stronger, whereas Charlie tasted more delicate, subtle. He bobbed his head, went to town. Both Charlie and Miles had a hand on his head now, and he fucking loved it. Claimed by both his men.

"I'm damn close," Charlie said, his voice throaty.

"Me too. I'm shifting a gear up. Need to pound that ass."

Pounding, he did. The first thrust was so powerful, it rammed Charlie's cock into his mouth even deeper. Both guys let out a simultaneous groan of satisfaction. Brad braced himself, eagerly awaiting being filled on both ends. Miles' fingers dug in, his cock slamming home hard now. Brad's body shook with the intensity.

"Coming..." Charlie warned, a mere second before he fired off a round of hard thrusts into Brad's mouth. As if choreographed, Miles did the same in his ass. Charlie came first, flooding his mouth. Brad swallowed furiously, gave up when Miles came in his ass with a mighty roar. His body went slack, the cum dripping out of him everywhere.

Miles spun him on his back, attacked his mouth with a searing hot kiss. Brad moaned, rutted against him with his hard shaft. Miles swiped his mouth clean, fucking his mouth until Brad about ran out of breath.

"Fucking hell, you taste good," Miles told Charlie. He licked his lips. "I could taste you all over his mouth. Come here."

Their mouths met an inch away from Brad's, but the funny thing was that he wasn't jealous at all. He didn't even want in. No, he was fucking horny again, and getting more aroused by the second as those two started making slurping noises. His hand traveled to his dick, found it slick with precum and trembling with need. He jacked himself off with furious, hard strokes.

"Fuuuuuck," he sighed only twenty, maybe thirty seconds later, his ball emptying violently. The orgasm barreled through him, leaving him weak and panting. Holy fuck, he'd come twice in one day. That in itself was a fucking miracle.

"Was that good, babe?" Charlie asked, smiling.

"Fuck, yeah."

Miles nuzzled his neck from behind. "One last thing I forgot to tell you. From now on, you can't come without my permission, unless you're playing with Charlie. If you do come, I'll have to discipline you, you understand?"

Brad was a fucking mess with cum, snot, and saliva everywhere, not to speak of his ass that was stinging like a motherfucker. Yet he was the happiest and most relaxed he'd been in years. He leaned his head back, kissed his man on the mouth.

"Whatever you say, Daddy."

15

Josh woke up before Connor did, a rare occasion. At first, he wasn't sure what had woken him, but when he shifted slightly he knew. They'd had another session with Master Mark yesterday, and he'd taught Connor how to use a cane. Fuck, Josh's ass had been on fire, the pain beyond what he had experienced so far.

Connor had noticed it, had safe worded them both with a code yellow and had slowed down considerably. Josh had never been more aware of how well Connor could read him. Master Mark had been impressed, too, and had praised them both for how in tune they were.

It had just been too much, too overwhelming. It was a different kind of pain than spanking or paddling, much sharper and deeper. He'd flown high, soaring in subspace, until the pain had become too much. But damn, it had been a good session.

He loved going there with Connor, loved learning more about the Dom/sub lifestyle that brought them both so much pleasure and peace. They were experimenting with all kinds of things and were both learning more about their preferences.

The shibari, for instance, hadn't done much for either of them. Josh was by nature a patient man, but the slow process of tying him up hadn't fulfilled his craving for being used. Master Mark had taken some pictures of Josh after Connor had tied him up according to the instructions, and on an intellectual level Josh thought it beautiful, but emotionally it didn't do shit for him. Luckily, Connor had felt the same.

The cane, however, he definitely wanted to try again, and Master Mark had suggested they'd try a whip as well. Josh couldn't wait. The regular sessions he was now doing with Connor were helping tremendously in keeping his PTSD symptoms manageable.

He shifted again, his ass burning hot against the cool sheets. Connor had put lotion on it, as he always did after a session, but it sure didn't help much this time. Josh suspected he was sporting some serious marks.

Next to him, Connor groaned. "Why are you awake? It's too early, baby, go back to sleep."

"My ass hurts."

Connor turned on a soft lamp and took Josh back in his arms, his hand gently patting Josh's ass. He kissed Josh's head. "Was I too violent?"

Josh put his hand on Connor's chest, as always marveling in his man's sheer strength. "Nah. It's different, deeper, but it will help me focus throughout the day."

Connor's hand brushed his hair. "It will help you remember who you belong to as well," he said.

Josh smiled. "Yes, Connor. You know I'm yours, baby."

Connor's muscles tightened, and he was quiet for a few

seconds, apparently mulling something over. "Do you want him?" Connor asked.

Josh had a quick intake of breath. There was no doubt who the "him" was. He turned on his side so he could meet Connor's inquisitive gaze completely open. "Yes."

Connor swallowed. "You love him."

"Yes."

"Did you always?" It wasn't the most eloquent of questions, but Josh understood.

"I think I did, but I didn't know it. My love for Indy, it's different from what I feel for you, or for Noah. With Noah, it's this secure love, the knowledge that he's there. Aside from the fact that we fucked, he's like a brother to me, my rock and strong protector. With you... Fuck, Connor, my love for you is this big thing that fills me completely. You're a fire that consumes me whole, and I love it. Our love is bold, dominating, big, and demanding. Indy, he's..." Josh's eyes turning soft, dreamy. "He's the breeze that cools me down, that gives me air to breathe."

Connor's eyes widened as the truth hit him. "You don't love him, you're in love with him."

Josh bit his lip, but still met his eyes. "Please, don't be mad, Connor. I didn't do it on purpose."

"Do you still love me?"

He looked so insecure, and it broke Josh's heart. The last thing he wanted was to ever hurt this man. "Fuck, yes, babe. So very much. It's different, and I know I'm doing a sucky job of explaining it, but I love you both."

"Do you still want to be with me?"

Connor was holding his heart out, more vulnerable than Josh had ever seen him. "Yes," Josh whispered. "If you'll still have me."

Connor's blue eyes were full of doubt, much like they

had been when they had first met. "I don't know how to do this, how to love you less so I can let you go."

Panic filled Josh. "I don't want you to let me go."

Connor kissed him. Devoured was a more accurate description. Fuck, how could Connor think Josh would ever want to lose this? He wanted him, wanted them both. Connor's tongue attacked, dueled with Josh's until Josh surrendered, like he always did, letting Connor invade him.

Finally, Connor seemed to have his fill—at least for now. He pulled back, studied Josh once more. "I didn't mean letting you go, baby. I could never do that. I meant letting you go to him. What if you end up loving him more? What if you choose him?"

Tears filled Josh's eyes. "I'm not choosing. I love you both. I'm so sorry, Connor. I never meant for this to happen."

"I know, baby. I know. It's... I'm trying to understand it. I can see it, how much you need him, too. And he's a good man, baby, he is. What you two have is special, but... I'm not jealous so much as scared. I don't know how this would work."

Josh's heart rate slowed down a little. "I don't know, either. But we can figure it out together. You, me, Indy, and Noah."

Connor swallowed. "Noah, he's on board with this?"

Josh nodded. "Yeah. But it's easier for him, since he's shared Indy with me from the start."

"I don't get that, because he's crazy jealous if others so much as look at Indy."

Josh smiled, because it was so true. "I know, but Indy and me doesn't bother him."

"I don't think the sex would bother me," Connor said.

"Would you feel better if you could watch us? I know you like that."

Connor's cheeks flushed. "Don't get embarrassed, babe," Josh said softly. "I love it. Makes me feel less of a freak."

"I think I would like that, yes. How were you and Indy planning on moving forward?"

Josh gently shook his head. "We don't have a plan, baby. We're not doing anything until you're one hundred percent okay with it."

Connor kissed him softly. "I think I am, but baby, will you ask me permission when the time comes?"

"Yes, Connor. Always."

An hour or two later he was in the kitchen, preparing breakfast with Indy. Noah and Connor were already at the huge kitchen table, happily reading their newspaper. Josh loved Sunday mornings when they were all together for an unhurried, extensive breakfast.

Brad walked into the kitchen, his face predicting heavy thunderstorms. Max followed him, sticking close as always. Uh oh. Trouble in paradise, apparently.

Brad's meltdown a few days earlier had confirmed what Connor had reported from a conversation he'd witnessed between Brad and Miles about Charlie: the three of them were involved with each other, though the exact dynamics hadn't been clear. No wonder, as it had to be fucking complicated building something solid between three people. Josh would know, what with his heart belonging to Connor and Indy both.

The whole thing with Brad did seem to have had positive effects, though. Miles had told them he was experimenting with a daddy-dynamic with Brad and had asked them not to interfere. Josh had utter respect for Miles for figuring out that was what Brad needed, though it had to make their threesome even more complicated.

Still, Brad had come back, had basically moved into Miles' room with Charlie. At some point, they'd have to talk about long term arrangements, but for now, Noah and Indy didn't seem to mind to be in the guest room next door to him and Connor. On the contrary, sharing a bathroom had proven to be quite...entertaining. Connor's exhibitionist side was coming to the surface more and more, and Josh fucking loved it. Connor had displayed so many inhibitions, his proud, insecure man, but he was shredding them one by one.

"Good morning," he said to Brad, who quietly took a spot all the way at the end of the table.

"Morning," he replied, but Josh couldn't make out if he was curt or shy. Like him, Brad was an introvert, so Josh never took his gruffness personally. Then Brad shifted and a flash of pain painted his face. Josh bit back a grin, because he knew exactly what was causing Brad's mood. Apparently, someone had needed a reminder of who was in charge.

"Good morning," Miles offered, stepping into the kitchen as well, followed by Charlie.

Friendly greetings flew around the kitchen.

"Brad, what can I get you for breakfast?" Miles asked.

Hmm, interesting dynamic, Josh observed. Brad submitted to Miles, but he didn't take care of him as Josh did of Connor. It was the other way around. Again, this made sense. Brad didn't react to Miles' question, though.

Miles took two steps forward, yanked Brad up by his arm and was in his face. "I asked you a question. Are you gonna answer me or do you want to walk around with a red ass all day? Do not challenge me, boy, because I will spank the shit out of you all over again, and they'll all get to watch. I'll ask one more time: what can I get you for breakfast?"

Brad swallowed once, then his shoulders came down. "Scrambled eggs, please, with toast."

Miles didn't back off, stayed an inch away from him. Apparently, he wasn't satisfied yet.

Brad sighed, the embarrassment on his face clear. "Scrambled eggs, please, Daddy, with toast, please."

Miles nodded. "Sit your ass down and don't talk until breakfast is served." He waited till Brad had sat down again, avoiding everyone's eyes. "What would you like, love?" His tone to Charlie was completely different, full of kindness and love.

What did Charlie think of this dynamic, Josh wondered. He hadn't interfered when Miles had confronted Brad, and he looked relaxed, amused even.

Josh finished the bacon he'd been frying for Connor and Noah, to complement their eggs and sausage. Meanwhile, Indy was cutting fresh strawberries into small pieces, his tongue peeping out from between his lips.

"Here's your grease for the day," Josh said, serving Noah and Connor both a full platter. His man sure loved his bacon, as did Noah, but Josh only made it on the weekends. He wanted to watch out for their cholesterol and all that.

"Thanks, babe." Connor looked like he wanted to smack his ass, but thankfully remembered Josh was still smarting and held back.

Josh took out two tall glasses, while Indy grabbed the granola and the yogurt and handed Miles the eggs to start on their scrambled eggs. Josh made layers of strawberries, homemade granola, and greek yogurt. It looked nice, if he said so himself, and it would taste even better.

"Thanks, baby," Indy said and gave him a quick kiss on his cheek.

They took spots next to each other, their elbows touching.

Indy let out a sweet groan after the first bite. "Damn, this is good. Try this," he said to Noah, leaning over the table to hold out a bite for him on the spoon.

Noah took it, tasted. He shrugged. "I like my bacon better."

"Cavemen, that's what you two are. Regular fucking cavemen. Barbarians," Josh muttered.

Indy's hand found his, a gesture so simple, yet so profound. "It's delicious."

Josh smiled. "Thank you."

They ate in quiet companionship, while Miles served both his men scrambled eggs and toast. The man was pretty handy in the kitchen, Josh had to admit. He wasn't as good a cook as he himself was, but he could fix a decent breakfast or lunch.

Charlie got his plate with a smile, but Miles held it out to Brad, obviously waiting for him to say something. Wow, he was keeping him on a tight leash, huh?

"Thank you, Daddy," Brad said meekly.

"You're welcome. You can talk again."

Josh chewed slowly, studying them. "We should introduce them to Master Mark," he said to Connor.

"Master Mark?" Miles asked.

"He's a Dom who's teaching me and Connor about the Dom/sub relationship," Josh said.

"Really?" Miles said, leaning forward. "How does that work?"

Josh did a quick check in with Connor to see if he was okay with sharing this, and he got the nod. "You have to fill out this huge list of what you like and what your limits are. He has this basement that's basically a sex dungeon where you can play, or do a scene. He either watches and gives suggestions, you can ask him for specific demonstrations, or you can let him participate."

"He fucks you?" Brad asked, the first time he'd said anything after his run in with Miles.

"He merely observes with us," Connor said. "I usually don't like it when others touch Josh."

Josh smiled, noticing the word "usually." Connor had to be talking about Indy. "Do you like being spanked?" he asked Brad. They might as well discuss it in the open, right? After all, the guy was sitting with a sore ass in the kitchen, his daddy across from him.

Brad shrugged. "Kind of."

Josh frowned. "What do you mean? You either love it, or you don't."

Miles gave Josh a reassuring smile. "So far, Brad has only experienced disciplinary spankings. Daily. And he's well on his way to getting a second one today. He hasn't earned a pleasure-spanking yet."

Well, that made sense, considering their dynamic. "You'll love it," Josh assured Brad. "Trust me, if you already kind of like a real spanking, you'll love a pleasure-oriented one." He shot a radiant smile in Connor's direction. "Connor can get me to subspace in no time."

"What's that?" Charlie asked.

Josh smiled. Here he was, dishing out BDSM knowledge like he was an expert. Times certainly had changed. "It's a pain-pleasure modus in your brain where you mentally check out and reach a level where you can take anything. It's total peace, really. I can get there with a mix of steady pain and pleasure, for instance by spanking, or getting paddled, caned, maybe whipped, even fucked. Not everyone can reach it, apparently, but I don't know why."

"Connor whips you?" There was true horror on Charlie's face.

"We've only bought one recently, but we haven't tried it yet. It takes skill, so we have a session with Master Mark next week and he'll teach Connor."

"If you do it wrong, it can leave lasting marks. There's no way I'm hurting Josh, so I wanna get it right," Connor explained.

Charlie looked puzzled. "I don't understand. You are hurting him, aren't you?"

"There's a difference between hurting and pleasure-pain. My goal is to bring Josh pleasure through pain and a little humiliation, not humiliate or hurt him because I can. It's what he needs, and I love taking care of him that way."

"Is that what you and Miles are doing as well?" Charlie asked Brad. Oy, how was Brad gonna answer that one? Josh wondered if Brad had even figured it out himself. This shit wasn't easy, and they were just getting started.

Brad seemed to think about it for a bit, but he didn't look to Miles for help. "No, babe. I've been trying to analyze it, and I don't have the full picture yet, but I want Miles to discipline me. I hate it when he does, but I need it and crave it at the same time."

"Brad missed out on a lot of structure, love, and attention when he was young, and he's catching up now. He equals discipline with love—and it is, in many ways. I love providing this for him and taking care of him this way. But even then, it'll be a while before he stops rebelling," Miles said calmly.

Josh was amazed at Miles' insights in this. He would have never linked Brad's obviously traumatic childhood to his needs as an adult, but now that Miles explained it, it made total sense.

"But I would love to meet with this Master Mark," Brad said softly. "Can we please, Daddy?"

The surrender in his voice touched Josh. It showed how much he needed this, wanted this.

"Yeah, absolutely. I'd love it if you joined us," Miles said to Charlie.

Charlie nodded. "If I can observe at first. With my clothes on."

"Whatever you're comfortable with. You know how much fun it is to watch Brad squirm," Miles teased.

In an incredible childlike gesture, Brad stuck his tongue out at Miles. Fuck, Miles had been spot on. Brad really was still a boy in some aspects.

"Bradford," Miles said, his voice stern. Holy crap, even Josh had the urge to obey him when he spoke like that.

Brad smiled innocently. "Sorry, Daddy."

Miles crooked a finger. "Come here." Brad's smile disappeared. He'd apparently thought he'd get away with it, considering they were in company.

He reluctantly got up from the table and walked over to Miles.

"You earned yourself another spanking, boy. Now, tell me, why am I disciplining you?"

"How the fuck should I know?" Brad shot back.

He really was craving discipline. Fuck, he was like a teen, testing his boundaries. Well, he certainly was about to discover them.

"That's ten extra. You wanna try again?"

Brad sulked, then gave in. "Because I stuck out my tongue at you."

"Ten more. You won't be able to sit by the time I'm done."

For the first time, Josh saw fear on Brad's face. No, it was respect. He'd pushed against the limits, and his daddy had put his foot down. This was a man realizing he was about to pay the price for his stupidity. Josh felt sorry for him, yet envied him at the same time. "I disrespected you by sticking my tongue out, Daddy. I'm sorry."

"Okay, then. I accept your apologies, but you'll still have to face your punishment. How many is that?"

"Forty-five, Daddy."

"Bedroom, now."

Brad obeyed immediately. "Yes, Daddy."

Miles sent Charlie a sweet smile. "Charlie, love, do you want to watch or stay?"

Charlie quickly finished his eggs. "I'll watch. We're in this together."

Miles' smile widened. "Thank you, love. Brad needs you as much as he needs me, you know that."

Josh watched with a warm feeling in his belly as Miles and Charlie made their way to the bedroom, hand in hand.

16

Miles and his boys came back a short while later. Connor noted Brad's face was red and puffy. No wonder, with forty-five slaps. That hurt.

Brad wanted to sit down, but Miles stopped him to put a fluffy pillow on the chair.

"Thank you, Daddy," Brad said meekly.

"You're welcome, sweetheart." Miles kissed him on his head.

Connor had to bite back a grin. Someone had gotten a little lesson in respect. He genuinely liked Brad. The guy was wicked smart, and his care for Charlie was endearing, but Connor had wondered about him lashing out at Miles constantly from the start. It all made much more sense now, and Connor respected Miles for taking the role Brad obviously needed so desperately.

"So, Miles, can we boss Brad around as well, tell him to make food and shit?" he asked, trying to ease the tension a little.

Miles flashed a grin. "Sadly for you, no. He obeys only me, and I take care of him, not the other way around."

"Too bad. I'm dying for a cup of tea." One hard rule was that there was no coffee in his house. Luckily for him, neither Noah, nor Josh or Indy cared for it. He still couldn't stomach even the smell.

"You can make your own fucking tea," Brad snapped.

Connor raised his eyebrows at Miles. "Sorry, dude. I only discipline him for his interactions with me and Charlie, not with anyone else," the FBI agent said.

Connor shrugged. That actually made sense if you thought about it. "Okay, fair enough. Anyone else fancy tea?" Miles' hand shot up, as did Charlie's and Brad's. Connor sent Brad a dark look. "You can make your own fucking tea."

Brad looked shocked, until Connor burst out laughing. "Fuck, you're too easy."

Embarrassed, Brad joined in. Connor rose from his chair, slapped Brad playfully on his shoulder as he walked past him. "Just trying to get a feel for the rules here, bro."

"Fuck off, man. You got your own sub to boss around, what do you need me for?" Brad replied, smiling.

The doorbell rang. Connor frowned, checked his watch. Sunday morning, 11 am. Who the hell would be stopping by now? Blake and Aaron, maybe? "You expecting your brother?" he asked Brad.

"No. They're gone for the day," Charlie answered instead. "He's taking Aaron to the city."

Connor made eye contact with Miles, who nodded. He got up, walked to Connor's bedroom where the gun safe was. Connor had shown it to him shortly after he'd arrived, so Miles could put his gun in there when needed.

"Everyone, stay in the kitchen," Connor said.

Josh and Indy immediately reached for each other, and

Brad grabbed Charlie's hand. Noah shot Connor a look that said he would make sure they were okay.

Connor waited till he heard Miles open the safe, then walked toward the front door, where the door bell was rung for the second time. He looked through the glass.

Dammit. Zack Waitley. Out of uniform, that at least.

He opened the door, immediately blocking it with his foot. "Good morning, Officer. How can I help you?"

"So you know who I am," Waitley said.

"Yeah. You're the asshole who beat Charlie to a pulp."

"I know he's here."

"Yeah, so?" Connor wasn't gonna deny it. He'd figured Zack would find out sooner or later anyway.

"I want to see him."

"Tough shit, as he doesn't want to see you. Was that all?"

He blinked, and the next second Waitley had drawn his gun. Connor froze to the spot, but his mind was crystal clear. "Let me inside," Waitley demanded. "Now!"

"Don't be this stupid," Connor said. From the corner of his eye, he caught a movement. A few more seconds was all he needed. "Put the fucking gun down. You know this won't end well."

Waitley's eyes narrowed, and he stepped closer. "Move aside."

Connor dropped to the ground in one fluid move, startling Waitley.

"FBI, drop your weapon! Now!"

Fuck, Miles sounded authoritative as shit in FBI-mode, Connor thought as he rolled to the side, moving as far away from Waitley as possible.

"Drop your fucking weapon right now! Put your hands where I can see them!" Miles shouted.

Waitley paled and raised his hands, but still held on to

his gun. "This is Officer Waitley, Albany PD. I'm gonna turn around. Show me your badge."

"This is your last warning. I'm a federal agent, and I do not take orders from someone holding a gun. Put your weapon down, or I will shoot!"

Thank fuck Miles had put his vest on. The damn thing had a massive FBI logo on the front and back that would easily help identify him. That asshole Waitley would not be able to shoot him and pretend he didn't know he was dealing with a federal agent. For a few breathtaking seconds, Waitley hesitated, but then he finally lowered the gun to the ground.

"Kick it away and keep your hands up."

With a killing look at Connor, Waitley kicked the gun. Connor exhaled, as he slowly sat up. Holy fucking moly. That had been way too close.

"On your knees on the ground, hands behind your head," Miles ordered.

Waitley defiantly raised his chin. "Show me your badge."

Fuck, Connor wanted to hit him. Badly.

Miles stepped around him, still holding his gun trained on the man. "Special Agent Miles Hampton, FBI, badge number 9529537." He reached for his badge with his other hand, threw it on the ground in front of Waitley. "Connor, get me my phone."

Connor wasn't too happy about leaving him with that crazy fucker, so instead he pushed the door open, shouted inside. "Brad, Miles' phone please!"

Waitley had picked up the badge, was now studying it, his face falling. "You can get this anywhere online," he tried.

"Sure," Miles said, his voice dripping with sarcasm. "And I assume the standard issue FBI gun and the FBI vest come with it? Give it up, asshole."

Brad opened the door and handed Connor a phone.

"Step next to me, dial 911 and hold the phone up to my ear," Miles told Connor.

Connor nodded. Miles was not taking any chances, and he was playing this smart. As he dialed, Brad stood in the door.

"Brad, get inside," Miles told him. "Close the door. Charlie needs you."

The first words clearly got Brad's back up, but that last sentence did him in. His face softened and he nodded, doing as Miles had asked him. Thank fuck.

"Dispatch, this is FBI agent Miles James Hampton, Washington DC Office. My badge number is 9529537. Request for immediate police assistance at 762 Rt 148 to arrest Albany PD Police Officer Zachary Waitley for statutory rape, aggravated assault, domestic violence, attempted kidnapping, and burglary."

Connor didn't even attempt to suppress his smile. Miles was listing charges for no other reason than to piss Waitley thoroughly off. Police blotter would pick this up, and Waitley's reputation—if he had any left—was done.

"Suspect is in possession of a firearm, most likely his service weapon, and is in my custody awaiting arrest."

Connor could hear the dispatcher say something, but couldn't make out what.

"That's negative, dispatch. You can reach me at this number when necessary."

He signaled to Connor to disconnect.

"Connor, I need you to step inside for a minute, see if you can find any handcuffs. I didn't bring mine, but maybe you can look if you have some?"

Connor knew for a fact he didn't have any—not unless you counted the faux fur ones he used on Josh every now and then. He'd turned in his official ones when he turned in his badge. Miles wasn't stupid. He wanted him inside for a reason, which meant Connor would trust him.

"Sure thing. Be right back." He didn't look back, wondering what Miles was up to. It couldn't be good, at least, not for Waitley.

"Is Miles okay?" Brad asked as soon as Connor stepped inside. He was on the couch, holding a trembling Charlie. The tenderness Brad displayed toward that kid was amazing.

"Yeah, he's fine. How you holding up, kid?"

Charlie nodded, cuddled closer to Brad, who kissed him on his head. "I'm okay. Is he gone?"

"No. We're waiting for the cops to come arrest him. He's going to jail, Charlie. There's no way out for him now."

Noah was in the living room as well, but Connor didn't see Indy or Josh. "I sent them to our room to cuddle," Noah said.

Good. Josh didn't need to see this. He'd experienced enough violence to last him a lifetime, and it would only trigger his PTSD. "I'm gonna step back outside," Connor said. He'd given Miles time enough to do whatever he wanted to do, he figured.

"Did you need anything?" Noah asked, curious.

"No. Miles wanted a minute alone with Waitley."

Noah grinned. "Is he gonna be alive when you get back?"

"Probably. Minus a few teeth, maybe."

Charlie sat up suddenly. "He'd hit him?"

"Yeah, kid. He'd beat the shit out of him if he could. That's your man out there, protecting you," Connor said.

"He can kill the fucker for all I care," Brad said.

Connor nodded. His sentiments exactly, though he suspected the FBI agent wouldn't go quite that far. He was a federal agent, after all. Still, when he stepped outside, he wasn't surprised to find Waitley flat on the ground, Miles' foot holding down his neck.

"Can you believe this asshole tried to escape?" Miles said.

"Oh, no," Connor said. "I'm sorry you had to use force to restrain him."

"Yeah, me too."

In the distance, police sirens were closing in. Miles removed his foot, squatted down. "I need you to listen carefully, Waitley, because this is the part you need to remember. There will be charges, and there will be a lawsuit, and Charlie will testify to every little thing you did against him, including statutory rape. If you deny the charges, any of them, I will find you, and I will shove a baseball bat so far up your ass it will end up in your stomach. And I'm not talking about the handle, you feel me?" He got back up, coolly put his foot back on the man's neck. "Glad we had that conversation."

Connor nodded with satisfaction at the pure terror in Waitley's eyes.

Two cops from the local Sheriff's Department arrived, none that Connor knew. That made sense, because these were local cops, not Albany PD. They got out, their faces none too friendly. Connor spotted the body cams on them. Good, that could work in their favor. He was confident Miles would notice, too. The guy usually didn't miss much.

"Special Agent Miles Hampton, Washington Bureau of the FBI. Thank you for coming, officers. I appreciate your assistance."

Being professional went a long way with these guys, and Miles was smart showing them proper respect. They quickly introduced themselves.

"O'Connor. I was with the Albany PD until recently."

He got a respectful nod. It was how they rolled, the boys in blue.

"Get him up and handcuff him for now," the oldest cop gestured toward Waitley. His colleague dragged Waitley up. His face was looking a little worse than it had before, with dried blood on his nose and bruises starting to form on his dirtied face. He swayed as he stood, looking dazed as they handcuffed him and positioned him between them.

"So what happened? I understand he's one of us?"

"Zachary James Waitley, he's with Albany PD," Miles said business-like. "Over a month ago, he beat up his boyfriend, Charlie DiAngelo. Charlie has been staying at this residence to recover. Waitley had contacted him multiple times since, but Charlie refused to see him. Waitley has been trying to find him, going so far as to pull over and threaten Charlie's best friend. We have a dash cam video of that conversation."

The cop nodded. "We'd like to receive that, obviously. What happened this morning?"

"Around eleven, Officer Waitley rang the doorbell," Connor took over. "When I answered, he told me he wanted to see Charlie. I refused and informed him Charlie did not want to see him. At that point he pulled his gun and aimed it at me, demanding entrance into my home."

"This is your home?" the cop asked.

"Yes," Connor said, straightening his shoulders. He was not denying who he was. "I own it with my boyfriend and two friends of ours. We're roommates." Roommates with benefits, but he was pretty sure he should skip that part.

"I heard the commotion at the door," Miles said. "I proceeded to procure my gun and vest, exited from the back door. Connor managed to stall him long enough for me to surprise him from the other side. At first, he refused to put down his gun, but in the end, he surrendered. However, I asked Connor to step inside, see if he could find handcuffs, when Officer Waitley tried to overpower me. We had a short struggle, but I managed to subdue him."

Connor shot Waitley a quick look to see if he would contest it, but he kept silent. He was looking more alert, though.

The cop nodded. "Where's his gun?"

Connor pointed. "We left it where he kicked it away, to preserve finger prints. You'll find it's his service weapon."

The cop who'd been asking the question gestured to his colleague to get it. The guy used gloves to pick it up, put it in a bag. At least that was preserved. Connor felt the cops were pretty neutral at this point, not choosing a clear side.

"Where does the statutory rape charge come in?"

"Waitley has coerced Charlie into having sex with him since Charlie was fifteen," Miles said.

For the first time, Connor noted a clear reaction on the older cop's face, and it came pretty damn close to contempt. He quickly pulled his face back to a more neutral look, though. "Why were you at this residence?" he asked Miles.

"I was injured in a recent FBI operation and am recovering here. Connor's roommate Indy is a friend of mine."

"And Waitley's boyfriend, Charlie..."

"Ex-boyfriend," Miles interrupted him. "You don't think he'd stay with a guy who beat him, do you?"

The cop nodded. "Okay, ex-boyfriend. Is he here? Can he corroborate this?"

Connor was sure Miles had hoped to avoid this step, but Charlie would have to testify anyway. "I'll get him," he said.

The cop asked more questions as Connor walked back

inside. "Charlie, the cops need to speak with you for a second."

He was pale as a sheet, but he nodded. Brad got up, too. "You'll have to sit this one out, Brad. We don't wanna make it more complicated than it already is. Stay inside for now, okay? I'll take care of Charlie, I promise."

Connor felt like a giant compared to the frail body next to him. Charlie trembled slightly, and Connor put a soft hand on his shoulder. "Stay calm, kid, okay? Simply answer the questions."

Charlie nodded, still shaking. He walked up to the cops, Connor beside him, ignoring Waitley.

"You Charlie DiAngelo?" the same cop asked.

"Yes, sir."

"And you were in a relationship with Officer Waitley?"

"Yes, sir. Since I was fifteen."

It was a smart move from Charlie, immediately positioning himself as so much younger. With his small body and his young age, the cops would immediately spot the age difference. It suggested a certain mind set, one that would help Charlie. His polite deference to the cop didn't hurt either. Kid had smarts.

"Can you tell us what happened, Charlie?" The cop's tone was softer, kinder.

"Zack... He beat me up violently, sir, six weeks ago. Busted my eye, bruised a few ribs."

Waitley opened his mouth to say something, but Miles shot him a look that was so deadly, he must have thought better of it. The man had not been joking about that baseball bat. And Connor would fucking hold his beer while he did it.

"I'm so sorry to hear that, Charlie." The cop studied Charlie, seemed to gauge how seriously to take him.

"We have pictures, sir. Of what he did to me. I was afraid to go to the hospital, because he's a cop, and he'd threatened me before. But I was examined by a medical professional, and he took pictures, sir."

"Okay, we have enough to take him in. We'll sort out the exact charges later. Charlie, are you prepared to come down to the station later to give your statement?"

Charlie raised his head, straightened his back almost imperceptibly. "Yes, sir. He should be held accountable for what he did to me, sir."

The cop's eyes softened. "Call us in a bit to set up an appointment, okay?" He turned toward the other cop. "Take him in. Read him his rights, according to the letter. We don't want any room on this one."

He waited till his coworker was out of earshot, turned his body cam off. "It's a fucking sad day when we have to arrest one of our own for something like this. Fucking disgrace to the uniform."

"I couldn't agree more," Connor said. "Thank you for your assistance. I know this is hard."

The cop nodded. He placed a gentle hand on Charlie's shoulder. "I'm sorry, kid. Real sorry. You're doing the right thing, pressing charges. Stick to 'em, okay? Don't let anybody pressure you into dropping 'em." He sighed. "My oldest son is gay. Fucking got beat up at school for that. Middle school. They're brutal at that age."

"What middle school does he go to?" Charlie asked.

"Trenton Park. Why?"

"Tell him to talk to Mr. Kent, the math teacher. He'll help him find his way."

"I think that's who he has for math. Name sounds familiar."

Charlie smiled. "Tell your son to find him, he'll have his back."

"Thank you, Charlie. I appreciate that."

He gave Connor a strong hand shake, then turned to Miles. "Tried to escape, huh?"

Miles kept his face carefully blank. "Yes, Officer. Can you believe that?"

The cop laughed. "Oh, I totally can. I'll make sure to mention it in my report. We need the two of you to come by the station as well for your statements. Maybe you could bring in young Charlie here, give him the mental support he needs."

Connor dropped a soft hand on Charlie's shoulder, knowing that's what Miles wanted to do, but couldn't. "Don't worry, we've got his back."

17

W hen Charlie woke up, the room was brightly lit by the sun forcing itself through the curtains. He stretched, yawned. He'd slept surprisingly well the last week since Zack's crazy ass stunt.

Charlie still couldn't believe what had gotten into Zack that he'd been so incredibly stupid as to show up with a gun —his service weapon, more specifically—and threaten not just a former cop, but an FBI agent as well. Charlie had gone down to the station to make a statement, accompanied by Connor and Miles. It had been Connor who had held his hand—literally—as he cried his way through his detailed statement, since Miles had to stay in role to prevent from muddying the waters.

Charlie had told them everything, every little detail he could remember about what Zack had done to him, He'd shown them emails, texts, and direct messages from when he'd still been a minor, clearly showing Zack had been fucking him. He'd given them the pictures Noah had taken, presenting every bruise Zack had caused. And Connor had submitted a video Charlie had known nothing about. Apparently, Brad had been pulled over by Zack and had recorded how the cop had threatened him, too.

The cops he'd been talking to had been sympathetic, more than he had expected. He knew this was probably due to Miles' and Connor's presence. He'd heard enough stories to know that not every gay teen or man reporting a crime was taken this seriously. Still, he was grateful.

He formally pressed charges, assured them he would not change his mind and would testify against Zack when it came to trial—unless Zack took a plea bargain, which according to Connor was a realistic option. Cops didn't usually do well in the prison system, so Zack would most likely do anything to lessen his time, Connor had explained. Since there was a good chance Zack would be released on bail, Charlie had filed a restraining order.

He'd been completely exhausted when he'd gotten home, where Brad had been anxiously waiting for him. One look at Charlie's face, and Brad had taken him into their bedroom, had undressed him, and had held him so tenderly it had made Charlie's heart soar. Miles had quickly joined them, cuddling him from the other side, until Charlie had fallen asleep. He'd woken up twice in between to Brad sucking off Miles, but had slept through the night.

Ever since, his nightmares had been gone. It was as if the act of reporting them had freed his mind, or something, He wasn't sure, but he was damn grateful. It had been seven weeks since Zack had assaulted him, and for the first time, Charlie felt like himself again.

He'd even ventured outside again, though not alone. Restraining order or not, he still feared running into Zack. But at least he wasn't the sad hermit anymore he'd become the last few weeks. Though admittedly, being holed up with

Miles and Brad hadn't exactly been a hardship. He smiled as he thought of his men.

They were slowly finding their groove, the three of them. Brad pleasured them every chance he got—and thoroughly loved it. His erectile issues seemed to get better, as he usually got hard during their sexual activities. He still wouldn't allow Miles to touch his cock, but Charlie got him off easily—if Miles allowed it.

So far, he and Miles hadn't done anything else but kissing without Brad being present. They'd had ample opportunity for more, since Brad was gone on weekdays, but for some reason it hadn't happened. Charlie wasn't sure what held them back. Maybe it would take time to figure out who they were without Brad. He liked Miles and was definitely attracted to him, but he wasn't sure if it really was mutual. Miles seemed to be focused more on Brad, though he did clearly love hanging out with Charlie.

Charlie sighed. It was complicated, this threesome-shit, but exhilarating at the same time.

Miles and Brad were up already, of course. Both were early risers, though Miles more out of habit than by nature, Charlie suspected. He was a night owl himself—no wonder with his shows at Flirt.

The door opened softly, Brad sticking his head around the corner. A smile lit up his face. "Oh, good, you're awake."

He came into the room, jumped on the bed to hug Charlie. Charlie smiled as he was thoroughly kissed. "Are you happy to see me, babe?" he teased Brad.

Brad's smile faded a little. "I'm antsy," he said.

Charlie brushed a curl off his forehead. "What's wrong?"

"I don't know." Brad hid his face against Charlie's neck, which told Charlie he damn well knew what the issue was but was afraid to put it into words.

"Do I need to get Miles so he can spank it out of you?"

Fuck, Charlie loved it when Miles spanked Brad. The man seemed to have a finely tuned sensor when it came to Brad. He knew exactly where to draw the line and what Brad needed. It was amazing, considering how short they'd known each other.

"No," Brad protested. "Please, don't say anything."

Charlie held him, caressed his curls. "Tell me what's bothering you."

Brad let out a shuddering sigh. "Miles has been cleared for desk duty."

Well, that was to be expected. The guy hadn't fully recovered yet, but surely he'd be able to do paper work behind a desk. "Yeah, so?"

Brad moved his head, looked up at him with big eyes. "Charlie, that means he's going back to Washington."

Oh, damn. Charlie's face fell. He hadn't let the implications sink in. Miles didn't live here, technically. He was only staying with Indy and the others to recover. Now that he was back on duty, he'd have to return to DC. "Oh," he said. Then again, "Oh."

Brad hid his face against Charlie's neck again.

"Well," Charlie said. "I'm sure he's thought of something already."

"Yeah, like how fast he can get on a plane."

"Brad!"

Brad leaned back again, his face scowling. "Seriously, did you really think this was gonna last? He's gonna walk out on us, Charlie. They always do." A heavy shudder rippled through his body, and he buried his face again. "Nobody ever stays with me."

Charlie's heart broke, right then and there. The pain

behind Brad's words was so overwhelming, that he felt it physically.

"I'll stay with you." He said it quietly, but with determination.

"Oh, Charlie, you too will grow tired of me. Especially after Miles is gone."

The fact that Brad said it with such casual certainty hit Charlie more than anything else. Despite everything they had experienced together and with Miles, Brad was still convinced it would not last.

"No, I won't. I know you don't believe me, sweetie, but I won't. I love you, and it's the real thing. It always has been."

"I'm so tired..." Brad said, shuddering again. "Without Miles, I don't know how to go on."

He tensed, probably realizing how his words had to sound after Charlie's declaration. He disentangled himself, cupped Charlie's cheek. "I didn't mean it like that... I'm not saying you're not enough... It's just that... Oh, damn, I'm fucking this up. I'm sorry, Charlie."

He looked crestfallen. Charlie kissed the hand on his cheek. "It's okay, baby. I understand. You need Miles. He provides something you crave right now, maybe always."

He wasn't lying. He truly did understand. Bit by bit, Miles was breaking through Brad's defenses. Brad was fighting him every step of the way, but every time he surrendered to Miles, he revealed a little more of himself. The fact that he'd even opened up to Charlie right now, that was all because of Miles.

"I need you, too. I need both of you. God, I'm such a selfish piece of shit."

Charlie shook his head vehemently. "No, you're not. You're about the least selfish person I know. Damn it, babe, you're always trying to take care of everyone else. You're entitled to needing us. And we need you, too."

Brad sighed, fidgeted with his hands. "I hear you," he finally said. "I hear your words, but I find it hard to believe."

"I know. Wanna do something to cheer you up?"

Brad's eyes rose to meet Charlie's, lit up. 'Yes, please."

Unceremoniously, Charlie shoved his pajama pants down, revealing his morning wood. "Suck me off. I need to pee, but you can get rid of my woody first."

The eagerness on Brad's face was endearing. Charlie had never met anyone who got such deep contentment and satisfaction from pleasuring others. In less than two seconds, he had deep throated Charlie's cock.

Charlie shivered with pleasure, goosebumps forming on his arms. "Damn, babe, nobody sucks cock like you."

Brad moved his head back a little, used his tongue to follow the veins that wrapped around Charlie's cock all the way to the crown. He gently scraped the head with his teeth, a sensation that never failed to make Charlie moan. Fuck, Brad had his number down pat, didn't he?

With a slurping sound, his cock was sucked back into that mouth, that slick, hot throat. He let out another deep groan.

"Good morning, love," Miles said, stepping into the room. "I see you found good use for that mouth."

Charlie opened his eyes, let his head fall sideways and smiled. Miles kneeled on the bed, took Charlie's mouth in a kiss that was far too gentle and tame for Charlie's taste. He dragged Miles' head closer, pushed his tongue in the man's sweet mouth, and kissed him for real. Mmm, Miles tasted so good. He'd had strawberries in his granola for breakfast, the subtle taste still lingering in his mouth.

Charlie's nuts tightened, and he moaned hard into Miles' mouth as he came, flooding Brad's mouth with cum.

"Damn, that was sexy," Miles sighed, kissing him one last time for good measure. Brad released Charlie's cock, licked clean as always. "Thanks, honey," Charlie said, his heart softening as Brad beamed. "Wanna cuddle?"

Brad nodded, molded himself against Charlie's body. Charlie petted his head, stroking his soft curls. Miles found his eyes, raised an eyebrow. Of course, the man would sense something was off with Brad.

"I'm needy today," Brad said softly. "Daddy."

Charlie's face broke open in a wide smile. It was the first time ever that Brad had signaled his needs like this. What a huge leap of faith he'd taken.

Miles smiled, too, as he climbed over them both to spoon Brad from the other side. "Thank you for telling me, Brad. You're such a good boy for letting me know you need us. Can you tell me what you need from us? Do you want me to be strict today, to discipline you?"

Charlie almost held his breath waiting and hoping Brad would take the next step as well.

"I had a shitty week at school with all kinds of department meetings, which I detest, and my head is going crazy... Can you, like, make my decisions today, Daddy? I'm exhausted from thinking, and I need my mind to stop driving me crazy..."

"Absolutely, sweetheart. We'll take care of you, okay? You won't have to do anything or worry about anything. We've got you."

The relief on Brad's face was so pure, it hit Charlie deep in his heart. Once again, Miles had understood exactly what Brad had been trying to say.

"Have you had breakfast yet?" Miles asked.

Brad shook his head.

"Okay, let's start with some cereal for you then, and after breakfast, we'll hang out with the three of us. How's that sound?"

"Perfect, Daddy."

Five minutes later, Miles had installed Brad at the kitchen table with a bowl of his favorite cereal. Miles had set up his iPad for Brad with head phones, having Brad choose his favorite cartoons to watch.

"When you're done, can you please rinse your bowl and put it in the dishwasher? Charlie and I will be in our room, okay? Come find us, sweetheart."

Brad nodded happily before digging into his breakfast, smiling as he watched his cartoons. It was like watching an eight-year old in a grown man's body, and Charlie would be lying if it wasn't a bit eerie.

"Charlie, love, can you handle this? I can see you're trying to process," Miles said as soon as they were in the bedroom.

Charlie bit his lip. "Is this normal?"

Miles smiled. "Depends on your definition of normal. He's regressing today, which shows how much he has missed as a boy. The fact that he allows himself to go this deep shows me he's feeling safe, which is wonderful, and something we should be grateful for."

"I understand, and I love that you can offer this to him, but what do I need to do? I mean, it even feels weird that he sucked me off not fifteen minutes ago, you know?"

Miles nodded. "I can see why. We'll have to experiment to find out what works for him, that's all I can say. Maybe not engage in sexual activities if he's this deep under, unless he initiates it himself?"

Charlie's eyes dropped to Miles' groin, which showed

him fully aroused. "What about you?" he asked, somewhat shy. He and Miles had never talked about it much. Miles would jerk off regularly when Brad wasn't home, and that didn't bother Charlie at all, but he'd never offered to help Miles, and Miles had never asked.

Miles stuffed his hands into his pockets. "I'll jack off."

"I can help." The words were out of his mouth before he realized it.

"You don't have to, Charlie. With Brad it's different because he loves serving me, both of us. I don't want you to feel obligated to help me if you don't want to. My right hand works perfectly fine again."

He bit his lip again. "Do you want me?" he finally asked.

Miles' eyes shot wide open. "Yes! Of course, I do."

"It's hard to tell with you, because everything turns you on, no offense. And you haven't made a single move toward me, not even when Brad was at work."

Miles took his hands out of his pockets, stepped close to Charlie, pulled him in an embrace. Charlie hid his face against his chest. God, he loved that Miles was so much bigger and stronger than him. Such a turn on.

"I didn't want to pressure you, especially not after what happened to you. We haven't really talked about us, you know, about where you and I stand."

"I know, but I do want to fuck you. If you want me to, that is."

"Fuck, yes. Please. I haven't been fucked in ages. I'm dying for a good pounding."

Charlie grinned. "That can be arranged."

Miles leaned back, made eye contact. "Next time. Our first time should be with Brad present."

Charlie nodded. Then his smile faltered, and he swallowed. "But Miles, I'm not sure if I'll want to bottom again any time soon. It's...there's a lot of negative connotations with that for me right now."

"I understand, sweetie, and it's fine. We'll do whatever you're comfortable with, no pressure. As strange as it may sound coming from me, it's not about the sex for me, you know that, right?"

Charlie sighed with relief. "Yeah, I know, but... Just wanted to make sure. How about you jerk off while I watch for now? I love watching you when you come."

～

MILES HAD NEVER SEEN Brad so carefree and happy. After breakfast, he'd made him take a bubble bath, which had ended with him gently toweling Brad off and picking out clothes for him. Brad had truly and fully surrendered, letting Miles make every decision for him—and the joy on his face told Miles how much he had needed this.

He'd taken Brad and Charlie to a matinee of a new action flick, which turned out to be highly entertaining. Brad had eaten his way through a big tub of popcorn, aided by Charlie. Miles didn't care much for the stuff, but he'd loved watching the two boys enjoy themselves.

Obviously, lunch was a no-no after that much popcorn, so he'd sent Brad to their room for a nap. He'd tucked him in, kissing him on the forehead. Brad was halfway asleep already, but his heartfelt "Thank you, Daddy" had been the best reward Miles could have.

While Brad was asleep and Charlie was giving Aaron makeup lessons in the room he'd shared with Brad before, Miles figured it was a good opportunity to sit down with Connor and Noah.

"Guys, do you have a few minutes for me?" he asked.

They were both in the kitchen, Noah reading the newspaper and Connor doing something on his laptop. Indy and Josh were grocery shopping together.

"Sure," Noah said, putting his paper down.

Miles grabbed a seltzer from the fridge and sat down across from them. "Look, I wanted to thank you for your hospitality. I know it's been a lot more and a lot longer than you guys must have counted on when you offered. You invited me, and you got Charlie and Brad as well, and you have all been nothing but kind, so thank you."

Noah and Connor shared a look that had Miles squirm a little. Had he missed signals they'd been overstaying their welcome? Fuck, he hoped not. "Please, tell me we haven't abused your generosity. I've pitched in for the groceries and stuff, but I'm sure it was nowhere near what we cost you."

"No, it's all good," Noah reassured him. "We love having you stay with us."

Miles slowly exhaled, relief flooding through him.

"We heard you got cleared for desk duty," Connor said.

Miles sighed. "Yeah. I'm supposed to report in DC on Monday."

"You're not going," Noah said.

"No." He hadn't even fully realized it until he spoke the words out loud. "No, I'm not. Well, I'll probably be going on Monday, but it will be to hand in my resignation. I don't want to leave Brad and Charlie, and I can't ask them to come with me. DC is no place for them."

Connor nodded thoughtfully. "I had the impression you weren't too happy in your job even before you met them."

"No. It was meeting Indy that made me realize how lonely I was."

Noah smiled. "He has that effect on people."

"What's next for you, then?" Connor wanted to know.

"Brad is happy in his job, so we'll be staying here. Stability is key for him, I think."

Noah frowned. "He's having an off day, correct?"

"He took the initiative in telling me, so that's big progress. But yeah, he's regressing today, having a full-blown daddy-day. It's okay. I love taking care of him."

Connor shot him a look of pride. "You're phenomenal with him. Seriously man, you have like a sixth sense for him."

"Much like you have for Josh," Noah remarked.

Connor's face lit up. "You think?"

"Dude, the way you can read him when you're domming him, or during sex, that's uncanny. You know his limits and needs better than he does."

Miles could only guess how much this praise meant to Connor. He knew Noah and Josh had been involved before Noah had met Indy, so this was high praise indeed.

Both men smiled as they turned their attention back to Miles.

"Plus, Charlie has indicated he wants to start his show again at Flirt, and he has a job interview with a spa to start training as a beauty consultant. I think it would be perfect for him. So yeah, we're staying," Miles said.

"And what about you? Any ideas what you want to do?" Noah asked.

He took a deep breath. "Yes. I want to start a practice, counseling adolescents specifically."

Noah's eyebrows shot up. "You're qualified for that? I mean, you're an FBI agent."

Miles smiled. "I have a bachelor's and a master's in psychology, with a specialization in adolescent development. The FBI hired me for profiling initially, then trained me as field agent with the specific goal to use me to get to targets. You know, gain their confidence."

Noah's eyes narrowed. "They put you on Indy's case to get him to talk," he concluded.

"Yes. It didn't work. First of all, Indy was way too smart to trust anyone, including me. But also, because I liked him way too much to play this game. The whole thing went to hell before I had a chance to report this back to my boss, but my decision had been made."

"I thought you'd have a background in law or criminology or something," Noah said.

"Many agents do, but the FBI likes their agents to have different backgrounds. To answer your question, yes, technically I'm qualified, but I need to look into what I need to do to start a practice here in New York. I want to start small and build up experience."

Noah and Connor had another one of those meaningful looks. He could ask, but they'd tell him when they were ready, he figured.

"I'm working on my degree in psychology," Noah said.

"Indy told me. Pretty impressive career switch, from army medic to physician assistant and now this. How's it going?"

"I love the courses, but I'm trying to find a part time job to make some money. We started out with me and Connor working full time, but he quit the Albany PD, and I went back to school. Financially, something needs to change."

Miles nodded. That made sense. "What direction are you looking into?" he asked Connor.

"I don't know," Connor answered, frustration lacing his voice. "I'd prefer something with regular hours, because it's easier for Josh, but I haven't seen anything that appeals to me. I've looked into becoming a prison guard, since the penitentiary was hiring, but I dunno. Didn't seem like a good fit, even though they'd love to have former law enforcement."

Miles leaned forward. "And that casual job offer from the Sheriff's Department here?"

He'd overheard the sheriff talk to Connor when they'd come in with Charlie, about looking for a replacement for an officer who was retiring.

"No," Connor said with a finality that left no room for discussion. "I cannot go back to direct law enforcement again."

Noah frowned. "Why not, actually? I never thought to ask."

Something flashed over Connor's face, and in that second, Miles knew without a shadow of a doubt what the cop had done. He *was* behind the shooting on the Fitzpatricks, and he had too much honor to wear a badge again after being on that side of the law. And Noah didn't know. How the hell Josh and Connor had kept this from him, Miles had no idea, but Noah had no clue.

Then Connor's eyes met Miles' and Miles nodded, signaling he understood—and was okay with it. Relief filled the cop's eyes.

"I think after going undercover in an organization like the Fitzpatricks is a lot to deal with," Miles said. "I can imagine after an experience like that, you're ready for something else."

"Yeah, exactly," Connor said, obviously grateful for Miles' explanation.

"Brad said his school district was looking for a Head of Security, a new position for the entire school district. They want to get more serious about preventing crime in the schools, but also about doing shooter drills, preventing students from escalating into violence unnoticed, things like that. I think he mentioned it to me because he hoped I'd be interested."

Connor's eyes lit up. "That sounds interesting, actually. And you're sure you don't want to apply?"

Miles shook his head. "No. I wanna start using my degree. The part about working with school kids appeals to me, but everything else, not so much. I think it would fit you to a T."

"Thank you. I'll definitely look into it."

"So what about Josh and Indy?" Miles inquired. "What are their plans for the future?"

"I've recommended Josh for a part time position as a shooting instructor with the Albany PD," Connor said. "It's only a few hours a week, but that's enough for him. He likes to stay home and take care of the house. It's what's best for him, and it works for us 'cause all three of us hate household stuff, including Indy. He loves to cook with Josh, but that's it."

"And Indy? What are his aspirations now that he's free to do what he wants?"

Noah leaned back in his chair. "He's teaching some jiujitsu lessons at Blake's studio, but that's just a few hours a week. It's been a hell of an adjustment for him, going from his old life to being on the run for a long time, and now finally free. He's still finding his way, and we don't want to push him."

Miles loved how Noah spoke about we, meaning him and Connor. The way they were taking care of the two men they loved was truly special.

Connor leaned forward, put his arms on the table. "Miles, forgive us for asking a rude question, but would you happen to have any savings stashed away?"

He raised his eyebrows. "Erm, yeah, as a matter of fact, I do. I have an apartment in DC that's worth a bit, plus the money I inherited from my parents when they died, and I rarely have the opportunity to spend money, so my bank account is looking healthy. It's why I can afford to walk away from my job. But why are you asking?"

Connor smiled. "We have a proposition for you that we think you're gonna like."

18

B rad woke up from his nap feeling refreshed. He stretched, yawning. Fuck, he'd needed the extra hours of sleep. He was getting used to sharing a bed with the three of them, but he still woke up regularly. A quick check at the time informed him he'd slept for three hours. Wow. Quite the nap. Miles had been right to send him to bed.

Miles. Daddy. He tasted both names on his tongue. This morning, he'd needed him to be his daddy. Miles had taken such good care of him, exactly like he'd promised. Brad had felt differently the whole time. Happy. Carefree. Protected and safe. His head felt so much clearer now, lighter.

It was like a switch had been flipped in his mind, and now he was back to his normal setting where he could see Miles as his lover. It was interesting how that worked. Sometimes the boundaries were fluid, but today they'd been crystal clear. Miles had become daddy, and now he was Miles again. Huh. How about that?

He got dressed, made his way to the kitchen where Miles

was talking with Noah and Connor, while Josh and Indy were putting groceries away.

"Hey, sweetheart, did you sleep well?" Miles asked him.

He walked straight up to Miles, kissed him deeply. "Thank you," he said.

Miles looked stunned for a second, then smiled. "You're back."

"I am."

"You sure?"

"Yeah. My head's peaceful now."

"I'm so glad to hear that, baby. Excuse us," Miles told Noah and Connor. He got up, gave Brad a hard kiss. "I need you."

Fuck, he loved hearing those words. They made him all warm and tingly inside. His right hand dropped to Miles' crotch, where it encountered a rock hard cock. He put pressure on it. "I'm here."

He loved that Miles always asked, never assumed, even though he knew how much Brad loved this. It was always Brad's choice.

Miles yanked his head toward him and assaulted his mouth. He pushed until he'd backed Brad up against a wall, then started kissing the shit out of him while rutting against him.

"You guys maybe wanna get a room?" Connor asked, his voice a tad rough.

Brad tore his mouth away from Miles, panting. "Like you mind watching others have sex," he shot back at Connor.

Josh and Indy giggled. "He's got your number, baby," Josh said.

Brad wanted to say something, but apparently Miles was done waiting. "Bedroom. Now."

He grabbed Brad by his neck and half-dragged him into

the bedroom. "Charlie, get your ass in here!" he yelled over his shoulder.

A giggle sounded from the other room, and muted voices sounded. Who did Charlie have in there?

Brad lost his train of thought as he was pushed down on his knees as soon as they were in the bedroom. "Get that damn mouth around my cock and hurry the fuck up."

Miles unzipped with one hand and unceremoniously shoved his dick in Brad's face. The man had to be on edge to be this bossy, but fuck if Brad didn't love it.

He didn't tease him, knowing now wasn't the time, but deep throated him without delay. It took half a minute, max, before Miles released with a low moan, just as Charlie walked in.

"Someone was horny, I take it?" he chuckled.

Brad licked his lips. Fuck, he loved Miles' taste in his mouth. He grabbed Charlie's hand, pulled him to his knees right next to him and kissed him. Within seconds, Charlie pushed him flat on the ground and laid on top of Brad so they had a better angle. Charlie's tongue invaded his mouth, exploring every corner. God, he tasted so sweet. It was sloppy and sexy and so fucking hot.

"You taste like cum," Charlie giggled, before attacking him again, grinding his cock against Brad.

"Hey, you two, mind if we take this to the bed?" Miles complained.

Brad watched him over Charlie's shoulder, Miles' eyes cloudy with want. His cock was hard again. Or still hard, Brad wasn't sure and didn't care, either. He wanted it, preferably deep inside him. Or Charlie's. Or both. They hadn't fucked at all yesterday, and his hole was twitching to get stuffed.

He moaned into Charlie's mouth, impatient to get the

show on the road. Charlie tore his mouth away, his eyes twinkling. "Desperate for more?"

"Always."

Charlie smiled, one of those sweet smiles that made Brad's insides melt. "We've got you, baby. We'll use you as long and as much as you want."

He scrambled to his feet, then surprised Miles by stepping in for a kiss. He rose to his toes, but Miles still had to bend a little to reach him, until he simply lifted Charlie up. He held him with two possessive hands on his ass and kissed him deeply.

Brad watched them kiss as he undressed. Fuck, he loved seeing them so engrossed in each other, even if he was a little impatient. Not jealous, not feeling left out—just fucking impatient because he wanted them so much. Needed them.

He figured he could maybe entice them to speed things up and remove the last of his clothes, kneeling on the edge of the bed on all fours, his head low and his ass sticking in the air. That way, they would be in the perfect position to fuck him hard.

"Oh, fuck, honey, look at our boy all ready for us," Miles said, his voice throaty. "God, he's so perfectly wanton."

Charlie moaned. "I want to watch you fuck him."

Rustled noises filled the room as Miles and Charlie got undressed. Brad didn't watch, content to wait until they were ready for him.

The snap of the cap alerted him someone was getting lube. He couldn't suppress a shudder. Who would it be? Miles had at least another round in him, probably two, but Charlie had been pretty damn hard as well. He couldn't wait for what they had promised him. Both, at the same time.

Cold, slick fingers breached his hole without any

preamble, stretching him without much finesse. Miles. He recognized his long fingers. Brad shivered again, reveling in the fact that he could take it.

"Someday, I wanna take it slow with you, my love," Miles throaty voice sounded. "You deserve to be worshiped, and I want to kiss every inch of your skin, suck on every sweet spot of your perfect body. Right now, I need you something fierce, Brad. I need to be inside you."

"Take me, Miles. Please, fill me."

Miles' fingers disappeared, and Brad relaxed so Miles could enter him. He lined his cock up and surged in with one, deep thrust. It burned, all the way from his first ring to his very insides. He clenched his teeth, fighting back his body's urge to clamp shut. Miles didn't wait, but pulled halfway out before surging back in. So damn perfect, that fat cock stretching him. Fuck, he loved this. He loved him.

He loved him.

Brad's heart skipped a beat as realization hit. He'd fallen in love with Miles. When had that happened?

And he loved Charlie, too. He always had. He just hadn't allowed himself to feel it, to harbor even the faintest hope. He loved them both. What a hot mess this was.

Charlie lowered himself on the bed next to him, and Brad automatically turned his head toward him for a kiss.

"You are so beautiful when he's fucking you," Charlie sighed, brushing a curl off his forehead.

Brad bowed his head, nuzzled Charlie's neck. God, Miles was fucking him so deep, filling every cell of him, driving away that emptiness, that need. "You're beautiful, period."

He felt Charlie's gasp more than he heard it, looked up. "You think I'm beautiful?" Charlie asked, his eyes wide.

"I'm sorry for never telling you before..." He closed his eyes for a second as Miles shifted gears and hit his prostate full on. So. Damn. Perfect. "You're so beautiful that at times you take my breath away. There's moments when I look at you and can't believe that you're with me."

Miles slowed down, unexpectedly. Brad would've asked why, but Charlie was more important now. Charlie who had been his friend even when he'd been an ass and had kept him at bay. Charlie who loved him despite being a total fuck up and the biggest slut on the planet. Charlie, whom he loved, too.

"I love you," Brad said quietly. "I've loved you since the day I met you, but I was too scared to allow myself to feel it, let alone say it. God, I love you so much."

Charlie's eyes welled up. "It took you look enough," he said, before dragging his head in for a searing kiss. "I love you, Bradford Kent. You're mine, now. Forever."

Forever.

Brad's heart soared with hope. "I'm yours," he echoed. He didn't dare to add that wonderful, sadly-scary word to it, but he hoped. And maybe, for the first time, he believed it a little bit as well.

"Do you guys need a minute?" Miles asked.

Brad's eyes locked with Charlie's. This wasn't just the two of them. Miles was part of them, inextricably linked to both of them. Without him, it wouldn't work. Brad needed Miles as much as he needed Charlie. He saw this truth reflected in Charlie's eyes, as they both smiled.

"No," Charlie said. "On the contrary."

He gave Brad one last kiss, before sitting up. "I wanna watch you fuck him and come," he told Miles. Brad looked at them as they shared a quick kiss. "And when you've flooded his ass, I'm gonna add my load. Our Brad deserves a treat today since he's been such a good boy."

Miles grinned. "Damn, I like the sound of that."

So did Brad. He bowed his head again as Miles thrust back in with a content moan. Brad spread his hips wider, giving him full access. Miles fingers dug hard into his hips, probably resulting in bruises. Tears formed in Brad's eyes, but they had nothing to do with his ass being pounded, or the rough hands on his body. How had he gotten so lucky to find these two men? And more importantly, how the hell did he make sure to not fuck this up?

"Ohhhh!" Miles grunted as he came. He gave a few last strokes, his cock softening, before pulling out.

The cum was dripping out of Brad's ass when Charlie took over, thrusting inside with one deep push. Brad moaned, and his cock hardened.

"You're such a perfect little boy slut, you know that?" Charlie praised him. "Your mouth is heaven, and you're the best cock sucker I've ever met, but baby, your ass... Mmmm... It's dripping with Miles' load, and you're all hot and wet around my dick. You take cock so well, baby."

The words danced over Brad's skin. Charlie knew how to play him like nobody else, and fuck, he loved it. His cock did, too, standing fully erect now.

"Brad was right. You are beautiful, Charlie. And you fuck our boy so well." Miles' voice was hoarse.

Brad couldn't see them with his head buried in the mattress, but the slurping sounds told him they were kissing. Charlie's moves were a little uncoordinated, distracted by the kiss.

"He deserves it," Charlie said, breathless. "He deserves to be fucked long and hard and deep, don't you, baby?" He rammed in extra hard for good measure.

Brad whimpered. The pressure in his ball was getting unbearable. His hand sneaked between his legs before he remembered. He didn't want to disobey Miles. Not today. Not when he had been so perfect.

"Can I please come, Miles?"

Miles didn't answer immediately, but lowered himself on the bed, his face a mere inch away from Brad's. "How does he feel inside you?"

Brad thrashed his head, desperate for friction on his cock. "I wanna come so bad. Please, Miles."

"Tell me how you feel, baby."

"Dirty. Used. So fucking perfect. He's fucking your cum out of my ass, and...please, I need it."

Miles' head moved, and before Brad realized it, his mouth was around Brad's cock, taking him in.

"Oh, fuck!" He exploded in Miles' mouth within seconds, as his ball emptied with a force that sent powerful tremors through his entire body, leaving him shaking.

Behind him, Charlie came with a roar, overflowing his hole with more cum. Brad barely had the strength to wait till he pulled out, but Miles steadied him, then pulled his limp body on top of his as Brad collapsed. Charlie joined them, and they were a sticky mess of sweaty, satisfied men.

Brad's head rested on Miles' shoulder. Miles' hands were roaming his body, petting him everywhere. Charlie's head moved closer, until his head was next to Brad's, their breaths mingling.

"I love you," Charlie whispered, kissing his nose, then his mouth. A soft kiss, sweet.

Brad sighed. "I love you, too."

Every time he said the words, they became a little easier, a little less scary. Still, he couldn't say them to Miles. He felt them, but they were still too scary, too big with him.

"You've been such a good boy today, Brad. I'm proud of you," Miles said.

His hands were still caressing Brad everywhere, a sensation he'd never experienced before. Cold, hard fucking, he knew. This tender care, this was completely new. It did indescribable things to Brad's heart.

"If you're this good tomorrow, Charlie and I have something special planned for you."

"I'll be good. I promise."

For the first time, he didn't care about being too eager. They knew he wanted whatever they had planned, no need to pretend he didn't.

"You'd better be, because bratty boys don't get double-stuffed."

He gasped, his eyes finding Charlie's, who was grinning. "You want both our cocks in your hole, baby?" Charlie asked.

Talk about a stupid question. He held back the eye roll and the snarky comment, though. Fuck, no, he was not risking losing this privilege. "Yes, please," he said sweetly.

Miles chuckled. "Good reaction, smart ass."

"Full ass," Brad quipped. "Really, really full ass."

He shivered with anticipation, his cock reacting with fervor.

"Your ass is not the only one that's gonna get filled," Charlie said. His hand found Miles' and they linked hands on top of Brad's back. "Miles is desperate for some cock as well, and I'm happy to oblige."

The mental picture of Charlie fucking Miles was incredibly arousing. Fuck, he loved it when his two men got all sexy with each other. So far, it had been just kissing and the occasional hand job, but nothing more. Brad wanted them to be together, as much as he was with each of them. Maybe Charlie could fuck Miles, while he was inside Brad...Oh, fuck, yes.

Miles laughed, as his hand traveled to Brad's hard dick. "Someone is liking that idea. He's hard again, Charlie."

Brad moaned. Miles's thumb was spreading precum around his crown, teasing him.

"What do you say, Miles? Does our beautiful boy deserve another round?" Charlie asked. He unlinked from Miles' hand, slipped two fingers inside Brad's ass with ease.

Brad's hips bucked, his cock seeking friction against Miles' hand. Suddenly, Miles lifted him, repositioned him so their cocks were meshed together.

"He does, love. Fill that insatiable hole with your gorgeous cock."

Within seconds, Charlie had taken position on top of Brad's back, spreading his legs and sinking his cock inside. Miles' hand circled around both their cocks, slick enough to create a delicious friction. Because of their position, Charlie couldn't sink in as deep as before, but he was thrusting in with a delicious, steady rhythm that had Brad's insides squirm with pleasure.

"Love this," Brad mumbled, his body going on overload from all the sensations.

Charlie gently bit his neck, giving him goosebumps. Then Charlie's mouth found Miles, and they were kissing each other right next to Brad's ear. Sloppy, wet, slurping kisses. He turned his head, wanted in, and then three mouths met. It was completely uncoordinated and their noses and jaws bumped a few times, but it was the most perfect kiss ever. At some point, both their tongues were in his mouths, and he sucked and licked and teased and drooled, and it was so damn good.

Miles was jacking them off with tight pressure, and Charlie was fucking him in a delicious rhythm, and their tongues were everywhere, and... He bucked, thrashed, then flat-out screamed as he came again.

Miles held him, whispering words that didn't really register cuddling him, stroking his back and head and chest. Charlie fired off a furious round of thrusts, before he deposited another load of fluids inside Brad. He collapsed on the bed next to them, panting hard.

Brad was completely limp, spent, a boneless mass on top of Miles. God, everything hurt. His jaw ached from the blow jobs he'd given Miles, and the weird angles of the three-way kissing. His ass was fucked raw, burning and stinging. His cock was tender, not used to coming twice, and his ball throbbed.

When Miles' hand caressed his ass, he protested, "Enough."

The chest underneath his ear rumbled with a soft laugh. "I didn't know it was possible. Charlie, love, we've managed to fuck the life out of Brad."

Charlie let out a deep sigh. "Not just him. Fucking hell, I'm spent. I need a shower. Desperately."

"Why don't you use the bathroom here? I'll take care of Brad."

Brad couldn't even be bothered to open his eyes, let alone lift his head when Charlie and Miles shared a quick kiss. Charlie pecked him on his cheek. "Thanks, babe."

He merely hmm'd in response, too tired to use words. If he could've crawled closer to Miles, he would have, but he was already sprawled on top of the man as it was. His big hands were still gently caressing him, and there was a peace between them that hadn't been there before.

He wasn't sure how long they'd laid like that, before he finally spoke. "Do you like being my daddy?" He wasn't sure how to phrase it, but hopefully Miles would understand.

"I do, sweetheart. Very much."

"Was it something you'd been looking for?"

"No, it wasn't, which makes it all the more special to me. To be honest, I didn't think I would ever find what I needed."

"What did you need?"

Miles kissed his head. "It's easy to blame Casey for what went wrong between him and me, but it wouldn't be fair. My condition, it makes me needy, sexually speaking, and that wasn't his fault. I wanted someone who would satisfy me—and I didn't realize till later how impossible that desire was. I can't be satisfied. I'll never be satisfied, at least not physically. Casey was a willing bottom, and he did the best he could, but we didn't match emotionally. He was too pliant, too easy in a sense."

"Well, there's one problem you'll never have with me," Brad quipped.

"No. And I see that as a good thing. You challenge me, and I need that. As much as I hate your pain and hang ups, I love that you make me work for it. Loving you is hard work, Brad, but it's deeply fulfilling."

Brad's heart stumbled, fell. "L-l-l-loving me?"

Miles rolled them on their sides, cupped Brad's cheek as their eyes met. "Yes, loving you. I love you, sweetheart."

Miles eyes shone with the truth of his words. "I'm scared," Brad whispered.

"I know you are, and I understand. I'm a patient man, my love, so take your time."

Brad swallowed. "What about Charlie?"

"Hmm, it's complicated, isn't it? The two of you have something precious, anyone can see that. I wouldn't dare to come between you, but neither am I content to be on the sidelines, or merely involved with you. Charlie and I need to take it slow, but I love what we're building, don't you?"

Brad thought of the news Charlie had told him, about Miles being cleared for desk duty. It had been on the back of his mind all day. "Would the FBI be okay with you being involved with two men?"

Miles brushed his bottom lip with his thumb. "What's really bothering you, sweetheart?"

Miles' eyes wouldn't let him go, and he found the strength there to come clean. "Will you go back to DC? Leave us?"

"I should spank the shit out of your ass for even asking me that. No, Brad, I'm not leaving you and Charlie."

"Please, don't be mad at me. Charlie said you were cleared for desk duty."

"Oh, Brad, how can you think I would leave you two? I told you I love you minutes ago. I'm not mad, sweetheart. I know this is hard for you. I'd planned to talk to you two tomorrow, okay? We'll have a nice, adult conversation about where to go from here. But no, I'm not going back to my job."

Brad let out a sigh. "You can punish me if it makes you feel better," he offered.

"That's a bit of a grey area, isn't it? It's not supposed to make me feel better. It's supposed to help you. Would you feel better if I spanked you for not trusting me to take care of you?"

Brad considered it. He felt like crap for not trusting Miles, especially after the man had declared his love for him. Rationally, he could explain and understand his own distrust, but emotionally, he felt like shit for it. "Yeah, I think it would make me feel better. Easier to forgive myself."

Charlie stepped into the room, waves of his body wash

rolling over Brad. Charlie smelled like spring, whereas the two of them still stank of sex and cum.

"Charlie, love, I need you here for a few minutes because Brad needs a spanking, and I prefer to do that in your presence."

Charlie raised his eyebrows as he put on pink boxers. "What did he do?"

"Not trust me to keep my promise that I would take care of him. And you. I'm not leaving for DC, Charlie. We'll talk more about this tomorrow, but I'm quitting my job."

Charlie nodded. "I figured," he said simply.

Brad scoffed. "It's so fucking easy for him, being Mr. Sunshine."

"Brad," Miles warned, his tone suddenly a lot stricter. "Don't fault Charlie for doing what you should have done in the first place, or I'll double your punishment."

Anger rose up in Brad. Charlie hadn't sounded so confident that morning, when he and Brad has discussed Miles leaving. Now all of a sudden he got brownie points for saying he figured Miles would stay? Not fucking fair.

He rolled away from Miles, sat up. If he acted out now, Miles would not only make good on his promise to double his punishment, but he'd lose his reward tomorrow as well. Fuck, it was like being punished three times for the same stupid shit. He'd better take it, though. He was not losing his reward. Besides, he had a pretty damn perfect day, and he was not fucking up his evening.

He got off the bed. "Let's get this over with," he said, fighting hard to keep his tone acceptable.

Miles studied him for a few seconds, then nodded. "Okay."

He took position on the edge of the bed, and Brad lowered himself over his knee. He'd fucking take whatever

Miles wanted to dish out, and that was it. Miles wasted little time in prep, had a solid rhythm going within seconds. Brad clenched his teeth, determined not to show anything. He asked for this himself, fucking idiot that he was, so he'd damn well take it like a man.

Miles never stopped, handing out the twenty-five slaps in rapid succession till Brad's butt stung like a motherfucker. His eyes were bursting at the seams with tears, but he fought them back.

Miles set him on his feet. "We good?" he asked.

"Yeah. I'm gonna take a shower," Brad said. He didn't wait for Miles' reaction but walked straight into the bathroom, closing the door softly behind him. The tears didn't come until the hot jets hit his tender ass.

19

J osh grinned as Miles pretty much dragged Brad into the bedroom, calling for Charlie to join them. Seconds later, Charlie came rushing out of the guest bedroom, a broad smile on his face. "See you later, Aaron," he called out over his shoulder before disappearing into Miles' room.

Aaron came walking into the kitchen with a broad smile. "I think Charlie will be...otherwise engaged for a bit," he said.

"I think that's a safe bet," Connor affirmed dryly.

Josh studied his brother. Aaron was wearing shades of purple eyeshadow, ranging from very light to dark purple, and it accentuated his eyes in a stunning way, especially with the thick layer of mascara he seemed to be wearing. "That's a beautiful color on you," he said.

Aaron looked at his shirt. "This?"

"No, your eyes. Did Charlie do that?"

Aaron blushed. "No, I did, but with his instructions. You like it?"

Josh stepped closer, gently held Aaron's chin to study

him from all angles. "It's gorgeous, really brings out your eyes."

Aaron's face lit up like a Christmas tree, and it made Josh realize how much his brother needed affirmations like this. "Thank you."

"How have you been?"

"I have a job interview Tuesday," Aaron said, still beaming.

"That's awesome. What kind of job?"

"Policy Director with a small non-profit that wants to become more effective in lobbying on state level on behalf of LGBTQ youth. It's part time for now, but with the potential for more, and it's the kind of thing I would love to do. I fit all of their requirements, and they called me back immediately after I applied to schedule an interview, so I hope that means I stand a good chance of getting the job."

Aaron's face was animated as he talked, his gestures signaling how enthusiastic he was about this opportunity. "That sounds like a perfect fit with your skills and passions," Josh said. He spontaneously hugged his brother, receiving a tight embrace in return.

They stood smiling at each other as the unmistakable sounds of fucking drifted in from Miles' room. At first, their smiles widened, but then Josh cleared his throat. "Anyway, yeah, erm…"

"I gotta go," Aaron said. "Blake should be home from teaching, and I wanna… Yeah. I'm leaving."

Josh didn't hug him again, merely waved as Aaron pretty much dashed out the door. Fucking hell, Miles and his men were going at it. Not that he or anyone else had any rights to complain, because fuck knew they made noise when they had fun, but it made him horny as hell. It was a good thing he was wearing his cock cage, otherwise he would have been leaking by now.

He turned around to find Noah rearranging himself, while Indy grinned, his cheeks flushed. "Sounds like they're enjoying themselves," he remarked. "This could be a while, too, what with Miles' stamina and all."

"Okay, that's it," Connor growled. He reached for Josh's wrist and grabbed it, pulling him close, then yanked his pants down.

A wave of exhilaration rode through Josh. Holy fuck, Connor was gonna fuck him right here, right now, with Noah and Indy watching. It was the first time that he'd been this brazen, this intentional.

"Hand me the lube," Connor told Noah, who was closest to the kitchen counter where they always kept a bottle handy. Noah's face split open in a wide grin as he fulfilled Connor's request. "You're gonna let us watch, big guy?"

"I don't give a flying fuck what you do, but I'm damn horny, so I'm gonna fuck Josh until I'm satisfied... Feel free to watch, Flint. You may learn a thing or two."

Connor had truly found freedom. What a change it was in comparison to the insecure man Josh had met. He couldn't be happier for him, for them.

Seconds later, Connor had dropped his pants as well, and he bent Josh down over the table, his shirt still on. Josh turned his head sideways at Indy, who flashed him a sexy grin that he reciprocated.

Lubed fingers were inserted in his ass, and he pushed back. He kept his eyes fixed on Indy, who was subtly grinding his ass against Noah's cock. Josh expected him any second to... Noah's hands found Indy's pants, dragged them down in one move. Indy bent over the table right next to Josh, so close their arms were touching.

Josh reached out and took Indy's hand, kissed it as Connor impatiently prepped his ass. Josh was still loose from their early morning fuck, so it wouldn't take long. Indeed, seconds later Connor pulled out his fingers and replaced it with the Beast. Josh bore down as Connor pushed back in one, deep surge.

Josh moaned loudly, not holding back. Being filled like that was such a rush. It was burning, pain, pleasure, fullness, all wrapped into one. He held on to Indy's hand, his eyes never leaving Indy's as he adjusted to the huge cock breaching him.

Noah had fingers inside Indy now, but Josh had heard them fuck earlier as well, so that wouldn't take long either. Connor was fucking him slowly, deeply, every thrust maxing out. Indy's hand tensed as Noah slid inside him, but then he relaxed again.

There was something profound about watching your soulmate get fucked. Josh slid closer to Indy, who did the same. Their faces were pressed together, their breaths intermingling. Indy gasped into Josh's mouth, as his body shook with the force of Noah's thrust. They couldn't kiss, the impact of both their men too hard to stay still, but they couldn't have been closer.

Josh took in every moan, every soft gasp of pleasure, every groan as Indy was fucked thoroughly, and gave back his own pleasure equally. They were one in every way that matters, two souls merged.

Noah came first, grunted hard. How telling it was that he allowed himself this pleasure without always ensuring Indy came first. Noah, too, had found freedom. Indy's body shook with the tremors of Noah's release, but Indy kept smiling at Josh, their eyes transfixed on each other.

"Did you come?' Noah asked Indy.

"No, but that's okay."

Connor halted, buried balls deep in Josh. "Suck him off," he ordered.

Both their breaths caught at the same time. Was this for real? Was Connor telling them what they thought he was?

"Hurry the fuck up, Joshua, or he can watch you get your ass paddled."

Connor sounded gruff, but Josh recognized the sincerity. Emotion rolled through him, constricting his throat. It was happening. Connor was giving his blessing.

"Thank you, Connor," he said, his voice breaking. "Thank you so much."

Noah sat down on a chair, dragging Indy backward on his lap, his cock still inside him. "Like this," he said, shooting Josh a dirty smile. Like Josh cared how and where he got to suck Indy off. It was the fact that he could.

Connor pulled out, slapped his ass. "Get us two pillows."

Josh hurried into the living room, snatched two pillows from the couch and threw them on the floor in front of Indy. He kneeled, bent over and took Indy in, his friend's hands immediately reaching for his head, caressing his short hair. Noah grabbed Josh's arms, held him steady, as Connor kneeled behind him, lined up, and slammed back in with a powerful thrust.

Heaven. This was heaven.

"Oh, Josh," Indy sighed, pushing his dick deeper into Josh's mouth.

Because Indy was so much smaller than Connor, he could take him in all the way, suck him deep and tight. It was sweet and perfect, especially with Connor still fucking him—though he was careful not to jolt him too much, lest he injured Indy. That Connor was allowing this, sanctioning it, it made it all the more perfect.

Indy came fast, his fingers digging into Josh's skull as he filled his mouth with his release. Josh swallowed, tears forming in his eyes. He'd missed him so fucking much. He licked him clean, then let him go. Indy cradled Josh's head tenderly in his lap, while Connor intensified his thrusts, and Noah kept steadying him.

"I love you, Josh." Indy's voice was soft, rolling over him like a caress. More tears formed, rolled down. "I love you so, so much."

He couldn't find words that adequately expressed what he was feeling. It was simply too much. So he held on, content to let his tears speak for themselves, as Connor unloaded in his ass with a loud grunt.

He lay there for minutes after, even as Connor pulled out, unable to stand up because he didn't want this feeling to ever end. "Come on, baby," Indy said at a certain point.

Even the gentlest push from him spurred Josh into action, and he got up, stiff from the extended uncomfortable position. He looked like an idiot, probably, with his shirt still on, but his ass naked and his cock cage still on, but he didn't care.

Connor watched him with guarded eyes, already dressed again and sitting back at the table. Josh stumbled over, hugged him, pulling Connor's head close against his stomach. "Thank you, Connor. I love you." He kissed his head, then leaned over and kissed his mouth. "Thank you."

Connor smiled, his face breaking free from the tension that had been there before. "Go," he said. He reached for Josh's cock cage, took it off with steady hands. "It's okay. I love you, Josh. Always."

Indy took his hand, pulled him, and together they walked into Noah and Indy's bedroom. He was tired, emotionally more than physically. "Lay on your stomach," Indy said. "I'll clean you up."

He took his shirt off first, then crawled on the bed and plopped down. Seconds later, the bed moved as Indy crawled in beside him. He washed Josh's ass with a warm washcloth, returned to the bathroom where he presumably washed himself as well. By the time he came back, Josh's eyes were drifting shut. He hadn't even orgasmed, but he didn't need one. Everything he needed was right here, in this house.

Indy cuddled close and Josh reached for him, pulled him on top of him until he could no longer tell where his body ended and Indy's began. They fell asleep with their bodies and souls completely entwined.

FUCK, he loved Sunday mornings. Noah sighed with contentment as he took a sip of his tea, the newspaper laid out in front of him. He was starting with the sports section today, while Connor had the front page. They'd come to a silent agreement to share, and the first one got the front page. It was just the two of them in the kitchen for now, as everyone else was apparently still sleeping. A lovely, peaceful way to start the day.

Josh and Indy had napped together for an hour or two the day before after that intense kitchen fuck. When they'd come back, Josh had been worried about Connor, about him changing his mind on Josh and Indy together. Noah had seen it in the somewhat skittish way he'd approached Connor, but he needn't have worried. Connor was truly okay with it.

When he and Indy went to sleep yesterday evening,

there had been two people in his bed, but sometime during the night Josh had walked in, presumably to cuddle again with Indy. Apparently, Connor hadn't wanted to be left alone, and had followed suit. When Noah woke up, his bed had been filled to the max with four men.

He'd smiled, first with amusement, and then with love as he'd watched Indy and Josh completely entangled with each other. Connor had woken up at the same time, and they'd shared a look of understanding. They were crossing into new territory, the two of them, but it was strangely okay. They'd left Josh and Indy in bed together.

It had become more and more clear Connor got off on exhibitionism, both being watched while he fucked or worked Josh over, or watching others himself. It was one of the reasons why they'd done their proposal to Miles. Noah didn't mind watching or being watched. He didn't get as much a kick out of it as Connor did, but he'd be lying if it didn't exhilarate him a little.

Connor had come a long way, from being highly possessive of Josh to being willing to share him with Indy and to a certain degree, Noah. But it hadn't been as easy for him as for Noah, who was deeply jealous of anyone else even looking at Indy, but had no problems at all with Josh. How could he, when Indy had been willing to share him with Josh when they'd met? The three of them had always been together in a way.

Noah wasn't sure what had changed for Connor, but it seemed he had truly accepted Josh and Indy belonged together, as much as Connor belonged with Josh, and Noah belonged with Indy. Sure, it was unconventional and many people would have a strong opinion, but Noah couldn't care less. Anyone could see those two loved each other, and that the love didn't diminish the love they had for Connor and

Noah. The two of them had such big hearts, it held more than enough love for two people.

"You done staring at that paper, or were you planning on actually reading it?" Connor asked.

"Yeah, sorry. Lost in thought. Wanna trade?"

They switched sections, as Connor's phone rang. Noah frowned. Who would call Connor on a Sunday morning? Connor dug up his phone from under the newspaper. He looked at the screen, and his face went blank.

"O'Connor," he answered, listened.

"Yes, sir."

Tension in Connor's tone alerted Noah something was going on. Suddenly, Connor, the proud man who so rarely showed vulnerability, grabbed his hand, clung to him desperately. Noah steadied him with both hands, turning toward him.

What the fuck was going on? Was it his family? Surely, he wouldn't be so upset about that.

"How...? Connor stammered, then listened.

"When?"

More listening.

"Oh, God...Yes, Sir. I'll call to make arrangements. And I'll let you know if I can make it tonight, Sir. Thank you, Sir."

The phone dropped from his hands as he turned to Noah with a face as white as Noah had ever seen a patient look. He didn't ask. Connor would tell him as soon as he was able to.

"They've found him. They've found his body. Lucas." Connor swallowed. "They finally managed to find where the Taliban dumped his body. He's coming home."

Connor's breaths were shallow, fast. The guy was hyperventilating. No wonder after that shock.

Noah got up, yanked Connor's chair back. "Head between your legs, buddy, or you'll pass out."

Connor looked at him with clouded eyes, breaths still speeding up. Noah clamped his hand down on Connor's neck, pushed it down with force. The guy's heart was racing under Noah's hands. "Come on, big guy. You're not fainting on me here."

Connor let himself be pushed down. "That's better. Slow down, Connor. You're okay. Listen to me. Four counts breath in, four counts out. Breathe with me. One...two...three... four. And out....two...three...four."

He repeated this for a minute or two until Connor's breaths had found the rhythm. "You're doing good, man." His fingers curled around Connor's wrist. His pulse was still fast, but nowhere near where it had been. He was coming around.

Noah stepped around the chair, let go of Connor's neck. "Look at me, big guy. Let me see your face." Connor slowly raised his head. His color was coming back, too. "There you go. Good to have you back. You with me, Connor?"

Connor nodded, as his eyes refocused. "They found Lucas," he repeated. "They found him. I didn't think they would. Not anymore."

Noah nodded. "I know. I know."

Something broke in Connor, and Noah watched it happen. The tight band he'd tied around himself, containing his emotions about what had happened to him —it snapped. Noah knew Connor had never talked about what happened, not really. He'd been able to recount some basic facts, but it had been like listening to a robot. Now, the flood was coming, and Connor had to let it out.

"God, Noah, they just dumped his body somewhere, you

know? What the fuck did they care about some American Marine..."

Connor drew in another shuddering breath as he dragged a hand through his hair. Noah sat down again next to him and held his other hand tight.

"He was so fucking brave. They waterboarded us, did you know? Thought it was funny to use our own techniques on us. Fuck knows how they found enough water in that godforsaken place, but they did. Every day. He was so brave. In the end, he knew. He knew he wasn't gonna make it."

Connor's voice broke, and Noah felt himself tear up. The things this man had been through, it was unspeakable.

"His body wasn't as strong as mine, maybe, I don't know. His will was, though. They never got more out of him than his name, rank, and number. He never told them shit. He was my best friend. He knew about me, knew I was gay, and he didn't give a fuck. I held his body after he'd died. For hours."

A mighty tremor tore through Connor's body. Fuck, Noah wished Josh and Indy were here to help him, to help Connor. He needed them, all of them.

"It was so hot and his body got all bloated... And I still thought he was the most beautiful man on the planet. They left him with me for days, continuing their torture of me. Every time they brought me back to him, I threw up because of the smell. And yet I had to look at him. God, Noah, I loved him. I loved him so much."

Noah's eyes were filled with tears. Connor probably hadn't even realized the depth of his feelings for Lucas until right now. If he had, he would've said something to Josh and Noah would have known. It wasn't like there were any secrets between them. No, Connor had held all of this in, for way too long.

"I know, baby." The term of endearment flew easily out of his mouth.

And then Connor opened his mouth and screamed. Heart-wrenching, sobbing screams that originated in his very soul. Noah stepped closer to Connor, and the man slung two arms around Noah's waist, leaned on him with everything he had. And wailed. Noah held him close, tears rolling down his face.

Within seconds, footsteps came running from both bedrooms. Miles arrived first, weapon drawn. He disengaged it quickly when Noah shook his head, put it on the kitchen counter.

"Clear," Miles shouted out, presumably to Brad and Charlie. They arrived at the same time as Josh and Indy, both still putting on clothes as they came running in.

"They've found Lucas' body," Noah said. Nobody would need more details than that right now.

"Oh, God," Josh said, immediately stepping in behind Connor, hugging him from behind. Indy stepped up, too, kissing Connor's head. Connor never acknowledged their presence, but held on to Noah with all he had, sobbing loudly. It was disconcerting, yet at the same time humbling to see Connor leaning on Noah like this, finally surrendering to his emotions. God, the man had kept this in for so long.

Noah held him, aided by Josh and Indy until finally, Connor's sobs were dying down, his body trembling and shaking. Noah's hands cradled the cop's head, stroking his dark hair. He needed a haircut, Connor did. His hair was longer than Noah had ever seen on him.

Miles' boys had found shelter in his arms, one around each of them, as they huddled together and watched quietly, Max at their feet. He was a good man, the agent. Indy's instincts had been spot on, as usual. Miles had been so fucking lonely. The man probably hadn't even realized the depth of it until he'd moved into their crazy home. What a ride he'd been on. Noah was truly happy Miles had found a family with Brad and Charlie, and hopefully with the four of them.

It took a few minutes before Connor spoke. "His body is arriving at Andrews Air Force Base tonight. They're flying him in today, but it will be late. But I could be there, if I wanted to, to receive him. They told me I could be present when he arrives. I also need to make arrangements for the funeral. He'll be buried at Arlington, where he belonged. I need to call the office tomorrow and tell them what he'd want. I'm listed as his next of kin, you know."

He was babbling, Noah noted, another sign of Connor's emotional state. This man did not babble. Ever.

Noah looked up, locked eyes with Indy, then Josh. There was no way Connor was going by himself, but who would go with him?

"Noah will come with you," Josh said softly.

Connor raised his head and looked up at Josh, finally letting go of Noah's waist. Noah's shirt was drenched with the man's tears. "What about you?"

Josh bent over, kissed Connor gently. "I can't come with you, baby. It would trigger too much for me, and you need to focus on yourself now, not take care of me. Noah will come with you to Maryland, to be there when Lucas arrives."

Noah loved that Josh was deciding for him, for all of them. It said so much about the faith they had in each other. Then Indy bent over, too, kissed Connor just as gently, on his lips. "I'll take care of Josh, I promise."

Connor's hand cupped Indy's cheek for a second. "Thank you. He'll need..."

Indy nodded. "I know. I'll make sure he'll get what he needs."

"Come on, baby. Let's get you dressed," Josh said. He gently pulled Connor until the man got up from his chair, followed him into the bedroom.

Noah waited till they were out of earshot. "How will you...?" He couldn't find the words, didn't want to insult Indy by pretending he doubted him, or that he wouldn't know what Josh would need after this.

Indy hugged him tight. "Miles will help me. You take care of Connor, Noah. He needs you to lean on."

Miles. Yeah, that would work. He wouldn't have Connor's expertise, but the man had good instincts. He turned his head, made eye contact with him. Did he sense what was being asked of him?

"We'll take care of him," Miles said with confidence. Noah exhaled. Yeah, he understood.

n hour later, Noah and Connor left for Albany Airport, where they'd catch a flight to DC Josh had been able to book for them last minute by calling the airline directly. Indy's heart broke for Connor, who had looked like a fucking zombie as he got in the car. He hadn't even bickered with Noah about who was driving, their regular argument whenever they were going somewhere with the four of them. Indy sighed as the car disappeared out of sight.

He slowly made his way back inside, where Miles was apparently laying down the law with Brad. His face was inches away from Brad's, his voice deceptively calm, but more authoritative than Indy had ever heard him.

"I will not take any crap from you, today, do you understand me, boy?"

"Yes, Daddy." Brad's eyes were spewing, though.

"If I hear that mouth of yours say anything more I don't like, I will spank your ass so hard you won't be able to sit for days. And trust me, it won't be the kind of spanking where you'll get to come, you feel me?"

"Yes, Daddy."

"I know you're disappointed. So am I, and so is Charlie. But you're damn well gonna swallow it and get the fuck over yourself, or you won't get your reward for another month. Am I making myself clear?"

The last bit of defiance disappeared from Brad's face. Indy wasn't sure what the reward was Miles had been talking about, but it sure as hell had been an effective threat.

Brad bowed his head, his shoulders dropping. "Yes, daddy." He waited a beat, then added, "I'm sorry, Daddy."

"That's a good boy. Go apologize to Charlie, okay?"

Brad nodded. He seemed hesitant to leave. Miles smiled, opened his arms wide to pull him close and hug him, kissing his head. Brad mumbled something Indy couldn't make out.

"I know. Let it go, Brad. You apologized, and now it's good. I love you, sweetheart. Go make up with Charlie."

He sent Brad off with a smack on his ass. All rebellion was gone from his posture, Indy noted. Miles' approach seemed to be highly effective.

"What was that about?" Indy asked, curious.

Miles sighed. "We promised him we'd double-penetrate him today if he behaved yesterday. He did, but now I had to tell him we couldn't, because of Noah and Connor leaving. He didn't take it too well."

"DP? He'd like that?" Indy couldn't even begin to imagine. Maybe Charlie was small, like him, so combined with Miles' dick it would be doable. He'd seen Miles' cock, if not up close, and it wasn't exactly small. Then again, Josh loved taking Connor's cock and that thing was massive. To each his own, right?

Miles grinned. "He'd fucking love it. He's a dirty little

shit with an eager hole. Pretty sure DP will be heaven for him."

Yup, to each his own.

"Look, Indy, now that I have you by yourself for a second, two things. First of all, Brad had testicular cancer a while ago, and they had to remove one testicle. He's highly insecure about his appearance. Also, he has some ED issues, all psychological. It's getting better, but he can't always get hard when you'd expect him to. Could you give Josh and the others a heads up just so they know? I'd hate for him to feel insecure around you guys."

"Wow. So sorry to hear that, man. Is he okay now?"

Miles gave him a sad smile. "As far as the cancer, yes. The emotional stuff, that will take a while. Brad doesn't trust me enough to share openly with me. Yet."

Indy stepped closer, put his hand on Miles' arm. "He'll get there. I see some of myself in him, you know? He's so damaged, wounded. But he's making progress. You're being great with him, Miles. You're exactly what he needs."

"Thank you. He's exactly what I need, too."

Indy grinned, pulled back his hand. "You mean a guy whose sexual appetite rivals yours?"

"He's a little boy slut, always happy to be used. Can't deny that's a match made in heaven considering my cock is in constant need of attention. But I love him, Indy. I love everything about him."

"I know. I wasn't suggesting you only like him because he's easy. Anyway, what was the other thing you wanted to ask me?"

"Josh. What does he need? How can I help?"

"Josh's PTSD is exacerbated by stress. Any changes in his routine cause him stress, so today is a biggie for him because Connor is gone, and Connor is hurting, and both affect Josh. Right now, he's good, but I expect he'll struggle more as the day progresses."

Miles nodded. "Okay. What helps to relieve him of that stress?"

"A BDSM scene. It's one of the reasons why Connor works him over regularly. I mean, they both get off on it sexually, but it's also a massive stress releaser for him. After a deep session, he's usually episode-free for days, sometimes longer."

"How long has it been since his last session?"

Indy grimaced. "Almost a week. They had one planned for today. I mean, Connor spanked him a few times this week, but those were quickies, not a full-on session. I could call Master Mark and ask for a session, but I'm not sure if that would work as Josh needs a lot of trust to let go."

"What does he like?"

"What doesn't he like? Spanking, paddling, Connor has started caning and whipping him, too. His pain tolerance has gone up, he told me the other day. Sexually, he likes it hard and rough. He has a cock cage, but Connor also uses nipple clamps on him, butt plugs, and he ties him up, of course."

Miles' eyes softened. "Are you okay with all this? I've read your file, you know."

It was easy to forget sometimes how much Miles knew about him. In some areas, he knew way more than Noah, since he'd had access to Indy's elaborate statements to the DA. Sure, he'd told Noah and the others some of it, but not everything. Some of it was so painful that he wasn't sure he'd ever be ready to talk about it.

"Indy, if you ever want to talk... I'm here. Friend to friend, but with patient confidentiality. I wouldn't tell a soul."

Indy didn't think. He stepped up to Miles, hugged him tight. The bigger man's arms came around him as he held him close. "Thank you," Indy whispered. "It means a lot to me. One day, I'll take you up on your offer."

As he turned his head to kiss Miles' cheek, his body encountered Miles' groin, which was as hard as Indy had expected.

"I'm sorry," Miles said, wincing.

Indy reached out with both hands, grabbed his face and forced Miles to meet his eyes. "Dammit, Miles Hampton, that's the last time I ever want to hear you apologize for your cock, you hear me? To me, to Noah, to anyone of us. We. Don't. Fucking. Care." He nodded when he saw Miles had gotten the message, then added, "If I hear one more apology out of that mouth of yours, I will spank your ass so hard you won't be able to sit for days."

He giggled when Miles' eyes went wide for a second, before he recognized his own words to Brad. Miles laughed. "Yes, Daddy."

Indy let him go. "I oughta smack your ass for even trying to apologize again."

"Whose ass are we smacking?" Josh asked, walking in with his hair still wet from the shower he'd just taken.

"Miles'. If he ever dares to apologize for being hard."

Josh rolled his eyes. "Who cares?"

"I know, right?" Indy said, laughing when Miles held up his hands.

"Okay, okay, I'll stop. I promise."

Josh hugged Indy from behind, and Indy leaned back against him. "We could also smack yours if you want to. Or if you need us to."

Josh sighed. "Yeah, that'd be good. I'm antsy already. Maybe this afternoon?"

"Whatever you need, baby. We've got you."

"Are you okay with me doing this, Josh?" Miles asked.

Josh nodded. "Yeah. I trust you and I really need it. Can you do it?"

"Yes. We'll keep it simple, but make it intense enough to satisfy your needs. You'll have to talk me through your limits, and especially any hard limits you have. And I'll need to know your safe words."

"I'll safe word for him," Indy offered. "It's hard for Josh to relax otherwise, right, baby?"

Josh nodded. "I don't use safe words with Connor because he reads me like an open book. We've tried it, but I was too focused on determining whether or not I liked something to get to subspace. It's one of the reasons why we've build our sessions up so slowly in terms of intensity, because Connor sets a pace he's comfortable with for both of us."

"Indy, I have to ask again: are you okay with this? Can you handle this? I can't worry about you when I have to focus on Josh…"

Indy loved that he was so concerned, for both of them. "I'm good. It was hard for me at first, but I've seen enough of what they do by now to realize Josh craves it. I love watching him sink into subspace and bliss out."

"Okay, good. Josh, why don't you and I take some time right after lunch to walk me through your limits? Oh, and do you want Brad and Charlie to watch, or would you prefer it private?"

Josh sought Indy's eyes. "I don't mind them watching, but are you okay with that, baby?"

Indy shook his head. "This isn't about me. This is about you, what you need."

Josh bit his lip as he clearly pondered it. "Let them

watch. I think it would be good for them to see a scene, even a mild one like this, so they know what they're getting into when they have to decide on our proposal."

"Have you talked to them yet?" Indy asked Miles.

"No. I'd planned to today, but I'm not sure it would be the right timing now."

Indy sighed. "Maybe not. I don't know how this will affect Connor. But the proposal stands. We want you guys here. Just maybe wait a week or so till things have quieted down a bit?"

"Yeah, that sounds smart." Miles shot Josh a confident look as he put a hand on his shoulder, slow enough so Josh saw it coming. "We've got your back, Josh. I'm gonna check on Brad and Charlie, but I'll be right back, okay?"

CHARLIE LOVED CUDDLING WITH BRAD, especially when the two of them were naked, like now. It hadn't been the plan. Brad had come in to apologize after being quite rude when Miles had told him they'd have to change their plans for today. He'd been honestly sorry, and Charlie had accepted his apology with ease. The fact that Brad was apologizing in the first place was big.

Then Brad had wanted to be held, and one thing had led to another, and Brad had rimmed Charlie till he saw stars. Actual fucking stars, as he'd come so hard he'd been unable to move for a minute or two. He'd offered to suck Brad off, but he'd informed him he wasn't allowed to come, courtesy of Miles. So they had cuddled, both naked, simply talking and touching. It was absolutely perfect.

The three of them were perfect. Charlie hadn't realized how much he needed both: to be taken care of and feel protected, and to be bossy and toppy. With Miles, he had the first, and Brad allowed him the second... Well, Miles did, too, to some degree. Charlie felt the man secretly loved it when Charlie got all bossy, though he'd never admit it to Brad, obviously. Theirs was one of those combinations that sounded and looked all wrong, but was so wonderfully right.

The door opened and Charlie turned his head.

"Look at you two, all naked and gorgeous," Miles said.

Brad looked up. "Wanna join us?" he asked with puppy eyes.

"For a few minutes, yes, please. After that, I wanted to ask you to come to the kitchen, because we have something to discuss."

Brad tensed in Charlie's arms. "Is it something good?" he asked.

Miles made quick work of his clothes before he joined them on the bed, spooning Charlie from behind, effectively sandwiching him between himself and Brad. His cock was rock hard, poking Charlie in his back. He didn't mind at all, loving the sensation of that strong body behind him.

"It is, and thank you for asking so nicely, Brad."

Brad beamed and Charlie had to kiss him. Simply had to, because he was so cute, with tongue until they were both gasping for breath. Then he had to roll on top of him and rut against him, because that lean body felt so damn good underneath him, Brad's hands possessively on his ass, pressing him close. Charlie had come not a half hour ago, and yet he was so damn hard again, so horny.

Miles moaned. "God, the two of you are killing me." He had his hand on his cock, was fisting himself hard.

Charlie rolled from Brad straight onto Miles and kissed him. He tasted so different from Brad. Brad was sweet, somewhat timid, whereas Miles was all male, spicy, and so dominant. Their tongues fought, pushing each other back and forth.

Miles let go of his cock to grab Charlie's ass, his fingers digging into his ass cheeks. He moaned in his mouth. "You're so fucking sexy, baby. God, you make me so hard."

Charlie grinned, then attacked Miles' mouth once more. He pulled his legs up when he felt Brad nudge him, then Brad's mouth descended on Miles' cock between his legs. Charlie's cheeks were resting against Brad's curls, tickling his hole and balls.

"Oh, fuuuuck!" Miles grunted, undoubtedly distracted by Brad's mouth around his cock. Charlie used the distraction to grab the lube from the night stand. Miles had said they only had a few minutes, but he didn't need more than that. Someday, he wanted to take the time, but for now, he wanted his cock inside Miles, and it wouldn't take but a few minutes to come.

"Brad, babe, let go a sec," he told him.

Miles' cock plopped out of Brad's mouth with a slick noise.

"Hands and knees," Charlie ordered Miles. Miles raised one eyebrow, before turning around and getting in position. "Brad, get underneath him."

Miles' hole was beautifully pink. And tight. The man sighed as Charlie breached him with a finger.

"How long has it been?" Charlie asked.

"I dunno. A year, maybe?" Miles sounded apologetic.

Charlie smacked his ass, laughed. "Well, then you're gonna feel this the rest of the day. Open up for me, baby."

Miles bore down as Charlie added a second finger. Seconds later, Miles' ass clenched around his fingers as he came down Brad's throat. His body went slack, and Charlie used the opportunity to add a third finger. His hands were small, so he had to get in at least that before fucking him.

"You okay, baby?"

"Mmmm. Feels good. Burns, but good."

He kept moving and stretching till Miles' hole relaxed around his fingers. "Here we go, baby. Tell me when I need to stop, okay?"

That beautiful, pink pucker fought to keep him out at first, but Charlie kept pushing until the head of his cock made it past the first ring.

"Damn, you're tight." He gave an experimental shallow thrust. The pressure on his cock was incredible.

Brad laughed, crawled from underneath Miles. "I wanna see you take him."

Miles groaned.

"Open that sweet ass for me, honey," Charlie said, thrusting again. Miles shivered under his hands.

"God, you're so fucking hot like this," Brad said, his voice raw. "Both of you. It's fucking sexy."

Charlie inched in deeper, slowly but surely, until he finally bottomed out. "Fuck, you feel good," he told Miles.

He slowly pulled out, surged back in. Fuck, he'd missed this. He liked being fucked, at least when Zack had bothered to make it good for Charlie was well, but damn, it was so good to top again, first Brad and now Miles. His men.

He found a rhythm, slow, but deep. Miles was still so damn tight that he didn't want to pound too hard. He was gonna feel this anyway.

"You good, baby?" he checked.

"Yeah... Need to come... Please, Brad..."

Brad didn't need to be asked twice, as usual. He reached between them, found Miles' cock.

"Oh...thankyouthankyouthankyou...so close..."

Charlie smiled, sped up his own thrusts. The pressure in his balls increased, and shivers tingled down his spine. His fingers found Miles' hips, dug in for grip. He needed to... He pulled back, thrust in harder. Could Miles take it? A low moan indicated he could. Charlie surged in again, his balls slapping against Miles' ass.

The body underneath him spasmed, as Miles was coming all over the bed. Charlie let go, fucked him hard and deep for the last few thrusts, before unloading inside him. God, he'd forgotten how deeply satisfying it was to deposit your cum in another man's ass. Mark him.

Miles was his. And so was Brad. They belonged together, the three of them. His men. Miles, his protector, and Brad, his wanton little slut. Had there ever been a day when he hadn't wanted to fuck him? He'd loved him since the day he'd met him, even as a high school student. And now he was his. To love, to cherish, to hold, to take care of. And to fuck. Hot damn, he wanted to fuck him, too. He was still hard, not done by far.

He yanked Brad down by his ankle, turned him on his back, then launched himself on top of him. His cock was slick enough, and if not, Brad would love the burn.

"Pull your fucking legs up."

Brad obeyed immediately, a stunned expression on his face.

Charlie held his cock with one hand, found Brad's hole with the other. "Let me in," he demanded.

No finesse here, no going slow, or inching in. He pushed in, then slammed home. Brad cried out, tears forming in his eyes. His cock hardened instantly, testament to how much he loved being taken like this.

He was too small to kiss Brad while fucking him, so he latched on to his nipples instead, scraping first the left, and then the right one. Brad bucked beneath him, whimpering. Charlie needed to be deeper inside him, harder. He leaned back, folded Brad's legs almost double. Good thing the guy was flexible as could be.

"Oh, fuck, yes," Charlie moaned. "Miles' hole is so tight, but you, baby, you can take anything we dish out. My beautiful, beautiful boy slut... Look at you, all desperate for more."

He rammed in so hard, Brad's whole body moved an inch, until Miles steadied him, supported him. Brad's eyes drifted shut, an expression of pure lust on his face.

"You be a good boy, baby, you listen to me and your daddy, and I promise you we'll ravage that wanton hole of yours... We'll fuck you so hard, so deep, you'll think you've died and gone to heaven..."

Miles was jacking himself off furiously, keeping pace with Charlie's brutal rhythm as he fucked the living daylights out of Brad's ass.

"Paint him, Miles. Spray your cum all over our cum slut here. I'm gonna fill his hole with my load. Need to show him he's mine."

Miles let out a deep sigh, and ropes of thin cum spurted all over Brad. His chest, some on his face, his arms. He looked absolutely perfect.

Charlie angled his hips, aimed slightly to the right, knowing exactly where to hit Brad. Two, three, four hard strokes and Brad came without ever touching his cock, his cum flying on his own stomach and chest.

"Look at you, you dirty little shit. All covered in cum, that's exactly how you like it, isn't it?"

He sped up, the tingling in his balls signaling he was ready to unload.

"Open wide, baby. I'm gonna fill you, mark you, make you fucking mine."

He rabbitted in and out till his balls exploded, sending the last bit of cum his body had to offer with a violent spurt deep inside Brad.

He collapsed half across Brad, getting cum everywhere. He was still flying high when Miles dragged him off, claimed his mouth in a searing kiss.

Miles broke off their kiss, cupped his cheeks. "I love you, Charlie. I know it's fast, and complicated, and maybe you're not ready to hear it, but I love you."

His heart burst free. "I'm ready. I was born ready for you, for Brad, for us. I love you, Miles. I love you both so much."

21

"I thought you said a few minutes," Indy laughed as the three of them stepped into the kitchen.

"We got distracted," Miles shrugged unapologetically. He didn't think Indy needed more explanation than that. He was smart enough to fill in the details, right?

Brad smiled as he quietly took a seat at the table. He winced as he sat down, his ass undoubtedly rather tender from Charlie's not so gentle fucking minutes before. Miles had to admit he was feeling his own ass as well, but fuck, it had been worth it.

Fucking hell, Charlie had ravished Brad, and that after his enthusiastic pounding of Miles. Charlie was slowly getting back to his old self, it seemed: flirty, bossy, and sexy as fuck. God, the sight of him fucking Brad, Miles had never seen anything more erotic than that waif of a man fucking the shit out of Brad, completely bent double.

"Wait," Indy said. "Brad is sporting a sore ass, and so is Miles. Who did the fucking here?"

Charlie grinned. "That would be me," he said, beaming. "Not the bottom everybody pegs me for. And after my experiences this morning with these two, I'm not sure I'll ever bottom again."

Indy laughed. "Power to you, my man. How's your ass feel, big guy?" he asked Miles.

"Sore. It had been a while, and Charlie's equipment is not exactly proportionate to the rest of his body, if you catch my drift. Very much worth it, though. He fucks like he does everything else: with gusto."

"What did you want to talk to us about?" Brad asked.

It was a bit of an abrupt segue, but Miles understood. Brad was worried and when he was, his social skills suffered. "Josh needs a scene in a bit, and since Connor is not here, I'll do it. Is that okay with you guys?"

A flash of relief crossed over Brad's face, but Charlie answered first. "Does...does that mean you'll fuck him?"

Miles shook his head. "No, honey, absolutely not. Come here, both of you."

Within seconds, he had Charlie on one knee and Brad on the other. God, he loved holding his boys like this, feeling so deeply connected. "I wouldn't do that to us and to Josh, Connor, and Indy. No, Josh needs pain, and Indy..."

Miles wasn't sure how to put into words what he understood on such a deep level. Indy wasn't capable of dishing out pain, and especially not to Josh. Even though the kid understood Josh craved it and needed it, he'd seen too much cruelty, had experienced too much of it himself, to ever inflict pain willingly on someone else—let alone the guy he loved so much.

"I can't hurt Josh," Indy said softly. "Even when I know he needs it and wants it. I can't do it."

"Can you bear to watch?' Charlie asked, leaning back against Miles' chest, cheek to cheek with Brad who had already found his spot there.

"Yeah, because I can see how much he loves it."

"It's fine with me," Brad said. "I get it."

He would, wouldn't he? Even though his need was different, he'd understand what Josh got from it, Miles mused.

"Thank you," Indy said softly. "For allowing Miles to do this."

Miles had kept an eye on Josh throughout the discussion. At first, he'd been fully engaged, but now his eyes kept glazing over. Indy had shot him a few concerned looks as well. It was time to intervene.

"Josh, you still with us?" Miles asked, making sure to keep his voice kind.

Josh jerked. "Yeah. No. It's getting hard."

"Are you worried about Connor?" Indy asked.

Josh nodded. "I think he was in love with Lucas, only he never realized until now," he said quietly. 'He's losing him all over again, you know?"

"Oh, baby, I know." Indy crawled on Josh's lap, hugged him. "Do you need Miles to work you over now?"

"We said after lunch," Josh protested, his voice trembling.

Miles' heart broke for him, but that was not what the man needed right now. He brought his mouth close to Brad's ear. "Boy, I need you to be good right now, okay? Josh needs me, and I can't deal with any disobedience from you. Do you understand me?"

Brad nodded. "I'll be good, Daddy. I promise. Can we watch?"

"Yeah, sweetheart. Thank you for being a good boy."

Both his boys slinked off his lap, took their own seats again. Miles got up, steadied himself internally. "Let's go, Joshua."

Josh's head shot up. "What?"

"I'm not asking again. Bedroom, now."

For two seconds, Josh hesitated, his body shaking, but then he set Indy on his feet and rose. "Yes, sir."

"You have thirty seconds to get undressed. I want to see your clothes folded neatly, and you on your knees when I enter that room, is that understood?"

"Yes, sir."

Josh all but ran off.

"Indy, we haven't had time to discuss his limits, but I don't think he can wait. Give me a quick run down."

"No bodily fluids, no humiliation. He loves serving sexually, likes to be fucked hard, wants you to forbid him to come. He can take a lot in terms of pain, and he craves commands."

Miles processed this quickly. They'd have to keep it basic, since he wasn't experienced with the floggers and whip, or anything hardcore really. And of course, he wasn't engaging him sexually in any way. That would be up to Indy. A slow build up then, using increasing levels of intensity. "I need you with me at all times, Indy. You're his safe word, okay?"

Indy nodded.

"Can I use you? I mean, to have him pleasure you?"

"Yeah. I figured you would." Indy looked down for a second, suddenly insecure. "Miles, I can't fuck him the way he needs right now. My dick... I'm small, okay? It won't be enough."

Oh, boy. Poor kid. This was obviously a tender subject for Indy. He put his hand on Indy's shoulder. "Indy, love, you will always be what he needs, okay? We'll figure it out. Whatever you are comfortable with."

An idea formed in his head, one that had to work. "I want you all to keep your clothes on for now, until I say otherwise. Brad, sweetheart, I'm gonna need you, too. I'm counting on you to listen to me, boy."

Brad nodded eagerly. "Yes, Daddy."

When he walked into Connor and Josh's bedroom, Josh was naked, his cock hidden in his cock cage, on his knees, his hands folded behind his back. His clothes were neatly folded on top of the unmade bed. He shot Miles an insecure look.

"Eyes down. You only speak when I ask you a question."

"Yes, sir."

"That wasn't a question, Joshua. That's ten."

Josh opened his mouth, then thought better of it and closed it again, training his eyes on the floor. His body showed tension. His shoulders were pulled up, his limbs restless.

"Do you think an unmade bed is how you receive your Dom?"

Josh sighed. "No, sir."

"On that we agree. That's ten more. Make the bed, Joshua."

Josh shot to his feet, had the king size bed made in no time. When he was done, he gave Miles an insecure look.

"Eyes down, Joshua. Ten more. What's the count now?"

"Thirty, sir."

"Any particular reason you're not on your knees right now?"

He lowered himself instantly. "No, sir. Sorry, sir."

"That brings us to what, forty?"

A sigh. "Yes, sir."

"We're not off to a good start, are we?"

"No, sir."

"You'll have to try harder, then."

"Yes, sir. Dammit! Sorry, sir. That's fifty, sir."

The frustration on Josh's face was obvious, which had been Miles' goal. "I'll give you two options. We can do the fifty now, but we'll add twenty-five because you're off to such a bad start. Or we can do them later and give you the chance to earn deductions for good behavior. Which do you prefer, Joshua?"

"I'll take the seventy-five now, sir."

Miles almost smiled. Josh might not have disobeyed on purpose, but he was craving the punishment. It seemed Indy had been right. Josh was a bit of a pain slut.

"Are you sure, Joshua? Last chance."

"Yes, sir."

Miles shrugged. "Okay. Brad, come here please."

The other boys had been standing near the door, quietly watching. Brad's eyes widened in surprise, but he did listen. "Strip. You will take the seventy-five slaps Joshua here has racked up."

Josh's head shot up, horror painted on his face. "No! Sir, no! Please."

Miles' eyes were on Brad, though. How would his boy react? Brad swallowed, then proceeded to strip naked. His brave, brave boy. He really wanted to obey, even though his eyes were wide with fear.

"Good boy, Brad."

Shaking, Brad lowered himself over Miles' lap without him having to ask. He caressed his gorgeous ass, those perfect curves that were always inviting him in. "So proud of you, boy."

He turned to Josh. "Be quiet, Joshua. I never said what the seventy-five were, now did I?"

It was quiet, except for Brad's rapid breaths and Josh's gasp.

"I asked you a question, Joshua."

"No, sir, you didn't. I assumed..."

"Well, you assumed wrong, didn't you?"

"Yes, sir."

"So now you'll have to watch as Brad takes your punishment. You ready, Brad?"

"Yes, Daddy."

The quiet word sent stabs through Miles' heart. He was a total bastard for doing this to both of them. He couldn't deny the rush it gave him to see Brad submit to him in trust, though. He didn't dare look at Indy and Charlie, could only imagine the stress on their faces.

His hand came down hard, the sound of it connecting with Brad's ass echoing through the room. The slaps after that were hard, too, because he needed to create the impression he was hurting Brad. But after that, he slowly lessened, until he gently smacked Brad's cheeks, reddening them in the most beautiful way.

"That was twenty-five, boy. How's your ass feel?" He rubbed it soundly, which would make the sting worse for now.

"It hurts, Daddy. But it also feels good."

Brad wasn't lying, since his dick was hard, rubbing against Miles' leg. The look on Josh's face was pure jealousy. He wanted that spanking, and he wanted it bad.

"You ready for fifty more, boy?"

"Yes, Daddy."

Oh, the sweet sensation of submission. He loved Brad all the more for it. The trust he displayed here was phenomenal.

"You're being such a good boy, Brad. You're really making me proud. You have definitely earned a big reward later."

He gave Brad's ass one hard slap, watched with satisfaction as Josh clenched his fists.

"I'll tell you what, Joshua. I'll make you a deal. Brad has forty-nine more to go. I'll give them to you, but we'll have to double them. Let's make it one hundred, to round it off. What do you say: forty-nine for Brad or a hundred for you?"

"Hundred for me, sir."

Like there had ever been any doubt. "Okay, then. Bring me the paddle, Joshua."

Josh's eyes flew up, but he restrained himself. He got up, walked over to a cabinet in the corner and came back with a sturdy paddle. Miles tested it against his hand, Brad still draped across his lap. "One hundred with this beauty. That's gonna hurt, Joshua."

Josh sank to his knees again, his eyes downcast. It was the first sign he was surrendering, and it was beautiful.

"Want me to test this out on you, boy?" he asked Brad.

Brad looked at the paddle for a few seconds. "I trust you, Daddy."

Miles smiled, smacked his ass once, but held back. "How's that feel?"

"It's different. Hard."

Miles nudged Brad off his lap. "Let me set Josh up, and then we'll find something for you to do, okay?"

He walked over to what had to be a work out bench for Connor, considering the weights placed nearby. There was a towel over the seat edge. It would be perfect. He didn't want to put Josh on his lap, since the smell and feel of his body might be too distracting for him to relax. He put the towel on the seat itself, threw a pillow on the floor.

"Joshua, kneel here, arms around the back of the seat."

Josh obeyed without words. Miles tied his hands behind the seat with a piece of rope he'd spotted. He made sure the rope was tight, but not cutting off circulation. Next, he put a blind fold around Josh's eyes.

Josh trembled, but he didn't protest. Miles checked in with Indy, who nodded his approval. Miles put a chair close to Josh, so he'd be comfortable while paddling him.

"Spread your legs a little wider," he ordered him. "That's good. I want complete silence now, from everyone except Josh. Joshua, you have permission to make any sounds you want. Are you comfortable?"

"Yes, sir. Thank you, sir."

"You do not have to count or keep track. I'll do that for you. I want you to simply take your punishment, okay?"

"Yes, sir."

"Let's start."

He started gently, with smacks that would barely register with Josh, which was exactly the point. Josh shifted, restless, seeking more intensity. By the time Miles had reached twenty-five, Josh was settling in, his ass getting red and warm. Miles spread the hits out all over his cheeks and upper thighs, wanting to create a big a palette as possible.

All that time, Brad had been sitting on the floor, waiting. He too, had been restless, but he hadn't made a sound. Miles gestured him over with one finger, then put a finger on his mouth to indicate he wasn't to make a sound. Brad's face was pure delight when Miles pointed toward his crotch. His cock was so hard it physically hurt, and he breathed a breath of relief when Brad quietly liberated it from his boxers. Miles didn't miss a beat—literally—as that sweet mouth engulfed him, took him all the way in.

Josh groaned, then whimpered. He was feeling it now, the steady rhythms of smacks getting to him. Miles checked in with Indy again, who smiled at him. Charlie gestured to the bed and Miles nodded. He didn't need it anytime soon, so the boys could relax there.

Miles made no other sound than a small gasp as he

flooded Brad's mouth with an orgasm that bordered on painful. Brad looked up at him, cum dripping down his chin, a blissed expression on his face. Miles gave him a smile of gratitude and love, rubbed his head with his left hand while continuing the paddling with his right.

He'd lost track of the count with Josh. Not that it had ever been his goal to deliver one hundred exactly. The idea had to be to make it so much Josh wouldn't be able to count, and would be able to let go and surrender. It looked like he was well on his way, aided by the silence in the room, his blindfolds, and the smell of Connor on the towel his head was resting on.

When Josh's shoulders came down, and his body went still, Miles knew he'd reached subspace. Miles slowed down, continuing with light smacks to keep him in that happy place. He needed enough pain to stay there, but not so much it would yank him out. He was flying blind here, because he couldn't see Josh's face, so he'd have to trust his instincts. Luckily, he'd always been good at interpreting body language, and Josh's body was signaling complete submission and surrender.

After five minutes or so, he gestured Indy over. Indy raised his eyebrows, wanted to know what to do. Miles indicated he should fuck him, no prep, use lube only. Josh would be tight because of the spanking, and Indy's cock would do the trick. Indy smiled and Miles knew he understood.

Miles averted his eyes when Indy hesitantly stripped. He wasn't sure how comfortable Indy was with them watching. Brad turned his head the other way as well, content to stay kneeling with his face in Miles' crotch, nuzzling his cock and balls, completely relaxed. Miles' hand was softly caressing his curls, and Miles was pretty sure Brad was about to start purring.

He raised his eyes to find Charlie watching them with so much love pouring from his eyes, it made Miles' breath catch. How had he ever gotten this lucky to find not one, but two amazing men he wanted to spend the rest of his life with?

He kept spanking Josh until he saw Indy step up from the corners of his eyes. Only then did he put the paddle down, and he signaled his boys it was time to leave. They left quietly, as behind them sounds of Indy taking Josh filled the room, accentuated by small sighs and moans from them both. It sounded like Indy fucked him with more gentleness than Josh was used to, probably, but that was to be expected. The kid didn't have it in him to fuck hard, and that was fine. It would hurt anyway, with Josh's ass being so tender from the extensive paddling.

Miles made his way to their own bedroom, groaning with discomfort. Damn, his shoulder and arm hurt like a motherfucker from the massive workout they'd gotten. He collapsed on their bed, exhausted. Both of his boys were on him in seconds, a naked Brad cuddling close, while a still-dressed Charlie started massaging his sore arm and shoulder.

He kissed Brad's head, sent Charlie a grateful smile.

"I love you both so much."

THE SUN SHONE BRIGHT, reflecting brightly off the endless rows of white crosses on Arlington. Josh stood ramrod straight, not a crease out of place on his dress uniform, his boots shinier than they had ever been. All of their friends had made the journey, even Blake and Aaron, to support Connor.

Connor stood in the front. The sight of him in his dress Marine uniform had taken Josh's breath away. Connor had proudly worn his medals—more than Josh had even known he'd earned. He'd never talked about his Marine career before, other than some anecdotes, but to have earned those medals, he had to have been through hell and back.

Next to Connor, Noah was equally formal and solemn as Marines brought the last honor to Lucas. Noah had been an absolute rock this week for Connor to lean on. And Connor had leaned hard. He'd shared more in the last few days than in all the months Josh had known him, and most of it had been with Noah, but that hadn't bothered Josh. Connor wanted to protect him, and rightly so, since some of the details would have been too much for him to handle.

But it was him Connor had sought comfort with. He'd held him, cuddled him, and Connor had fucked him absolutely raw. Even now, standing here, Josh's ass was throbbing. Usually, they didn't fuck every day, simply because Josh's body needed time to recuperate from taking him. The last couple of days, it had been daily, and sometimes even more than once per day. Josh had done it with love, more than willing to sacrifice some physical comfort to be there for Connor.

It seemed sacrilegious to think of sex at an occasion like this, but Josh had to. If he focused on what was happening in front of him, he'd lose it. It triggered too much inside him. Sex it was, then.

As much as he had loved taking care of Connor this week, he had reached his limit of what he could handle, at least physically. He wasn't sure how to tell Connor, though.

He'd always been there when Josh had needed him, so how could he say no when the tables were turned?

The wail of "Taps" broke through Josh's thoughts, and he shivered. Fuck, he loved and hated that piece of music with equal fervor. It was so hauntingly beautiful, but so fucking heartbreaking at the same time.

On his left side, Indy brushed Josh's hand with his pinkie. They couldn't hold hands, not here, not with so many military men present. And not while Josh was in uniform. He respected the uniform and all it stood for too much for that. But that tiny little touch steadied him nevertheless.

The pallbearers folded the flag, every move perfectly executed. Josh's throat was too tight to swallow. That could have been Noah right there. He'd come so damn close to losing him.

Indy's hand nudged his again, pulling him back. He had to think of something else.

The Marine holding the flag approached Connor, offered him the flag. "On behalf of the President of the United States, the Commandant of the Marine Corps, and a grateful nation, please accept this flag as a symbol of our appreciation for your loved one's service to Country and Corps." Connor nodded, accepted it with a stony face.

Josh managed to hold it together till it was all over. Indy and the others were standing near the front, leaving Josh standing a bit to the side. Connor was still talking to a few of his former Marines when loud talking erupted behind the group. Josh turned. A group of tourists was taking pictures of the graves, laughing and joking. Josh clenched his fists, but before he could say or do anything, a lone figure in the back marched toward them.

"Be quiet!" his voice thundered. "You will respect the

sanctity of this place and the sacrifices made by those buried here."

Josh recognized him on instance. Behind him, one of the Marines yelled: "Attention!"

All military men and women snapped to attention. To the last man, including Noah, Connor, and Josh himself, they saluted General Flint. Instant silence descended upon the place. Even the birds seemed scared to sing. The tourists slinked off hurriedly, casting worried glances over their shoulders until they were out of sight.

General Flint marched to the front of the group. "As you were."

His face softened as he approached Connor, but Josh tensed up. The last time they had seen each other was when Connor had booted him out of that hospital waiting room when Noah had his surgery. Only later had Josh understood how Connor had gotten rid of the man—by threatening to go public with the truth about what had happened to his unit.

The General stepped in front of Connor, who still stood ramrod straight. "Sergeant O'Connor."

Connor didn't even blink. "General."

"At ease, Sergeant. I'm sorry...for your loss. I understand he was your best friend."

Josh's breath stopped at that long pause. Noah's dad was saying more than standard words. He was apologizing to Connor in a way Josh had never thought possible. Noah's face showed the same shock Josh was feeling. Even Connor looked startled for a second or two. Then he, too, accepted the hand extended to him.

"Thank you, sir. He was. The best Marine I've ever known and an even better friend."

Josh caught the baffled looks of the other Marines

present. Few people knew about General Flint's involvement in the operation that led to Lucas and Connor being captured. But even those who did must have been wondering why a general would show up to a Marine's funeral.

Then Connor's CO stepped up, gave the General a crisp salute, which he returned promptly. "General Flint. On behalf of the United States Marine Corps, our deepest thanks for your relentless efforts in retrieving Corporal Martins' body."

Josh's eyes widened, and he shared a quick what-the-fuck look with Noah. His dad had been involved in finding Lucas' body? Everyone stood straight as the two men exchanged soft words.

Noah broke rank first, walked toward his dad with unsteady paces on the uneven ground. Josh trailed behind him, wanting to make sure he was okay.

"Dad," Noah said. Josh held back a chuckle as Marines all around him suddenly checked the name on Noah's uniform to make sure they'd heard it right. "Thank you for coming."

His dad nodded. "It was the right thing to do." He lowered his voice, making sure only Noah, Connor, and Josh could hear it. "I kept in the back, though. Didn't want to distract anyone. This wasn't about me."

"No, but it means a lot to Connor that you showed up. And to me."

"Noah..." The general seemed to search for words. "I would love to come see your new house."

It was the clearest attempt at reconciliation Josh had ever seen the man make.

"You know I live there with my boyfriend, right? And with Josh and Connor?" Noah asked.

His dad nodded. "Yes. I'd like to meet Indy, but not here. Not like this."

Josh understood. The man who'd defended *don't ask don't tell* could not be seen in public with his gay son and boyfriend. The fact that he even wanted to meet Indy in private was a big gesture, though. You couldn't expect miracles here, only small steps in the right direction. Would his own parents ever even make a gesture like that? He doubted it. As far as they were concerned, Josh was dead. Aaron, too.

At that exact moment, Aaron appeared at his side, sporting the insecure look he usually had when he was near Josh, as if he was expecting a blow. How long would it take before Aaron would feel safe with him and not expect Josh to reject him? It stabbed through Josh's heart that this was what he had caused. He'd started to rebuild his relationship with Aaron, but it would take a long time before Aaron would fully trust him.

He turned toward Aaron, sent him a soft smile. "Hey, bro. Thanks for coming today."

The smile Aaron sent back was staggering. He was indeed a little puppy, so eager to please. "We wanted to be here for Connor. And for you."

"I'm holding up okay," Josh answered the question Aaron was probably afraid to ask. "But I could use a little distraction now."

"Want me to get Indy for you? Or Noah?" Aaron offered.

"Nah. Just talk to me. How did your job interview go? I'm sorry, I forgot to ask this week, but—"

"It's okay, Josh, I get it. You had other things to worry about." Aaron's voice was kind, and Josh felt his sincerity. "I got the job. They called me Friday to tell me. I start in a week."

Josh's face broke open in a smile. "That's awesome! I'm

so happy for you."

"Me too. I'm really excited, because it's such a great cause, and it's the kind of work I love."

Josh hugged him briefly.

"How have you been?" Aaron asked. "Not this week, I mean, but like, in general?"

It wasn't the most articulate of questions, but Josh understood the sentiment behind it. "I'm relatively good. This week has been hard, obviously, most of all for Connor, but shit like this affects me too." He hesitated. He wasn't used to explaining himself to others, but maybe Aaron deserved more than finding things out weeks later. "Indy and I, we're together now, too. Like, I'm with Connor and he's with Noah, but we're together as well if that makes sense."

Aaron sent him a sweet smile. "A polyamorous relation," he said. "That makes total sense for you all."

Josh couldn't hide his surprise. "How do you know about...?"

Aaron blushed a little, but didn't avoid Josh's eyes. "I'm educating myself about all kinds of things, including the many options on the gender and sexuality spectrum, but also about different sexual kinks and preferences. I wanted to know more about puppy play, that's how it started, and I kind of went down a rabbit hole from there."

Josh grinned. "There's plenty of kink to go around," he said.

"Josh, I'm happy for you and Indy. It's obvious how much you love each other, and you're blessed that Noah and Connor can see it, too."

Blessed. It was a word Josh hadn't heard or used in a long time, but it was strangely fitting. He was blessed in every single way.

22

H e was still not okay. It was the day after Connor had buried Lucas, and he felt like ants were crawling under his skin. What the fuck did he have to do to feel normal again?

He'd talked. For the first time ever, he had talked. He'd shared memories of Lucas with Noah, but also with Josh and Indy, even with Miles and his boys. Something would happen that would trigger a memory and he'd talk.

How they'd met in boot camp, became friends. His wicked sense of humor, always pulling pranks. How Lucas had struggled with reading, being severely dyslexic, but he'd been so proud to finish high school, then become a Marine. How much he'd loved his mom, who'd raised him as a single parent after his dad had walked out on them when Lucas was still a toddler. She'd died during his first tour, her body surrendering to the cancer she'd been fighting for years.

He shared with Josh how Lucas must have known Connor was gay, but never said a word, and never treated him any differently. He'd been straight, Lucas himself. Not a womanizer by any standard, but definitely straight. And still, Connor had loved him. He hadn't fully realized how much he'd loved him until now.

"I'm sorry for not telling you," he'd told Josh in bed sometime that week. "I didn't mean to keep it from you."

"Oh, baby, there's nothing to say sorry for. You didn't lie to me. You didn't know. Our mind protects us that way, and I understand."

Connor had sighed. "He called me Boston. He was from Connecticut, and he always laughed at my thick accent, so he started calling me Boston. He never went back to Connor."

He'd teared up, remembering the last time Lucas had been dragged off. "You'll be okay, Boston!" he'd shouted out as he'd been hauled off to his death. Not something he could share with Josh. His sweet, nurturing Josh who was doing everything he could to be there for Connor, but who had to be protected from the gruesome details.

So Connor had talked to Noah about the torture, as best as he could. They'd sat outside in the garden, nature in full bloom around them, as Connor recounted what had been done to him, to them. Noah had listened, throwing in an occasional supportive word here and there, but nothing more than that. No advice, no well-meaning clichés, simply presence. Connor had talked more than he had in his entire life, and it had been good. But still, that restlessness wouldn't disappear.

He'd never been more grateful for the family he was now a part of. They had rallied around him, supported him and Josh. Fuck, the way Miles had taken care of Josh together with Indy when Connor and Noah went to Andrews, it had been phenomenal. Josh had needed the pain, and Miles and Indy had stepped in.

Truth be told, Connor had hardly thought about Josh

that day. His mind had been so full with Lucas, it was like he'd had no capacity for anything else. Should he feel guilty about that? Probably.

"It's okay, Connor," Noah had said.

He'd turned his head. "Hmm?"

"It's okay to be selfish right now. You're grieving. Josh understands."

Josh would. The man knew about pain, about coping. He was the strongest man Connor knew, with the exception of Indy. Those two, what they had walked through, it was phenomenal.

"But he's okay. Josh is okay. Miles worked him over good with the paddle. Indy texted pictures, if you want to see them?"

It was funny how Indy and Noah communicated. Josh would text Connor sometimes, but they were either short to-the-point messages relaying some information, or a simple "I love you" in a few variations. Indy and Noah texted entire stories, complete with pictures and whatnot.

Noah dug his phone out, handed it to Connor. He looked at the pics of a sleeping Josh, spread out on his stomach, his face showing the bliss of a post-subspace peace, and smiled. "Hot damn, that's one wicked red ass. Beautiful."

One thing was certain after seeing that picture: he would not be able to fuck Josh, and selfish as it was, he was bummed. He was restless, in the mood to fuck really, really hard. Let off some steam. But there was no way, not with what Josh had endured already. It would have done Josh good, no doubt. He'd been due a session anyway, and with the stress of what had happened, he would have needed a solid level of pain to cope.

And if Indy had fucked him, he would have let Josh come afterward, at least twice, because that's how Indy rolled. The kid was no pushover, but he was way too tender-hearted for a Dom. Even denying Josh an orgasm would feel cruel to him. No, Josh would not be in any mood or condition for sex. He'd be willing to if Connor asked, but it would not be good for him. He handed Noah his phone back, sighed.

"You okay?" Noah asked.

"Yeah." He pondered it for a bit, then decided to level with him. "Was hoping for a hard fuck when I got back, but looking at that pic, that's not gonna happen."

"He would do it, if you asked him."

Connor shook his head. "No. I won't ask him. I will never put him in a position where he'd feel he can't say no."

"You're a good man, O'Connor," Noah said, banging a right onto their driveway. "Honorable."

Maybe, but he was also horny as fuck now. Oh, well. He'd live.

When they walked in, Miles was in the living room with his two boys, watching a movie. Thank fuck they didn't ask any of the obligatory "How did it go" questions.

Connor walked straight into his bedroom, where Josh was sleeping on his stomach, Indy reading a book in bed next to him. Indy got off the bed as he spotted them. He walked out, closed the door softly behind him.

"How is he?" Connor asked.

"He's good," Indy said. But how are you?"

Connor shrugged. He had no fucking idea how to answer that question.

Indy reached out his arms and when Connor hugged him, simply jumped up. He caught him easily—the kid weighed nothing—and held him close. He loved how affectionate Indy was with him now. It was such a dramatic change from the skittish boy who'd been scared of even being touched. Yet every time Indy hugged him like this, the truth of what he'd done to him stabbed Connor through the heart. He still hadn't told him.

Indy rubbed his cheek against Connor's. "I'm so sorry for you, Connor."

"Yeah."

When he put Indy back down, the kid made contact with his massive hard on, which had come back with a vengeance after seeing Josh. "Sorry," Connor mumbled.

"You can't fuck him," Indy said, crossing his arms.

"I know, little firecracker. I know. I saw the pictures. Is he okay now?"

"Miles was awesome. Used only the paddle, but so slowly and so long he had Josh squirming, begging for more. I fucked him twice, then had him suck me off a third time before I allowed him to come."

Huh. Indy had more Dom skills than Connor had given him credit for. "Thank you for taking care of our man," he said, meaning every word. He rearranged his cock, trying to get it to settle down.

Indy beamed. "Always my pleasure. I took a bath with him, then rubbed his ass with that lotion you always use. You know, the aloe one."

Connor nodded. "Good. That'll help."

"I wasn't sure if he needed a cooling pack or not, and he fell asleep before I could ask."

"Nah. Let him be for now. The longer the burn lingers, the longer it'll help him to keep his head clear."

Behind them, the door opened. "Connor," Josh said simply. He'd put on some boxers and walked straight into Connor's arms, hugging him tenderly. "I love you."

No empty words from Josh either. He understood loss.

They all did. Connor kissed Josh's soft lips. "How are you, baby? Did Miles work you over good?"

He put his hand on Josh's ass, slipping under his boxers to gently rub the skin that was searing hot under his hand. Josh winced.

"Fuck, yes. When he started paddling me, I thought he was joking, it was so gentle. But after like fifty strokes or so, my ass was on fire. I lost track after that, completely sank into subspace."

Miles stepped into the hallway, grinning. "I used the water drip method. Small drops seem harmless, but water that drips for a long time will win from a rock. Plus, I blindfolded him, made the room silent, and had him lie facedown on a towel you had used before, Connor. I didn't want him to be reminded who was in the room with him, and risk yanking him out of his zone."

Connor sent him a grateful look. "Thank you."

Josh had gone back to bed almost immediately, Indy staying with him, so Connor had bunked with Noah. He didn't even want to be close to Josh, too scared he'd lose his control. He'd jacked off, furiously, and had willed himself to sleep. And he'd made it up the days after, had sought Josh out again and again in the hopes of getting rid of this restlessness, this itch inside him that wouldn't leave him alone.

Noah had gently told him it was time to let go. Letting go. How did Connor do that? How did you let go of someone who you only now discovered you loved? Lucas had been dead for years, but it felt to Connor like it happened yesterday.

He sighed as he walked into the living room, where Josh and Indy were cuddling on the couch, their limbs entwined, both reading a book. Noah was taking a shower after physical therapy. Miles and his boys were in their bedroom, judging by the sounds, clearly having fun. Connor's cock stirred.

Josh looked up from his book with a soft smile. "Hey, baby."

He was so beautiful. They'd been together for over six months now, but there were times where the sheer sight of Josh took his breath away. "I love you," Connor told him.

"I love you, too," Josh said, his smile widening. It should feel strange, somehow, to express this while Josh was in the arms of his other lover, but it didn't. Indy watched them with a sweet smile on his face.

"Can I steal him from you?" Connor asked.

Both Indy and Josh froze, then shared a look that made Connor feel like an outsider for the first time since the early stages of his relationship with Josh.

"Connor..." Josh started. He untangled himself from Indy, but reached out for Indy's hand. Connor's stomach sank. What the hell was going on? He jammed his hands in his pockets, bracing himself for what was coming. Whatever it was, it couldn't be good.

"I need a break," Josh said, and Connor could swear he felt his heart break. His breath came in painful gasps that sent waves of hurt through him. "It's just too much, baby. I'm hurting."

"Dammit, so am I," Connor snapped.

Josh's eyes widened. "I'm sorry, but I—"

"You're sorry? Fuck you, Josh. I've always been there for you no matter what, and now that I need you, you're rejecting me? I'm drowning, and I fucking need you!"

The words were out of Connor's mouth before he knew it, and Josh reeled back from the impact, tears forming in his eyes. Indy jumped up from the couch in front of Connor, fearless in full attack mode. Connor had to admire the kid's guts to face a man twice his size. "Back the fuck off," Indy bit out.

Connor raised his hands in surrender, just as Noah came running in from the one bedroom on his crutches, wearing only boxers, and Miles from the other bedroom, buck-naked, both no doubt alerted by the yelling.

"What the hell?" Noah asked. "What is going on?"

"Ask Josh," Connor said bitter. "He decided that right now was the perfect time to break up with me."

There was a collective gasp in the room, but then Josh got up from the couch, eyes blazing. "I'm not breaking up with you, you idiot. I'm telling you I need a break from sex with you. I know you're hurting, and I know sex makes you feel better for a bit, but I need a break. My ass hurts, and you're in no condition to do a scene, so I'm saying no."

He wasn't breaking up with Connor. That one thought hit him first, before reality sunk in. "I hurt you?" Connor asked, his voice breaking. "Oh God, Josh, did I hurt you?"

The distance between them right now stabbed his heart. What had he done?

Josh took a step toward him. "You needed me, and it was okay, because I loved being there for you, but now I need a break."

Pain unlike anything else Connor had ever felt wrapped around his heart. He'd hurt the man he loved more than anything else. He took a faltering step backward. "I'm sorry, Josh. I'm so sorry. I'll... Yeah, I understand. I'll leave you alone."

Eyes blinded by tears, he walked out of the room, through the kitchen into the garden. He held it together until he was away from all of them, until no one could witness his shame.

"WHAT THE FUCK JUST HAPPENED?" Noah asked, dragging a hand through his hair.

Josh let out a shuddering sigh. "I think I fucked up. He thought I was breaking up with him. God, Noah, he looked like I shot him straight through the heart... What the hell did I do? I'll go talk to him."

Noah held him back. "Let me do it. He's in so much pain right now, and he's lashing out. Sound familiar?"

"No." Indy squared his shoulders. "I'll do it. I'll talk to him. I made it worse just now by reacting too aggressively. I'll fix this."

Josh hesitated for a second, then surrendered and kissed the top of Indy's head. "Thank you."

Indy found him in the garden, sitting by himself in a chair all the way in the back. Connor's shoulders were shaking. He was crying. This big, proud man was crying. Indy's heart filled with empathy. He grabbed a chair and made his way over.

Connor looked up when he heard Indy approach, his eyes red and his face blotchy. "Is Josh okay? I'm so sorry, Indy... Is he okay?"

Indy sat down across from him. "He's good, Connor. Are you?"

Connor leaned back in his chair, wiping the tears from his eyes. For a long time he sat, and Indy watched. Waited.

"How did you do it?" Connor finally asked. "How did you let go of what happened to you?"

His blue eyes met Indy's, so full of pain that Indy's heart clenched. God, this man was suffering. He had to try and help him.

"When my mother handed me over to Duncan, I was...

cautiously optimistic. He was powerful, he was hot, and I was gay, so I figured it couldn't be all that bad. Turns out, I was wrong. Boy, was I wrong. It was bad, and it got worse through the years as he started using more and became aggressive and unpredictable. I went through stages. I was livid for a while, but it didn't get me anything, except a couple of beatings. Then I tried numb, but there's only so long that works. So finally, I decided I had to accept this was the reality—for now. But I started plotting and planning, determined to get away. Well, you know how that turned out. When I was on the run, the thing I struggled most with wasn't what had been done to me. That was so heinous, that I was okay with being livid about it. It was my own role in it all that I wrestled with the most. The crimes I knew about but didn't prevent or report. The people who got hurt with me standing by. That's what I had to learn to forgive myself for. It's not what's been done to us by others that kills us on the inside, Connor. It's what we do to ourselves."

Connor's face had paled as Indy spoke until he was white as a ghost.

"Indy..."

It sounded like a plea, a broken cry from a suffering man. Connor let himself fall forward on his knees, kneeling in front of Indy.

"Oh God, Indy..."

Indy reached out and put his hand on Connor's head. "What did you do to yourself, Connor? What's tormenting you?"

A sob escaped from Connor's lips before he pulled himself together. "I knew," he managed, his voice hoarse and broken. "I heard rumors about you, about Duncan acquiring a young boy for himself. A teen. I knew, Indy...and I did nothing."

Indy's heart contracted painfully, but not because of what Connor was saying. He had suspected Connor had heard at least rumors, considering Duncan had been his cousin. It was the unimaginable pain on Connor's face, the depth of the remorse and regret in his eyes. It was the rejection he was counting on that showed in his hunched shoulders, his dejected posture. This was a man expecting to be broken.

"I could have stopped it all, could have prevented so much suffering for you, if only I had...if only I had been strong and courageous enough to say something, to do something. I failed you, Indy. I caused you so much pain and suffering."

Indy put his finger under Connor's chin to lift his head. "No, you didn't. You did not cause any of it, Connor. That's all on Duncan and his men, not you."

"But if I had—"

"It wouldn't have made a difference. Even if you'd gone to the cops, had reported it, do you really think it would have made a lick of difference? Duncan woulda denied it, my mother would've sworn up and down nothing was going on, and I sure as fuck didn't have the balls back then to speak up against Duncan. I was too scared of what he'd do to me—and we both know what he woulda done to you, to me, to anyone coming out against him. He would've killed you, Connor, and your parents with you. I did stand up against him, and he did almost manage to kill me, remember?"

Connor stared at him as if he couldn't believe what he was seeing. His mouth opened and closed a few times before he finally spoke. "You're not angry with me?"

Indy bent over and kissed his head. "No. I never was. It

was never on your conscience, only on Duncan's, on that of his men. They did this, not you."

"I thought for sure you would never even look at me again if you knew... I was so afraid of losing you all, of losing Josh."

Indy shook his head. "Don't you realize how much Josh loves you? You could never lose him."

"You forgive me?"

The incredulity was thick, and Indy had to take it away. "I forgave you the day Josh fell in love with you. His happiness trumps everything else, and he loves you so much...and you love him. You're so good for him. But Connor, even if I had been upset, don't you realize you redeemed yourself?" Indy cupped Connor's cheeks, making sure the man listened. "Connor, you set me free. That was you and Josh, and I'll never, ever be able to express my thanks for that."

"It was all Josh," Connor whispered. "God, you should've seen it, Indy. I was right there in the room when he shot them, and he took them out in seconds. It was phenomenal. I wasn't even scared, because I knew he wasn't gonna miss."

"Oh, Connor, that was you as much as him. Don't you see? Josh could not have done it had you not believed in him this much. It was your faith in him, in his skills and abilities, that gave him wings."

A hint of a smile broke through on Connor's face and Indy let his hands fall. "You're a sneaky one," Connor said. "I told you we were never gonna speak about it again, and yet you got me to admit a hell of a lot more than I had ever planned on."

Indy shrugged, smiling back. "Deal with it."

Connor unfolded his legs to sit cross-legged on the grass. "How do I do that, Indy? How do I deal with this?"

"What you and I have been through, it's not the same.

You lost someone you loved in a very traumatic way. Correct me if I'm wrong, Connor, but I don't think you're struggling with what happened to you. I think you're struggling with what happened to Lucas."

The itch under his skin broke free. "I was so helpless... Every day they would come for us, and every day I knew there was a real chance he was not coming back. I was never scared for me, always for him."

"I know. This is what Josh feels, too, don't you realize? His biggest trauma isn't what happened to him. It's what happened to Noah, while he was watching."

Connor swallowed visibly and Indy saw understanding dawning in his eyes. "Do I talk about this with him? I'm so scared of triggering him, of making his symptoms worse."

Indy 's eyes filled with tears all over again. The fact that he and Connor could share their love for Josh, could take care of him together, it was...everything. "I don't know, honestly. You could ask Noah, or Josh's therapist. But let him see this. It will help him see he is lovable despite his trauma, you know? And maybe you could take the step of going into counseling yourself. I know it's something I need to do... I'm just trying to find the courage."

Connor looked at Indy with love. "You are wise beyond your years, you know that? It was hard for me at first, to accept that you and Noah were such a huge part of Josh's life. But the more I got to know you, the easier that became. Now, I consider myself lucky to have the two of you in my life. You keep saying how much Josh loves me and I him, and it's true, but he loves you just as much and you love him. I vow to never be your competitor, Indy. I will never keep him from you, or you from him. I want us to love him together."

He rose and extended a hand to Indy, who let himself be pulled into Connor's big arms. "I promise the same, Boston."

Connor pushed him back to meet his eyes. "Boston?"

"If you're okay with it, I'd like to start calling you Boston. I think it's a fitting tribute to Lucas, and also to the wicked special relationship you and I have, sharing not just a background, but Josh."

Connor's eyes filled up all over again. "I'd love that. Thank you."

23

B rad thought he'd been very patient. Sure, he'd acted out when Connor had gotten that call because he knew it meant he wasn't gonna get his reward, and that had been selfish. He'd realized it after, especially once he'd seen how devastated Connor had been.

So he'd been a good boy the rest of that day. Josh had needed Miles, and Brad had been happy to do his part. He hadn't complained once, had obeyed every order Miles had given him.

Hell, he'd been good the whole week after. He'd taken care of Miles every chance he got, had made sure the man was as satisfied as he could be, realistically speaking. He'd let both Miles and Charlie fuck him whenever they wanted to. Not that that was a hardship, fuck no. He loved it when they used him, appreciated the sensation of a slightly tender ass when he went to work in the mornings.

Miles only had to spank him twice, and both were debatable offenses in Brad's mind. Really, Miles could be a tad sensitive to any suggestion of disrespect. But since the spankings weren't entirely unpleasant—though Brad still hadn't made up his mind whether he looked forward to them or feared them—he'd taken them without complaint.

He'd helped Josh out a few times with laundry, knowing he was struggling to take care of Connor. Brad had seen the laundry baskets overflowing and had quietly stepped in, making sure there were enough clean sheets and towels.

He'd also done some grocery shopping for Indy when he'd been short on supplies and had been too busy making sure everyone was okay to go to the store. Brad had stopped by the store on his way home and had worked down the entire list that had been on the refrigerator in the kitchen.

Miles hadn't commented on Brad's efforts to contribute to their...household? He wasn't sure what to call it, but he was determined to not be a bother any more than he'd already been. He felt like he was teetering on the edge of a cliff already, that any second now, they'd all grow tired of him.

But now it was Friday evening, and Brad was exhausted. The end of the school year was always stressful and this year was no different. God, he'd love nothing more than another one of those daddy-days, where Miles took care of him and his mind could find total peace. Even the idea made his eyes grow a little misty, but he knew it wasn't gonna happen. Miles didn't have time for that anymore. Or energy. Or maybe the will.

Brad parked his car in the broad driveway, making sure not to block anyone else. It could get busy with so many cars. Well, it was only temporary, right? They never had the discussion Miles had promised about the future, so Brad had no idea what would happen. And as time had passed, he'd started wondering if maybe Miles had changed his mind about being with Brad, about being his daddy. He sure hadn't had much time for Brad this week.

Brad sighed as he walked in the door, his shoulders low. The living room was empty, but he heard voices in the kitchen. He dumped his backpack near the front door, then picked it up again to put it in their room. Miles was being a total hypocrite about that, of course, considering he was a first-class slob, but Brad was not risking Miles getting upset with him. He already felt like it was slipping through his fingers, so he was doing everything he could to hold on to it.

He kicked off his shoes, then neatly put them in the closet. Miles had forgotten to hang up his towels, of course, so after taking a piss, Brad quickly tidied up the bathroom. Before he left, he made the bed, then checked to make sure the room looked in order.

When he walked into the kitchen, everyone was sitting at the big kitchen table, and for some reason he felt like an outsider. Josh was on Connor's lap and Charlie was cuddling with Miles, and Noah and Indy were laughing, and Brad felt so damn alone he could cry. He was never gonna fit in here or anywhere else.

"Hi, sweetheart," Miles said when he spotted him.

Brad looked at him, this beautiful man who had so much patience with him. He wanted nothing more than to crawl on his lap, into his arms, to seek protection and shelter. But he couldn't, could he? Because Miles was growing tired of him being needy all the time. Miles preferred sweet and sassy Charlie, who didn't have all these issues. Gorgeous Charlie who took Brad's breath away every time he looked at him, and who'd stolen his heart so many years ago.

He watched them, these two men he loved so much and who would be so perfectly happy if it wasn't for him and his stupid fuck-ups. He hadn't realized he'd taken a step back until the kitchen fell quiet, and concern replaced the warmth on Miles' face. He took another step back, every breath painful. He couldn't do this, couldn't bear to wait for that ax to fall.

He turned around, but before he could move again, Miles' voice rung out. "Brad, no!"

There was enough authority in it that Brad listened. He slowly turned back around. Miles gently pushed Charlie off his lap and walked toward Brad. "Why are you walking away, sweetheart?"

"You know why," Brad managed, his eyes trained on the floor. "I'll never be good enough."

He heard Charlie gasp. "Good enough for what?" Miles asked in a slightly unsteady voice.

Brad raised his eyes. "I tried so hard this week to be good. I was there for you and Charlie, and I did laundry for Josh, and helped Indy with grocery shopping, and I made sure our room was tidy and the bed was made, and I fucking listened to every command you gave me...and it was still not enough!"

Shock filled Miles' eyes. "You...what? Brad, I have no idea—"

"No, you don't. You promised me you would take care of me, but I know you're already tired of me, so why don't you just come out and say it?"

Miles reeled back as if Brad had hit him. "How could you... Brad, sweetheart, I'm not tired of you. How could you even think that?"

"You're blaming me now for thinking that?" Brad scoffed. "Then where were you? Where were you when I did everything you asked, everything that was needed, everything that I could think of..." His voice broke. "To make you love me and keep me, and you didn't even see it... You didn't see me."

He no longer tried to hold back the tears that were determined to fall. "None of you did. Connor was grieving and Josh was taking care of him, while Indy was making sure Josh was alright, and Noah tried to be there for all three of them. And Charlie was busy preparing for his first performance back at Flirt, and you Miles, you could barely be bothered to make sure I stuck to the rules you gave me. You only spanked me twice, and you promised me a reward and never gave it to me."

He wiped away his tears impatiently. "So I get it, okay? I get that I'm too much, more than you signed up for."

"Oh God, Brad..." Miles sounded so broken that Brad felt sorry for the man for a second. "I fucked up, didn't I?"

Brad jammed his hands into the pockets of his jeans and shrugged, unsure of what to say. Was there even anything left to say?

"I had a lot going on this week, trying to put some things into motion for us, and I had planned on telling you both tonight, but I fucked up. You're right, Brad. I didn't give you the attention you deserved and needed this week. I got distracted, and I'm so sorry... I didn't see that you were making yourself invisible again and I should have."

"We all missed it," Indy spoke up. "I thought Noah had picked up the groceries."

"And I figured Indy had done laundry," Josh said.

"And I honestly thought Josh had been a sweetheart and had made the bed and cleaned our bathroom," Charlie said in a timid voice. "I'm so sorry, baby. I feel awful."

"We all do," Indy said.

"But sweetheart, it wasn't because you're too much, or because I'm tired of you. You were a good boy this week, but I failed you. I'm so sorry."

The regret on Miles' face was real, even Brad could see

that. His heart was a little lighter. "I hate feeling like I'm invisible," he whispered.

"I know, sweetheart. I feel awful. It's my fault, though, not yours. I love you, Brad. You're not too much or too needy. Will you please forgive me?"

Brad was in his arms before he'd even finished the words, and he exhaled shakily as Miles' strong arms enveloped him. "I love you, sweetheart," Miles whispered into his curls. "I love you so much, and I'm so damn sorry."

Then Charlie stepped into their embrace and hugged Brad as well. "I love you," he said in a tearful voice. "And I'm sorry for being selfish this week."

They stood until Brad felt the darkness pull away inside of him. "Daddy," he said softly, gathering courage to voice his request. "Do you think you could maybe spank me every morning when we get up? Just a quick spank so I know that you see me?"

Miles pushed back slightly so he could see Brad's face. "I'd love that, sweetheart. Thank you for asking me. I'm so proud of you."

Brad gave him a careful smile. "What did you want to tell us?"

Miles gave him a quick kiss, then did the same to Charlie. "Guys, I need five minutes with my boys, and we'll be right back, okay?" he told the others.

"Five minutes my ass," Noah mumbled, amusement lacing his voice.

"Well, Miles is an easy target," Indy remarked dryly.

The jokes were still passing around as Miles led them into the bedroom and closed the door behind them.

"Are we truly okay?" he asked, looking at both of them.

Charlie's bottom lip trembled. "I feel so bad for Brad."

"It's okay," Brad muttered.

"No, it's not okay. We did you wrong, and that is not okay, sweetheart. And Charlie and I should feel bad for a bit, because we love you and we accidentally hurt you. But we promise to do better, right, honey?"

Charlie nodded, and Brad couldn't help but hug him. "I love you," he told Charlie, kissing him everywhere. "I forgive you."

He didn't stop until Charlie found his mouth and gave him one of those toe-curling kisses that made Brad's insides go gooey.

'I love watching you two," Miles sighed. "Brad, you were right. We promised you a reward and we never followed up on that. I blame myself for not realizing you would interpret that as us rejecting you, or you not being good enough to get the reward. Tomorrow, Charlie has his show at Flirt, but Sunday we will spend in bed, the three of us, and we'll do whatever you want, Brad. I promise."

Brad's face lit up. "Really?"

"I can't wait," Charlie said, grabbing Brad's hand first, then Miles. "I wanna share this with you."

"Oh, same here," Miles sighed. "The thought alone makes me so damn hard. Not that I needed any help in that department anyway."

Brad beamed, unable to find words.

"But Brad, you also deserve a little reward right now, for speaking up and telling us how you felt. So pick one thing you wanna do in the next, say, three minutes. How can we make you feel good right now?"

He didn't even need to think. "I want you to spank me while I suck you off. Please, Daddy, I need to feel you."

Miles' smile was broad as he unbuckled and slid his jeans and underwear down in one motion. Brad yanked down his pants so fast the button went flying, but he didn't care. He was on Miles' lap as soon as he'd positioned himself on the bed.

When that first slap came, he exhaled. Fuck, he needed this. It centered him, grounded him, somehow. He nuzzled Miles' cock, his balls, breathed in deeply the scent that had become so familiar. He felt the stress leaving him as he gave a few tentative licks, then sucked that gorgeous cock right in.

Miles let out one of his low groans, telling Brad he wouldn't need to do much to make his daddy come. They only had a few minutes anyway, so that was perfect. As Miles slapped, Brad sucked in perfect tandem rhythm, until Miles tensed and came with a soft moan. Brad swallowed his load, humming happily, his mind so much more peaceful now that he'd been reminded he was not alone.

Miles lifted him up to cuddle. "Was that good for you, sweetheart?"

Brad nodded. Charlie joined them, holding Brad as well, and the last bit of frustration left him. "Thank you," he said quietly. "I needed that."

"Good. Now, let's go 'cause the others are waiting, and we have some exciting news we want to share with you."

Miles didn't give Brad's nerves the opportunity to reappear, because as soon as they entered the kitchen, he pulled Brad on the chair right next to him and held his hand, Charlie on Brad's other side.

Indy sent him a soft smile. "Listen, we wanted to talk to you guys about something. Noah and Connor already discussed it with Miles, and at first he wanted to ask you in private, but we thought it might be better if it came from all of us."

Miles squeezed Brad's hand, a reminder for him to take a breath. Where was this going?

"The four of us, we wanted to ask you three to move in with us. Permanently. Or at least, for the foreseeable future."

Wait, what? Brad's head shot up.

"We want to add a wing to the house where you could build a spacious bedroom and bathroom for the three of you. You'd have your own private entrance and exit, but the kitchen and living room would be common areas. We'd also add a little to the current in-law suite, the one where you guys are staying now. That would be our room, for the four of us. We want to add a few feet to the bedroom so we can have a bed custom made for us, and we want to create a second en-suite room, which would be a play room."

"By playroom we mean a sex room, basically," Josh explained. "Connor and I will be using this a lot, obviously, but it would also be available to you. We're looking to put some benches there, a whipping cross, a flogging wall, and some other really cool stuff, but also a lot of toys."

How a guy that looked so cute and sweet could talk about hardcore shit like that without breaking a sweat was a mystery to Brad. The whipping and flogging sounded scary and not at all like something he wanted to explore, but some of the other stuff they could maybe try out together? He bit his lip. What did Indy mean exactly with moving in?

"You're gonna share a room with the four of you?" Charlie asked.

Indy and Josh shared another one of those looks. "Yeah," Indy said. "Noah and I are together, but I'm also with Josh, and he's with Connor. We've talked about it, and we all agree we want to share one room. Josh and I, we really like sleeping in the same bed, and both of our guys got tired of waking up alone."

"But Noah and Connor are not, like, together?" Brad

couldn't blame Charlie for asking. He wasn't sure exactly of where the boundaries were either, if there even were any.

"No. But they're completely okay with this," Josh said. "Plus, Connor is an exhibitionist who likes to watch and show off, and Noah simply doesn't care either way, so it meshes really well."

Brad's head dazzled. It made sense what Josh and Indy were saying, but why would they need the three of them? He cleared his throat. "No offense, but what would you need us for?"

Josh smiled. "First of all, we really like you. All three of you. You fit in really well with us, and that's not easy. We know we're freaks in many aspects, but you guys don't seem to mind."

"Hell, they're as bad as us," Indy snorted.

"True," Miles spoke up for the first time. He was watching Brad and Charlie, gauging their reaction it seemed. "There are also some practical reasons, to be fair. Financially, the four of them are in a bit of a limbo since Noah went back to school, and Connor quit his job," Miles explained. "Indy is still figuring out where to go next, and Josh prefers to mostly stay home, aside from his part time job as a shooting instructor. Adding the three of us to the mix would help financially. Brad, you have a stable income, and Charlie, if your application is accepted, as I'm sure it will be, you'll have income as well. Splitting all costs between the seven of us will lessen the burdens for all of us. I have enough money put away to last me a while and to contribute the remodeling and renovation costs."

"I can contribute as well," Brad jumped in. "I saved up since I started working, so I've got a nest egg."

Miles' eyes softened and his lips curved in one of those

smiles that made Brad's insides dance. "Thank you, Brad. I really appreciate you saying that."

Brad's insides burned with want. To live with these people, to be a part of their circle, it was more than he could have ever dreamed of.

"What about my behavior?" he dared ask. "Will you kick me out if I misbehave?"

Josh's "No" mixed with Indy's "Never".

Indy pushed his chair back. He got up and kneeled in front of Brad. "I need you to listen to me. You were dealt a shitty hand in life, much like I was. We didn't ask for the shit that happened to us, but it did. I know you feel damaged and unworthy, because so did I. I still do at times. But Brad, you are worthy to be loved. You're a good man, a kind man. You're broken and damaged, but it will heal, I promise you. We will love you and have patience with you, even if you act out or misbehave. We will never, ever reject you, let alone kick you out. If you guys move in, you're part of our family, and families stick together no matter what."

He bit his lip. "What if I regress again, like a while back, or get all emotional and needy like today?"

Indy smiled reassuringly. "Then Daddy Miles will be there for you. And if you're being a little brat when he's not there, Daddy Noah and Daddy Connor will set you straight. We've got your back, okay?"

"Personally, I think that whole daddy-shit is hot as fuck," Josh remarked. "And I love watching Miles spank your ass, even though I was jealous as fuck."

Brad couldn't help it. He laughed. "You're all bat-shit crazy!"

"Right back atcha, dude," Indy said, taking his seat again.

"How do you feel about this, Charlie?" Miles asked.

Charlie looked around the kitchen, then pointed toward the living room. "If we find a different spot for that mini office you have there, we could put in a second big couch. One with washable covers."

Brad snorted.

"We also need a second cooking range," Josh said. "And another washer and dryer. With the amount of bed linens we use every day, I can't keep up if it's just one."

"I can bring mine," Brad said. "My duplex is a rental, but the washer and dryer are mine and they're brand new. High efficiency or some shit."

"That would work," Josh said.

"One thing I insist on is that Brad doesn't do any household work. Nothing. No cooking, no cleaning, no laundry. If we were to make a cleaning roster or something, I'll take his shifts." Miles' voice was firm.

Brad flew out of his chair, attacked Miles with a hug. Words wouldn't come, but Miles hugged him so tight Brad knew he understood. "I promised I'd take care of you, and I will, sweetheart. I will not allow you to become invisible ever again."

He sat on Miles' lap, put his head against his shoulder. "Thank you, Daddy."

"I don't mind cleaning and laundry," Josh said. "Indy loves to help with cooking."

"I can cook as well," Charlie offered. "And I love shopping, even if it's for groceries, as long as I don't have to carry all that shit inside. This body was not built to haul cargo."

They went back and forth with ideas, plans, practical details until Brad's head was dizzy. He couldn't believe this proposal. They wanted them to move in. They wanted him. Noah and Connor, too. Even with all his hang ups, fucked-up as he was, they still wanted him. Indy had said Noah and

Connor were even willing to be his daddies, too, if he needed them.

Fuck, the idea of Connor spanking him with those big, meaty hands excited and terrified him in equal measures. That would hurt for certain, but maybe also in a good way? Hmm, maybe he should experiment more with that Dom/sub shit.

"Are you still with us, Brad?" Charlie asked, yanking him out of his thoughts. He was still on Miles' lap, resting against his broad chest.

"Are we really doing this?" he asked softly.

"Do you want to move in here, sweetheart? You don't need to decide now. It's a big step."

"I know. What do you think, Charlie?"

Charlie got up, lowered himself on Miles' other knee, so that Miles had his arms around them both. Brad sighed with happiness at having both his men so close. "I would love it," Charlie said. "You know I'm a people person, so I love the idea of sharing a house with so many people. But Brad, honey, if this is too much for you, I'd be just as happy somewhere else with the three of us."

Brad smiled, leaned over to give Charlie a quick kiss.

"What about you, Miles?" Charlie asked.

"I'd love it. It's been surreal these last few weeks, being around people who accept me without judgment. I don't think I realized how lonely and touch-starved I was until I came here. But as Charlie said, Brad, if you're not comfortable with this, we'll find a place for the three of us."

Brad swallowed, looking down at the floor. He had to ask. Had to know for certain. "If I said no, you wouldn't move in here with just Charlie?"

Miles lifted his chin up with one finger, forced him to make eye contact. "No, sweetheart. I'm so proud of you for asking, though, instead of assuming and working yourself up over it. We're a family, the three of us. Families make decisions together, so if this is not what you want, we'll find something else. But we're together, the three of us."

Tension he hadn't even realized had been in his body seeped out. "I love you," Brad said quietly, the words finally coming out to Miles as well. "I love you both so much."

"Oh, Brad," Miles sighed, "You have no idea how happy those words make me. I've been waiting forever to hear them. I love you, sweetheart."

They shared a sloppy three-way kiss, as the others in the kitchen watched with sweet smiles.

"I really, really want to move in," Brad said, his heart suddenly ten times lighter. "But Josh, do you think we could maybe create a small room for you and me? We're the only introverts here, and sometimes I just need to be alone, where it's quiet. My head gets too messy when I don't have that."

Miles let out a soft gasp. "Is that why you've been acting out sometimes? Because you needed time alone?"

Brad shrugged. "Maybe. I dunno. I've lived alone for years, so alone time was all I knew. Since I started coming here, I haven't had much opportunity to be by myself. I didn't realize it until we were talking about this."

Indy and Josh looked at each other. "What if we built a little garden shed? I mean, insulated and with heating and cooling and all, but a quiet place away from the house?" Indy slowly said. "It would just be for Brad and Josh, and everyone else who'd want to use it would have to ask their permission."

Brad's mouth dropped open. "You'd do that for me? For us, I mean?"

"Brad, baby, we'd do it if it were just for you. We want you here. We want this to work, for you to be happy."

They really, really wanted him. He belonged here. He had a family. For the first time in his life, he had a family who loved him and wanted him, who had chosen him. They saw him, all of him, and they still wanted him to stay.

"Daddy, I wanna stay here and never leave. Can we please stay?"

Amidst happy exclamations from the others, Brad only heard one thing: his daddy's sweet, strong voice. "Yes, boy, we can."

24

Blake was honestly happy that Charlie was up to performing again, but he'd be lying if he said he was looking forward to spending the night at Flirt. He'd go, obviously, since Charlie needed all their support. It had taken him time to find the courage to perform again, after what Zack had done to him. For a while, Blake had feared Charlie would develop agoraphobia, but luckily, he'd slowly started going outside again after he's formally pressed charges against Zack.

Blake's main reason why he was tense about the night was that he feared seeing Brad again. They hadn't talked since that emotional confrontation in Brad's house. Fuck, Blake was still reeling from the blow Brad had dealt him. He'd never known Brad had wanted to go with Benjamin, that he had deeply desired to be adopted as well. In hindsight, it made total sense, and it only reinforced Blake's deep sense of failing him.

Aaron put his head on Blake's shoulder. "Are you okay?"

Blake's eyes warmed as he took in Aaron's appearance. He was wearing the flowery top they'd picked out at Macy's, with the ridiculously tight and low riding jeans. His puppy had bedazzled—his words—a pair of white Chuck Taylors with pink pompoms, glitter, and whatnot, and he looked absolutely edible. His sparkling pink eyeshadow matched his outfit, as did the shiny stuff he'd put on his lips.

He turned toward Aaron, kissed him softly on his lips. "Every time I look at you, you take my breath away, puppy," he said. He had to raise his voice to rise above the thumping beats drifting up from the dance floor below them. The thin plexiglass separation filtered some noise, but the music was still loud.

Aaron's face lit up like a lightbulb in a dark room. "I feel pretty."

"You're gorgeous," Blake assured him.

"I agree," Indy said, joining them with Noah, who looked positively out of his element. "Those jeans are absolutely indecent, and I fucking love them."

Noah shot him a dark look. "If you ever show up wearing one of those, I'll hand you over to Connor for a solid spanking," he threatened.

Indy merely laughed. "Don't mind him," he told Aaron, who beamed after Indy's praise. "He gets jealous in places like this."

"And with good reason. I left you alone for one minute, and you had three guys on your ass, "Noah grumbled.

Indy raised a finger, his eyes narrowing. "Who I told to fuck off, didn't I? Chill the fuck out, Noah. We're here to have fun."

Blake suppressed a chuckle. Fuck, he loved that kid. He literally didn't take shit from anyone, including his own boyfriend. He still had to get used to his short hair, though. It was such a different look than the long, feminine curls he'd had before.

"You dance, Aaron?" Indy turned back to Aaron.

Aaron nodded eagerly. "I love it."

"Good. Let's leave Grumpy and Moody here to stew, while you and me have some fun on the dance floor. Josh should be here any minute as well, and I'm sure he'll join us, too."

Blake watched with amusement as Indy took Aaron's hand and dragged him downstairs to the dance floor. "I can't believe how far he's come," he said to Noah. "A few months ago, he couldn't bear to be touched and look at him now."

Noah's face broke open in a proud smile. "It's a fucking miracle. Can't claim credit, though. It's all him, and a bit of group effort from all of us."

They watched as Aaron and Indy found a relatively empty spot on the dance floor, started swaying and dipping their bodies to the beat.

"I could say the same for Aaron," Noah said.

"Hmm. True. He's still got a ways to go, but he's more stable now."

"The puppy thing, is it working for him?"

There was no judgment in Noah's voice, nor any trace of sensationalism. He was truly curious, Blake noted. "Yeah. It took me a while to realize that was what he needed, but it does wonders for him. There are days where he functions normal, so to speak, but other days he's selfishly needy, and needs my constant attention and care. I've done a bit of research, and there are way more extreme versions of puppy play, but this works for us." He smiled, remembering the hour they spent together earlier that day. "I did build him a little portable play pen, though, and he loved it. We spend an hour every now and then playing there, and it's exactly what he needs."

"That's good." Noah gave him a careful look. "You know about Brad and Miles?"

Blake sighed. "Yeah. Charlie gave me a heads up. It's hard for me to think about my little brother that way, but I understand why he needs it."

"Miles is a good man, Blake, I swear. We've gotten to know him pretty well these last few weeks, and he's solid."

Blake considered taking a cheap shot at the man's insatiable dick, but let it slide. Too cheap. "Is...is it working, you think?"

"For Brad, you mean? I think so. Miles is keeping him on a pretty tight leash. He spanks the shit out of him, but Brad takes it well. He needs it, man, there's no denying it. The way he mouths off to Miles, it's like watching a teenager rebel against his dad. A week or two ago he had a bit of an off day, I guess, and he regressed. Miles fed him, bathed him, took him to the movies, made him take a nap, the whole nine yards. It was phenomenal to watch his patience with Brad. I respect the shit out of him, honestly."

"That's good. Well, it fits right in with the whole kinky thing you guys had going anyway, right?"

Noah grinned. "You heard about that, too, huh?"

"Indy and Josh? Yeah. I suspected it before, to be honest. I never could figure out what the four of you were to each other. Close, that much was obvious. You and Connor fuck-buddies, too?"

Noah laughed. "Fuck, no."

A meaty hand slapped his shoulder with considerable force, and Blake jumped up. "Flint here is not man enough to take my cock," Connor said, his eyes sparkling.

Blake let his eyes drop to the man's groin. "I heard rumors."

"Trust me. They're all true...and then some," Noah said. "That monster isn't gonna get nowhere near my ass."

It was clear Noah and Connor both enjoyed this alpha posturing they had going.

"I take it this is where us men hang out while the boys play downstairs?" Miles joined them.

Blake turned his head to watch the dance floor. Josh and Brad had arrived, joining Indy and Aaron, exchanging hugs all around. It was telling that Brad was considered one of the boys, though he was only two years younger than Miles, and older than Noah and Josh.

"Charlie is in his dressing room getting ready," Miles said. "I can't wait to see him."

They all focused on watching their boys.

"Aaron looks stunning," Miles said.

Huh, interesting. Blake hadn't expected the FBI agent to appreciate more feminine types, let alone a bit of cross dressing. He gave himself a mental slap. Duh. The man was involved with Charlie. Of course he wouldn't have an issue with Aaron being feminine.

"He does, doesn't he? I love that top on him," Blake said with pride.

"You're not the only one," Noah remarked, pointing to two lumberjack-type guys who were closing in on Aaron. Blake's heart rate sped up. He'd better make it downstairs fast.

"Wait," Noah said, grabbing his arm. "Indy's got this."

Blake should have known that the smallest of the four boys on the dance floor was also the fiercest, and the most protective. Indy had stepped in front of Aaron, Brad flanking him, and his body language made clear he was telling the two men to take a hike.

One of them reached out to Indy with his hand, and

Blake laughed. The idiot had no idea who he was messing with. Indy's hand shot out, grabbed the man's hand and twisted it. His heart warmed when he saw Brad take up a defensive position as well. He only had a yellow belt, but he was ready to defend his friends. Even Josh stood half in front of his brother, a hand on his shoulder.

The guy said something to Indy, his face half distorted in pain. Holy fuck, Indy stepped even closer to him, clearly laying down the law. He let go of the guy, and the two slinked off, their figurative tail between their legs.

Aaron was shaken up. Should he go down? Blake was still debating with himself, as Brad and Indy hugged him, then pointed upstairs to where Blake and the others were standing. Blake raised his hand, then jerked his chin to signal if Aaron was okay. His puppy squared his shoulders, nodded. They resumed dancing, Aaron hesitantly at first, then with more confidence. People around them had witnessed the exchange, and some admiring and respectful glances were sent in Indy's direction.

"That's my boy," Noah said with unmistakable pride.

Connor slapped his shoulder. "Damn right. Little firecracker could beat them all up if he wanted to."

Blake sighed with relief. "Aaron, he's vulnerable," he said. "Men pick up on it easily. I don't know what to do about it."

"Nothing." Miles' eyes were kind. "It's who he is. You can't change that without robbing him of that innocence he has."

"He was a virgin when I met him," Blake said, surprising himself with revealing that to these men. "In more ways than one."

"It's precious, that kind of naiveté. Rare, too," Noah agreed.

"Hmm." Aaron was now dancing with Brad, their bodies plastered together. He was dipping and swaying, those hips gyrating in a highly suggestive manner, the top of his crack showing every time his top twirled. He had no idea how sexy he was, how many eyes were fixated on him.

"He's safe with those boys," Connor said. "Indy is protective, and Brad, he'd never interpret it the wrong way. Besides, I'm surprised he can still walk after the way Miles and Charlie worked him over this afternoon."

Blake's face crunched. "Fuck off, O'Connor, that's my little brother."

Connor grinned. "Sorry, forgot for a second."

He couldn't think about his brother having sex too much without being weirded out, but truth be told he was grateful Brad had found a way to satisfy his needs. Fuck knew he'd been living dangerously, letting strangers fuck him left and right. This way, at least he was with men who respected him, cared for him. And the match between his insatiable brother and the man who had a sexual appetite that rivaled his was perfect. The fact that Miles could apparently fulfill the daddy-role Brad craved as well made it even better.

"I love him."

He looked up at Miles' quiet words.

"Brad. I'm in love with him. Thought you should know, since he's your little brother."

Blake blinked slowly, cleared his throat. "That's good. Does he...does he love you, too?"

"Yes, he does."

The man's quiet confidence left little room for doubt. "And Charlie?"

"It's complicated, but we're together, the three of us. Actually, we're moving in with these guys here permanently." Miles shared the plans for renovating the ranch to fit all of their needs. Blake couldn't help but smile. It was crazy in a sense, but it fit them all to a T. And fuck, he was happy for Brad.

"I...Thank you. For telling me, but especially for taking care of my brother. I love him, you know, and it's... As I said, I fucked up terribly with him, and I want the best for him. I'm grateful you're taking care of him."

Miles' face lit up with so much love, any remaining doubt about the man's feelings dissipated. "It's no hardship, Blake. He's special, your brother. And he's getting what he's always wanted, a family."

Blake's eyes grew misty. "Yeah. That's... that's good. Do you think that he'll forgive me?"

Miles' hand clamped down on his shoulder. "He already has. He misses you, but he's scared to reconnect because he thinks you're angry with him. Come by the house sometime this week. He'd love that. Just not tomorrow. We've got... something planned."

Blake didn't ask, pretty sure he really didn't want to know. "Thank you. I will. I miss him." He got distracted by the music dimming. "It's Charlie's time," he said. "We need to go downstairs."

By the time they made it downstairs, everyone else had, too. It took them a few minutes to reunite with the boys. Blake breathed easier once he had Aaron in his arms. He was sweaty, happy, and handsy, apparently craving Blake's touch. Blake smiled, held him close, petting his head and neck. "Settle down, puppy. I'm right here."

Aaron pressed up against him, seeking his mouth. The kiss was anything but short and sweet, and it resulted in a few whistles from people around them. Blake couldn't care less. It was all in good form, and he'd witnessed far, far worse here.

The lights dimmed. Blake had seen Charlie perform a few times, and every time was a treat. The kid was a talented performer. He turned Aaron with his back against him, pulled him close.

"Good evening Flirt! A special welcome to all twinks! Lumberjacks! Daddies! Power bottoms! Hipsters!"

Blake smiled at the familiar roll call, groups of people responding by echoing the label they identified with. It was a long list, but it never failed to get a great response.

"Soldiers!"

"Hooah!" Josh and Noah responded loudly, aided by a few others.

"Marines!"

"Oorah!" Connor's booming voice rung out, and people around them turned their heads, nodded in respect.

"And last but not least: all you sexual deviants!"

He nudged Aaron, and they replied laughing: "Deviants!"

Turned out they'd all responded, which made Josh and Indy have a fit of giggles. Those two were worse than teenage girls sometimes.

"Please welcome on stage...the one and only...the unforgettable, insatiable, unbelievable, improbable...Lady Lucy!"

Charlie's song boomed through the speakers, an up-tempo, sexy version of "Man-eater". The crowd burst out in the lyrics: "Oh, here she comes, watch out boys, she'll chew you up!"

Charlie was unrecognizable in his drag outfit, as he sauntered onto the stage. The slender, elvish man had transformed in a sex goddess, with fake blond hair, fake boobs pressed into a pink, short dress with sequins that sparkled, massive lashes and thick makeup, and a pair of pink platform heels Blake still couldn't believe Charlie could walk in.

He knew how to play the crowds, pretending to be flattered and shy while waiting till everyone was done catcalling and whistling. When they finally stopped, he quipped: "I didn't quite catch that, what was that?" His reward was a small encore.

Next to Blake, Miles watched, enraptured, Brad pulled close to his body. "God, he's perfect," Blake heard him say to Brad, who stood beaming proudly.

Brad waited till it was quiet before he called out: "Hey, sexy!"

Charlie smiled, recognized his voice. "That's one of my boyfriends," he said, earning another laugh from the crowd. "Laugh all you want, but this girl is so sexy she needs two men to satisfy her!"

A man in the front shouted out a rude remark about her sexual preferences. "Tuttuttut," he shushed him. "A lady never tells."

The crowd laughed, with some yelling out for more details.

"Suffice it to say their nicknames are Big..." He held up his hands a good ten inches apart. "...And Bigger." He indicated fifteen inches, and the crowd went wild.

"He's talking about you, O'Connor," Noah joked, bumping Connor's shoulder good-naturedly.

"He sure as hell wasn't talking about you," the former cop shot right back.

Blake caught an eye roll between Josh and Indy and grinned. Aaron shifted restlessly in his arms. He ground his ass against Blake's cock with enough pressure to make him hard in seconds.

He brought his mouth close to Aaron's ear. "What's wrong?" He slipped his left hand under Aaron's top, wriggled it into his jeans to tease his crack. "Does Sexy Aaron need a good, hard fuck?"

Aaron's head dropped back against him as he moaned softly, and at the same time opened his legs to give Blake room to play. The temptation to finger-fuck him was great, but they both needed more than that. He'd been busy with a tournament this week and hadn't given Aaron enough attention, at least sexually speaking. No wonder his puppy needed his hole filled. His anal fixation was still a big thing, and Blake had forgotten to put the butt plug in he'd bought for him.

"Right after the show, I'll take your sweet ass in the bathroom, okay? But we gotta watch the show first. Now, behave, puppy, and stop teasing me."

Charlie had transitioned into his first song, a pitch-perfect rendition of Lady Gaga's "Born this Way".

Brad met his eyes, gave him a tentative smile. Blake smiled back, and was relieved to see Brad's smile widen. It seemed Miles had been right, that all would be good between them. Thank fuck. Now all he had to do was try and mend bridges with Burke who was still being a stubborn ass.

Indy and Josh were dancing to the song and pulled Brad between them. Brad had become part of their group, Blake realized. He fit in with them. He smiled as he thought about what Miles had told him. The agent was right. It would provide Brad with the family he needed and had wanted for so long.

Blake watched as Charlie gave a flawless performance. His puppy remained restless and kept grinding against him, but it wasn't too bad. The promise of a solid fuck usually helped, if it didn't take too long.

As always Charlie closed off with Queen's epic "We Are the Champions", a big-time crowd-pleaser.

"Let's go," he told Aaron. "We'll beat the crowds at the bathrooms."

Noah spotted them leaving, raised his eyebrows. Blake winked. Noah would know where he and Aaron were headed, no doubt, and Blake didn't care.

Aaron beelined straight for the fuck stalls, where they did indeed beat the crowds and walked straight in. Blake locked the door, and when he turned around, Aaron had lowered his jeans, and stood bent over at the sink. He'd kicked off one leg of his jeans, so he could spread his legs.

Blake would smile, but he didn't want Aaron to take it the wrong way. He should never experience shame over his needs. Instead, Blake grabbed lube from his wallet.

"Do you have it bad, puppy?" His voice was warm, kind. "I'm gonna take care of you."

Aaron whimpered in response, his eyes closed, and his body trembling.

Blake lubed up his cock as fast as he could, didn't bother to grease Aaron's hole. When he was like this, he didn't need it. He'd want to feel it, would welcome the burn.

"I'm here. Hold tight."

He entered him hard, not stopping till he'd bottomed out. Aaron's moan bordered on a scream, but it wasn't in pain. It was relief. Blake pulled out almost entirely, drove back in hard.

"Blake!" Aaron's voice broke.

He held Aaron's hips as he fucked him hard and deep, exactly as he had promised. Aaron came in under a minute, but Blake didn't stop. He was nowhere near done, and neither was Aaron.

He didn't speak, the only sounds audible the slaps of his

body against Aaron's as he fucked him, the slicking sounds of his wet cock in Aaron's channel, and the music that filtered through the doors. People were talking loudly outside, so a line was forming of people who wanted to fuck as well. Well, they'd have to wait until he was done.

The second time, Aaron did actually scream, and outside people laughed and commented. Blake didn't give a shit. He released the tight hold he'd had on his own needs and came without making a sound, his orgasm barreling through him.

Aaron shuddered, still breathing hard. "You good now?" Blake asked.

"Yeah."

Blake smiled now, wiping off his cock with a hand towelette. Aaron pulled his jeans up without cleaning himself. He loved the sensation of cum in his ass, he'd told Blake once. There was something inherently dirty about it, but Blake loved knowing that he'd marked him. Aaron would feel him the rest of the night, and somehow, that was deeply satisfying.

When he was dressed again, Aaron turned around, his face devoid of the stress he'd shown earlier. "Thank you," he said.

Blake grabbed his head, kissed him deeply. "Always. I love fucking you, and I love taking care of you even more. I love you, puppy."

Aaron all but melted against him. "I love you, too."

EPILOGUE

ne Hundred Days Later

INDY WOKE up wrapped around Josh, Noah and Connor already up. Josh looked at him with beaming eyes, a soft smile playing on his lips. "Good morning, baby."

Indy leaned up on his elbow for a kiss. "Good morning... Did you sleep well or were you as excited as I was?"

Josh grinned. "It feels like Christmas morning to me."

"I know, right? It's the weirdest feeling..." Indy leaned in for another kiss, then disentangled himself from Josh.

Indy looked around their bedroom as he threw on some sweatpants and a shirt. The contractor had done an amazing job with the renovation. He had added a few square feet to the former in-law wing, making it big enough for the huge bed they'd ordered custom-made. They had also added a second shower to the bathroom, and had created a second walk-in closet.

And, of course, he'd built a play room Josh and Connor made good use of. Indy still couldn't stand to watch when Connor whipped or caned Josh, even though he knew Josh craved it, but he loved seeing the bliss Josh experienced afterward.

It had become their sanctuary, this house, and especially this room. They'd all found their place, both literally and figuratively. Noah and Connor on the outsides of the bed with Indy and Josh in the middle. Indy loved that whenever he woke up, someone was always holding him, touching him. Josh's nightmares were gone for good, too.

On the other side of the house, the contractor had built another wing, slightly smaller than this one, but roomy enough to comfortably house Miles, Brad, and Charlie. Watching the three of them making their relationship work had been a joy.

Brad had rebelled hard at times, and Miles had patiently been there for him. Even Noah and Connor had stepped up at times to give Brad the stability and discipline that he needed. Miles had to go through a week training upstate a few weeks ago, and Connor had taken over Brad's daily morning spanking to make sure Brad knew he was not invisible. It was heartwarming to see that Brad was slowly, but surely getting better at trusting he was loved and wanted.

Charlie had blossomed into a sassy, spunky, but super sweet guy whose biggest joy was loving his two men. He loved his job as a beauty consultant, and still did monthly performances at Flirt.

Indy sighed as he thought of Miles. The former FBI agent was developing a counseling practice working with teens. Recently, he'd been asked by the school district to help train teachers in recognizing mental issues in students, and Indy couldn't have been prouder of the man.

It was also clear that Brad wasn't the only one who loved having a family again. Miles had become close with Noah and Connor, the three of them hanging out a lot. Miles and Noah loved having long conversations about psychology, Miles cheering Noah on every chance he got for Noah to finish his degree. The safety Miles experienced at home, being able to be himself, had made a huge difference for him as well. And he doted on Charlie and Brad, the love between the three of them healing for all.

"You ready?" Josh asked, snapping Indy out of his thoughts.

"Yeah." He sighed. "They're gonna react well, right?" His stomach rolled a little.

Josh quickly closed the distance between them and gave him a gentle hug. "You really worried about that?"

Indy's stomach settled as Josh's hug steadied him. "A little." His voice sounded muffled, his mouth against Josh's shirt.

Josh let go and grabbed his chin. "Indy, Noah loves you. Don't you ever doubt that. And you know he's more than fine with us."

Indy nodded. He did know—on a rational level. Still, there was this flutter in his stomach, this deep-down fear that Noah would reject him anyway. "Let's go," he said, not wanting to bring Josh down. "We've got a plan to execute."

His nerves wouldn't go away the rest of the day. When they started the preparations for the barbecue party, they were back in full swing. He pushed them down as he let Aaron and Blake in, helped set everything up outside, then prepared the side dishes with Josh, Aaron eager to help as well.

It was a gorgeous autumn day, the sky crystal blue with soft white wisps of clouds in the distance. The men were laughing and eating, catching up and joking around. Aaron was at Blake's feet, more confident than ever before. He was excelling at his new job, making local and even statewide headlines for his work. Brad was playing chess with Noah, Max sleeping at his feet as usual, while Connor and Miles were talking about Connor's job at the school district, Charlie content to simply sit on Miles' lap.

Indy felt Josh behind him before he saw him, then Josh's arms came around him. "You ready, baby?"

Indy nodded. "Ready as I'll ever be."

Josh handed him the small box, and hand in hand they made their way to their family, their tribe.

"Everyone," Josh said, then waited till the conversations had stopped. "Indy and I have something we want to say."

He squeezed Indy's hand, and suddenly those nerves were gone, and Indy's heart filled with so much love it felt like it would burst.

"I don't know if you realized what day it is today, Noah," he said.

Noah frowned, shook his head.

"It's exactly a year ago that I met you and Josh, and even Connor for the first time."

Recognition lit up on Noah's face, and he smiled, but stayed silent, sensing apparently that Indy had more to say.

"In hindsight, that was the best day of my life, even if I didn't realize it at the time. Meeting you changed my life in so many ways, that I can't even put it into words."

"It was the best day of my life, too," Josh took over. "Because that day changed everything for me, for us. It was the start of a new chapter, and looking back, it's hard to imagine my life before that day. Meeting Indy was the catalyst for a lot of changes, all of them good. We would not be sitting here with this company, if not for that day."

"That doesn't mean this year was easy, because it wasn't," Indy said. "We all paid the price for the crimes of others... and we came damn close to losing some of us. I'll be forever grateful to what you all have endured and sacrificed because of me."

His voice choked, and Josh squeezed his hand again.

"It was also not easy because all of us, we didn't take the easy route to love. We found love in unexpected ways and forms, and that was often a struggle in itself," Josh said. "It's what makes us a family: to be able to see and accept that love comes in many shapes and forms. And no one knows that better than Connor and Noah, who had the courage to set Indy and me free."

This was it, Indy realized. This was the cue he and Josh had agreed on. Peace descend in his heart, as he let go of Josh and reached for that small box. They kneeled at the same time, and an audible gasp sounded in the garden as the others realized what was happening.

Indy opened the small box at the same time Josh did, and they both held it out to their men.

"Noah Flint, I love you more than words can say, and I want nothing more than to have your name. Will you marry me?"

Next to him, Josh repeated his words for Connor. Then all Indy could see was Noah's face, lighting up like the sun, radiating with so much love it would've brought Indy to his knees if he hadn't been there already.

"Yes! Oh, yes, Indy, hell yes."

Noah came out of his chair, dragged Indy to his feet and kissed him senseless. Those strong arms held him so tight it felt as if Noah never wanted to let go.

"God, I love you," Noah breathed in his ear. He leaned back. "Are you sure this is what you want? I wanted to ask you a hundred times already, but I didn't want to make you feel like you had to choose between me and Josh."

Similar words were uttered by Connor at the same time, and Indy and Josh smiled at each other. They'd guessed it right when they had discussed it.

"We both agreed that we want your names. For us, it's enough to be together. We don't need anything else. But we want to make it official with you," Indy said.

"We'll do it together," Noah said with a quick look at Connor. "Right, Connor? Same day wedding, the four of us."

Connor nodded, his eyes suspiciously moist. "There's nothing that would make me happier."

Then they kissed and hugged, and the others stepped into congratulate with even more hugs and kisses, and Indy's heart swelled inside his chest.

He'd found love when he never expected it.

He'd found a family he'd never dared imagine.

Life was pretty damn good.

THE STORY CONTINUES in *No Angel*, where we see the men celebrate the holidays...and come together for a special celebration... Start reading now!

DON'T MISS NO ANGEL

Our favorite men are back...and they're celebrating the holidays in true No Shame style.

It's time to say *I do*, and Indy couldn't be more excited. Side by side with Noah, Josh, and Connor, he's proud to take his vows with their friends watching.

But his post-wedding bliss is rudely interrupted when his past once again comes back to haunt him. And not just him, Connor gets some shocking news as well that leaves him reeling.

Before they can all share the best Christmas ever, they'll need to come together as one family.

No Angel is the fifth book in the No Shame series, a continuing series that needs to be read in order (start with No Filter). You can expect the usual sexy shenanigans, some suspense, and a whole lotta love and emotions as we reconnect with all characters from the previous books.

FREEBIES

If you love FREE stuff, head on over to my website where I offer bonus scenes for several of my books. Grab them here: https://www.noraphoenix.com/free-stuff/

BOOKS BY NORA PHOENIX

🎧 indicates book is also available as audio book

Forty-seven Series

An emotional daddy kink duology with a younger Daddy and an older boy. Also includes first time gay, loads of hurt/comfort, and best friend's father.

- **Clean Start at Forty-Seven**
- **New Daddy at Forty-Seven**

The Foster Brother Series

They met in foster care. Now they're brothers. Nothing can come between them, not even when they find love...

- **Jilted**
- **Hired**

White House Men

A romantic suspense series set in the White House that

Books by Nora Phoenix

combines romance with suspense, a dash of kink, and all the feels.

- **Press** (rivals fall in love in an impossible love) 🎧
- **Friends** (friends to lovers between an FBI and a Secret Service agent) 🎧
- **Click** (a sexy first-time romance with an age gap and an awkward virgin) 🎧
- **Serve** (a high heat MMM romance with age gap and D/s play) 🎧
- **Care** (the president's son falls for his tutor; age gap and daddy kink) 🎧
- **Puzzle** (a CIA analyst meets his match in a nerdy forensic accountant) 🎧
- **Heal** (can the president find love again with a sunshine man half his age?) 🎧

No Regrets Series

Sexy, kinky, emotional, with a touch of suspense, the No Regrets series is a spin off from the No Shame series that can be read on its own.

- **No Surrender** (bisexual awakening, first time gay, D/s play) 🎧

Perfect Hands Series

Raw, emotional, both sweet and sexy, with a solid dash of kink, that's the Perfect Hands series. All books can be read as standalones.

- **Firm Hand** (daddy care with a younger daddy and an older boy) 🎧
- **Gentle Hand** (sweet daddy care with age play) 🎧

- **Naughty Hand** (a holiday novella to read after Firm Hand and Gentle Hand) 🎧
- **Slow Hand** (a Dom who never wanted to be a Daddy takes in two abused boys) 🎧
- **Healing Hand** (a broken boy finds the perfect Daddy) 🎧

No Shame Series

If you love steamy MM romance with a little twist, you'll love the No Shame series. Sexy, emotional, with a bit of suspense and all the feels. Make sure to read in order, as this is a series with a continuing storyline.

- **No Filter** 🎧
- **No Limits** 🎧
- **No Fear** 🎧
- **No Shame** 🎧
- **No Angel** 🎧

And for all the fun, grab the **No Shame box set** 🎧 which includes all five books plus exclusive bonus chapters and deleted scenes.

Irresistible Omegas Series

An mpreg series with all the heat, epic world building, poly romances (the first two books are MMMM and the rest of the series is MMM), a bit of suspense, and characters that will stay with you for a long time. This is a continuing series, so read in order.

- **Alpha's Sacrifice** 🎧
- **Alpha's Submission** 🎧
- **Beta's Surrender** 🎧

- **Alpha's Pride**
- **Beta's Strength**
- **Omega's Protector**
- **Alpha's Obedience**
- **Omega's Power**
- **Beta's Love**
- **Omega's Truth**

Or grab *the first box set*, which contains books 1-3 plus exclusive bonus material and *the second box set*, which has books 4-6 and exclusive extras.

Ballsy Boys Series

Sexy porn stars looking for real love! Expect plenty of steam, but all the feels as well. They can be read as stand-alones, but are more fun when read in order.

- **Ballsy** (free prequel)
- **Rebel**
- **Tank**
- **Heart**
- **Campy**
- **Pixie**

Or grab *the box set*, which contains all five books plus an exclusive bonus novella!

Kinky Boys Series

Super sexy, slightly kinky, with all the feels.

- **Daddy**
- **Ziggy**

Ignite Series

An epic dystopian sci-fi trilogy (one book out, two more to follow) where three men have to not only escape a government that wants to jail them for being gay but aliens as well. Slow burn MMM romance.

- **Ignite** 🎧
- **Smolder** 🎧
- **Burn** 🎧

Now also available in a *box set* 🎧, which includes all three books, bonus chapters, and a bonus novella.

Stand Alones

I also have a few stand alones, so check these out!

- **Professor Daddy** (sexy daddy kink between a college prof and his student. Age gap, no ABDL) 🎧
- **Out to Win** (two men meet at a TV singing contest) 🎧
- **Captain Silver Fox** (falling for the boss on a cruise ship) 🎧
- **Coming Out on Top** (snowed in, age gap, size difference, and a bossy twink) 🎧
- **Ranger** (struggling Army vet meets a sunshiney animal trainer - cowritten with K.M. Neuhold) 🎧

Books in German

Quite a few of my books have been translated into German, with more to come!

Liebe im Weißen Haus

- **Henleys Liebe** (Press)
- **Seths Freundschaft** (Friends)
- **Calix' Fürsorge** (Click)
- **Denalis Hingabe** (Serve)
- **Kenns Daddy** (Care)

Indys Männer

- **Indys Flucht** No Filter)
- **Josh Wunsch** (No Limits)
- **Aarons Handler** (No Fear)
- **Brads Bedürfnisse** (No Shame)
- **Indys Weihnachten** (No Angel)

Wanders Männer (No Regrets series)

- **Burkes Veränderung** (No Surrender)

Mein Daddy Dom

- **Daddy Rhys** (Firm Hand)
- **Daddy Brendan** (Gentle Hand)
- **Weihnachten mit den Daddys** (Naughty Hand)
- **Daddy Ford** (Slow Hand)
- **Daddy Gale** (Healing Hand)

Das Hayes Rudel

- **Lidons Angebot** (Alpha's Sacrifice)
- **Enars Unterordnung** (Alpha's Submission)
- **Lars' Hingabe** (Beta's Surrender)
- **Brays Stolz** (Alpha's Pride)
- **Keans Stärke** (Beta's Strength)

- **Gias Beschützer** (Omega's Protector)
- **Levs Gehorsam** (Alpha's Obedience)
- **Sivneys Macht** (Omega's Power)
- **Lucans Liebe** (Beta's Love)
- **Sandos Wahrheit** (Omega's Truth)

Standalones

- **Mein Professor Daddy** (Professor Daddy)
- **Eingeschneit mit dem Bären** (Coming Out on Top)
- **Eine Nacht mit dem Kapitän** (Captain Silver Fox)
- **Judahs Dilemma** (Out to Win)
- **Ranger** (Ranger, cowritten with K.M. Neuhold)

Books in Italian

- **L'Occasione Della Vita** (Out to Win)
- **Posizioni Inaspettate** (Coming Out on Top)
- **Baciare il Capitano** (Captain Silver Fox)
- **Professor Daddy** (Professor Daddy)
- **Ranger** (Ranger, cowritten with K.M. Neuhold)
- **L'offerta di Lidon** (Alpha's Sacrifice)
- **La Sottomissione di Enar** (Alpha's Submission)
- **La Resa di Lars** (Beta's Surrender)
- **L'orgoglio di Bray** (Alpha's Pride)
- **La Forza die Kean** (Beta's Strength)

Books in French

- **Le Garçon du Professeur** - Professor Daddy
- **Positions Inattendues** (Coming Out on Top)

- **Une Nuit avec le Capitaine** (Captain Silver Fox)
- **Une Main de Fer** (Firm Hand)
- **Une Main de Velours** (Gentle Hand)
- **Une Main Coquine** (Naughty Hand)
- **Une Main Prudente** (Slow Hand)
- **La Sacrifice de l'Alpha** (Alpha's Sacrifice)
- **La Soumission de l'Alpha** (Alpha's Submission)
- **La Capitulation du Bêta** (Beta's Surrender)
- **Enflammer** (Ignite)
- **Brûler** (Smolder)
- **Ballsy Boys: Rebel** (Rebel)
- **Ballsy Boys: Tank** (Tank)

Books in Spanish

- **Con Mano Firme** - Spanish - Firm Hand

MORE ABOUT NORA PHOENIX

Would you like the long or the short version of my bio?

The short? You got it.

I write steamy gay romance books and I love it. I also love reading books. Books are everything.

How was that?

A little more detail? Gotcha.

I started writing my first stories when I was a teen...on a freaking typewriter. I still have these, and they're adorably romantic. And bad, haha. Fear of failing kept me from following my dream to become a romance author, so you can imagine how proud and ecstatic I am that I finally over-came my fears and self doubt and did it. I adore my genre because I love writing and reading about flawed, strong men who are just a tad broken..but find their happy ever after anyway.

My favorite books to read are pretty much all MM/gay romances as long as it has a happy end. Kink is a plus... Aside from that, I also read a lot of nonfiction and not just books on writing. Popular psychology is a favorite topic of mine and so are self help and sociology.

Hobbies? Ain't nobody got time for that. Just kidding. I love traveling, spending time near the ocean, and hiking. But I love books more.

Come hang out with me in my Facebook Group Nora's Nook where I share previews, sneak peeks, freebies, fun stuff, and much more: https://www.facebook.com/groups/norasnook/

My weekly newsletter not only gives you updates, exclusive content, and all the inside news on what I'm working on, but also lists the best new releases, 99c deals, and freebies in gay romance for that weekend. Load up your Kindle for less money! Sign up here: http://www.noraphoenix.com/newsletter/

You can also stalk me on Twitter: @NoraFromBHR

On Instagram:

https://www.instagram.com/nora.phoenix/

On Bookbub:

https://www.bookbub.com/profile/nora-phoenix

ACKNOWLEDGMENTS

I can't believe I did it: four books in four months. Wow, what a ride.

A heartfelt thank you to every single one of my readers. I can't express in words how much your love for my books means to me. The Nookies in my FB reader group deserve a special mention since you guys rock.

Amanda, Kyleen, Michele, Tania, and Vicki, thanks so much for beta reading this book. I so appreciated the feedback, and you made this book better.

Vicki, thank you for the gorgeous fresh cover. I love it.

Last but not least, a special thank you to my GBF and his BF. The fact that you guys are both reading my books makes me giddy...and proud. You've always believed in me, so thank you from the bottom of my heart.